TENNIS SHOES
A D V E N T U R E S E R I E S
WARRIORS OF
CUMORAH

TENNIS SHOES
ADVENTURE SERIES

WARRIORS OF
CUMORAH

a novel

Chris Heimerdinger

Covenant Communications, Inc.

Covenant®

Cover illustration by Joe Flores

Cover design copyrighted 2001 by Covenant Communications, Inc.

Published by Covenant Communications, Inc.
American Fork, Utah

Printed in Canada
First Printing: October 2001

08 07 06 05 04 03   10 9 8 7 6 5 4 3 2

ISBN 1-57734-922-9

AUTHOR'S NOTE

In this novel, I have decided to include endnotes for some of the chapters to offer additional insight. These notes are found at the end of the book. For the most part, this story is purely fantasy and is strictly intended to entertain. Nevertheless, there are many names, settings, and details that are based on historical research and actual historical figures. It is my hope that these chapter notes will enhance the readers' enjoyment of the story and help to inspire a greater appreciation for some of the remarkable settings wherein the story takes place.

Chris Heimerdinger

PRONOUNCIATION GUIDE AND QUICK REFERENCE GLOSSARY

Abu-Walid (ab-oo-wal-eed')
Agouti (a-gow'-ti)—small Mesoamerican animal
Ahau (ah-how')—"lord" or "king"
Ahmen (ah'-men)—"royal"
Ajul (ah-hool')—"master"
Al-Arabah (al-a-ra'-bah)
Al-Farabi (al-far-a'-bee)
Allah (all-ah')— "The God"
Atlatl (at-lat'-l)— "spearthrower"
Bacchanalian (Bak-a-nay'-lee-on)—Roman festival of dance, decadence, and revelry
Balam (ball-om')—"jaguar"
Catemaco (cat-i-maw'-ko)— city and lake located in the Tuxtla mountains, state of Veracruz, Mexico
Cauac (ku-awk')—"owl"
Cenote (sin-oh'-tae)—sinkhole, considered by Mayans a doorway to the Underworld
Chac (chawk)—Mayan god of rain; also means "red"
Chan (chawn)—"sky"
Chanim (chan-eem')—"faster"
Chilan (chill-an')—"shaman"
Chorti (chore-tee')—Mayan dialect
Coatimundi (coat-e-moon'-dee)—Mesoamerican animal similar to anteater
Cocao (co-cow')—"cocoa-bean"
Copáli (co-pa'-lee)—"sacred resin"

Copal'in (co-pa'-lin)

Cumorah (cu-mor'-uh)

Ephesus (eff'-a-sus)—city in ancient Turkey

Felsina (fell-see'-nah)—Roman city

Gerizim (Ger-i-zeem')—hill in ancient Samaria

Hapai-Zin (hop-eye-zin')

Hazim (ha-zeem')

Huehue Tlapallan (way-way lap-all-an')—ancient land mentioned by Aztec historian Ixtlilxochitl, located in the present-day Tuxtla mountains of Veracruz, Mexico

Hunahpu (Hoo-nah'-poo)—Hero Twin of Mayan legends

Huracan (hur'-a-can)—Mayan god from Popal Vuh

Iqui (ick-kwee')—"wind"

Itzamna (it-zahm'-nah)—highest god of the Mayans

Ix-Chel (ish-chel')—Mayan goddess

Ixtlilxochitl (isht-lil-sho-chee'-tul)—Aztec historian

Jaguarundi (jag-war-oon'-di)—Mesoamerican cat, smaller than a jaguar

Jolom (hole-om')—"skull"

Julu-Tlé (ju-lute-lay')

Kalomte (kal-om'-tae)—"emperor"

Kaminaljuyu (Kam-in-al-hu-yoo')—ancient archeological site located in present-day Guatemala City

Kanalha (kan-al'-ha)

Kinkajous (kink'-a-joos)—small Mesoamerican animal

Kukalcan (kuk-al-kan')—"feathered serpent"

Kux-Wach (kush-wach')—"weasel face"

Lamanai (läm-an-eye')—"submerged crocodile"

Ma'an (Muh'-un)

Mahucatah (maw-hu-ca-tah')—"traveler" or "wanderer"

Maw (maw)—Mayan deity of the Underworld

Men (men)—"eagle"

Nabatean (nab-a-tay'-an)

Nun-Yax-Ayin (noon-yash-eye-een')—"Lord-Blue-Crocodile" or "Blue-Green-First-Crocodile," Son of Spearthrower Owl, king from Teotihuacan.

Oaxaca (wah-hock'-uh)—state and city in Mexico

Olmeca (ol-mek'-uh)—ancient people of Mesoamerica, "people of the rubber tree"

Paal Kaba (paul ka-ba')—sacred name or given name

Paca (paw'-ca)— small Mesoamerican animal

Pacawli (paw-cow'-li)

Paolo (pow'-low)

Popal Vuh (pope-al-voo')—sacred book of Mayans

Puteoli (poo-ti-o'-lee)—Roman city

Quetzal (ket-zall')—sacred bird of Guatemala with beautiful blue-green plumes

Quiché (ki-quay')—Mayan dialect

Quillkiah (quill-ki'-uh)

Riki-Kool (ree-kee-ko-owl')

Santiago Tuxtla (san-tee-a-go-tooxt'-la)—Mexican city in the state of Veracruz, sits just below the Hill Vigia

Seibalche (see-bal-chay')

Shika (shee'-ka)

Sinai (sigh'-nigh)

Siyah K'ak (see-ya k-awk')—"Fire Is Born," Kalomte (emperor) at Tikal from A.D. 378 to A.D. 402

Tapir (tap'-ur)—Mesoamerican cameloid, also found in South America

Tehuantepec (te-hoo-wan'-te-pek)—ancient city in central Mexico

Tikal (tee-kal')—Mayan City, "place of spirit voices"

Tz'ikin (zi-keen')

Uaxactun (wash-ak-toon')—Mayan city

Vigia (Vee-hee'-ah)—"lookout"

Wadi-Musa (wa-dee-moo'-sah)

Xbalanque (Sh-bal-an'-kay)—Hero twin of Mayan legends

Xibalba (shi-bal'-ba)—Mayan underworld

Yak (yak)—"fox"

Yax-Chaac-Xoc (yash-chalk-shok')—"First Scaffold Shark," King of Tikal beginning at around 223 A.D. Considered the founder of the dynasty of Tikal kings.

Yucatecan (yoo-ka-tek'-an)—Mayan dialect

Yusuf al-Sa'id (yu-sef-al-sa-eed')

PROLOGUE

We are all droplets of water in an endlessly shifting sea of history—the relentless succession of events, one thing leading to another, interdependent, and each one vital to the ultimate outcome. We don't often think about it that way—to think that because a butterfly flapped its wings in China, there were hurricanes in Florida. Or to think that because a man forgot his wallet, he was late for work; and because he was late for work, he ran a stoplight; and because he ran a stoplight, he crashed into your car; and because he crashed into your car, it changed your life forever. And all because a man forgot his wallet.

Yes, it's me, Jim Hawkins. Resident philosopher. In my veins still surges the blood of an adventurer, but alas, I'm afraid the greater part of that title, at least for now, belongs to the young. But I can still philosophize, can't I? About the shifting sea of history?

But before you think I've grown too old and over the hill, let me remind you that I'm only forty-eight. I'm a brand-new father as well! My beautiful, strapping son was born on July 5, a little less than two years after my wife, Sabrina, and I were wed. She actually went into labor while watching fireworks the previous night from the front porch of our new home in Provo, Utah. We named him Gidgiddonihah Teancum Hawkins, but we'll call him Gid for short, in memory of a great warrior who saved the lives of my loved ones more than once.

Not long ago I thought I'd never again gaze into the face of a newborn baby that was my own. But life can take some funny twists sometimes. And so often it relates to our individual choices. Sabrina and I *chose* to have this child, and because we made that choice, the ramifications could well change the history of the world. During the course of my life I must have made a billion choices, each one with potentially eternal consequences.

I've sometimes imagined the setting for the Final Judgment. I've wondered if it will be like one of those little choose-your-own adventure books marketed to young adolescents. You know the ones I mean—the books where the character reaches a certain crossroad in the plot where it says, "If you decide to battle the Imperial Forces, turn to page 211. If you decide to escape in your galactic speeder, turn to page 134." I've imagined myself standing at some sort of podium watching a movie of my life—that is to say, my life as it *could* have been. When I reach a certain juncture where I made an unwise decision, the film will show what *might* have happened if I'd selected a better option. Not an easy movie to watch, I'm sure. But the object lesson of how our individual choices affected things throughout history might be invaluable in our quest to become more like God.

In the case of my family, we've frequently found ourselves in extraordinary positions, faced with extraordinary choices. Because of a certain cave in northern Wyoming, the very real prospect of permanently altering world history has been a continual part of our lives. Back in the beginning, back when Garth and I went on our very first adventure among the Nephites, we had always understood that we should never try to deliberately change the outcome of historical events. Not unless it looked like our interference might have unintentionally *caused* the change, in which case we'd done everything we could to set things right.

Until now our family has never had a loose cannon—no family member who'd set out with the specific objective of altering history. Perhaps it should have come as no surprise, then, that the ones who would set in motion such things were the two family members who may have felt the most displaced in the modern world. After all, they'd been born in a very different age. As a result, they'd felt a very strong attachment to the *people* of that age, and a strong incentive to keep those people from making the unwise decisions that led to their destruction. But alas, these persons were still very young. And we all know the reckless, impetuous ideas that can sometimes enter the minds of youth.

What I *didn't* expect was that, because of certain discoveries that were about to be made, my oldest son, Harry, would *also* seek to change the outcome of certain events. But I suppose this really shouldn't have surprised me either. After all, the event that he would seek to change was one that he felt should have never occurred in the first place—the death of a friend, a tragedy for which he had always blamed himself.

And who could have known that these decisions would place so many of us in such precarious circumstances—the most precarious of our lives? And that not just *our* fate would hang in the balance, but the fate of history itself, as well as the delicate balance of space and time . . . ?

PART I:

THE RETURN
OF THE ROMAN

CHAPTER 1

Hi!

My name is Rebecca Plimpton, but you can call me Becky. That is, you could call me Becky *if you ever met me, but since you're doing the reading and I'm doing all the talking, you can just know that* most *people call me Becky.*

I'm ten years old—but don't let that scare you off. My dad says I've always been very percoshus . . . precotious . . . (excuse me while I look it up in my dictionary). Precocious! *That's the word! That means I know a lot more than most girls my age, so don't worry. I intend to tell a good story with lots of details and lots of action—and absolutely none of it made up. It all happened! Honest!*

Many of you already know my mom and dad, Garth and Jenny Plimpton. My Uncle Jim, my cousins Harry, Melody, and Meagan told you all of the other stories, but they said I could tell this one. Or at least half of it. So why would they trust someone as young as me with something as incredible as this? I think it has something to do with my "gift."

What gift is that, you may ask? Well, I'll tell you. But please don't think I'm boasting. It's not the kinda thing a person ought to brag about. Actually . . . I'd better not tell you yet. It will only be confusing. It'll be a lot better if I just let it come out over the course of the story. Just keep it in the back of your mind for now. Is that okay?

First I'll tell you about myself. I might just be one of the most unique persons you've ever met. You see, I wasn't born here. That is to say, I wasn't born in the twenty-first century. Now don't stop reading! I'm totally serious! I was actually born in 31 A.D. But before you go thinking I'm two thousand years old, let me explain.

A long time ago, when they were just kids, my dad and my Uncle Jim discovered this secret cave that took them way back into the times of the

Nephites and Lamanites. They met Teancum and Captain Moroni and lots of other cool people. Later on, some Gadianton robbers (those are bad guys) came to modern times. My Uncle Jim ended up destroying a really evil sword made by a guy named Akish at a place in Mexico called El Cerro Vigia—a hill that a long time ago used to be called Cumorah. Also remember that name—Cumorah—because later it becomes very important.

Anyway, it was shortly after all that stuff took place that my mom and dad got married. Mom says my dad was sort of a geek when he was young, but he grew up to be rather handsome and dubinair—deboneir (sorry, I gotta use my dictionary again) debonair, so my mom fell in love with him. (I won't tell you when I'm using the dictionary anymore—just know that I gotta use it a lot!)

The problem was that Mom and Dad didn't think they could have any children. This made Mom really sad and she got awfully depressed. My dad loved her so much that he decided to take her to a special place that might cheer her up. That place was back in Nephite times.

Now we get to the part where I was born. Except, I wasn't the first one born. I have a brother named Joshua who's two years older than me, but I'll tell you about him later. I was born in the city of Zarahemla on the banks of the River Sidon in the year 31 A.D. For the first three years of my life I didn't know about anybody else besides Nephites and Lamanites. I never saw a television, never played a video game, never turned on a light switch, and never cooked a hot dog in the microwave. I never even knew what a hot dog was! Although I've eaten quite a few since that time. Hot dogs are sort of my weakness. Like Superman and Kryptonite.

My family sometimes asks me how much I remember about the Nephites and they're always surprised to learn that I remember a lot. I remember one event most particularly—the coming of Jesus Christ. I remember when He came down out of the clouds. I remember when He healed Harry and made him walk again. I remember when Mom and Dad took me up to meet Him and He hugged me and I got to look into His eyes. And I remember when the angels came down from heaven and circled around me and Josh and the other children in a ring of fire. Yes, I remember everything. Dad says that makes me more accountable than other girls—which is kinda scary, but not really. Because I already know that I love my Savior with all my heart and I'd never want to do anything to make Him sad.

I bet you want to know what I look like. I have blonde hair like my mom and freckles on both cheeks like my dad—or at least like he used to have when he was my age. Joshua, on the other hand, has flaming red hair like Dad and skin that gets really tan like Mom. (Which makes me a little jealous since I just get sunburned.) I'm kinda short for most ten-year-old girls, but I've been told that I have especially pretty green eyes—and who am I to argue? (I'm grinning mischievously.)

Now I'll tell you about Joshua. As I guess you'd expect for somebody born in 29 A.D., Joshua was a little different than most other kids. For that reason he didn't have that many friends. He absolutely hated Nintendo and never really liked television or movies. Instead, he preferred playing outside and exploring in the hills and building things in the dirt. I knew why, of course. That's all he did for the first five years of his life!

Dad would remind him that the Savior was lonely too, and that He was spat upon and reviled and treated terribly by the people who should have loved him. I think that worked for a while. But over the last year—ever since Josh started the Fifth Grade (he was a year behind most other kids since he didn't start Kindergarten till he was six)—the kids had started treating him worse than ever, challenging him to fight and pushing him down. That's when Josh made a remarkable discovery. By sending one or two good punches to the nose, a kid would almost magically stop teasing him! Unfortunately, my brother, like me, is not very big, so he ended up having to fight almost every boy in school. Most of the time he won, too. In fact, I can't think of a time that he lost— although there were a few draws. That is to say, the teachers sometimes managed to reach him before he could blacken both of the other kid's eyes.

Needless to say, Joshua spent a lot of time in the principal's office. He even got suspended for a week last spring. My parents were tearing their hair out trying to figure out what to do about him. It wasn't just the fighting. They wanted him to start taking school more seriously too. Josh didn't like school very much. He didn't see much use for it. What was the point of learning how to add fractions or diagram a sentence? How could that help you to build a better obsidian knife or hunt a jaguar? That was my brother's favorite hobby. Not the hunting part, but making ancient weapons. My brother would get more excited if he opened his Christmas present and found a big block of shiny obsidian than if he found a Gameboy or a new CD.

Joshua had Nephites on the brain. He talked about them, daydreamed about them, and missed them very badly. Nobody read the Book of

Mormon the way my brother read it. To him it was like a book of adventures, or a newspaper from home. Sometimes when Joshua got depressed, he'd talk to me about running away and going back to that cave near Cody, Wyoming. If he went on long enough, I'd start to cry. I'd tell him if he ever left me I'd be devastated. He was my brother, my best friend, and it was his job to take care of me and protect me till the day I got married, and if he let me down I'd beat the living daylights out of him. This usually shut him up. Joshua knew better than to hit a girl, which meant I could almost always get in a few good slugs before he got away.

But even I didn't know how deep his obsession with Nephites really was until one afternoon in August. It was just a month and a half after the birth of Uncle Jim and Aunt Sabrina's baby boy—who, by the way, was the cutest baby I'd ever seen. The whole family was gathered at Uncle Jim's house for Sunday dinner, all except Harry, who was due to come home from his mission to Athens, Greece, in just two weeks. This fact was particularly exciting for a certain girl, named Mary Symeon, who lived in my uncle's home. Like me, Mary had been born in ancient times. She'd come home with Harry and Meagan after their last adventure in first-century Israel. She had the most gorgeous eyes and beautiful long black hair I'd ever seen. Uncle Jim and Aunt Sabrina had become her legal sponsors. Somehow they'd helped her to obtain something called refugee status and she was now working hard to learn to read English and become an American citizen. Jim said it was a nightmare to get through all the red tape over that one. He was convinced that it could only have been done by the hand of God.

Most family members were eating in the living room. This included Steffanie and her new fiancé, Michael Collins, a twenty-four-year-old Accounting major at the Y. He was handsome and all, but to me he was kinda dull. Especially when compared to adventurous, outgoing Steffanie. But maybe that's what Steffanie felt she needed—someone to bring her back down to earth. Besides, who was I to advise my cousin on her love life?

Meagan was also there with her new boyfriend, Ryan Champion. I loved that name! Ryan Champion. He was tall and blond, with dreamy blue eyes. Ryan had just graduated from high school. His family had moved to Arizona that summer, but he'd stayed behind to go to BYU in the fall. I know the fact that Meagan had a steady boyfriend might raise a few eyebrows. In my opinion she was very much in love with somebody else, but that somebody hadn't been seen or heard from in over two years.

Joshua and I had carried our paper plates piled with barbecued ribs and mashed potatoes out onto the back porch. Marcos and Melody were also outside with their two-year-old boy, Carter, whom they'd adopted six months earlier through LDS Family Services. He was an adorable little tyke with a Hispanic background, like Marcos. Melody was constantly chasing Carter to keep him from pulling up Aunt Sabrina's pansies or from abusing Melody's little dog, Pill. Melody finally decided to hold the dog on her lap to protect it.

Joshua sat there staring at Marcos for a long time. He had mixed feelings about Marcos. I mean, he loved Marcos and all. He just didn't understand him. They'd had many conversations about life among the Nephites. Marcos would tell him stories about serving as a missionary in Bountiful after the visit of the Savior. I think, deep down, my brother wondered why Marcos was here.

To me that was easy to understand. The answer came with a capital M—Melody! And besides, Marcos hadn't actually been born among the Nephites. He was born in this century. He'd just spent a good part of his youth in ancient times, being raised under the thumb of his wicked father, Jacob Moon. Joshua would try to get Marcos to talk about the days before he was converted to the gospel—when he'd lived the life of a full-fledged Gadianton. But Marcos avoided that subject like the plague. This irked my brother terribly. He considered Marcos an important link to understanding the Nephite world, and he didn't like it when he wouldn't answer all of his questions.

I could tell that just such a question was on Joshua's mind that evening.

"Marcos," he finally began, "can I ask you something?"

"Go ahead," said Marcos warily, like he always sounded when Joshua asked if he could ask something.

"How come if the Gadianton robbers were wiped out during all the earthquakes and stuff before the Savior appeared—how come a couple hundred years later they started showing up again? Where would they have learned all that Gadianton stuff if it had all been destroyed?"

"Satan has a way of reintroducing such things when the people are wicked," said Marcos plainly.

"Have you ever thought about going back and warning them?"

"What do you mean?"

"I mean finding out exactly who was the first person to start teaching all that Gadianton garbage and, I don't know, stab him in the heart like Teancum did to Amalickiah."

"Joshua, that's terrible," said Melody. *"You can't just execute someone before they're guilty of anything."*

"Why not?" said Joshua. *"We already know what they're going to do!"*

"Because it's not right," she continued. *"Heavenly Father knows everything* we're *gonna do too. Why doesn't He just send down a lightning bolt and kill* everybody *who might do something evil?"*

"Good question," said Joshua. *"Why doesn't He?"*

I set down my rib bone and decided to chime in. Sometimes the wisdom of a ten-year-old girl can go a long ways. "I think I know. Because if He did that, there'd be no reason to come down to earth. He could never test us to see if we'd do what Jesus wants us to do."

"Becky's exactly right," said Melody.

"I don't agree," said Joshua. *"Think of all the people you could save. You might save the whole Nephite nation!"*

"I don't think so," said Marcos. *"If you stopped the first person who became a Gadianton, Satan would just find someone else."*

"We'll stop them too!"

Marcos shook his head. "The secret works of Gadianton are only the consequence of a wickedness that already exists among the people."

"How come you don't go back and help the Nephites to keep from becoming wicked?"

"Why can't I carry on that same fight here in this day?" asked Marcos, *sure that this would settle the argument.*

But Marcos forgot who he was talking to. "Because you're a Nephite! *It's your* duty *to help them!"*

"He's only half *Nephite,"* said Melody. *"Marcos has already done* tons *of things to help the Nephites. Joshua, you're sounding awfully rude."*

Joshua backed down, hemming and hawing. "Yeah . . . yeah, I guess you're right . . . Sorry."

But Joshua's words had gotten to Marcos a little bit. I think he did feel guilty. But the next thing Melody said seemed to shake him out of it.

"Would you have Marcos leave me and little Carter?" she added. *"Raising a family is pretty important, too."*

"Okay, okay," said Joshua impatiently. *"I said I was sorry."*

"I'm not sure I could do much anyway," said Marcos. *"If I went back in time now, I'd likely find myself in the midst of the generation that*

remained faithful to Christ. Serious wickedness didn't start to appear again until two hundred years after the Savior was born."

"Not only that," I added after licking the barbecue sauce from my fingers, "but Meagan said the Rainbow Room may have fizzled out. For all we know it doesn't even work anymore. Frost Cave might just be a regular cave now, like any other cave."

"I don't believe it," said Joshua stubbornly. "Anyway, Meagan was talking about the Galaxy Room. *The Galaxy Room may have nothing to do with the* Rainbow Room. *And what does it matter if the Nephites are still in the time when they're faithful to Christ? That may be the* best *time to warn them. You could tell them exactly what'll happen if they don't stay righteous."*

"Nephite prophets have already foretold what would happen if they rejected the Savior and His gospel," said Marcos.

"But that was just general *stuff," said Joshua. "I'm talking about* details. *Tell them exactly when the Gadiantons will start becoming powerful again. Tell them everything you can about Mormon and Moroni. Tell them about the Hill Cumorah! That way they'll know that they shouldn't gather there. Or at least that they shouldn't try to fight a battle. Instead, they should just head north, settle in Utah or something. Or better yet, California. That way they won't have to deal with snow."*

"Joshua," said Marcos. "You can't just change the destiny of a nation."

My brother's face got really red, like he was about to explode. "What do you mean! *Of* course *you can! Isn't that what Harry and Meagan did? Didn't they save the scroll of Matthew and all those other scrolls? Didn't that* change the destiny of a nation? Didn't it change a *lot of nations?"*

Marcos realized he'd said the wrong thing. "That's not what I mean, Josh. I mean . . ." He looked to Melody for help. "Tell me what I mean."

But it wasn't Melody who answered. Meagan was standing in the patio doorway. She'd overheard the last part of the conversation. "What he means—" She came outside to join us. "—is that what happened to us was different. Harry and I might have been the ones who almost screwed things up in the first *place. The pivotal moment may have been when we took the scroll of Matthew out of that cave near Qumran. Harry and I were just fixing a problem we may have created."*

"How can you be so sure that you didn't change history?" asked Joshua. "How can you know that if you hadn't gone back, we'd even have *the book of Matthew?"*

Meagan shrugged. "I guess I can't be sure. But at the time, I felt strongly that if we didn't fix what we'd messed up, those books might be lost forever."

"You see?" said Josh. "Why can't I feel just as strongly about this? The Nephites are my people. Why can't I want to save them from being destroyed? What's wrong with wanting—?"

Josh stopped talking. My dad had appeared in the doorway.

"What's everyone talking about?" he asked.

Melody pointed at Joshua. "Uncle Garth, explain to him why he can't go back in time and save the Nephites from being destroyed at Cumorah."

I think Melody was kinda trying to show how silly Joshua sounded. But, boy, you should've seen the look on my dad's face. He turned as white as a sheet. Joshua stared at the ground.

"Uh, yes," Dad said finally. "I'll have to do that."

Joshua grabbed up his plate, and without looking at anyone, slipped into the house. Dad smiled weakly, as if to say, "Don't worry, I've got everything under control," and went back inside. Meagan let out a little whistle, letting everyone know how relieved she was that that was over.

Grateful to change the subject, Melody said to Meagan, "Where's Ryan?"

"Who knows?" said Meagan. "Am I my boyfriend's keeper?"

Melody raised her eyebrows, continuing to wait for an answer.

Meagan sighed, "He had to go to work. I hate businesses that make teenagers work on Sunday. I say boycott them all! At least . . . that's my opinion."

"You seem to have a lot of opinions when it comes to Ryan," said Melody with a wink. "How long have you two been dating?"

"A little over three months. Ever since the end of school."

"Do you think he'll ask you to marry him?" I asked.

Meagan widened her eyes. "Gracious, Becky! You wanna get me married off already? I'm not even out of high school!"

What she'd said was true. I'd often heard Meagan say that she might've graduated last year. But she'd decided to repeat her sophomore year so she wouldn't lose a chance to earn some academic scholarships. As it was, Meagan was already being offered scholarships from all over the country.

"Besides," Meagan added, "I already told you, I'm not getting married."

Melody laughed. "That's what Steffanie used to say too. And I'm sure you'll go right on saying it until the right one comes along."

"Or comes back," chuckled Marcos.

He saw the look on everyone's face and regretted his words immediately. Melody looked like she wanted to bite his head off. Meagan just shuffled her feet.

Marcos cleared his throat. "Well, I'm batting a thousand this evening. I think I need more mashed potatoes."

He tossed his rib bones to an excited Pill as he went inside. Meagan sat down on the patio's bottom step, but her eyes looked far away.

"Do you think about him?" Melody asked.

"Who?" said Meagan. "Apollus? No! Hardly at all anymore. He made his choice. He went off to explore the world. I'd have probably done the same thing in his shoes. Besides, can you really see me spending the rest of my life with a Roman*?"*

"Doesn't seem any more strange than me spending my life with a Nephite," said Melody.

"Half Nephite," Meagan corrected.

I spoke up again. "Where do you think Apollus went? Do you think he might've gone back to Roman times?"

"Nah, I doubt it," said Meagan. "He was having too much fun on Harry's motorcycle." She tried to laugh, but it came out weird. "I don't know. Maybe he did *go back. That's probably where he belonged."*

"I think he still loves you," I said.

Meagan was looking really uncomfortable. "Let's not talk about this anymore. It's all water under the bridge. And it doesn't matter anyway. I'm a different person today than I was two years ago. Apollus needs to find his own way. Make his own destiny. That's exactly what he's doing."

I raised my eyebrows. "Are you saying you don't . . . love Apollus anymore?"

"She said she didn't want to talk about it," said Melody.

Meagan just grinned at me—the kind of grin that older girls always give younger girls to tell them they're too young to know anything.

"Sure I love him," Meagan said. "A part of me will always love him. But not *that* way. *I was only sixteen! Besides, it's not as if I have any shortage of boyfriends. Don't you like Ryan, Becky?"*

"Oh, yes," I said with a sigh. "I think he's wonderful. But . . . well . . . he's no Apollus."

Meagan became irritated. "Just who do you think Apollus is? You're obviously remembering someone different than I *remember. Apollus is coarse, he's arrogant . . . his perceptions are absolutely* primitive *when it* comes to women. I mean, I realize all men have to be trained before they can become good husbands, but give me a break! I just don't think I'd have the energy to train someone like Apollus. I'd rather start with a Labrador than a Timber Wolf."

I didn't say anything else. The whole thing was just too confusing and disturbing. Maybe Meagan was right. What did a ten-year-old know about love? Melody acted as if she understood Meagan better than anybody. After all, she knew all about waiting for the one you love to come back. I don't think Melody believed what Meagan had said, but I wasn't so sure. To me she sounded pretty convincing.

Right then Mary, Steffanie, and Steffanie's fiancé, Michael, came outside. They talked about the wedding, of course. Steffanie and Michael planned to get married on December 27, just two days after Christmas. By then Harry would be home. Just two more weeks! That was the subject that came up next—a subject that only caused Mary to blush.

Everybody fully expected Harry and Mary to get married soon after Harry got home. There was even talk of making it a double wedding again, like Uncle Jim and Aunt Sabrina, and Marcos and Melody. But in the end, everybody seemed to agree that they ought to wait for Harry to return and at least give him some say about his own future.

The car was very quiet as we drove the three blocks to our house later that night. I could tell Dad was still stewing over the things Joshua had said on the patio, and Joshua was bracing himself for a lecture.

Finally, Dad began. "Joshua, I know you love the Nephite people, and I know you think you should try and save them—"

"We should all try and save them!" Josh interrupted. "C'mon, Dad! What would it really take? Just a few history books. We could give them a copy of the Book of Mormon."

Mom's face suddenly looked as stricken as Dad's. "Joshua, do you even know what you're saying? You can't give the Nephites a copy of the Book of Mormon."

"Why not? They already have most of it, don't they? I thought the Book of Mormon was just a shorter version of all the Nephite records for a thousand years."

"Yes," said Dad, "but—Joshua, this conversation is ridiculous! What would Mormon and Moroni do if the Nephites already had a copy of the book they wrote?"

"It might make it a lot easier to write."

"We have no right to change history. None whatsoever. And even on those rare *occasions when we've done it, it was only to fix things. Any other motive would be . . . well, it might be* devastating. *What do you think would happen if even one person got killed because of something we did? Even accidentally? Millions of people might suddenly disappear from the face of the earth!"*

We pulled into the driveway.

"I don't think you really believe that," said Joshua. "You and Uncle Jim are always saying that God is in control of everything. He wouldn't allow that to happen."

"And there's a good point," said Dad, attempting to end the discussion once and for all. "God is *in control. Everything in history is just the way our Heavenly Father knew it would be. He didn't* make *it that way; He just* foresaw *it. And you can't change it. No matter how hard you try. God won't let it happen."*

Mom turned around at that instant and faced Joshua sternly. I didn't think I'd ever seen *her so stern. "I don't want to hear anymore about this. You make me a promise right now, Joshua Plimpton. You promise me that you won't sneak off and go back to that cave."*

"Huh?" Joshua looked mystified. "You really think I'd do that?"

"You're just about the same age as your father when he *did it."*

"Didn't you sneak off too?" I asked Mom.

She scowled at me with a look that said if she wanted to hear my opinion she'd ask for it.

"I learned the hard way," she declared. "I will not have my son doing the same foolish things. Do you understand?"

"Don't go ballistic," said Josh. "How would I get there anyway? Ride my skateboard?"

Mom narrowed her eyes. "I'm not so naïve. You'd find a way. A boy will always *find a way. Now you promise me, Joshua. Say it!"*

Josh looked defeated and glum. Finally he blurted, "All right! I promise!" He got out of the car and stomped into the house. Mom breathed a sigh of relief. She knew Josh was capable of a lot of things, but he'd never yet broken a promise.

Finally Mom said to Dad, "I knew I'd have to ask him to make that promise one day. I've known it ever since the day we left Bountiful. It's part of him, Garth. It's rooted in his soul. And you and Jim are no help. All your stories. Why wouldn't *he fantasize about saving the Nephites? All his life he's identified them as* his people. *He considers himself* one *of them!"*

"I know," said Dad. "And because of it, I'm not sure how long he'll be able to keep that promise."

"Just a few more years," said Mom closing her eyes, as if in prayer. "That's all I ask."

CHAPTER 2

I am Apollus Brutus Severillus, a centurion in the Fifth Legion of the empire of Rome, born in the eight hundred and fifth year since the founding of the great city on the Tiber, or as I have also come to know it, the year of our Lord, 52 A.D. But now I am a stranger in a strange land, an Odysseus seeking his place in a new and foreign world. I cannot explain the miracles that have transpired to bring me here. But here I am, and my eyes have been wide with wonder ever since.

After that fateful April night when I bade farewell to Meagan Sorenson and her family, I rode south upon the motorcycle that had been given to me by Harry Hawkins. How I've loved this machine! I loved how it made me one with the wind. I had taken with me only a small pack with light provisions, and about one hundred dollars worth of new-world paper money, also acquired from Harry in exchange for my Centurion's helmet. It was clear that I would have no need of it here. But I retained my sword. New world or not, no soldier of Rome should ever be without his blade.

I rode for several hours, finally bringing my mount to a halt at the side of the highway and rolling out my bedding in the grass. By morning I was hungry, but choosing not to deplete my small store of rations, I fashioned a crude lance using a sapling and my short blade. After secreting my motorcycle in the brush, I stalked several head of deer on a nearby hillside. A short time later I had slain my quarry. I was just in the process of skinning it when the automobile of a policeman rolled off to the side of the road.

I waited for him warily as he approached, my sword near at hand in case he tried to claim my prize for himself. As he arrived and discerned the method that I had used to bring the animal down, he scratched his head in amazement.

He indicated my lance. "You killed that with *this?*"

"I had no bow. But I'm adept enough with a javelin when I need to be."

"Unbelievable. I've come up empty three years in a row—and you bag one with a *spear!*"

"You're welcome to share breakfast with me if you like. When we're through, I'll take a few strips off the shoulder and you're welcome to the rest."

"Are you serious?"

I waved him off modestly. "No thanks necessary. Just one warrior to another."

"I'm afraid I'm going to have to cite you for hunting out of season."

"'Out of season?'"

"Poaching."

"Is this imperial land?"

"Very funny. What's your name?"

"Apollus Brutus Severillus."

"No kidding," he said flatly. "Where are you from?"

This was where the matter got rather sticky. The man wanted addresses, places of birth, and many other strange things that sounded rude and invasive. When I told him I was a native son of Italy, he asked if I possessed something green—a card or something. He then asked if I spoke Italian, though I assumed he meant Latin.

"Isn't that what we're both speaking?"

He became quite agitated. I cursed myself, remembering suddenly what Meagan had explained about the miracle of languages that accompanied a traveler to this world. The policeman no longer believed my story. He asked if I was an escaped prisoner of some sort. Perhaps I should have slain him with my blade at that moment, but as a newly baptized and ordained Christian, I knew this wasn't right. I decided to cooperate and allowed him to drive me to the police head-quarters of his village.

They made a picture of me and pressed my ink-covered fingers to paper. Then they asked me all the same questions and again found my answers unsatisfactory.

Four days! That's how long they kept me in a prison cell. I truly regretted having not slain the policeman when I had the chance, but at least I found the food palatable. Truthfully, it was highly satisfying. I acquired a particular taste for french-fried potatoes dipped in mayonnaise. After discovering that my "fingerprints"—as they put it—did not match any known criminal, I was placed before a judge and told that I should pay a seven-hundred-and-fifty-dollar fine. After discovering that I had only ninety-two dollars and seventeen cents to my name (I'd spent a small amount on fuel) the judge threw up his hands, charged me for time already served, and commanded that I get my sorry backside out of his courtroom.

I was forced to walk back to the place where I had secreted my motorcycle. From there I continued southward, arriving some hours later at a glittering city with more lights than I had ever seen in any foreign capital, including Rome or Alexandria. I gawked in wonder at all of the flashing signs and tall, shimmering buildings with statues and illuminated pictures of women standing fifty feet tall. Like women in a Bacchanalian revelry, many of them wore only the scantiest of garments and had feathers and frills coming out of their heads. Thousands upon thousands of motorized cars galloped back and forth in a desperate rush. It was perhaps the most frenetic vista I had ever witnessed, and yet its decadence exceeded even that of Corinth or Athens. Greasy and fast-talking men stood upon the sidewalks handing out obscene little books, the ink of which stained my fingers. I may not have been able to read the words, but their intent was clear enough. The air itself in this place was repulsive and suffocating. I took my meal at an establishment that exactly resembled a place Meagan and Harry had introduced me to in Salt Lake City called "Arby's," and again mounted my motorcycle.

This time I rode east, into the rising sun. I rode far and fast, taking no thought for my destination. At a place with the tongue-twisting name of Albuquerque, my money and fuel ran dry. For the first time I felt true loneliness. I yearned in my heart to return to the world I knew, and the sites and people I understood. But I would not be defeated by this mysterious and resplendent land. I would conquer it like any other adversary, and prove that I could survive without aid or charity.

I was fortunate at this time to befriend a group of men who called themselves "immigrants" from a land called Mexico. They appeared quite destitute compared to the rest of the populace, and reminded me of the refugees I'd seen in the hovels and backwashes of Judea. Most had traveled a long distance seeking work, after which they planned to return to their country of origin to live a more comfortable life with their families. I got along with these men remarkably well. I saw in them an opportunity to repent somewhat of the tyranny I'd perpetuated as a Roman. Besides, they respected me. One evening when a drunken man accosted their women, I sliced his leather belt with a single well-aimed stroke and sent him shimmying off with his trousers around his ankles. After that, the immigrants felt a degree of safety and protection in my presence. They also felt I spoke their language surprisingly well for a "gringo."

In their company I found various opportunities for employment that did not require something called a "social security number." It was hard work, honest work, and always in the open air under a gleaming sky. It reminded me of my boyhood, harvesting fruit on my grandfather's estate in Felsina, and for the first time since arriving in this new world I had friends of my own making.

I became particularly close to a man named Heliodoro Paiz. He was a simple man, and a hard worker who'd left his family back in a Mexican village called San Andrés Tuxtla. At the end of the harvest season I traveled with him back to his native land, and subsisted for a time by the grace and hospitality of his family. Nevertheless, I remained quite an oddity to the local denizens. Here was a gringo who spoke perfect "Spanish," was known for his skills as a fighter, and also as a defender of the weak. My fame caught the attention of a local businessman named Domingo Guzman. He was a good man who controlled vast tracts of land for growing an unusual crop called sugar cane and another called pineapple. He was having considerable trouble at that time with harassment. Several of his fields had been burned and many of his workers had been threatened with physical harm. The perpetrator was a foreign fruit company who for years had tried to purchase Domingo's land or drive him out of business. I was hired as a kind of plantation policeman. My job was to protect his workers and property.

There were several altercations over the course of the next few months, all of which ended with my adversaries face down in the mud or slithering back to the holes out of which they had crawled. The harassment soon ended, and Domingo kept me on as his personal bodyguard and plantation foreman.

The subject of my background rarely came up, perhaps because those who sought to know were too frightened to ask—an anonymity that I was all too happy to perpetuate. Some would ask Domingo for information, but he would tell them that I was a very private man. Over the months, I think even Domingo began to see me as a relic from the past. We grew quite close and he treated me like a son, but the questions from the people of the village continued.

Many thought I was an old-fashioned western cowboy, especially when I told them that I had come from a village in Wyoming called Cody. Others felt I could only have been an American fugitive, ducking the law and hiding out in the jungles of southern Mexico. Others postulated more interesting theories. Once I let slip that I had been a soldier in a faraway land, and once, while disciplining an indolent worker, I shouted that "as his Centurion he was obligated to obey!"

Behind my back some began to call me "the Roman," or "the Centurion." They would whisper that I was "crazy" or "dangerous," and some even suspected that I was a kind of demon.

However, I remained a religious man, and as often as I could I attended worship services in the local churches. But the ceremonies were quite different from those I remembered with Meagan and Harry and the others. The tutors of my new Christian religion had failed to mention all of the different denominations and variations of worship by those who professed the doctrine of Jesus Christ. As I tried to explain to people about the ceremonies that I recalled—partaking of bread and water, preachers from the midst of the congregation, the laying on of hands for gifts and blessings, or having three successive meetings, one in which the men and women were separated—I was told that my church sounded like the Pentecostal faith. But after attending one of their meetings, I knew this wasn't the church I was familiar with.

Most of those around me belonged to the "Catholic Church," but few attended regular weekly meetings. Most attended only on holidays or special occasions. Regrettably, I adopted much the same habit. It all became very confusing, but nothing could take from me the feelings that I'd had in the presence of Meagan and Harry, Garth and Jim, or the apostle named John the Beloved. I knew that Jesus Christ was my Savior. I just began to doubt the purpose of uniting to any particular sect.

During this period many women sought my affections, but I did not forget the covenants I had made when I was baptized. I would often think of Meagan Sorenson. Her memory gave me strength. But I was not a fool. I knew that any declarations of love that she'd expressed were the ramblings of a young girl. Yes, she was in love with me. She loved my "uniqueness." She loved how I was an exotic warrior from a strange world, and she was infatuated because I had saved her life. But I felt she was no different than the young girls in so many conquered provinces who worshipped soldiers only because they were Romans, and Rome was the ultimate symbol of power and strength.

Though I was still a young man of twenty-two years, I'd been around enough to know that such infatuations wear off quickly. Those very "differences" that they once found so attractive soon become the thing they most detest. In the end, they all go back to what is familiar, a man they understand, not someone whose moods and customs are so unpredictable.

So while I dreamed of the amber-eyed girl I'd come to know on the slopes of Gerizim, on the roads of Judea, and on the decks of the ships that crossed the Middle Sea, and though I had promised her that one day I would come back to find her, I had no intention of ever seeing her again. It wasn't fair to ask her to love a man like me. We were such different creatures. I was a man of violence and a rolling stone. Perhaps it was *because* I loved her that I also knew she deserved far better.

It was during the third summer of my sojourn in the new world that a most unusual event transpired. I was taking my evening meal at a local cantina at the edge of the town of San Andrés. It was raining hard. I found the slap of raindrops on the wooden roof relaxing as I consumed my tortillas with chorizo sausage and cheese. Only one other table was occupied. I thought nothing of the American seated in the corner, smoking his tobacco cigarette, and enjoying a bottle of Coca-Cola. Picking out an American wasn't difficult here. They were normally better dressed, often wearing a colorful shirt, the armpits and neckline soaked in sweat, and the customary sunglasses. This man also wore sunglasses, even though he was sitting in the shade, and he had on a wide-brimmed hat with a reptile-skin band. On the seat beside him was a canvas bag. He was an older man, thin, but reasonably fit, with graying hair. His face was long and drooping. Even through the lenses of his gold-rimmed sunglasses I could tell he was watching me.

At first I ignored him. Just another tourist who found it curious to see a gringo dressed like a plantation worker. But then he spoke and my efforts to ignore him became impossible.

"Certainly do get a lot of rain down here," he said.

"It's the season," I replied, returning to my meal.

"You speak English," he observed.

I glanced around to see if anyone else was listening. I had learned never to speak in the company of two men who spoke varying languages. The experience had often sparked a debate about which language I was really speaking. But as we appeared to be alone, I replied, "Yes."

I felt I knew his next question: *What was a gringo like me doing in a place like this?* But I wasn't in the mood. I studied my plate to see if I could justify leaving. Sadly, my meal was only half-consumed, and this cantina did serve good chorizo. But the man's next question surprised me.

"You're the one, aren't you?"

I cocked an eyebrow. "Pardon?"

"The one they all talk about around here called Apollus the Roman—the American who speaks two languages in the same sentence, depending on who might be listening."

I set my tortilla back onto my plate. I was aware that many locals found me a curiosity, but I had no idea that my celebrity status merited the attention of American tourists. And no one had *ever* been so bold as to mention my gift of languages—at least, not to my face. I started to rise. Half-consumed or not, dinner was over.

"Please," said the man. "I didn't mean to offend you. I've been looking for you. They told me this was where you often came to eat your dinner."

I remained standing, glowering down at him. "You were looking for me? Why?"

"Relax. Sit down—please. I don't bite. I might have taken no interest in your story at all, except that I also heard where you were from."

I sat down cautiously. "What did you hear?"

"I heard that you were from Cody, Wyoming. Is it true?" He continued to peer at me through his gold-rimmed sunglasses.

The soldier in me was on full alert. "What is that to you?"

"I'm also from Cody. Lived there almost ten years. I worked in law enforcement. What was your address?"

I pretended to take an interest in my food again. "I don't remember."

"Don't remember, eh? Cody is a pretty small town. There are not that many streets. Do you remember the street?"

I felt I should have known. Cody was the first village in the new world that I'd ever seen. My memory of it was still quite vivid. Unfortunately, I'd never learned the name of any of its streets. I decided to mention one of its landmarks.

"I lived near the airport," I replied. "I liked to eat their hamburgers."

The man chuckled. "I'd never thought of the Airport Cafe as one of Cody's finer restaurants."

"Why do you want to know these things?" I said abruptly. "Who are you?"

He shrugged. "Just making casual conversation, friend. Two men from the same hometown. I thought we might have something in common. Something to reminisce about."

No matter what he said, I knew this was no casual conversation. There was something disquieting, almost menacing, about this man. I looked at him a little closer than I had before. A notion flashed in my mind. No, he *couldn't* be . . . could he? Was it possible that he was also a stranger out of time? It was *my* turn to ask questions.

"You're from Cody, Wyoming?"

"That's right. I still own a small cabin there, though I hardly ever see it. In my business I have to travel quite a bit. I make it a habit to come down here a couple times a year. Right now I'm staying in Catemaco at the Hotel De Los Brujos."

Hotel De Los Brujos. It was an odd name for an inn. Hotel of the Warlock. Everyone around here knew that Catemaco, a town and lake a few miles to the west, was a popular stomping ground for people who professed to practice witchcraft. They held several festivals at different times of the year. Many of these witches were foreigners from the United States, and also other parts of the world. Was it possible that these festivals might attract witches from other *centuries?*

"What business are you in?" I asked.

The question made his eyes light up with pleasure. "I'm a dealer in rare antiquities. Unusual items. Things purported to have supernatural powers. Crystal balls. Indian charms. That sort of thing. You might say I have a special knack for such items—knowing when something's power is real and when it's fake."

"Oh? And how often do you find that an item's power is real?"

"More often than you'd think."

He reached toward the canvas bag, unzipped it partially, and pulled out an odd-looking trinket that looked like a ring with a dark purple stone. The metal was so wide it would have covered the wearer's entire knuckle joint, making it impossible to bend the finger.

"Cleopatra's Amethyst," he declared. "Said to have been used by the Egyptian queen herself to seduce and control Mark Antony."

"Oh?"

"Fake. No powers whatsoever. I would wager that no spell was ever conducted upon it. But it is of some antiquity, so the chances are good that I can still pawn it off on some unsuspecting dolt." His hand went back to the bag. "Now *this* is a little more intriguing."

He pulled out a strange silver head, about the size of a grapefruit, molded in the same fashion as many of the ancient *Olmeca* heads that one saw in village plazas and museums of this area. Normally these heads were made of granite, stood to the height of a man, and weighed thousands of pounds. This smaller silver sample had the same oriental-looking features and rounded battle helmet, but its eyes were inset with dark red stones.

"There is some power here. Not an exorbitant amount, but it can help to locate certain things that one might lose. Its principal value is its age, for everyone knows that a spell grows stronger with age. The silver ore that made it is from a quarry very near here on a mount that the ancients once called Ephraim Hill."

"This is all very interesting, but—"

"In my lifetime I've only held one item of truly great power. By coincidence, this item happened to have been forged using the same silver ore. But alas, it is long dead. The power is gone. However, I recently acquired another item that I also find intensely curious. I got it from an old Indian villager in Santiago Tuxtla. But unfortunately I haven't been able to make much use of it. Strange as it seems," he chuckled uneasily, "I don't think the item *likes* me very much."

I was afraid he was softening me up for a sales pitch. Since I really had no interest in such wares, I steered the conversation back to a subject that might help me learn who he *really* was.

"You say you lived in Cody for ten years? Where were you born?"

"I was actually born in *Casper*, Wyoming." He leaned forward. "But keep fishing, my friend. Maybe you'll finally ask the *right* question."

I narrowed my gaze. I'd heard enough of this. It was time to go. What did it matter who he was or what nonsense he carried in his canvas bag? If he was a Roman or someone else who had traveled through the cave, what was that to me? He had his own business, and I wanted him to stay out of mine.

As he sensed my agitation, he laughed again, this time from the belly. "I know what you're thinking. You're wrong, however. I'm not a traveler who likes to explore *old caves*, if you get my drift. But I also know a few things about you that you'd probably prefer I *didn't* know. For one, I know that you're no Roman Centurion."

I pulled in my chin.

"No," he added thoughtfully. "I suspect you're from a slightly different era. Does the word *Nephite* mean anything to you?"

Nephite. It was a name the Hawkinses had used. A race of people. That warrior, Gidgiddonihah—the one who had died in Athens—*he* was a Nephite. And those other men—Jashon, Heshlon, and the rest who'd sailed with us back to Judea. They were also Nephites. The boy, Jesse, and the young man, Micah, had taken a different tunnel and gone to their world. I tried to recall the name of their city. Zarahemla. Yes, I knew all about the Nephites. But why would this man ask me if I knew what the word meant?

"Ah," he said with note of satisfaction, "You *do* know that word. I knew that I wouldn't be disappointed. But I suspect a word that you know even better is the word *Gadianton*."

His tongue had caressed the word, like something sweet. I shook my head. This was a word I did *not* know. Or did not remember.

He sat back. "Oh, don't play coy with me. Why else would a Nephite who had traveled through the cave come down to the area of Lake Catemaco and the Hill Vigia if he was not a follower of Gadianton?"

I said nothing. Just stared at the man. I decided it wasn't the right moment to confess that I didn't understand. I first wanted to hear more of what he had to say.

He continued, "I wasn't certain at first, but when I heard a few more details about you, I decided I had to meet you for myself. I wasn't absolutely sure until I heard you speak. You see, I'm fairly fluent in both Spanish and English. Most of my Spanish I learned in a Mexican prison where I was sentenced for fifteen years. My native language is English, so naturally that's the language that I hear in my mind—that is, if I don't think about it. But when I concentrate—when I really focus on the sound of your voice—there are moments when I could swear that you're speaking Spanish. That's how I know. You see, I've met men like you before. It was almost a quarter century ago. I followed these men from Cody, Wyoming, all the way down to this region of the world. We were both pursuing the same thing—an ancient sword of magnificent power. Does this ring a bell?"

Again, I didn't react.

He smiled widely, and I saw that one of his teeth on the right side had been broken off. It looked just like a fang. A brown and rotten fang. "Yes, I thought so. What I wanted you to know is that *I am one of you.*"

He proceeded to make several gestures with his hands—odd gestures where he crossed his fingers and touched them to different parts of his face—never taking his eyes off mine. I hadn't the vaguest idea what he was doing, but still I said nothing.

"Do you believe me now?" He put out his hand. "The name is Finlay. Todd Finlay."

I looked at the hand, but I didn't take it. He let it drop to his side.

"You can trust me," he assured. "I'm here to help you. But first you must help me. I would like to show you the item that I acquired from the old Indian. I feel you might be able to tell me a few things about its origin that no one else in this world would know." His hand brushed against the collar of his shirt. The thing he wished to show me was apparently hanging around his neck, hidden. "But not here," he added, glancing around suspiciously despite the fact that we appeared to be alone. "And first I would like you to tell me why you have come to this world. What is your mission?"

We stared at each other for a long moment. I decided to play Mr. Finlay's game a little longer.

"Why don't you take a guess? What do you *think* it is?"

His expression relaxed. He took a drink of his Coca-Cola. "I'm afraid I wouldn't know that. But I know what it *isn't*. Or at least what I *hope* it isn't. I hope you haven't come here looking for the sword of Akish. I've been to the summit of Vigia a hundred times, scraping at the soil, yearning to hold that piece of metal in my hands again." He sighed longingly. "It just isn't there. I still feel as if that sword is a part of me. Something continues to draws me to it. But there's no power anymore. As I said before, the sword is dead."

"I see. Well then, I guess my mission was a waste of time."

He looked at me strangely. I was afraid I'd said the wrong thing. Unfortunately, my next statement mucked things up even worse.

"I'll have to go home and tell Gadianton that he's out of luck."

His frown sunk even deeper. "I thought . . . Gadianton was dead."

"Yes," I said quickly. "He is. But his spirit lives on, yes? His, uh . . . his mystique."

Finlay's face reddened. He leaned forward, eyes lethal, voice low. "Show me the sign."

My muscles went rigid—a natural reaction when I suspected someone might be about to attack. "What sign is that?"

He suddenly looked agitated. "You're no Gadianton. What are you?"

Now it was *my* turn to lean forward, my eyes like dagger blades. "I am a Roman—a Centurion of the Fifth Legion, and I could kill you with a snap of my wrist—so don't toy with me."

"A different time?" he gasped. "A different place?"

I pulled a face, not quite sure what he meant.

He went on. "Are you saying to me that this cave . . . Are you saying that it has the power to transport men from *other* places and times? I'd always thought it was limited to . . . I hadn't *realized* that it might also—"

"I wouldn't know about any of that."

"Who brought you here?" he asked sharply. "Who led you up through those tunnels?"

I hesitated. This was not a question I wished to answer.

"Was it *him?*" he asked. "Was it Jim Hawkins? Or was it Mr. Plimpton?"

I was unsuccessful at masking my surprise.

"So you *do* know them. Well, so do I. I know all about them. Everything I *need* to know. Was it them who brought you here?"

I decided to lie, cover my tracks as best I could. "I don't know those people. Actually, I don't understand a word you've been saying. I've just been listening for my own entertainment. But I'm afraid I'm not having fun anymore."

I tossed some pesos on the table and got up to leave. But I'd hardly stepped outside and put my shoe in the muddy street when a hand grabbed my arm. I faced the American again, and even with the rain falling all around us, I could smell the foul breath of his rotten tooth.

"I've *been* there," Finlay said. "I've been to the cave. I've explored every tunnel. *I can't find it!* Tell me where it is! Where is the passage that leads to other places and times? *Tell me!*"

I gripped the man's hand firmly and removed it from my sleeve. Then I slammed it back against his chest. My expression became as cold and intimidating as I could make it.

"Touch me again and you'll regret it."

"I'll pay you. I'll give you anything you ask. I'll even give you—" He hesitated, but then his hand reached inside his collar. "I'll even trade you for something more valuable than anything you could possibly own. Something that may change your life forever."

"You have nothing I want."

But then he reached inside his shirt and pulled out the thing that had been hanging around his neck. I squinted my eyes to take it in. It was as curious-looking an object as I'd ever seen—two glistening white stones, almost opaque, fastened inside some kind of silver rim. The rain splashed off the stones and seemed somehow to disturb the way the light reflected off the two surfaces. Or was it that it affected the way the light emitted from within? I wasn't sure.

"They are called 'seers,'" said Finlay, emphasizing the "s" sound like a serpent. "The Indian told me they are from the ancient worlds. The same ancient worlds that can only be reached through the caves of Spirit Mountain. They are said to possess many deep and marvelous powers. If you tell me what I wish to know, I will give them to you."

I shook my head. "I'm not interested in your magic."

"Oh, but it's not *my* magic," he insisted. "They mean nothing to me. As I was explaining, the stones don't seem to like me. They are far choosier than the Sword of Akish. Who could blame them? I am old and ugly. But perhaps they would be more accommodating to a strong, able-bodied man like you. And even if their powers stay dormant, who could deny their enchanting beauty? There is great value and wealth in this alone, wouldn't you say? You could be a rich man."

I realized I was still staring into them. I mentally shook myself and looked squarely back at Finlay. "Keep them," I said firmly.

His shoulders dropped. He looked utterly desolate and defeated. "Please," he begged softly.

I raised my finger to his face, speaking slowly so that he did not mistake my meaning. "I don't want to see you again, Mr. Finlay. Don't come near me. Don't speak to me. Or it will not be a pleasant memory. Do you understand?"

I walked away, leaving him standing alone in the mud. But before I'd rounded the corner, I heard his voice call out again over the clatter of the downpour. "If you won't tell me, I know who will!"

I turned again, peering back through the thick, blurring sheets of rain. But the street before the cantina was empty. The American tourist with the brown hat and gold-rimmed sunglasses was gone.

CHAPTER 3

The parents were going away! Isn't that every kid's dream? Well, actually I was going to miss them very much. But hey, it was only for a week. Dad was going to some kind of archeology convention in Austin, Texas, and he was dragging (I mean taking) my mother with him. Supposedly there was gonna be some extra time. They hadn't had a vacation together in years. Not that Texas sounded all that romantic to me, but they got a really nice hotel, and besides, there were some aunts and cousins of my mom's who lived nearby.

At first I thought we were gonna stay with Uncle Jim and Aunt Sabrina, but with the new baby and all, and because Jim was headed out of town for two days for some computer convention, the lot of babysitter fell to Mary.

Josh and I had mixed feelings about this. I mean, we liked Mary and all. She was a sweet, pretty girl, but . . . well, to be quite honest, she could be a real stick-in-the-mud sometimes. She was just so serious *all the time. She'd been working night and day for two years trying to learn how to read English, and learn everything else about the twenty-first century. I think she wanted to impress Harry when he came home. It surprised everybody how quickly she picked up on things.   The problem was that she'd forgotten how to relax, and she didn't feel comfortable watching anybody else relax or have fun either.*

She had a real problem with a lot of the habits and customs people had in modern times. Like wearing makeup. Back in Israel the only ones who wore lipstick and rouge and stuff were girls from the bad part of the village. Only after she saw that everybody *wore makeup now, did she give it a try. The first time was before Harry left on his mission. Steffanie had given her a makeover and all the girls were in total awe of how beau-tiful she was. She coulda been a Hollywood model!—except that she was probably too short. But when Harry finally saw her, he acted so shocked that Mary immediately went into the bathroom and washed it all off. Harry stood outside the bathroom door trying to apologize, saying how nice she'd looked and that he'd just been taken by surprise, but she never wore makeup again until after Harry had left on his mission. And then it was just a little at a time—a little foundation, a little lipstick, and so on. By now she'd gotten kinda used to it, but she still didn't understand why anybody should have to waste so much time in the bathroom everyday.*

And that went along with her biggest *problem. She was overwhelmed by how much* stuff *people had. All her life she'd never owned more than two outfits—the one she was wearing and another one being washed. Before the end of her first month in the twenty-first century, Meagan and Steffanie had loaded her down with so many clothes that Uncle Jim had to buy her a new dresser.*

But it was how spoiled *everybody was that really seemed to upset her. She felt like the only thing anyone ever talked about was getting more stuff, or comparing their stuff with other people's stuff, or trying to earn more money so they could get rid of their old stuff and buy new stuff. She found it incredible how much people* wasted!*—food, clothes, shoes, every-thing! She told us once that half of the things we threw into the garbage—including the plastic garbage liner itself—would have been considered prized possessions by many of the people in her day.*

One thing she had no patience for was hearing people complain about being bored or how there was nothing to do. She wondered how this was possible in such a rich, colorful world and once she said to Uncle Jim, "I think it may be better to have nothing. When you have nothing, you trea-sure the things that God *treasures, like loved ones, and service, and easing one another's burdens."*

But even so, Mary was now talking about going out and getting a job. She was starting to feel uncomfortable about Uncle Jim having to support her all the time. I don't think it would have been strange at all in her world for the father of the boy she hoped to marry to take care of her. But TV and magazines and the way people always talked (not in our family, but everywhere else) made her feel like she wasn't doing what was right. There was something else too. But if I tell you this you gotta realize that I'm not a mind reader—it was just a suspicion. I think she was afraid that Harry might not really want to marry her.

Once I heard Meagan tell Aunt Sabrina that one of the girls in our ward had called Mary "Harry's future squaw." The girl didn't realize that Mary had overheard. When Mary asked Meagan what she meant, Meagan tried to brush it off and say that the girl was just jealous. But Mary kept asking, so Meagan, in the kindest way that she could think of, tried to explain to her what rude people in our day thought that a squaw was—someone who cooked and sewed and walked behind the husband and chewed rawhide till it was soft.

Mary was confused at first, wondering why this was so bad. In many ways that was what girls did in ancient Jerusalem too. But after she figured out that the girl was insulting *her, she was deeply hurt. She started to think that in this day and age there must not be much use for a girl like that. She wanted to be* useful *to her husband, and wasn't sure that she could be very useful to Harry the way she was. So she worked hard to learn how to be a twenty-first-century woman. It would have crushed her if she thought Harry would marry her only because he felt sorry for her. But I think that's just how she was starting to feel.*

But back to the babysitter thing—at least there was a silver lining. You see, Mary had just gotten her driver's license! Can you believe it? Three years ago she was grinding wheat in ancient Israel and now she was driving a car! To Mary, getting a driver's license was a very big deal—much bigger than it was for most new drivers. She'd forced Meagan to help her practically memorize the test booklet, while Uncle Jim spent many hours teaching her how to drive.

Joshua and I were excited. This meant that our babysitter had wheels! Her car wasn't exactly the prettiest thing I'd ever seen. Uncle Jim had found her this old wagon-looking thing in the newspaper. How did my uncle put it? Oh, yeah—"twenty gallons to the mile instead of twenty miles to the gallon." But that didn't matter to us. Now we could go anywhere! *Lagoon, Trafalga, Seven Peaks, Park City, Provo Towne Center—you name it, we could go. The first place at the top of our list was Lagoon. The really cool thing about it was that Mom and Dad left on Monday, so we could go to Lagoon on Tuesday— normally the slowest day of the week. No long lines! We wanted to ride everything twice—and certain things, like Rattlesnake Rapids, the Rocket, and Colossus* three *times. The problem was convincing Mary.*

After we'd explained to her what Lagoon was, she replied, "Is there nothing more useful to do with your day than to spend it at a park for amusements? Isn't there work around here that you could accomplish to please your parents?"

Somebody needed to teach this girl how to lighten up. Joshua and I decided to take it on as a personal mission.

"I promise, Mary," I said, "if we can go to Lagoon today, we'll work all day tomorrow. We'll weed the whole backyard!"

"You'll have fun!*" Joshua added. "You must remember what it's like to have fun, don't you?"*

Mary bristled at that. "Pleasure and satisfaction are gained from hard work. How can you consider such frivolous activities to be fun?"

We could tell this was going to be a long week.

Joshua tried a different tactic. "Harry will be home in eight days. I guarantee you he wouldn't *think such activities are frivolous. He* loves *Lagoon. He'll probably try and take you there himself. I think you better practice having fun for a day, Mary. A* whole day—*or Harry might get bored out of his gourd."*

That hit the right nerve. With much reluctance, she agreed to take us. Mary was quite nervous during the drive there. She'd never been to an amusement park and wasn't sure what to expect. The way we described it didn't help her attitude very much. She'd seen a roller coaster on TV, but the sight of it only scared her to death. She had no idea why anybody would ever ride such a thing for enjoyment!

We arrived at about 11 A.M. We paid the extra money to park close to the entrance, because that was how Dad always did it. It wasn't as slow as I'd hoped. If this was slow, I'd have hated to see what it was like on Saturday!

As we were standing in line to buy tickets, I remember seeing an old man in a wheelchair pushing himself across the hot parking lot. The sight made me feel kinda guilty, knowing it would've been nice to let someone like that park where we were parked. As I looked over at handicapped parking, most of those spots were filled too, so the poor man had had to wheel himself all the way from who knows where. He made it up to the ticket place okay though, so I felt better.

Mary's eyes were wide with all of the swirls of color, the sounds of loud music, the bells and whistles, the mountains of cotton candy and popcorn, and all of the other sights as you walk into the park. She crinkled her nose at the way some of the girls were dressed and shook her head as she listened to many of the children whining and crying because their parents wouldn't buy them things.

"Hey, the Terror Ride!" shouted Joshua as we rounded the corner. "Come on! The line isn't very long!"

But Mary took one look at the ghoulish faces and the skeleton playing the piano on the outside of the building and said, "I don't think so."

"Huh?" said Joshua.

"Why would anybody try to make such evil, terrible images into something fun?"

Joshua and I looked at each other. "Just like Mom," we said at the exact same time. Then we laughed and moved on to the roller coaster.

Mary refused to stand in line with us at first.

"Oh, c'mon," said Joshua. "The roller coaster is Harry's favorite."

"You think you can use that argument on me every time?" asked Mary.

"It's worth a try," said Joshua.

At last Mary sighed and got in line. The whole time she was kinda pale. When we climbed into the roller coaster, she looked absolutely scared to death—especially as it steadily clicked its way to the top of that long, steep hill. Then whooosh! We were off like a rocket! By the end, Mary was laughing and screaming along with everybody else, even if there were tears in her eyes.

As we climbed out and made our way down the ramp, Joshua asked her, "So what did you think?"

She hesitated, then quipped, "So silly to build a ride that goes absolutely nowhere except back to the place where it started."

Ho boy, I thought. Then I saw the sparkle in her eyes. She wasn't about to admit it, but I think she enjoyed it.

After that we rode anything and everything. We walked the whole length of the park back and forth, and ate the junkiest junk food a person can ever eat. By the end of the afternoon, Joshua and I felt wonderful and awful all at the same time. Mary's favorite ride seemed to be the bumper cars. Don't get me wrong—she kept wearing her sour face—yet that innocent girl from ancient Jerusalem was an absolute menace on the bumper-car floor. And sneaky too, ramming into Josh and I from out of nowhere, then grinning that tight, mischievous grin. She could say whatever she wanted, but I think she was having the time of her life. By late afternoon, Mary was still going strong, unlike Mom and Dad who always hinted that it was time to go home about now.

As we were headed back to the other end of the park to ride the Wild Mouse I noticed the old man in the wheelchair whom I'd seen in the ticket line. He was still alone. His chair was parked next to the game area where you throw basketballs. He tried to throw a basketball up and hit the hoop, but the poor man's ball didn't even make it all the way to the rim. He just didn't have the strength.

He noticed us walking by and called us over.

"Excuse me," he said, "but could you children help me?"

We moved in closer.

He explained, "I promised my granddaughter that I would win her one of those dragon things. Do you see it?"

He was pointing at a big, green, stuffed dragon with red fins coming down its back and a shiny purple belly. It was the biggest prize in the booth.

"I wonder if you two could help me win it. I promise I'll pay all of the fees. You just keep throwing basketballs until we get the prize."

The guy who ran the game said, "Yeah, c'mon, you three. Help the guy out. Be a good samaritan."

I frowned at the greedy game operator. He wouldn't have cared who threw the basketballs.

Mary looked at the baskets and shook her head. "You two go ahead. I'll just watch."

"Ah, give it a try, Mary," said Josh. "Here, I'll show you how."

Joshua stepped up to the line. He pretended to spit into both his hands and rub them together. Then he said to the old man, "How far did ya get?"

"Not very far, I'm afraid. I've been playing for about fifteen minutes and I haven't hit a single basket."

That pulled at my heart. It was so sweet—just an old man trying to win a prize for his granddaughter.

"Where's your granddaughter now?" I asked him.

"She was here with us earlier today. My son-in-law won her that dragon. But then as we got out to the car she discovered that someone had stolen it. I'm afraid it broke her heart. I decided to come back and see if I could win her another one. Go on. All three of you. Please. Just keep throwing as many baskets as you can until we win."

The race was on. Mary was frowning as she stepped up to the line. She missed her first three baskets, then turned back to the grandfather and said, "Wouldn't it be easier if you just bought her the toy?"

The game operator shook his head, "I couldn't give it away like that. Those are the last ones left. Someone has to win it fair and square."

Nobody said anything about giving *it away. What a jerk! He was just hoping we'd pay out a lot more money than the stupid thing was worth.*

So all of us kept tossing basketballs.

After missing her next three shots, Mary said to the grandfather, "You must love your granddaughter a great deal."

His face lit up. "She's Grandpa's sweetheart. Not much younger than this little girl right here. What's your name, honey?"

"Becky," I said. "This is my brother, Josh. And this is Mary, our babysitter."

"That's wonderful. Where are you all from?"

"Provo," I answered.

Just then a siren went off and Joshua shouted, "Hey! Three in a row! I win!"

The man running the booth handed Joshua a scrawny-looking dog. Josh pulled a face. The man explained, "With each win you trade in what you had before and graduate to something bigger."

"How many wins till we get the dragon?" I asked.

"Just four more times."

What a con man! But the grandfather in the wheelchair kept shelling out more dollars.

"I think you two are wasting all his money," Josh said to Mary and me playfully. "Just let me win the prizes."

"Oh, now," said the old man. "I want all of you to have fun. Everybody. Go on, Becky and Mary. Keep throwing."

"It's your money," I said, smiling warmly.

He tipped his brown hat like a big-hearted cowboy.

Another siren went off. Mary let out a squeal, then quickly recovered her composure. She'd won the game! A moment later, Joshua's siren went off again.

Mary took a break and said to the grandfather, "What's your name, sir?"

"It's . . . Bernard. Cody Bernard."

"Cody?" Mary repeated. "Isn't that also the name of a city?"

"Why, yes," he answered. "There's a Cody, Wyoming. I think there's also a Cody, Nebraska. Cody, Wyoming, is the most famous, though. Named for William F. Cody—'Buffalo Bill.' Why? Have you been to Cody?"

"Yes," said Mary skittishly. "But it's been several years."

"Gorgeous town. I haven't been there in a long while either."

"I got it again!" cried Joshua.

Just one more win and we'd have the dragon. I was feeling very jealous. I really wanted to do my part. As of yet I'd only gotten two basket-balls total. Mr. Bernard had easily spent over twenty-five dollars on us.

"What will you do after you win the dragon?" asked Mary.

"Go home, I suppose. Give the prize to my granddaughter. But first I might get me some of those old-fashioned french fries. I sure do love those fries."

"Why don't you come with us?" asked Joshua. "It's time for dinner anyway, isn't it, Mary?"

"That's awfully kind," said Mr. Bernard. "But, I wouldn't want to intrude—"

"Don't even concern yourself," said Mary. "We'd be honored to have you."

"Well, if you put it that way . . ."

I was feeling the suspense. I'd just made two baskets in a row.

"Just one more," I said, "and I win!"

"No chance," said Joshua.

"Shhh!" said Mary, helping me to concentrate.

I stuck my tongue in the corner of my mouth, focusing hard. I threw the basketball up, but all I saw was it hitting the rim. Then I closed my eyes, afraid to look. The siren rang out. I'd made it! Mary and Joshua started clapping and Mr. Bernard made a loud whistle with his fingers. The game operator handed me the big green dragon. Proudly, I set it onto Mr. Bernard's lap.

Even though he was wearing sunglasses with gold frames, I could still see his eyes through the lenses and I swear there was a big twinkle in them. He gave me a really wide grin. I winced a little as I saw that one of his teeth was brown and broken, like it was rotten.

"Congratulations, Becky," he said. "You're the big prizewinner."

"What about me?" squawked Joshua. "I won three times!"

"And you too, Joshua. Yes, you two are quite the pair. I'll bet your father is proud to have children as lovely as the two of you. He'd probably do anything in the world for you."

We continued to congratulate one another.

Mr. Bernard sat back and said a little more quietly, "Yes, probably anything in the world."

CHAPTER 4

For the first twenty-four hours all I did was stew over the words of my conversation at the cantina. Finlay's statements continued to torment me. Not just the general conversation, which I would have found disturbing enough, but . . .

There was something about the *surprise* in his voice when he realized that I wasn't a Gadianton or a Nephite, but that I'd come from an entirely different place and time. It was as if he'd felt his mind illuminated to ideas or possibilities that he'd never considered. There was also something about the stones—the two white stones set in the silver frames that hung around his neck. I'd never seen seers before. Normally such was the stuff of magicians and charlatans, but these were different, and I wasn't quite sure how.

His most disturbing words that day were the ones he spoke regarding Jim Hawkins and Garth Plimpton: *So you* do *know them. Well, so do I. I know all about them. Everything I need to know.* I also couldn't escape the connection between these words and his final sentence—*"If you won't tell me, I know who will."* If indeed he had been referring to Jim or Garth, I feared they might be in danger.

The following morning I searched for Finlay again, even riding my motorcycle ten leagues—that is to say, thirty or forty kilometers—to the *Hotel of the Warlock* in Catemaco. To my surprise and alarm, I learned that he'd left the night before, despite the fact that he'd already paid the innkeeper for two additional days.

That afternoon I strode into the antechamber at the villa of Domingo Guzman and told him that I would be leaving within the hour. When I couldn't give him any kind of estimate on my return, he was deeply disappointed, but because of the urgency in my manner, he did not attempt to talk me out of it.

My long journey back to the United States began. For three days I rode hour after hour, the wind whipping at my leather jacket, the bugs and debris collecting on the visor of my helmet. I was given no trouble at the border since my appearance and accent convinced them I was a citizen of America. I stopped as infrequently as possible, only to ask directions or to catch a few hours sleep here and there along the roadside. I lost more hours of precious time by riding all the way into Salt Lake City, only to discover that Jim Hawkins no longer lived at his villa in West Valley. Fortunately, the new owner was gracious enough to provide me with his new address, though I hardly understood the numbers and words—962 Plum Orchard Lane.

"He gave it to me so's I could forward any mail," the man explained. "Plum Orchard Lane is one of those streets east of the University."

"University?" I repeated.

"BYU. At least I *think* that's what he said. It's been two years." He looked me up and down one more time. "What was your name again?"

"Apollus Severillus." Ever since my arrest for poaching, I'd stuck to using only my forename and cognomen.

"You sure you're an old friend? I'd hate to give out his address to just anybody. You're not a bill collector, are you?" He laughed uneasily.

"No," I said. "Just a friend. One last question . . ."

"Yes?"

"Where is Provo?"

He gave me general directions to this village, assuring me that it wasn't many leagues. The written language of this world was still undecipherable to me. Several more times I stopped to ask directions, always showing the small piece of paper on which the man had written the address. To my credit, I had at least learned the new world's symbols for numbers, so upon reaching the correct neighborhood and street, I had only to search out the house with a nine, a six, and a two.

Upon finding myself within three or four houses of my destination, I discovered that my heart was pounding faster than usual. I'd been so consumed with just getting here that I hadn't given much thought to the emotions I might feel, or how my return might be received upon my arrival. *First let me talk to Jim*, I thought. Let me deliver my message. Then I could prepare myself for Meagan. Perhaps such a reunion wouldn't be necessary. Did she even live here? How old was she now? Eighteen? Nineteen? At what age did a young woman strike out on her own? Among the Romans it would not have been until she was wed. But here . . . I didn't know.

Perhaps it was best, I thought, not to see her at all. I could ride away again without stirring up any trouble. And yet . . . I confess, I felt a definite twinge of anxiousness. Even nervousness.

What foul emotions! I'd faced the most dangerous opponents that a soldier of the Empire could face. Why should I feel nervous about something as trifling as this?

At last I found the house with the designated numbers and parked my motorcycle in the street. The place looked uncommonly quiet. The front window was open, but no one was visible within. A large, rugged-looking vehicle was parked in front. Otherwise, there was no evidence that anyone was inside.

Cursing myself and shaking off all feelings of trepidation, I strode up the cement sidewalk and climbed the two steps to the front door. My fist hesitated for an instant, then I rapped four times.

Footsteps shuffled inside. Someone was definitely home. My chest tightened. All at once the door swung open. But the person standing there I didn't recognize. It was a man, perhaps a year or two younger than me, with the blonde-haired and blue-eyed countenance of a Germanic tribesman. He was about my height, but with a notably slighter build. The young man scrutinized me suspiciously.

"Can we help you?" he asked.

I began to think I'd made a mistake. "I must have the wrong house," I said. "I'm looking to find Jim Hawkins."

"Oh," said the young man, and I sensed that he was a little relieved. "Brother Hawkins isn't here right now. He's in Las Vegas till Thursday."

This took me a bit off guard. "Who are you?" I asked stiffly.

He took slight offense at my question and challenged back with, "Who are *you?*"

I found his query equally irritating, and narrowed my gaze. "What about other family members? Are they at home?"

A female voice spoke from somewhere behind him. "Who is it, Ryan?"

My heart tightened into a fist. I knew that voice. It was Meagan.

"He won't say," Ryan called back inside.

Then she appeared. Her eyes settled upon me and she stopped sharply. Her mouth fell open. I attempted a smile, but it was weak. I gazed into her dark eyes. She was more beautiful than I even remembered. When we'd first met, her hair had been black. Now it was a bright, reddish blonde, floating on her shoulders, looking as alive as any other part of her glowing complexion. Stronger feelings than I'd anticipated stirred up inside me.

Her eyes clouded with tears as she whispered, "Apollus."

"Hello, Meagan."

The man named Ryan frowned.

Meagan announced my name again, this time at the top of her voice. "Apollus!"

She threw her arms around my neck and embraced me with all her strength. I embraced her in return. Then all at once she stopped. She released me and suddenly looked awkward, her face blushing brightly. She glanced back at Ryan, who stood there, squirming.

Meagan tried to compose herself and said, "Ryan Champion, I'd like you meet an old friend, Apollus Brutus Severillus."

"How are ya?" Ryan said without a grain of enthusiasm.

Looking beyond him into the house, I saw Sabrina crossing toward the door. I brushed past Ryan, knocking him aside slightly, and swooped down to hug her.

"Oh, Apollus!" she cried. "Welcome back!"

Moments later I was also getting my first look at the new addition to the Hawkins family—a fine-looking son with his mother's blue eyes and his father's strong jawline (well, as strong as might be expected in an infant). Even as young as he was, I told them he appeared to have all the makings of a new Hawkins adventurer. Meagan looked as if she was bursting at the seams with questions, but Ryan's presence caused her to hold back. The young man hadn't said another word, just looked on, sucking at the inside of his cheeks. At last Meagan took his hand and said, "Ryan, why don't you go and buy the movie tickets for tonight. Then come back. Is that all right?"

It didn't look "all right" with him at all. But he sighed through his nose and said curtly, "Fine." Glumly, he turned and walked out the door.

Meagan watched him go, then she faced me again, her head still shaking in wonder, and once again threw her arms around me. "Oh, Apollus, I can't believe it! I can't *believe* it! Where have you been? Two years!" She leaned back and all at once her expression flushed with anger. "Why didn't you contact us? Didn't you think we'd be worried about you? I've been—we've *all* been *sick* with worry! *How could you do that to us?*" She was surprisingly furious.

Sabrina came to my rescue. "Meagan, it's all right."

"Sorry," I said evenly, searching for something more, but finding no words.

"Sorry?" Meagan repeated. "*Sorry?* That's all you have to say to the people who cared about you for so many—?"

"Honey, please—" said Sabrina.

"*Where have you been!?*" Meagan demanded.

"Mexico," I said.

"*Mexico?*"

"Yes. I worked for a large landowner. He grew pineapples and sugar cane."

She narrowed one eye. "You were a pineapple picker?"

I bristled a little. "I was a sentry for his plantation."

"Mexico!" she repeated with a rush of breath, as if the very idea would have never occurred to her.

"I know I should have contacted you sooner. I just . . . wouldn't have known what to say."

She didn't accept this for an instant. "We knew each other for a year, Apollus! What did you think I expected you to say? We just wanted to know you were all right—that you weren't dead, lying in some morgue somewhere with a John Doe tag on your toe. If only you knew how often—" She stopped herself, overwhelmed by anger and frustration.

Sabrina touched her daughter's arm. Only now did I realize the grave pain that I had caused them. But even if I'd understood the courier or postal systems of this world, what would I have written? Of course I'd watched people speaking into those boxes called telephones, but I still hardly understood how to use them, and I certainly didn't trust them.

"I'm sorry about all of it," I said again. "But I'm here now. There was no choice."

"No choice?" asked Sabrina curiously.

Meagan's eyebrows drew together as well.

"What I mean to say is, I had to make sure everything was all right. That no one was in danger."

"Why would we be in danger?" asked Meagan.

"You're *not*," I said. "That is to say, you're *probably* not. I came because I had to make sure. I had to talk to Jim."

"About what?" Meagan persisted.

"Jim won't be back until Thursday," said Sabrina.

"Then Garth. I could just as easily talk to Garth."

"They're out of town too," said Meagan. "All but the two kids. Garth and Jenny went to Texas until Saturday night."

I frowned heavily. What kind of terrible fortune was this? Again I cursed myself for not trying to call them on a telephone before my departure. Domingo might have helped me. But what would I have said? I'd felt strongly that this matter had to be discussed in person.

"Can we reach them with a telephone?" I asked.

Sabrina nodded. "Jim should be back at the hotel later tonight. What's so urgent?"

I began soberly, "I met a man in Mexico. A very unusual man. My impression was that he was a witch—or some other kind of shaman. He knew about the cave. He also knew Garth and Jim."

"He knew about the cave?" asked Meagan, her voice filled with dismay. "Was he a Nephite? Or a Roman?"

"I don't think he was either one. He told me that he was born in this world."

"What did he say about Jim and Garth?" asked Sabrina.

"Only that he knew them. And that it must have been one of them who guided me here. You see, he discerned that I was not from this place and time."

"How did he do that?" asked Meagan.

"I'm not quite sure, but . . . well, my peculiarities are no secret to the people of the village where I live. This man drew his own conclusions. At first he accused me of being a shaman like himself—a 'Gadianton' is the word that he used."

Their eyes widened with alarm. "This man was a Gadianton robber?" asked Sabrina.

"Yes, I think so, but . . ." I sat down heavily in a chair. "No, I really don't know for sure. That's why I need to talk to Garth or Jim."

"What made you think we might be in danger?" asked Meagan.

I pondered this, wondering how to answer. How could I explain that I was acting—what is the phrase?—on a "hunch?"

"It was the things he said. Or perhaps it was one of the things *I* said. He told me that he had visited the cave near Cody, Wyoming, and had searched for the passage to the 'miracle rooms,' but his search had availed him nothing. He implored me to tell him where this passage was, but I refused. His last words before he fled into the rainstorm were, 'If you won't tell me, I know who will.'"

"And you think he meant . . . us?" asked Sabrina.

I nodded tentatively. "I think he believes Jim and Garth are the only other ones who know the way."

Meagan sat down as well, struggling to comprehend. "But if this man was so desperate to find the secret passage, why hasn't he searched out Jim or Garth before now?"

"I think he *has* searched them out," I said. "He acted as if he knew all about them. Perhaps he was just waiting for the right moment. Or a strong enough reason. I may have given him that reason."

"What do you mean?" asked Sabrina.

"Until our conversation he seemed to think that only Nephites or Gadiantons could make this journey through the cave. When he realized that I was neither—but that I might actually be a Roman—his interest in finding the hidden passage appeared to swell, almost to desperation. He even offered to trade for the information—offering an unusual pair of stones that hung around his neck."

"Pair of stones?" asked Meagan.

"They were white, almost translucent, set in silver loops in much the same manner as the eyeglasses worn by people in this world."

Meagan had an odd look on her face. "Did he give these stones a name?"

I shook my head. "No, but he called them 'seers.'"

Her eyes widened. *"Seer stones?"* She looked at Sabrina, whose curiosity had also been piqued.

"And he gave them no other name?" Meagan continued. "Nothing like 'Urim and Thummim?'"

I shook my head.

"Don't be ridiculous, Meagan. No Gadianton—from this century *or* the past—would ever be in possession of something like that." Sabrina scoffed.

Meagan was not satisfied by this. She asked me, "What did he tell you about them?"

"He said they had marvelous powers. But he did not elaborate."

"Why would he think that you would trade information about the cave for these stones?"

I shrugged. "I'm not sure. I had the impression that he had gotten very little use out of them himself, as if he wasn't quite sure how they worked. Actually, he said that the stones did not 'like' him."

"Didn't 'like' him? That almost sounds like he treated these stones as . . . pets."

I nodded tentatively. "He inferred that they operated on magic, but he was quick to point out that it was not *his* magic."

"Whose magic was it?"

Again, I shook my head.

"What was this man's name?" asked Sabrina.

"Finlay," I replied. "Tom or Todd Finlay or something."

Their faces were blank. It was a name they didn't recognize.

I continued, "He kept mentioning a sword . . . a sword that had been destroyed. He was far more consumed with this sword than anything else, including the stones about his neck."

The worry lines deepened in Sabrina's face. "Jim once told me about a sword."

Meagan's face brightened. "That's right! The Sword of Coriantumr! Jim told us that he destroyed it at the summit of that hill in Mexico—El Cerro Vigia."

"Yes!" I said excitedly. "Only Finlay called the sword something else." I strained to remember. "The Sword of Akish or . . . Anyway, this man seemed obsessed by this object. He even suspected that this had been the entire reason I had come to this world—to somehow lay my hands on it."

"But what does this sword have to do with making him more determined to find the Rainbow Room or the Galaxy Room?" asked Sabrina.

"That's one of the questions I wanted to ask Jim."

Meagan chewed her upper lip, determined to solve the riddle. "I think I might have an answer. Or at least an idea." She turned to Sabrina. "Jim told us that this sword was originally brought here by Gadiantons, didn't he?"

Sabrina nodded. "He said it was an evil sword—a tool used by evil men in ancient times."

"That's right," said Meagan. "But Jim destroyed it at the top of Vigia in *this* century. What if this man, after learning from Apollus that Frost Cave might be the means of visiting different places and times—places besides the Nephites in the first century B.C. . . ." She stopped herself. "No, it's a stupid idea."

"What?" Sabrina demanded. "I'm in the *mood* for stupid ideas."

"What if . . ." She thought another moment, making sure the thought was clear in her mind. "What if Mr. Finlay somehow got the idea that he might travel back to a century before the sword was brought here and try to get it back again? What if he thought all he needed was someone to take him deep inside the cavern—show him the secret route down to the Galaxy Room?"

We stared at Meagan, trying to take it all in.

"See, I told you it was a stupid idea."

"Stupid or not," said Sabrina, "it would explain why Apollus felt we might be in danger."

"But the Galaxy Room doesn't work like that," said Meagan. "It can't be used to bounce around to any century you want . . . Can it?"

"It doesn't matter," I said. "What matters is what Finlay might *believe*."

"Do you think he might try to make Jim or Garth the same offer that he made to you?" asked Meagan. "In other words, trade the stones for the information?"

I thought about this, then shook my head decisively. "I think he now has serious doubts if the stones are any kind of commodity for negotiation. The next time, I fear he will try to bargain with something more substantial. Something he is certain that we would not refuse."

The reality of that sank in. Meagan turned quickly to her mother. "Is there any way to reach Jim before he gets back to his hotel?"

Sabrina shook her head. "I don't know how. I tried his cell phone earlier to ask about a bill, but he didn't answer."

"Doesn't your service carry that far?"

"It's not our service," said Sabrina. "Jim has a bad habit of leaving the cell phone in the car."

"What if we called the convention center and had him paged?" Meagan suggested.

"What about Garth?" I asked. "Is he at a place where we might call him?"

"Mary might have a number," said Sabrina. "She's over there right now, babysitting."

"No, she's not," said Meagan. "She took the kids to Lagoon today."

"Lagoon?" I asked.

Meagan started to explain. "It's an amusement park with—never mind. It's about an hour from here."

Sabrina moved toward the telephone. "I'll try to reach the convention center to have Jim paged. It's nearly six. They're probably starting to close up shop."

"What about Garth's children and Mary?" I asked.

Meagan shook her head. "We'd never reach them now." She smirked. "Knowing Josh and Becky, we probably wouldn't reach them until very late." She looked at me, and her expression grew serious. "Do you think they might be in danger?"

I gaped at her, feeling uncertain. The fear in my heart was swelling again—the same fear that had urged me to make this long journey in the first place.

CHAPTER 5

Mr. Bernard was a riot. All through dinner as we sat in the shade by the merry-go-round he told these stupid, silly jokes that weren't even that funny. It was just cute the way he told them, like, "Why was Six afraid of Seven? Because Seven Eight Nine." Or, "Why did the monster spit out the clown? 'Cause he tasted funny."

Half the time we answered the joke for him, which always caused him to snap his fingers, make a silly ugh! *sound, and say, "Thought sure I'd get ya with that one!"*

After we were nearly finished with dinner, Joshua sat across the table eating some pistachio nuts. Dad called that one of Joshua's trademarks. He always filled his front pockets with pistachios. He bit one open and asked Mr. Bernard, "What happened to your legs?"

"Joshua!" I scolded. Even I was old enough to know that such a question was in bad taste.

But Mr. Bernard didn't even flinch. "I was shot while I was on duty."

"You were a policeman?" asked Joshua.

"That's right. The bullet is still lodged in my back. I make out okay. I can even stand for a few minutes if I use a cane."

Shyly, I asked him, "Does . . . the bullet hurt?"

"Sometimes," he said. "Mostly at night when I try to sleep. Truth is . . . I haven't slept much for the past twenty-five years."

"Twenty-five years!" cried Joshua. "That's impossible!"

"Oh, I lie down," said Mr. Bernard, his eyes gazing a long ways off. "But I don't sleep."

"That sounds terrible," said Mary.

He waved this away. "Ah, it's nothing. In fact, I'll tell you something. In a way, that bullet saved my life. Taught me what was really important. Family. Togetherness. And the Man Upstairs." He whispered the last part and pointed quickly up at the sky, like it was a big secret.

"That's beautiful," said Mary. "I admire your courage."

"Well, thank you, Mary. You're a sweetheart. And I must say, it looks like you're doing a smash-up job taking care of these kids."

Mary blushed a little. "Oh, they're no trouble." She mussed Joshua's hair. "Are ya?"

Mr. Bernard sighed. "Well it's starting to get late."

"Are you kidding?" said Joshua. "It's not even dark yet."

"Oh, that's all right," said Mr. Bernard. "I'm sure you three young-sters have better things to do than hang around with a broken-down old man."

"Don't be ridiculous," said Mary.

"No, I really better be going."

He picked up his big green and purple dragon from the picnic table and placed it on his lap in the wheelchair. It was easy to see that it would be difficult for him to push the wheels on his wheelchair and hold onto the dragon at the same time.

"Would you like us to help you to your car?" asked Mary.

"No, no. I'm sure I can manage." But then the dragon fell off his lap and bounced onto the ground.

I quickly picked it up and gave it back.

"I insist," said Mary. "In fact, maybe we should all think about *getting home."*

"Oh, please!" Joshua pleaded. "The party's just getting started!"

"I'm sorry, Joshua," said Mary.

"Just one or two more rides. Please?*"*

"It's perfectly all right," said Mr. Bernard. "I'll tell you what. If you promise to help wheel me out, I'll tag along for a little while."

"Are you sure?" asked Mary.

"I have a saying that I live by," said Mr. Bernard. "Nothing makes you feel younger than being around the young."

That settled it. He was coming with us. Joshua and I took turns pushing him. The wheelchair really wasn't that hard to push and it felt good to be of service. Our last two rides ended up being Jet Star 2 and the old *Lagoon roller coaster, which was my personal favorite. Each time we got off a ride, Mr. Bernard was waiting with a big smile.*

"*Looks like you survived another one,*" *he said.*

You know that feeling that you sometimes get when things aren't quite right? Well, I never got that feeling—except once. It was while we were wheeling Mr. Bernard out toward the front entrance. It was just this dark, uncomfortable feeling that came over my body.

But there was no reason for it! It wasn't as if Mr. Bernard had ever said or done anything weird. He was just this kind, crippled old man. Besides, Mary and Joshua didn't think anything was wrong. Or if they did, they never said anything about it. Maybe because they thought the same thing that I did—that the feeling was silly, so they ignored it.

As we reached the edge of the parking lot, Mary asked him, "Where did you park your car?"

"*Truck, actually,*" *he said.* "*I think it's at the end of this row. Where's your* chariot *parked?*"

"*Right over there,*" *I said.*

"*I'll tell you what,*" *said Mr. Bernard.* "*Why don't you youngsters wheel me out to my truck, and Mary, you can fetch your car and bring it down to pick 'em up.*"

Mary hesitated a little. "*Well, I—I don't know if—*"

"*I'll tell you what,*" *said Mr. Bernard.* "*We'll get started and you can catch up in about thirty seconds. Just drive alongside us.*"

"*It's all right, Mary,*" *said Joshua.* "*We'll race you there!*"

And with that, Joshua rolled the wheelchair down the little lip on the curb and out into Lagoon's wide-open parking lot. I had to run to catch up.

"*Be careful, Joshua!*" *I called out.*

"*Hey!*" *laughed Mr. Bernard.* "*And I thought I wasn't goin' on any rides today!*"

I glanced back at Mary, who had walked over to her car and was now looking in her purse for the keys. Then I turned back.

"*Joshua slow down!*" *I said sternly.*

He slowed down to a fast walk. "*All right, all right. I just want to beat Mary.*"

"*You're doin' fine,*" *said Mr. Bernard.* "*Just fine.*"

As we got closer to the end of the row of parked cars, I asked Mr. Bernard, "Which one is yours?"

"That one," he pointed toward a truck in the very last stall.

I was expecting to see a pickup truck, but this looked more like a van. Actually, like a moving van. It looked old, and it wasn't very big, at least compared to the moving van that Uncle Jim and Aunt Sabrina used when they moved to our neighborhood, and there was no company name on it. Mr. Bernard handed me his stuffed dragon and said, "Why don't you put this on the front seat and grab my cane. All right?"

I opened the front door and did as he said. His cane was heavy, made out of polished wood with knots in it and everything. After I pulled it out, I looked back at Mary. She was pretty far away, but I could tell that she hadn't climbed into her car yet. In fact, she still seemed to be looking for the keys. It almost looked like she'd dumped all of the stuff inside her purse out onto the hood. I wasn't too worried. After all, she'd told us that Uncle Jim had taught her a trick—hiding an extra pair under the floormat. It didn't occur to me that this wasn't going to do her much good if the doors were locked. I carried the cane around back, where Joshua had wheeled Mr. Bernard.

"How come you drive a moving van?" I heard Joshua ask.

"It's just for today," he explained. "My son moved here from out of state. I gotta get it back in the morning. Becky, why don't you unlatch that little do-hickey at the back and slide up the door. We'll put the wheel-chair inside, then you two can help me around to the front seat."

I looked at the rear door. It was sorta ratty-looking with spaces between some of the slats. I unlatched the little bolt and Joshua pushed up. The door screeched as it rolled up into the roof. The back of the truck was totally empty, except for a single open padlock lying just inside—one of those padlocks with a long neck loop.

"Okay, you two," said Mr. Bernard. "Now why don't you help me to stand up, then you'll probably have to work together to pick up that wheelchair and put it inside."

"I won't need any help," said Joshua as he got underneath one of Mr. Bernard's arms.

I got under the other one and we helped Mr. Bernard to stand.

"You'd be surprised," said Mr. Bernard, leaning against the cane, his legs wobbly. "A wheelchair is a rather heavy article. You can fold it up by stepping on that thing at the back there."

I stepped on it and folded it together. Joshua took one side and made a little groan. It wasn't as light as he thought. I grabbed the other side.

"If you can," said Mr. Bernard, "set it all the way down inside."

We set it on the edge, then Joshua climbed up. I took one last look back toward the front of Lagoon. Mary was no longer standing by the car. That's weird, I thought. Then I saw her. She was moving quickly toward us down the row of cars, but she was still only halfway.

"I think Mary lost the keys," I said.

Mr. Bernard ignored that. "Hurry, hurry!" he said impatiently. "My family has likely sent out the Marines to look for me. Set it in as far in as you can."

We carried it toward the back wall. Just before we set it down, I turned to look at Mr. Bernard. I only saw his face for a second, but I'll remember that look forever. He wasn't leaning on the cane anymore. He was standing straight. His expression was cold and frightening, like it wasn't even Mr. Bernard's face anymore. His hand whipped out and grabbed the padlock. Then he yanked down on a cord from the roof. The rear door screeched closed and the inside went totally dark expect for a couple of narrow strips of light coming through the slits. Footsteps ran around to the front of the truck.

At first I didn't know what to think. My thoughts were racing. Was he playing a joke on us? But then the driver's side door opened and closed and I heard someone scream. It was Mary. The truck's engine roared and we lurched forward. I grabbed onto my brother for balance, but both of us fell onto the floor. The truck made a sharp turn and Joshua and I were jerked to the right.

"What's happening, Joshua?" I cried. "What's going on?"

"I don't know! I don't know!"

"What's Mr. Bernard doing? Where's he taking us?"

The truck tore around another corner and threw us to the left.

"Mary!" Joshua shouted. "MARY!"

But Mary didn't answer, and we could no longer hear her screams.

* * *

A few moments after Sabrina had called the convention center where Jim Hawkins was conducting his business, he called us back. There were two separate telephone boxes on the first floor of the Hawkins' household. Sabrina held one of the "receiver" parts to her ear, while Meagan and I stood close together and listened on the other.

"*Todd Finlay?*" Jim exclaimed after I'd told him what had transpired and reported the man's name. "*Yes*, I know that name! It's been—goodness!—twenty-five years! Todd Finlay was a cop in Cody, Wyoming. After I found the Sword of Coriantumr on the canyon rim, he stole it from the police station. He turned up in Utah a few months later as the head of a UFO cult called the Bernardians. The sword seemed to be guiding him every step of the way. He was obsessed with it—totally controlled by it. He followed us down to Mexico. He tried to kill me at the Hotel Castellano in Santiago Tuxtla."

Sabrina's face darkened further with fear and anxiety. "Jim, why didn't you tell me about any of this?"

"I thought I had," he said. "I guess I never went into detail. The Mexican police arrested him. Since he was arrested with a gun in his hands I assumed they sent him to a nice Mexican prison, but I haven't heard a thing about him since that day. Apollus, you did the right thing to come back and tell us. Todd Finlay is potentially a very dangerous man."

"What about the stones?" Meagan said to me. "Tell him about the stones."

At her insistence, I repeated for Jim the details of the incident when Todd had tried to pay me for information about the cave with the two white stones. Afterwards, the line on Jim's end was silent.

Meagan, speaking into my receiver, repeated some of the information for emphasis. "Two white stones set in silver rims like eyeglasses. What does that sound like?"

"I know what you're getting at, Meagan," said Jim. "But the idea is ludicrous. How would Todd Finlay have ever gotten his hands on an Urim and Thummim? It's inconceivable. Todd Finlay has never been through the cave. As far as I know, he never even had direct contact with the Gadiantons who came seeking after the sword. Not that I ever saw any Gadiantons with that kind of item either."

"Is there any way he could have obtained it in modern times?" asked Sabrina.

"No," said Jim. "After Joseph Smith used the Urim and Thummim to help him translate the Book of Mormon, he didn't seem to need them as much. They were given back to the Angel Moroni with the gold plates."

Meagan broke in. "That's always what everybody has *assumed*. But there really isn't any definitive statement."

I stopped this course of speculation. "Todd Finlay definitely stated that they'd been sold to him by an old Indian in the village of Santiago Tuxtla. This Indian told him that they were from the caves of Spirit Mountain."

"What caves are those?" asked Sabrina.

"Spirit Mountain Cavern is another name for Frost Cave," said Jim. "An Indian name. Did Todd ever tell you the name of this old Indian in Santiago Tuxtla?"

"He never said," I replied.

"Did he say where this Indian got the stones?"

"No," I replied.

Everyone was thoughtful for another moment. I, of course, was extremely curious as to what exactly an "Urim and Thummim" was, but other matters seemed to weigh far more heavily.

"What do you think we should do, Jim?" Sabrina asked urgently.

"Try to get everyone together at the same location," he advised. "In fact, take everyone over to Marcos and Melody's in Salt Lake. Finlay might not know my daughter's married name, so he won't be able to look up the address in the phone book. Get hold of Garth and Jenny if you can. I'm headed to the airport as soon as I hang up this phone. I'll take the first flight available. We'll decide what to do next when I get there. Apollus, did you say Finlay left Mexico a full day before you?"

"Possibly," I said with regret. "But he may not have traveled as swiftly."

"Let's hope you're right," said Jim. "Because if Todd Finlay somehow got it into his head that there might be a way to get that sword back, there's no telling what he might do, or how determined he might become."

Jim expressed his farewells. There was a click and his voice disappeared. Meagan and Sabrina set down their own receivers. Their expressions were both grave and tense. Sabrina snatched up her phone again and said, "I'll call Melody, then I'll try the Plimptons again."

"We should go and get Mary and the children now," I insisted.

"Lagoon is a big place," said Meagan. "There's thousands of

people. Besides, you might pass them on the highway as they're driving back, making the trip a complete a waste of time."

At that instant the front door was thrown open. I turned abruptly, but it was only the young German tribesman, Ryan, having returned from his errand.

"Okay," he said to Meagan. "All set. The eight-thirty show starts in forty-five minutes, so we better—"

"Ryan," Meagan interrupted. She approached him. "We can't go. Something's come up."

"What do you mean? I bought tickets—"

She struggled to explain, "We, uh, we're having a little emergency. We'll have to do this another night."

Ryan looked at me, his eyes flecked with anger. "What kind of emergency? I don't understand."

"It would take too long to explain," said Meagan.

"Did someone get hurt? Maybe I can help."

I realized Meagan wasn't sufficiently making her point. I stepped toward the young man. "I think you had better go. We have everything well in hand."

This advice wasn't received very well. Ryan's face reddened with ire and the muscles in his neck tensed. "What's going on here? Who do you think you are? I was the one here for the *last* Hawkins family emergency." He looked at Meagan. "Wasn't it me who helped drive your mother to the hospital when she started having the baby? Wasn't it me who got hold of Jim? You trusted me then, didn't you?"

Meagan sighed. "Yes, Ryan. But this is—"

"Would you like me to put this person outside?" I asked Meagan.

She came between us and put her hands out to stop my forward progress. "No, Apollus—don't!"

"Put *me* outside?" Ryan said defensively. "You've gotta be kidding! Will somebody please tell me what's going on here?"

Meagan went back to him, trying to quell his temper. "Ryan, it's all right. I'll explain everything to you tomorrow. I promise."

"If *you* want me to leave, I'll leave," said Ryan crossly. "But no one else is going to ask me. So? Do you want me outa here?"

Meagan looked unsure how to respond. I was becoming more and more annoyed. Wasn't there enough tension without having to deal with this irritating insect? As Meagan glanced at me again, I raised my eyebrows to indicate that I was still perfectly willing to carry this person's hindquarters to the door.

But then we heard Sabrina, who was still talking on the phone in the adjoining room. "Hold on, Melody. I have a call on the other line." She pushed something on the front of the phone, then said, "Hello? . . . Mary!"

Our attentions were riveted immediately.

"Mary, what's wrong?" Sabrina asked frantically. "Mary—Mary slow down. I can't understand what you're . . . *Who* took them? . . . Oh no! OH NO!"

My stomach dropped. The blood left Sabrina's face.

"Where are you?" she continued. "You don't *know?* But I thought—! . . . What? . . .You're *what?* . . . Mary wait! You can't—! Mary, *don't! Do not try to do this!* You have to call the police! *Mary? MARY!*"

Sabrina, her face still as white as Tuscan marble, lowered the phone and looked at the rest of us.

"He took the children!" she said gravely, her hands shaking, her eyes filling with tears.

"How?" asked Meagan. "I don't understand—"

"She couldn't explain! She hung up the phone!"

Meagan was also near hysterics. "Why would she hang up?"

"She said she was at a gas station. She couldn't talk because he was leaving. She'd broken her car window. She was—"

"*Who* was leaving?" I demanded. "You mean *Finlay* was leaving? She was watching Todd Finlay *drive away?*"

Sabrina nodded. "Mary is trying to follow him!"

CHAPTER 6

As we rolled to a stop, Mr. Bernard's voice yelled from the front of the truck. "Nobody make a sound. Do you hear me? I don't want to hear a peep out of either one of you, or I swear by the fires of hell that I'll kill you both. Do you understand?"

Joshua and I were huddled together in the corner—the back corner—as far away from the front of the truck and that voice as we could get. It was such a horrible voice. It didn't even seem like Mr. Bernard's voice anymore. How could it belong to the same man who'd joked with us and said such kind things? But it was his voice—the exact same person. And that's what made it the most frightening. Because only the most wicked and evil person I could imagine would have pretended to be a crippled man for an entire day and playacted his part so well. This meant that we had no idea who Cody Bernard—if that was his real name—really was, or what he was going to do with us.

I'd been crying for over an hour while Josh struggled to make me feel better. He was trying to be brave and not cry himself, but I could tell that he was having to fight hard not to. We heard the door on the driver's side open and close and then Mr. Bernard fumbling with what sounded like a gas pump. I didn't hear anybody else. If I had heard somebody, I might've started screaming in spite of Mr. Bernard's warning—screaming as loud and as long as I possibly could. But I didn't dare. And neither did Joshua, although Joshua was brave enough to stand up on his two feet as quietly as he could. He pressed his eyes really close to one of the slats on the back door. He was trying to see outside, find out where we were.

He stood there for a long time, bending up and bending down, trying to see every angle. At last he quietly sat back down beside me.

"Where are we?" I asked in a whisper so quiet that Joshua barely heard even from a few inches away.

He shook his head like he wasn't sure, and yet I could tell something had seemed familiar to him. I knew we'd just climbed a big, long hill, because the truck coughed and chugged, like it was having a lot of trouble.

"I think . . ." he started.

"What?"

"The mountain over that way has paths on it, like a ski resort."

I thought a second. "Park City?"

"Yeah!" he whispered. I was afraid he'd whispered too loudly and we both became very quiet again. I didn't hear anything outside anymore. Had Mr. Bernard gone inside to pay for the gas? This might've been our best chance to start screaming and making a riot, but I still didn't dare. I was too scared.

At least I had the guts to do what Josh had done. I stood on my feet and went over to the thin gap. The light coming through it was getting dimmer. It was almost dark outside. I had to get up on my toes to see out the way Josh had seen. I looked off to the left and saw the mountain with paths cut through the trees, like ski runs. I was convinced now it was definitely Park City. But why had Mr. Bernard brought us here? Where was he going after he filled up the truck with gas?

I tried to get up even higher on my tippy toes and see off to the right. I could see part of the building that must have been the gas station. There was another building beyond it, across the street, that looked like another gas station. I also saw the "M" sign of a McDonalds, but it was quite a ways away. There were cars at the other gas station, but there didn't seem to be anybody else pumping gas where we were. It became obvious why when I saw the signs. Gas here was a full five cents more expensive. Mr. Bernard had decided it was more important to keep us away from people than it was to save a little money.

As I bent my neck a little bit more, something else at the other gas station caught my eye.

"Joshua!" I whispered.

"Shhh!" he said.

My whisper was too loud, so I leaned closer to him. "Give me a boost. I wanna see across the street a little better."

He was taller than me, so he was able to see at the angle I wanted without getting a boost. Just like a boy, I thought. Because I said I wanted to see something, he had to see it first.

"What did you want to see?" he whispered.

"Across the street. That other gas station."

"So?"

"Just give me a boost!" I whispered sternly.

He wrapped his arms around my waist and lifted me up. He didn't hold me very steady—but I still managed to catch another glimpse of what I'd seen before. Now I felt sure! I made a little gasp. Just then we heard the driver's side door open and close. The engine roared to life. With hardly a pause, the truck shifted into gear and Josh and I were thrown off balance. We fell to the floor. A tiny shriek squeaked out of my throat.

Mr. Bernard's fist pounded on the wall. "I said be quiet *back there!*"

We remained still for about a minute. Joshua watched me. He knew I'd seen something, but he didn't dare ask. Finally, the truck pulled out onto a highway or something, and the engine got loud enough that we felt sure our whispers weren't going to be heard no matter how hard Mr. Bernard tried to listen.

I couldn't keep it in any longer. "I saw her car!" I said excitedly.

"Whose car?"

"Mary's!"

"What are you talking about?"

"It was at that other gas station!"

"You saw Mary's white Monte Carlo?"

"It was parked behind that van, so you may not have seen it."

"If it was parked behind a van, how did you see it?"

"I did Joshua! Cross my heart! I saw the front of it."

His shoulders drooped. "How could you tell from just that?"

"'Cause of the license plate."

"You memorized Mary's license plate?"

"No, but it was crooked. Remember how her license was sort of lopsided?"

"No."

"Oh, Josh, it was her! I know it!"

He got back onto his feet and stuck his nose into that gap again. He tried as hard as he could to get an angle on the highway, but the truck was going over a hill, so he couldn't see anything.

"Did you see Mary?" he asked.

"No," I replied. "But it was her car."

"But you said she'd locked her keys in the car. How could she follow us if she didn't have any keys?"

I frowned. I'd sort of forgotten about that. How would she have followed us? Unless . . . unless somehow she got inside the car and got those extra keys. But what were the chances of that? She'd have had to bust out her own car window. I just couldn't see Mary doing that. Besides, what would she have busted it out with? My heart sank. Maybe it wasn't her car, but just wishful thinking.

Then Josh, still peering though that little slit, let out a gasp of his own. "I don't believe it!"

"What?"

"I think you were right!" He waved wildly for me to come see.

I tried to see, but I was still too short. Joshua picked me up again by the waist.

"Fourth or fifth car back," he whispered.

Our truck was going over another hill, so the fourth or fifth car back was blocked by a camper truck. But then, almost as if he'd been inspired, the driver of the camper switched lanes and I could see it. It was almost completely dark. Most of the cars had turned on their headlights, making it hard to tell colors. But Mary's headlights were still off. I could see quite clearly that it was a white car shaped exactly like Mary's. I could also see one person's shadow inside. Something about that shadow looked just like Mary.

But even as our hearts were cheering, I had to wonder what Mary thought she was doing. Did she expect to break that padlock and rescue us? And what if Mr. Bernard saw her? A chill went through me. Mary could get herself killed.

We stood looking through that crack for another half hour, checking and rechecking to make sure it was really Mary. Soon it was too dark to see anymore. Joshua and I settled back into the corner and huddled close together.

My tears felt like they were gonna start again. "Where is he taking us?" I asked Joshua. "He seemed so nice. Why is he doing this to us?"

Joshua growled, "I should have pushed that wheelchair right into a parked car. You should've taken that cane and whacked him right over the head."

Lots of things ran through our minds that we might have done differently. There just didn't seem to be any way that we could've known.

Quietly, I said to Joshua, "Do you think he's going to hurt us?"

"Just let him try," my big brother answered. "It'll be the sorriest thing he ever tried to do. I'll make sure of that."

But even as he tried to sound tough, I could still feel him shivering a little in the darkness.

* * *

Panic and commotion engulfed the Hawkins household. My own feelings of guilt were keen and devastating. I was the one who'd failed to follow my instincts for a full twenty-four hours—a hesitation that now looked as if it might have catastrophic consequences.

But the most vexing questions remained unanswered. Why would Todd Finlay take captive these two children? From what I understood, young Becky and Joshua Plimpton had been toddlers when they'd visited the cave—certainly too young to remember the secrets that Finlay wished to learn. They must have only been bait, I decided. Finlay would use them to lure Garth or Jim to his lair, then he would force either of these men to reveal the way to the hidden tunnel that led down to the miracle rooms.

"Where was Mary calling from?" Meagan inquired desperately.

Sabrina was overwrought. "I don't know. It was Call Waiting. Caller I.D. didn't get the number."

"Has she called the police yet?" asked Ryan.

"She made it sound like there wasn't time. I'm not even sure she knows how."

Ryan crunched his forehead, perplexed. "Doesn't know *how?*"

"I'll call them from here. I have to call *Jim!*" Sabrina raised the phone, but Meagan took her by the shoulders.

"Did Mary say anything that might give us a hint about where she is?"

Sabrina tried to concentrate. "Something about . . . back to Salt Lake . . . then up a canyon."

"Parley's Canyon," said Ryan. "The man could be headed east."

I gave Ryan a sideways glance. There was no getting rid of this gadfly now. He knew the details of this crisis as well as any of us—all except the motives. I'd always respected the Hawkins' advice that the secrets of the cave should be kept private. Ryan wasn't going to learn anything more from me. I wondered if it might be best to knock him unconscious with a blow to the head in the hopes that the resulting delirium would convince him that he'd misunderstood what had transpired.

Ryan asked, "Did she say what kind of car he was driving? Or a license number?"

Sabrina shook her head. "Nothing."

"If he's headed east," Meagan continued, "that means the gas station she called from was in Park City. Maybe even Evanston."

"Then we should go to these places and find her," I said. "If she's attempting to follow Finlay, she's risking her life."

"Don't you think this is a matter for the police?" asked Ryan.

I scowled at him. "Where I come from, we handle such problems ourselves."

"Where's that? Dodge City, Mr. Dillon?"

How I wanted to deliver that blow! It would be so satisfying.

"I think Apollus may be right," said Meagan. She turned to her mother. "We could take the other cell phone so that if Mary calls here again, you can let us know where she is. We'd be the first ones to reach her."

Sabrina shook her head vigorously. "We don't know anything about this situation. This man could be armed. He could hurt the children—"

Meagan spoke boldly. "That's why we have to go, Mom! It's *Mary!* It's Becky and Joshua! If he's taking them where I *think* he's taking them, it's imperative that we catch up to him. If we don't—" her voice cracked, "—we might never see them again."

Sabrina didn't seem to be in a frame of mind to deal with such ideas. "I'm calling the police," she declared and began pressing more numbers on the phone.

I faced Meagan. "We can't waste anymore time. We need to pursue Mary immediately."

"And how do you propose to do that, cowboy?" said Ryan. "On your motorcycle? Do you even know what Mary's car looks like?"

I raised a finger to Ryan's face. "You have become a considerable pest. I advise you to keep your mouth shut, *Ryan Champion,* and leave this to those of the proper mettle."

"Stop it! Both of you!" said Meagan. "This isn't helping!"

Sabrina went into the other room so she could hear herself talking. Ryan's nostrils flared. I could see his mind cogitating. In the end his basic male instinct won out—that is, his desire not to appear the coward.

"All right then," said Ryan, sighing huskily. "We'll take my 4-Runner. We'll take the cell phone. When we get to Park City, we'll call back here to see if there's been any more word from Mary."

Courageous or not, I saw no need to burden ourselves with an untested nuisance. "Your services aren't required," I replied.

"Yes, they are," said Meagan. "Ryan has the only available car. If we're going to do this we need to go *now*. Every minute may be taking them further away."

"Then let's do it," said Ryan resolutely, his hand already reaching into his pocket for the keys.

"You two get in the 4-Runner," said Meagan. "I'll get the cell phone and explain to Mom. I'll promise her we won't try anything foolish."

She physically pushed Ryan and me toward the door, urging us along. We eyed one another narrowly as we stepped outside.

"You heard the lady," said Ryan. "You get in back."

First I approached the travel pack on my motorcycle. After untying the straps, I pulled out my Centurion's sword and scabbard. Ryan watched as I hefted it, his eyebrow cocked in utter disbelief.

"What the heck is that?"

"Something you obviously don't understand," I replied.

"You're bringing *that?* What do you plan to do? Chop the kidnapper's head off?"

"Or yours," I said, my expression unflinching.

To that he did not reply. In fact he may have swallowed his tonsils.

CHAPTER 7

I wish I could say how long we drove. It seemed like forever. With every hour I knew we were getting farther and farther away from our families. Farther and farther from anybody who might be trying to find us. That is, except for Mary.

It was totally dark now, so we had no way of knowing if Mary was back there anymore. We kept looking out that narrow slit in the back door to make sure there were headlights following us, but a lot of times it was too hard to tell. We'd left the highway somewhere and started traveling on two-lane roads. Sometimes we would peer through that gap and see headlights and sometimes we wouldn't. Both of us began to think Mary had lost us. Even something as simple as needing gas or having car trouble would have thrown her off our trail forever. But at least maybe she could give our parents or the police or whoever some idea of where Mr. Bernard was going.

As for Josh and me, the first clue about our destination came to us sometime in the middle of the night. I had been dozing on the floor. Not sleeping, really. It was impossible to sleep with everything that was happening. But my eyes were closed and my thoughts were drifting when Joshua nudged me and said, "Thermopolis Hot Springs."

"Huh?"

"I just saw a lighted sign. It said Thermopolis Hot Springs. The sign *was behind us so we already passed it. But do you know what this means?"*

I shook my head. "Should I?"

"It means we're in Wyoming. Remember when we went to visit Uncle Spencer and Aunt Louise? Dad said he was going to take us swimming there, but we ran out of time. Thermopolis is on the way to Cody."

I perked up a little. "You think he's taking us to Cody?"

"I don't know."

Our imaginations started spinning. We both knew perfectly well that right above Cody, Wyoming, was the cave that could take us back to Nephite times. This was really bizarre. I started having strange thoughts.

"What if . . ." I could hardly get the question out. "What if Mr. Bernard is a Gadianton?"

The question made Joshua stiffen with dread. We knew the story of how Melody had been kidnapped by Jacob of the Moon and taken to the ancient city of Jacobugath.

"You don't think he's planning to take us back to Nephite times, do you?" asked Joshua. There was a strange note of excitement in Joshua's voice.

I shook my head. "I don't know, Josh."

"Wowww . . ." he sighed. "If he is a Gadianton and if he is trying to take us back to Nephite times . . . and if we were to escape . . ."

Now his imagination was getting carried away. "It's no use trying to figure it out," I said. "We're just gonna have to wait and see. Or wait till somebody tells us."

Our thoughts turned to the man sitting up front. He'd hardly said a word to us except for that first time we'd filled up with gas, and also the second time we'd filled up with gas, but that was only to bark the same threat about keeping quiet. I was getting so thirsty. Joshua still had some pistachio nuts in his pocket, but I refused to eat any, afraid they'd only make me thirstier. Still, being thirsty wasn't the worst thing. I had to go to the bathroom really bad. How long did he intend to keep us in here like this? Was he just gonna starve and torture us for days? I couldn't take it anymore. I got a sudden burst of bravery, marched up to the front of the truck, and banged on the wall.

There was no reply, so I banged again.

"Shut up back there!" the voice snapped.

"I have to go to the bathroom!" I called out.

"We'll be there in another hour. You can go then."

"I've already been holding it for an hour! I can't wait any longer!"

It seemed like he took forever to answer, but then he said in a low growl, "You'd be surprised how long you can wait."

A shiver went through me, like he was talking about more than just waiting to go to the bathroom. I went back and sat down by Josh. Surprisingly, I really didn't have to go anymore. Is that what happens when you get terrified? I'd always thought it was exactly the opposite. Or maybe it was an answer to a prayer.

That's what I'd been doing much of the time—praying. Joshua prayed a lot too. He didn't act like he was scared at all anymore—not since we'd passed that sign about Thermopolis. I hoped that was because his prayers had comforted him. I hated to think he was getting excited by the idea of finally getting his wish to visit the Nephites. That would mean he was temporarily bonkers, and who wants to believe that about their brother?

The truck kept on going for another hour. Towards the end of the trip we turned off some kind of main road and began climbing a dirt road that went up a steep hill.

"Cedar Mountain!" Joshua whispered. "We're climbing toward the cave!"

It seemed like we were climbing and climbing for hours on a road that took a lot of sharp turns. I'd never climbed Cedar Mountain in a car, so I couldn't be positive if it was this place or not. All I knew was that my stomach was beginning to hurt again from being scared.

The truck seemed to turn off onto a dirt road that was even worse than the first one. We held on as the truck went over some sharp bumps. A half minute later, we jerked to a stop. Joshua and I sat still. The driver's door opened and closed. We could hear Mr. Bernard coughing. His footsteps came around to the back of the truck. We saw a glimmer of light through the slits. Mr. Bernard had a flashlight. As he began tinkering with the padlock, Josh and I stood up. I was holding Joshua's hand. My grip was really tight.

A few seconds later, the door started to lift. But it didn't go up all the way—only a couple inches. Joshua's arm made a slight jerk, almost as if he was thinking about trying to escape. But he stopped himself and waited.

Suddenly two pieces of black cloth were tossed into the four-inch gap.

"Put 'em over your heads," Mr. Bernard ordered. "Then stand back to back. I'll take you to the outhouse one at a time. Don't think about trying anything. I don't need both of you. You understand? Only one of you. And I won't hesitate to cut one of your throats if the other causes me any trouble. Is that clear?"

"Yes," I said, my voice a peep.

"Yes," said Josh.

My hands trembled as I picked up one of the black cloth things. It was some sort of bag. There were even strings that could be pulled tight.

Josh and I took one last look at each other in the dim light. He tried to smile to make me feel better. I smiled back weakly. Then Joshua put the black bag over his head. I did the same. We stood back to back.

"It's on," said Josh.

The rear door slid up all the way. Mr. Bernard grabbed onto my arm. He pulled me roughly out of the truck and set me hard on the ground. Then I heard him close the door again and lock it shut.

"Just walk," Mr. Bernard said to me.

He held me under the arm, his nails digging in. I tripped on rocks a couple times, but Mr. Bernard kept me from falling. Finally, I heard some hinges squeak. I was pushed inside a hollow sounding room. The hinges squeaked again as the door was closed.

"Hurry up!" Mr. Bernard barked from the other side.

There was no way I was gonna try and go to the bathroom with that bag over my head. I pulled it off. It was still so dark it hardly made any difference, but Mr. Bernard's flashlight was shining through the cracks of the outhouse door. After I was finished, I pulled the bag back down on my face. He led me back to the truck and Joshua got his turn. He was taken away, the door slid back down, and the padlock clicked. Now I was all alone. I shivered again with fear. I was so afraid Joshua was going to try something stupid and get killed. But a few minutes later, he and Mr. Bernard returned. The rear door slid up. I looked out and saw them. I also saw a little bit of the surrounding area. Just below us was the silhouette of a small, scruffy-looking cabin. It was a clear night. Beyond the cabin were some trees. And beyond the trees there was a big valley and some lights—like a small town.

Mr. Bernard's face filled with rage. "Get that bag back on! I'll kill you! Get it on, you little—!"

Tears sprang from my eyes as he continued cussing and shouting. Crying uncontrollably, I fumbled to pull the bag back over my head. Then I backed away and bumped into the rear wall. I sank down and turned my face into it. The rear door slid down again with a crash and the padlock snapped shut. The terrible voice of Mr. Bernard fell silent. I felt Joshua's arms come around me. He pulled the bag off my head one more time and held me as I cried.

"It's okay," he whispered. "He's gone again. He's gone."

But I didn't stop crying. I couldn't help it. "He's going to kill us, isn't he?"

"No. We'll be okay."

"Yes, he is. He's going to murder us and no one will ever know—!"

"Shh! He won't. *We'll be okay, Becky. He won't hurt us. I* know *he won't."*

"You know?*" I asked. "How?"*

"Because some things you just know. And this is one of those things."

He sounded so sure. I didn't understand. But he was my big brother. So I believed him, and soon I was able to stop crying.

* * *

Meagan finally connected with a second phone call to her house sometime after midnight. Her mother answered. Apparently Jim had already arrived home in Utah, traveling by airplane. Sabrina reported that he'd only remained at home for about an hour. Then he went back to the Salt Lake City airport to pick up Garth and his wife, Jenny, who had also taken the first flight home, terrified to think of their children, Becky and Joshua, in the hands of a madman. According to Sabrina, the policemen had accompanied Jim to the airport when he went to get Garth. There were also policeman staying at their home—special policemen that Meagan called the F.B.I. From Meagan's side of the conversation it sounded as if the Hawkins household was an anthill of military activity. I found this somewhat perplexing. In Rome it was not uncommon for a man of importance, or his wife or children, to be carried away to a distant land for ransom, but it was never a matter that civil authorities paid much attention to. That is, unless they were bribed with sums nearly equivalent to the ransom. Generally, the victims were forced to pay. Bandits in some districts had found it to be a very lucrative business, which was undoubtedly the reason that many aristocrats and patricians paid high sums of money for retired soldiers and former gladiators to serve as bodyguards.

The problem in this case was that no ransom had been demanded. I gathered from Meagan's side of the conversation that Todd Finlay had made no effort to contact Garth or Jim or anyone else. Neither had anyone heard again from Mary. The mystery appeared to be deepening, and tensions were mounting.

This was especially true for the three of us as we rolled hour after hour into the wilderness of Wyoming. Ryan had been under the impression that our journey would end at the village called Park City, after which we would turn around and go home. Meagan's pleadings had induced Ryan to continue driving eastward, but a few hours later when we left the main highway and started toward the north, his tolerance began to wear thin. It was in a Wyoming municipality called Riverton, after Meagan's second phone call home, that Ryan's patience reached the breaking point.

"I'm turning around," he said.

"Please, Ryan," said Meagan. "Just a little further."

"It's two in the morning! We have no evidence at all that Mary even went this way."

"She *did.* It's the only way she *could* have gone. You have to trust us."

"That's all I've been hearing for five hours," said Ryan. "I deserve to know where we're going and how long it will take to get there. And I don't need anymore 'bravery' speeches from Clint Eastwood in the backseat."

"As I've said," I repeated calmly, "you're free to get out whenever you like."

"It's my car!" Ryan protested. "Maybe *you'd* like to get out. Maybe you could *walk* to wherever you're going. I'm sure you'd do just fine living off sagebrush and roadkill—"

"Stop it!" said Meagan. "You two are intolerable! Did you forget that two lives are at stake? *Three* with Mary."

"I'd just like an explanation," said Ryan. "If you have a final destination in mind, then tell me!"

"Cody," Meagan confessed.

"Where's that?"

"It's another three hours or so. I promise, Ryan, if we don't find Mary or the children between here and Cody, we'll turn around and go home."

"How big is this town?"

"About ten thousand people."

"What makes you think the kidnapper would take the children there?"

"That's where you have to trust us," said Meagan. "I can't give you all the details."

"Is it top secret? Would you have to kill me if you told me?"

"It's just too involved," Meagan said. "Jim knew Todd Finlay from a long time ago. That's all I can say. It's a personal family matter, and I don't think Jim would want me telling just anybody."

"Just anybody? We've been going out for four months. I was there to take your mother to the hospital. Now I'm 'just anybody?'"

"That's not what I meant." She glanced at me, then dropped her face to her hands and massaged her forehead. "Ho, boy. Mama told me there'd be days like this."

"Apparently *Apollus* knows all these secrets," Ryan grumbled. "What gives *him* such high security clearance?"

"Apollus is . . . a longtime family friend," Meagan defended awkwardly.

"Well, why didn't ya say so? Longtime family friend. That explains everything. Thank you so much."

I remained quiet, but there was a definite grin on my countenance. I wasn't sure what was more entertaining—listening to Ryan's jealous sarcasm or watching Meagan squirm as she tried to deal with the politics of two potential suitors. Not that I would have put myself in that category. For many reasons, I still didn't feel it was an appropriate ambition. But even if I *had* been in the running for this maiden's hand, I certainly wouldn't have felt any competition from this yapping mongrel. Unless of course my innate instincts for perceiving feminine wiles had been thrown completely out of scale and women now preferred calves over bulls.

Ryan sighed deflatedly. "It just seems so hopeless. We've chased down two white cars already. One not even a Monte Carlo. It's so hard to tell with the headlights and . . ."

"*I* can tell," said Meagan confidently. "And no other cars have even been close."

"Are you having difficulty staying awake?" I asked Ryan. "Perhaps I should drive."

Meagan gave me a curious look. "You know how to drive, Apollus?"

"I've observed it closely. It can't be that difficult."

Meagan glanced at Ryan, fearing, I think, that her question and my response might have been judged unusual.

Indeed, that was how Ryan reacted. "All right. That's it. What's going on here? Who is this guy, Meagan? The Dodge City/Clint Eastwood thing was a *joke*. Now I'm starting to wonder if he really *was* chipped out of an iceberg!"

"He just . . . grew up a little differently than you and me," she hedged. "That's all."

"Where? In a bomb shelter?" He faced me directly, "You mean to tell me you've never driven a car?"

"I prefer motorcycles," I responded.

Meagan tried another angle. "He's been in Mexico for the last few years."

"Oh?" said Ryan. "Is that where he got that silly-looking sword? A tourist novelty?"

That raised my ire. "Tourist novelty? That weapon is cast from the finest Noricum steel! Only centurions in the Fighting Fifth may wield—!"

Meagan eyes were *begging* me to shut up. So I did, but only with great huffs of temper. Did no one in this world have an eye for fine metalwork? Maybe he'd appreciate it better if I set it against his pearl-white throat.

"Sorry!" said Ryan with as much sincerity as a Corsican trader. "I didn't think you'd take it personally. Then again, I've heard you 'Centurions' are rather touchy."

He was mocking me! How dare he mock me! This boy would learn some manners—that was a promise. But Ryan was spared some much-deserved pain as Meagan gasped and began pointing frantically.

"Stop! Slow down! That's Mary! That's her car!"

On the right side of the road sat a large, white car. We overshot it considerably before Ryan reined in his 4-Runner and brought us to a halt. The vehicle appeared abandoned. The window on the driver's side had been broken out. It was Meagan again whose falcon eye spotted a lone figure nearly a quarter league ahead. She was wandering away from us, down the road, in the moonlight.

"Over there! See? Drive!"

Ryan did as instructed. A moment later our headlight beams were illuminating the figure of a young woman with dark hair, wearing a light yellow dress. Mary turned, startled, as we pulled off the road beside her. Meagan was quick to leap out of the door and embrace her.

"Mary!"

"Meagan! I don't believe it!"

Both girls were shedding tears of relief and delight as Ryan and I got out of the carriage and gathered around.

"Are you all right?" Meagan asked.

"Yes. I ran out of gas. Can you imagine it? I followed them all this way, and—But what else could I do?" More tears sprang from her eyes. "Oh, Meagan! It's all my fault! I'm so ashamed! I'm so sorry!" She noticed me for the first time. "Apollus?"

"Yes, Mary."

She threw her arms around my neck. "But how—? When did you—?"

"I arrived this afternoon. I came to warn everyone of the danger, but I was too late. If this is anyone's fault, it's mine."

"How did you break the side window on your car?" asked Ryan.

"I *had* to break it," said Mary. "The man who took them—he stole my keys. I smashed the window with a wooden cane that he left behind on the asphalt."

"Where was the man going?" Meagan asked. "Where is he taking them? Do you have any idea?"

To our surprise, Mary replied, "Yes! I *do* know. But I only found out a few moments ago."

"What do you mean?"

"Here!" She reached into her purse and pulled out a slip of paper. "I'm such a fool. I poured the whole thing out at Lagoon looking for my keys and didn't even notice it—not until my car ran out of gas and I was searching for my penlight. It's been in there all along! He slipped it in, most likely at the same instant that he took my car keys."

Meagan took the slip of paper and unfolded it. She read the characters aloud.

> *To Garth Plimpton or Jim Hawkins,*
> *You once had something of mine. Now I have something of yours. I always knew it would be worth my while to keep track of your whereabouts all these years. I don't wish to hurt anybody, but if you don't tell me the secret I wish to know, you will force me to take action that I will deeply regret. You will meet me tomorrow in the entranceway. I'm certain you know the entranceway that I'm referring to. And remember, I*

*have a very wide view. If either one of you does not come
alone, what is yours will be lost forever. Do not show this
note to the police. And do not try anything stupid.*

*Your old friend,
Todd Finlay*

"I can't believe I missed it," Mary continued to lament. "The note
says 'tomorrow.' That's *today!*"

"How long have you been stranded here?" asked Meagan.

"I don't know. An hour. I was going to walk until I found a
phone."

"So Todd Finlay is only an hour ahead of us?" I asked.

Ryan chimed in. "What's this great secret that the kidnapper
wants to know? What entranceway is he talking about?"

"It's . . . it's a cave," said Meagan reluctantly.

"A cave? Are you serious?"

"If he's only a hour ahead of us, we might still overtake him," I
pointed out.

"I have to call Jim," said Meagan.

Ryan was still befuddled. "He wants to hold a meeting in a *cave?*"

I ignored his question. "If the parchment says tomorrow, he
surely meant after daylight. If we can arrive at the mountain before
sunrise, we may be able to reach the cave well before Finlay."

"Wait just a minute," said Ryan. "The note says Jim and Garth
are to come alone. It says he'll be watching for them."

"But not in darkness," I said. "We have to keep going. There isn't
much time."

"Now *wait!*" cried Ryan, sounding quite desperate. "*Just wait!* Am
I the only one who thinks this might be dangerous and stupid?"

I made a scowl. "Apparently you are."

"Jim or Garth will know what's best," said Mary.

At that instant Meagan growled at the cell phone. "We're out of
battery power!"

"Did you bring a charger?" asked Ryan.

"Of course not," she said, self-effacing. "You think I'd be that smart?"

"Then we should find a pay phone," said Mary.

"But afterwards we'll continue on to Cody, right?" I asked. "I won't miss such a perfect opportunity to resolve this problem quickly and cleanly."

Ryan stepped closer. "*Quickly and cleanly?* Did it ever occur to you that you might get those children killed?"

I stepped even closer—right up to his nose. "I'm growing weary of listening to the advice of a coward. How in Jupiter did you ever merit a name like Champion?"

He shoved me back a step. "You're crazy, Apollus! Crazy as a—!"

That was the last sound he made. With a quick motion, I grabbed him by the back of the head and snapped my fist at the base of his skull. The poor fellow was out like a candle. He crumpled to the ground.

"*Apollus!*" Meagan shrieked. "What did you *do* to him?" She rushed to his side and gathered him up.

"He attacked me."

"You were in his face! You call that an *attack?*"

"He's been nothing but a whining, simpering malcontent since we left Salt Lake City."

"Don't you think that's understandable? He knows nothing about the cave! Nothing about you or Mary! Don't you think you'd be a little freaked out by all of this too?"

Her words stung, but I wasn't certain if it was because I felt guilty for what I'd done, or because it was now clear that Meagan did, in fact, have feelings for this grub worm. Perhaps it was only the sympathy one might shower upon the vanquished, but it stung me all the same.

"Carry him to the car," Meagan commanded. "I can't believe you, Apollus! A centurion in the Fifth Legion of Rome and you act more like a spoiled rotten child!"

Steam pumped in and out of my nostrils like I was an Arabian stallion. I was being reprimanded by a *woman!* I took Ryan under both arms and hefted him into the backseat. He was already coming to as I set him in place. Meagan opened the driver's side.

"Stay in back with him!" she ordered. "Mary, take shotgun. We'll have to come back for your car later."

Now I had the additional humiliation of my opponent's groggy head nestled against my shoulder as Meagan turned the wheel and we pulled quickly back onto the highway.

CHAPTER 8

We drove to a small desert village called Shoshoni, where Meagan placed her next call home. Mary had climbed out of the car with Meagan so that she might listen in on the conversation, and perhaps offer additional insight. I remained in the backseat with Ryan, watching the two girls closely as they stood at the pay phone along the side of the small, dilapidated gas station whose lights had been doused for the night.

Ryan had become fully cognizant now. He sat on the opposite side of the vehicle, saying nothing. At last, he posed a question, his tone more curious than angry.

"What did you do to me?"

"Only what I felt was necessary," I replied, "in self defense."

"It was a good one," he confessed, rubbing the back of his neck. "I wasn't expecting it."

"That was your weakness," I said plainly, not attempting to sound so much rude as instructional.

He didn't seem to appreciate the critique. "Next time I'll be sure not to make the same mistake."

I gave him a disbelieving look. Was this a modest challenge? My, my, but this one could be a glutton for punishment! "For your health's sake," I said flatly, "I would recommend that you don't."

He didn't reply to that. I continued to watch Mary and Meagan. Meagan was now speaking animatedly on the phone. Occasionally a gust of wind would blow up the desert dust around them.

"Tell me something, Apollus," said Ryan finally. "How long have you known Meagan?"

"Long enough."

"Funny she never mentioned you before. You must not have made a lasting impression."

I didn't respond. He was fishing for information on a subject that was none of his business. Meagan hung up the phone. She and Mary returned to the car. Mary spoke to Meagan with urgency as they opened their doors.

"But you didn't read him the note!" she pointed out to her.

"I *couldn't*," said Meagan. "Jim hinted to me that there were other people listening to the conversation. He wants us to go to his Uncle Spencer's house."

"Where is that?" I inquired.

"It's in Cody. He used to live on a farm, but last year he and his wife moved into a condominium. Jim is going to call us there in the morning. By then he thinks he can get away from the house and talk in private."

"Wait a second," said Ryan. "By 'other people listening' I assume you mean the police. You don't think Jim wants the police to hear the contents of that note?"

Meagan sounded impatient. "You heard what the note said. I don't think Jim would want to take a chance that the police might interfere."

"Police are *supposed* to interfere!"

"You don't understand what's going on, Ryan!" Meagan flared. "I want to read Jim the note when no one else is listening. Then he can talk to Garth and they can decide for themselves what they want to do."

"By then I hope to have decided the matter for them," I said, stroking the hilt of my sword.

Ryan made a little whistle, shaking his head. "Unbelievable."

The boy with the look of a German tribesman reassumed his place at the helm of the car, waving off Meagan's concerns that he still might not be well enough to drive. But I think he may have somewhat regretted the choice as Meagan climbed into the backseat beside me.

For three more hours we continued northward, driving ever faster at my urging. I felt it was imperative that we reach the mountain before sunrise. If I could arrive at the cave before Todd Finlay, I might secret myself in any of the various side tunnels or chambers and wait for the right moment to strike.

It was nearly five A.M. when we rolled into the quiet village of Cody. A few villagers were out and about, but for the most part the town was asleep. We passed through it and continued on to Cedar Mountain. As we pulled up to the base of the mountain and parked, Meagan was acting nervous and agitated.

"Apollus, I don't feel good about this. Maybe we should just go to Spencer and Louise's condo and wait for Jim's call."

"You go to the uncle's home," I said. "I will go to the cave."

"What if Todd Finlay is already at the cave, waiting and watching. If he sees you . . ."

"He *won't* see me," I said.

There was a slight break in her voice as she said, "If anything should happen to you, Apollus . . . or the children . . ."

"It won't." I looked directly into her eyes to stress my reassurance.

A twinge of the deep feelings I still had for this girl returned at that instant. I'd almost forgotten the spell those dark brown eyes could cast on me. I shook it off. I could not afford to be distracted.

Ryan was watching us closely. This exchange was too much for his young pride. Something about the sweet strain in Meagan's voice—the strain of a damsel about to send a lover into battle—ignited in Ryan that masculine spark that I had begun to think did not reside in the hearts of this century's men.

"All right," he said to me succinctly. "I'll go with you."

"Don't be ridiculous," said Meagan. "Apollus is trained for this kind of thing. You're not."

I looked at Ryan, my face likely betraying some satisfaction.

Ryan tried not to appear put out. "Trained with a *sword?* That'll come in real handy if Todd Finlay has a gun. I'll keep a lookout and watch his back. That way I can warn him if I see something that he doesn't."

"I'll do better alone," I growled.

"I'm sure you will," said Ryan. "But I'm going anyway."

I flashed my teeth threateningly. "Do I need to render you unconscious a second time?"

"You could try," said Ryan, unflinching. "But if you allow it, Kimosabe, I might just save your life."

I wasn't quite sure what he had called me, but it sounded quite feminine and insulting. Before I could react, Mary abruptly changed the subject. She indicated the top of the mountain. "What are those lights?"

Meagan craned her neck to see up the slope. At the summit were several sets of red lights. One of them was blinking. "I think there's some transmission stations at the top. The flashing one might be for airplanes. I've never seen this mountain at night, so I'm not sure."

"If somebody regularly maintains the equipment up there," said Ryan, "maybe we should drive a little further."

"That's not necessary," I said.

"No, no, I think Ryan's right," said Meagan. "If people go up there regularly, the sight of a car on this road might not be that big of a deal."

Ryan started rolling forward. I opened my mouth to protest. But then I glanced toward the east. A deep band of magenta light was forming against the hills. The sun was rising. Reaching that cave as quickly as possible now seemed the most exigent strategy.

"Hurry," I said. "If that sun gets any higher, it might be too late."

* * *

It had been quiet for a long time. Maybe two hours. I was a little calmer now, and as I laid there against my brother's shoulder I think I actually got some sleep. But it wasn't for very long. Joshua nudged me.

"Becky, are you awake?" he whispered.

"Yes," I said sleepily.

He waited a second, then said, "I've been thinking."

"About what?"

"About escaping."

"Really," I said, unimpressed. "I think you were dreaming, Joshua."

"I don't think so," he said. "I came up with an idea. To escape, all we need is a weapon, right?"

"What do you mean?"

"We just have to find some way to attack Mr. Bernard. To knock him out or hurt him so he can't hurt us."

"Okay," I said doubtfully. "So?"

"We have to do it quick. Right when he opens that door again. We can't think about it. We just have to do it."

"But we don't have a weapon."

"I think we do," he said confidently.

"There's nothing else in here," I said. "Just you and me and some pistachio shells."

"No, that's not all.

"Well, the wheelchair—"

"Bingo," said Joshua.

"The wheelchair?"

"Exactly. Here's my idea. When Mr. Bernard comes back, we pick that wheelchair up over our heads. We lift it high enough so he won't see it until the last second. Then when he raises up that door, we clobber him with it."

I sighed in disappointment. "That sounds silly."

Joshua's chest sank. He'd obviously put a lot of thought into this. "No, it isn't, Becky. It's the last thing he'll expect. He'll just think we're standing there. He'll tell us to put the bags over our heads again, but we won't really do it. Then when the door gets just high enough, we'll throw the wheelchair down on top of him. It's heavy enough that I bet it will knock him out cold."

"Joshua, you're gonna get us killed," I whispered harshly. "Besides, the wheelchair is too heavy. He'll hear us trying to lift it."

"Not if we're quiet."

"Joshua, it's too dangerous—"

He grabbed me by the shoulders. "Becky, listen to me. It's a good idea. And it may be our best chance. I know it sounds dangerous, but Becky . . . I think Mr. Bernard is crazy."

"Well, no doubt."

"No, I mean really crazy. Like he's not in control of his own soul anymore. Something else has taken over. I don't know why he brought us here, or what he wants, but I believe if we don't do this, something really awful could happen."

I frowned in anger. "You just told me a little while ago that we would be okay."

"That's right," said Joshua. "We will be. That's why I want to try this. I think it's the best way to guarantee that we'll be okay—that we'll be able to escape. You have to trust me. I'm your big brother. I won't let you down. Have I ever let you down on something like this?"

"When has there ever been anything like this?"

"Becky, I'm serious. I really want to try this."

Now I started to shake. "Joshua, I'm too scared. I could never hold up that thing."

"We'll be holding it up together. All the way up over our heads."

"What if he doesn't come back? What if he just stays in that cabin and leaves us in here all day."

"Then we have nothing to lose. We'll just wait until the right moment."

My shivering increased. I took a deep breath and tried to steady my nerves. As I looked up at the back door, it seemed to me that it was getting lighter outside. The sun was coming up.

"Oh, Joshua, are you sure about this?"

"Yes," he said. "If we do it just right, it should work. *And like I said, I feel it's our best chance. Maybe our* only *chance."*

Joshua took my little question as if I'd given my permission. He moved over to where the wheelchair was still laying in the darkness. He found it and tried to budge it. It made a scraping sound against the floor. He stopped and found another grip. "You have to help me, Becky. Let's just see if we can lift it."

I went over to him and we did it. But it was awfully noisy. Joshua made us practice again, this time lifting it so it didn't make any noise.

"All the way up," he whispered.

So with our muscles straining, we lifted the wheelchair all the way up over our heads. Boy, it was heavy! It was also lopsided, because I was shorter than Joshua.

"Now down," he said, his voice squeaking from strain.

We set it down, but it was impossible not to make a noise as our muscles gave out at the last second and the chair came down with a thud. We sat back on our elbows and listened. It was harder to hear as we heaved for breath, but it didn't sound like Mr. Bernard had been disturbed. Still, I knew he'd have heard us for sure if he'd been standing right outside the truck.

"We can't do it," I panted. "He'll know what we're doing."

"No, he won't. We just have to be more careful. We can do it, Becky. I know *we can."*

My brother. I loved him with all my heart. I had a hard time refusing him. He just seemed so sure all the time. And come to think of it, what he'd said before was sort of right. Whenever he talked like this, whenever he said he knew *something was true, I'd never known him to be wrong.* Please Heavenly Father, *I prayed.* Don't let this be the first time.

We lay there resting for another minute. Joshua had wanted to practice lifting the wheelchair again, but we never got the chance. I heard a door opening—the door of the cabin. I heard coughing—Mr. Bernard's cough. It was light enough now that I could see Joshua's face. His eyes were looking straight at me, wide and determined. He motioned me and gripped his side of the wheelchair.

My heart started pounding. I hesitated. I almost chickened out. But then I did as he directed and grabbed the other side. I realized this might be a total waste of energy. Mr. Bernard might not even come over to the truck. Or even if he unlocked it, he might just raise it up enough to throw in some water or stale bread or something. We'd just be left there holding up the wheelchair and he'd never even know what we had been doing. Somehow that thought gave me courage. If he never saw what we were doing, what did it matter? What did we have to lose?

We raised up the wheelchair over our heads. It made a few squeaks and rattles, but I felt sure it wasn't noisy enough to be heard from outside. Mr. Bernard's footsteps came up behind the truck.

"All right," he said through the door. "Get those bags over your heads. We going on a little walk before it gets any lighter."

Joshua and I looked at each other for confidence. We were holding the wheelchair up over our heads like a couple of weightlifters. I fought to keep my balance. My heart was hammering so hard I thought it would break out of my chest. My arms were shaking like leaves, but I couldn't tell if it was because of the weight or just because I was so terrified. Joshua sent me a small nod—just a nod to say everything would be okay. Heavenly Father please, *I cried in my heart.* Don't let us get killed while doing this insane thing!

"Are they on?" came the voice from the other side.

I looked at Josh again. He turned his face into his shoulder a little to muffle his voice, as if the bag were really over his head.

"Yes," he answered.

We heard Mr. Bernard fiddling with the padlock. My muscles were straining. It wasn't fear that was making my arms shake now. It was plain heaviness. My muscles were giving out. I could feel my elbows starting to buckle. Just a few seconds longer! *I told myself.*

But then suddenly the weight on my arms lightened. I realized Joshua was holding up the chair almost by himself, every ounce of his concentration focused on that back door. He had adrenaline *inside him—that was a word Uncle Jim used a lot. Either it was adrenaline or else an angel had taken my place in holding up that wheelchair.*

The rear door started to lift. One inch, two inches . . . I saw Mr. Bernard's hand. He was holding a large bag, like a gym bag. It was open slightly and I could see some rope dangling out of the top. Suddenly, with a mighty push, the whole rear door flew up into the roof of the truck. Mr. Bernard's body, neck, and cold, lifeless eyes fell into view.

At first he looked confused, but then his eyebrows shot up. Joshua let out a terrible yell and threw down that wheelchair with all his might. I helped too, throwing it forward right at Mr. Bernard's head. He dropped the gym bag and tried to bring up his arms, but the wheelchair hit him smack in the face and chest. He let out a gruesome ugh! *and tripped backwards. The wheelchair crushed him to the ground.*

"Go!" shouted Joshua.

We leapt from the back of the truck and landed on our feet. Joshua landed perfectly, his legs already running. When I landed, though, I fell forward onto my hands and knees. I glanced over at Mr. Bernard. Oh, why did I do that? He looked disoriented. His glasses had fallen off and there was a small trickle of blood coming out of his nose. He fought to push the wheelchair off of the top of him. Then in an instant he seemed fully alert—looking straight at me!

I lunged to get away, but Mr. Bernard's hand grabbed my ankle. His grip was like iron. It sent ice shooting up my leg and spine. I shrieked in terror as he pulled me back, dragging me flat onto my chest.

"Joshua!" I screamed.

Mr. Bernard rolled himself over to where he could grab me with his other hand. I saw his nose again. It was bleeding badly now, almost gushing, and the blood appeared to have gotten in one of his eyes. That was the instant that saved me—the instant he wiped his eye with his sleeve before latching onto me with his other hand. Joshua returned and buried his shoe in Mr. Bernard's ribs. My ankle broke free.

"Run!" Joshua cried.

I strained to get to my feet and start running, but out of the corner of my eye, I saw Mr. Bernard reach out toward Joshua. I continued forward, dashing up the dirt road that led away from the cabin.

"Run, Becky!" Joshua cried again.

But something was wrong. Joshua's voice wasn't right behind me. I turned back. The sight was horrible! Mr. Bernard had pinned Joshua to the ground. He had one hand around Joshua's wrist and the other gripping Joshua's hair. My brother was helpless!

"Keep running!" Joshua shouted again.

My mind was filled with panic. How could I run? How could I leave my brother behind? But even in the dim light I saw a desperate look in Joshua's eye. He was pleading with me in silence, begging *me to do as he asked. What else could I do? I did exactly what he told me. Tears washed over my eyes as I turned and fled. I ran as fast as I could—faster than I'd ever run before. I left my brother—left him behind with a crazy man!—and I wondered if I'd ever see him alive again.*

CHAPTER 9

Ryan turned yet another corner in the endless series of switch-backs that led up the mountain. At last the headlights illuminated a forested trail leading westward toward some cliffs. At the head of the trail stood a brightly painted sign etched in white characters.

"That's it," said Meagan. "Spirit Mountain Cave. That sign is new."

"Interesting," I noted. "That's the name that the old Indian used—the one who gave Finlay the stones."

"I thought it was called Frost Cave," said Mary.

"Jim said it has several names," said Meagan. "He believes that Spirit Mountain may be its Indian name."

"It was named by the people of India?" asked Mary.

"Native American," Meagan corrected. "Stop here, Ryan. Turn off the headlights."

He did so and the car's engine shut off. I prepared to get out.

"Wait," said Ryan. "If it's a cave, shouldn't we take flashlights? I have two in back."

"Yes," said Meagan. "And rope."

"Rope?"

"For climbing."

Ryan screwed up his face, perplexed. "We're going to be doing some climbing?"

Meagan hesitated, seeming to weigh in her mind how much she should tell him. "Probably not. But take it just in case."

"I have some nylon cord," said Ryan. "I use it to tie things to the rack."

I was becoming impatient with all the chatter. "We're losing time!" I climbed out of the car and strapped the sword around my waist. A stiff wind was kicking up out of the west, and I could tell by the pale color of the night sky that it was thick with clouds.

Ryan climbed out and went quickly to the rear of the car, opening the back. "Hang on."

I waited grudgingly. I did not want company on this mission. I feared Ryan's presence might prove a serious liability. But I realized that it might be more of a liability to have him dawdling after me at a distance. If we could only reach the cave unseen, then I could tuck him away in some nook or cranny—hog-tied, if necessary—where he'd be safely out of trouble.

"Okay, I'm ready," said Ryan, looping some rope around his shoulder and filling his hands with two flashlights. He turned one of them on.

"*Not now!*" I said harshly.

He snapped it off. "Sorry. Just making sure the battery worked. Wouldn't do us much good if—"

I faced him straight on. "You will do precisely as I say at all times. Is that clear?"

"Crystal," he said smartly, offering what appeared to be a Roman salute. "I'm at your command, Centurion."

The appropriateness of the reply put me off guard and I nearly returned the salute. Then I scowled, realizing he was mocking me again. Meagan had climbed over the seat and taken over the helm of Ryan's car.

"We'll wait here a few minutes," she said through the open window.

"No," I said. "Go to the home of Jim's uncle."

"But how will we know if anything has happened?" asked Mary.

"When Jim calls, tell him the contents of the note. I do not doubt that he or Garth will fly to the Cody airport on the first available airplane. Tell them to come to the cave as instructed. By then, I hope to have everything well in hand."

I turned back into the wind and started rapidly down the trail. Ryan followed closely in the increasing light.

* * *

What had I done? I'd abandoned my brother. I could never forgive myself. Joshua would have never abandoned me. And yet my legs were still moving fast, tears streaking my face as I threw myself forward into the wind. I kept to the main road—there seemed to be nowhere else to go. I didn't seem to have any choice but to keep running down the mountain until I reached a building or the highway where somebody would find me, or where I could hide. Any second I expected Mr. Bernard's moving van to come barreling down the dirt road and him to jump out and try to grab me. I was prepared to jump off the road and hide if I heard it coming, but if he saw me, I felt sure I could never outrun him. I was already panting so hard that I was about to faint.

Then I did *hear a car engine. But it wasn't behind me. It was in* front *of me. I came around some pine trees and saw an SUV—sort of like the one Meagan's boyfriend, Ryan, drove. It was trying to make a U-turn and go back down the mountain.*

I didn't care who it was. I began waving my hands and yelling, "Wait! Help! Stop! Help!"

The car had turned completely around and was starting to roll away from me. It was about to drive off before I could reach it! With all the air in my lungs I yelled, "WAIT!"

Suddenly the car hit its brakes. Heads inside of it began looking around. The license plate said "Utah." The passenger side door flew open and out stepped—it was too good to be true!—Mary!

The sight was so surprising and startling that I couldn't speak. Then the door on the driver's side opened and out flew Meagan. They'd found me! They'd followed us! It was a complete and total miracle!

I fell into Mary's arms, crying uncontrollably.

"Becky! Are you all right?"

I nodded, still unable to speak, and began pointing back up the road. "Joshua!" I stammered.

"Where is he?"

"H-he has him!"

"Who? Todd Finlay?"

"Mr. Bernard! H-he was going to hurt him!"

Meagan and Mary looked back in the other direction, their eyes filled with dread. I couldn't figure out what they were looking at. "He's up that way!" I reminded them.

"But Apollus and Ryan have gone to the cave!" said Mary.

I couldn't see anyone in the direction that they were looking, and the wind was blowing hard in our faces. I felt a few drops of rain too, and clouds were starting to curl around the top of the mountain, making the cliffs harder to see even though it was getting light.

Meagan made a quick decision. "Get in the car," she told us. "Show us, Becky. Show us where!"

As we got into the SUV Meagan started yanking on the gearshift and switching from gas to brakes as she fought to turn the car back around. I was still shaking uncontrollably.

I continued rambling, "I g-got away. But he was hurting Joshua!"

"How far away is it?" Meagan asked.

"Just up there," I said.

Mary sounded frantic. "Meagan, what are you going to do? If he sees us—!"

"She said he was going to hurt him!" Meagan shouted back.

We sped up the road and reached the turnoff. I was terrified. What were we going to do? Judging by the way Meagan was driving, she was ready to plow into Mr. Bernard and run him over. I could see the tiny cabin through the trees, as well as the moving van. But I couldn't see Joshua or Mr. Bernard.

"They were right over there," I said.

"How long ago?"

I shook my head. "I-I don't know for sure."

Meagan punched the gas. The SUV shot up the little road—really no more than two tire tracks—bouncing hard as Meagan refused to slow down for bumps. But as we reached the cabin and pulled up behind the moving van, there was still no sign of Joshua or Mr. Bernard. Everything looked the same. The back of the van was still sitting open. The cabin looked quiet too. The way the cabin's front door was slapping in the wind, it didn't look like anyone was inside there either. Meagan jumped out of the car and started yelling.

"Joshua! Joshua!"

The wind carried her voice right back into her face. I looked around desperately in the woods. It was nearly light outside, but the clouds were making it hard to see very far. There was no sign of anybody else. Where could they have gone?

As Meagan came back from looking in the cabin, she asked the same question. "What happened to them? Where did they go?"

I got out of the car and walked over behind the moving van. The wheelchair was still lying on its side on the ground, but the gym bag with the rope and other stuff was gone. Despite the wind and dust, I could still see blood on some of the rocks.

"That's from Mr. Bernard's nose," I said. "We threw the wheelchair down on top of him."

"His name is Todd Finlay," said Meagan, speaking loudly now to be heard over the wind.

I was just turning back to face Mary when something flashed out of the corner of my eye. It was near the wheelchair, just over the other side and almost sitting underneath its rubber wheel. I stopped and stared at it. I'm not quite sure why. I wouldn't have thought something shiny could have ever caught my attention like that under the circumstances. But it did, and I moved closer to pick it up.

Meagan saw what I was doing, and even with the wind howling like it was, I heard her let out a little gasp. I reached down and lifted the object into my hand. It was one of the strangest things I'd ever seen—a pair of shiny white stones, almost transparent, surrounded by silver frames in the shape of a figure eight. The object appeared to be some sort of necklace. Attached at either end were leather strings that would make it easy to tie around the neck. I thought I remembered the kidnapper wearing something around his neck, but it was mostly hidden under his shirt. As I stared into those shiny white stones I got the queerest feeling. It was like—I'm not sure—it was like the stones were lighter than they should've been. Or maybe I was lighter. I really can't explain it.

Meagan reached out and touched it. Mary also noticed what we were doing and came over to see. As Meagan's fingers ran along the surface of the two stones, her face looked totally engrossed.

"What is it?" Mary asked.

"I don't know," I answered.

Meagan wasn't so quick to answer, as if she knew something that we didn't. Or thought she knew.

"I think it's . . . seer stones," she answered.

"Seer stones?" said Mary. She sounded surprised, but not as if she was unfamiliar with the word. "Where did they come from?"

Meagan turned to me. "Was Todd Finlay wearing this?"

"I-I think so," I said, unsure. "It might've fallen off when we hit him with the wheelchair. Or maybe when he was fighting with Joshua."

"It's beautiful," said Mary.

"I can wear it," I said, and I brought up the leather strings and began to tie it around my neck. "I'll bring it."

Meagan looked like she was about to object to that. Maybe she thought that it might be safer if she carried it. But as I finished tying it off, Meagan nodded and seemed to feel there wasn't any harm in my keeping it for the time being.

"All right," said Meagan. "You wear it. Be careful with it, Becky."

"Okay," I said.

Mary changed the subject. "What did Mr. Finlay tell you, Becky?" She opened her handbag and took out a small piece of paper. "Finlay put this note in my purse. He said he brought you and Joshua here to try and convince your father to tell him a secret. Did he mention any of this to you?"

I shook my head, "He didn't tell us anything."

"Did he talk about the cave?" asked Meagan. "We think he wants to know the secret passageway through the cave."

"Frost Cave?" I replied.

"Yes," said Meagan. "It's not very far from here."

"If that's all he wanted to know, why didn't he just ask us?" I said.

That seemed to surprise Meagan. "You mean you and Joshua still remember the way?"

"Joshua does," I said. "Or I think he does."

Meagan looked at Mary. "He's taken him to the cave."

Mary looked startled. "Do you think they would have reached it before Apollus and Ryan?"

Meagan gazed off toward some cliffs that sat a short distance below the cabin. We could hardly see the outline. The rain clouds seemed to be swallowing up the whole mountain. But we could make out that there was a little path leading down through the trees.

Meagan asked me again, "Becky, concentrate. How long ago did you escape?"

I tried to think. "Fifteen or ten minutes."

Meagan thought out loud. "If that path leads rights down to the cave . . ."

Mary finished the thought for her. " . . . Finlay might have reached it before Apollus and Ryan."

"We have to warn them!" said Meagan.

Meagan scrambled down the little path that led toward the cliffs. Mary and I followed, our hearts pounding. It was starting to rain even harder. I felt frightened and confused. But as I held Mary's hand and followed her down the path at a run, I realized that some of the fright seemed to be . . . How can I describe it? . . . absorbed by the stones. All I knew was that having them on made me feel better. But I still wondered if we were doing something insane. I'd been trying to get completely away from this man. Now we were trying to catch up to him—and catch up to Joshua. And hope that by the time we did, it wouldn't be too late to prevent something horrible from happening.

* * *

"Stop," I said to Ryan, and stuck out my arm like a tree branch.

He stopped even before he collided with my arm. He'd heard it too—voices over the steady cry of the wind. The voices were somewhere below us and closer to the face of the cliff. The clouds had completely engulfed us now. The cliffs ahead were like ghostly visages, further blurred by streaks of rain.

I led the way to a place where we could see the broken wooden walkway that led to the cave's mouth. But the fog bank was preventing us from seeing any details. This was turning into quite an early-morning storm.

"There!" said Ryan.

I tried to follow his finger and peer into the pale mist, but I shook my head, unable to—

Then I saw it. Just a flash of color really. It appeared as though someone—perhaps it was *two* people—had disappeared behind one of the rocky outcroppings that hid the entrance of the cave.

"Who was it?" I asked Ryan, hoping he'd had an instant more to interpret the flash of color.

"I couldn't tell," he replied. "This fog! Would there be other hikers visiting this cave?"

"Doubtful," I replied. "Not at this hour. Or in this weather."

My voice had an edge of discouragement. If indeed it was Finlay and the children, my worst fears had been realized and we had arrived at the cave too late. And only by five frustrating minutes! Finlay definitely had the advantage if he was already in place at the cave's mouth. It was almost pointless to continue. Our lives were in Finlay's hands. But then I considered the weather. The cloudbank and the screaming wind might potentially erase his advantage.

"Let's move in," I said, and started down toward the dilapidated walkway.

Reluctantly, Ryan remained close behind. The rain was pelting my face. I was glad of it. The more rain, the better. It obscured our vision, but it also obscured theirs. We crept along the walkway until we reached some stairs carved into the rock. Our level of caution increased. The cave was very close. My ears were attuned to every sound that did not resemble the wind. As we neared the place where the trail dropped down onto the stone platform at the cave's mouth, I drew my sword from its sheath.

Ryan seemed quite agitated. I had the feeling that he wanted to toss my sword down the mountain, convinced it was utterly useless in these circumstances. I suppose I understood his reservations. I knew about guns, and I knew their advantages over steel. But if by chance this villain had no gun, there was no other weapon that would have made him my equal.

I edged forward, keeping close to the wall until I could see the cavern mouth. To my surprise there was a new gate over the entrance. It looked considerably more impregnable than the one that had been there two years earlier. Adding to my dismay, the only entry point was a small square hole about the height and width of my forearm. To breach it a person would practically have to crawl, catching themselves with their hands. The position would be terribly awkward, leaving me vulnerable to attack for several precious seconds.

But as I peered through the tight crisscross of steel grating, there was no sign of movement within. I couldn't trust this. After all, from the outside looking in, my vision could only register a gaping black void. But it still seemed to me that I should have perceived some kind of movement. The wind was my worst enemy now. If I couldn't trust my eyes, I wished I could have trusted my ears.

It was the point of no return. If I stepped away from this wall, I would make myself an open target. And yet it hardly seemed wise to reveal our presence. *Oh well*, I thought resignedly. As a soldier, I'd faced such moments before. There was no other choice but to take the risk. I prepared to jump down onto the stone platform.

Ryan grabbed my arm. "What are you doing?"

"I'm going in," I said.

"Don't you think this might be a good time to negotiate?"

"A Roman does not negotiate."

The phrase slipped out. Ryan's face went blank. Then it twisted. He looked at me as if I'd completely lost my mind. His voice suddenly became soothing, like a parent trying to talk a small child into putting down a dangerous object before they hurt themselves.

"Apollus, you're not well. You need help."

I brushed this off angrily. "If you're not here to fight, then don't interfere."

I turned away, but before I could leap down onto the stone platform, Ryan called out loudly, "Finlay!"

I turned back, enraged. As I lunged to throw my hand over his mouth, he cried again, "Finlay, are you in—?"

My palm encased his mouth and my sword came to his throat. "What are you *doing?*" I seethed. "*You've given us away!*"

I don't think he'd expected such a quick or violent reaction. His eyes were like goose eggs as he considered that this crazy Roman might actually cut his throat. Yet I was hardly paying attention to him. I was listening for a reaction from the cave. There was none. Ryan's shout had not drawn any response. Slowly, I released my grip on his face and continued gazing into the hollow stillness. As soon as I set him loose, Ryan scrambled away from me, down the cliff wall.

"What's wrong with you, man!"

"Be silent!" I shot back.

My concentration was still set upon the entrance. I felt sure that even in this wind Ryan's shout should have been heard. In particular, I listened for a child's voice, sending up a cry of warning. Was Todd Finlay determined to wait until we tried to enter before he attacked? Or had he already ventured so deeply into the tunnel that he really hadn't heard Ryan's shout? That would not have made sense. According to Mary's note, he would be waiting directly at the entrance.

My options still seemed limited. There was still no choice but to step out into the open. Only now I faced the added danger of an alerted enemy. I sent Ryan another searing glance, then braced myself and jumped down onto the platform.

I stood there in full view of the cavern for several seconds. Still, there was no movement. No bullet from the darkness. I glanced to my right and looked over the ledge, wondering if perhaps the people we'd seen had fallen off or climbed down a different way.

Carefully, Ryan climbed down onto the platform behind me. He acted more wary of me than anything in the cave. At this point I preferred to pretend he wasn't there, but as we stepped toward the tight opening, I felt compelled to issue one more warning.

"Make another sound and I *will* shut that mouth of yours for good."

He put up his hands submissively, as if to reassure me. To get through the opening I was forced to resheath my weapon and unfasten my scabbard. I leaned it against the metal grating where I could easily retrieve it. Then, as efficiently as I could, I leaned into the hole backwards and gripped the metal grating above. Then I pulled my legs through the square hole and landed flat upon my feet. But as I looked back through the grating, I realized Ryan had snatched up my sword.

I reached back through the opening. "Hand it over," I said sternly.

He backed up several steps and shook his head. "I don't think so, Kimosabe. This chunk of metal has gone to your head. You're gonna get somebody killed."

I stood there in total indignation. It was the ultimate offense! No soldier would ever forgive this. No rational Roman would hesitate to *kill* such an offender. And for him to do it *now*—in the face of such potential danger! Would anyone have objected if I tore this person apart with my bare hands?

"Give it to me now," I threatened, "or I swear they'll carry you out of here limb by limb."

"That's what I'm talking about," said Ryan. "You're not thinking rationally. This is not a game, Apollus. You're not a Roman Centurion. And I'm not James Bond. The lives of two children are at stake here. I'm not willing to put those lives in the hands of a mental case with delusions of being a Roman swordfighter."

My fists remained clenched with fury. Nevertheless, I had the presence of mind to calm my voice. "All right," I said, conceding defeat.

"You're assessment is correct. Perhaps I have taken this game too far. I'm not a Roman swordfighter and that isn't a real Roman sword. I apologize for threatening you. But two lives *are* at stake, and that blade is the only weapon we have. If you insist, I will allow you to carry it."

His eyes studied me carefully. He felt that I was at enough of a disadvantage now that I could finally be interrogated. "If you're not a Roman sword fighter, will you tell me who and what you really are?"

"Meagan already told you. I came from Mexico. I worked there as a bodyguard for a plantation owner."

"A bodyguard? Is that where you got this so-called 'special training' that Meagan mentioned?"

"Yes," I said. "Now, please. Get inside the cave before anyone hears us and returns."

"One more question," said Ryan. "What is this secret that Todd Finlay wants to know so badly? You know what it is, don't you?"

"Yes," I confessed. "I know what it is."

"Will you tell me?"

"I can't," I said. "I have to *show* you. It's here in this cave."

He waited another minute, considering. I backed away to make him feel he could enter the cave without my interference. He stepped up to the entry hole.

"You'll really show me?" he asked again.

I nodded reluctantly. "There's no reason to keep it from you now."

He leaned the sword against the grating, just as I had done. The flashlights and rope were dropped inside. He tried not to take his eyes off me as he climbed through, but as he pulled his legs through, there was one vulnerable moment when he had to turn away. That was all it took. I struck like an Egyptian cobra.

One minute later Meagan's twenty-first century boyfriend was bundled up and hog-tied as neatly as a festival pig.

CHAPTER 10

The trail we took dropped down a steep ravine and then connected up with a wider trail that led toward the cliffs where the cave was hidden. Meagan commented that it was definitely a faster route than the one Apollus and Ryan had taken. She felt certain Joshua and Mr. Bernard—that is, Mr. Finlay—would have reached the cave before them.

I was so out of breath by the time we arrived at the old broken-down wooden walkway that my lungs hurt. Not only that, but I don't think I was fully awake anymore. My legs might've been working, but half the time I almost felt like I was dreaming. I was so tired. Except for a couple hours of restless dozing, I'd been up nearly the whole night. I hadn't eaten since yesterday and I was still so thirsty. But somehow I found the strength and managed to keep up with Meagan and Mary. Again, I wondered if part of my strength came from the seer stones.

Meagan slowed us down as we got closer to the entrance. We couldn't see or hear anybody outside. Meagan told us to be quiet and walk carefully, afraid we might come upon some kind of meeting or fight between Apollus and Ryan and Mr. Finlay. Meagan picked up a big, gnarly-looking stick that she could use as a club. Mary grabbed a hefty rock. I kept right behind them.

At last we reached a place where we could look around the corner and see the steel gate over the entrance. Meagan motioned us to stay back while she crept up close and watched. After a minute, she called toward the tunnel in a loud whisper, "Apollus!"

A loud answer came back right away.

"Meagan! I'm here!"

It was her boyfriend, Ryan. Meagan jumped down onto the ledge and rushed up to the little entrance hole in the gate. She stopped in surprise.

"What happened?" Meagan asked.

"It was your creepy friend, Julius Spartacus Romanicus Ceasar! Just get me outa this!"

Mary and I climbed down and followed Meagan up to the gate. Ryan was right inside, lying on his stomach with his hands and feet tied together behind his back. Boy, did he look mad.

Meagan climbed into the hole. "Where's Apollus?"

"How should I know?" Ryan said in great irritation, struggling against the ropes. "He's only been gone a minute. Untie me!"

Meagan started undoing knots as Mary and I climbed into the cave.

"Apollus did this to you?" Meagan asked again, still in disbelief.

"Yes!" Ryan barked. "He attacked me as I was coming through the opening. Again, he did it when I wasn't expecting it. Oooo, if I ever get that guy face-to-face on even ground!"

"But why did he do it?"

"Because he's crazy! A total lunatic! Under what rock did you find that whacko?"

"Where's Joshua and Mr. Finlay?" I asked.

"We didn't see them," said Ryan. "Well, I take that back. We saw somebody. But nobody was inside the entrance when we got here."

"And Apollus went after them alone?" asked Meagan.

"Yes, alone," Ryan snapped, sounding insulted and humiliated. He added sarcastically, "Oh, but don't worry. He has his trusty sword!"

Meagan untied the last knot and Ryan's hands came apart. He rolled over and began hastily untying his feet. He did a double take as he glanced up at me. "Becky!" He looked at Meagan. "Where did you find her?"

"I got away," I said. "Thanks to Joshua."

"Finlay still has Joshua?" asked Ryan.

"Yes," said Mary. "What do you mean you saw somebody?"

"It was hard to tell with all this fog and wind," said Ryan. "But it looked like somebody may have gone into the cave ahead of us."

Meagan saw a flashlight on the ground and picked it up. "Come on," she said. "We have to follow them."

"It's time to call the police," said Ryan stubbornly. "Apollus is gonna get himself and everybody else killed. I think he really believes he's some kind of Roman Centurion!"

"Don't underestimate Apollus," said Meagan. "He's trying to save Joshua's life."

Now Ryan was thoroughly offended. "What do you think I was trying to do before I got bushwhacked?"

Meagan stepped up close to him. "I already told you, Ryan, you don't understand what's going on here. But there's no time to fill you in. If you want to leave and get the police, then go. Maybe that's a good idea. I'm guessing Apollus did what he did to you because you wouldn't just shut up and do what you were told. Am I right?"

Ryan opened and closed his mouth, unable to reply.

"That's what I thought," said Meagan. "So what do you wanna do? Do you want to go back to your car and bring the police?"

Ryan hesitated. His face got serious. In an instant he shook off any feelings of humiliation and said, to our surprise, "I'm staying with you."

Meagan softened a little, then got stern-faced. "Then stop trying to tell anybody what to do—especially Apollus. He may be a little rough around the edges, but if anybody can save Joshua's life, it's him."

Again, Ryan looked insulted. He hissed and turned away. He was still steaming inside, but as Meagan had requested, he kept his mouth shut. Meagan looked glad. I don't think she wanted to hurt his feelings, but she said what had to be said.

"Now let's go." Meagan flipped on the flashlight and led the way deeper into the cave.

* * *

A rope had been tied off at the usual place where the cave floor dropped into a deep pit. I grabbed onto it and yanked. It was a sturdy knot, and appeared to hang directly over the ingress that went underneath the floor a few yards down the wall. If indeed somebody had entered the cave before us, they didn't appear to have wasted any time.

I began to hear the echo of voices behind me. I stood and shined the light back into the tunnel. Another flashlight beam soon flashed into view, and behind it I could clearly make out the face of Meagan. Behind her was Ryan, still looking appropriately peeved. They were followed by Mary and—this was a surprise—little Rebecca!

"Apollus! What's happening?" Meagan inquired.

"Is the boy safe as well?" I asked.

"No," said Mary. "We feel sure he's still with Mr. Finlay. Have you seen any sign of them?"

I indicated the rope. "It appears that someone has climbed down to the ledge below. But how would Finlay have known about the secret tunnel?"

"Joshua would have told him," Becky said.

"How did *he* know?" I asked, dumbfounded.

"Don't you remember, Apollus?" said Becky. "Joshua and I were here before—when we were little."

Ryan examined the place where the rope had been tied off. "They were likely here just a few minutes ago." He paid me a searing look. "If you hadn't wasted so much time, we might have stopped them."

"If *you* hadn't taken my sword, you yipping cur—!"

"That's enough!" barked Meagan. "What are we going to do?"

"I'm going after them," I said without hesitation.

Ryan turned to Becky. "Does Finlay have a gun?"

She shook her head. "I never saw one. But I think he has a knife."

Mary said to me, "Apollus, if you're going, I think we all should go—at least for a short distance."

"Why?" I asked in dismay.

"Finlay has already found what he wanted," said Mary. "He has no reason anymore not to let Joshua go. We have to find him before they get much deeper—hopefully long before they reach the Rainbow Room."

"Rainbow *what?*" asked Ryan.

Mary ignored him and kept explaining to me, "We have to convince him that he doesn't *need* Joshua—that he can find his way now without anyone's help."

Meagan broke in. "Mary, do you realize what could happen if a man like Todd Finlay found the Rainbow Room or the Galaxy Room?"

"It's too late to think about that now," said Mary stubbornly. "We'll leave it in God's hands. It's all we can do. My only concern now is saving Joshua."

"That's why I should go alone," I said.

"That's exactly why you *shouldn't* go alone," said Mary. "If Finlay discovers that he's being pursued by a man like you, he may feel compelled to keep Joshua close just to protect himself. He won't let Joshua go until he feels he's reached his final destination."

Meagan caught the gist of Mary's strategy. "And if Finlay is looking for what I *think* he's looking for, he never *will* reach that destination. Or if he does, he'll be very disappointed."

Ryan was exasperated. "Would somebody please explain to me what's going on?"

We continued to ignore him.

"That's why I think we should go as a group," said Mary. "As a family. Finlay might be more willing to release Joshua to women and children than to a Roman warrior bent on killing him. I feel strongly that this can be done without violence."

"Violence is all a man like Finlay understands," I scoffed.

"You may be right," said Mary. "But he's also an old man. A twisted, corrupted old man. I believe he'll only hurt Joshua if you force him to—if he feels he has no other choice. You should come, Apollus, but not with the rest of us. You should hang back behind us a little ways."

"This is ridiculous," I spat. "It's the strategy of a woman."

Meagan raised her eyebrows and said, "Maybe the strategy of a woman is what this situation needs. It's not always necessary to charge in with a sword and chop everybody's head off."

Ryan got a smug look on his face. I wanted to wipe it off with my fist.

Meagan continued, "If we can convince Finlay to let Joshua go, I don't care what happens from there. You can keep pursuing him if you'd like, before he reaches the ancient worlds."

"*What?*" Ryan was at the edge of sensibility. "*What?* I must be losing my mind! Ancient worlds? *What is everyone talking about?*"

Meagan faced him. I thought she might slap him to bring him to his senses. Instead she took him roughly by the shoulders, as if losing all patience with his persistent density. "Oh, Ryan, *figure it out!* There's no time to explain it all! This cave is a time tunnel! Apollus really *is* a Roman soldier! Could you please just put two and two together and get hold of yourself? Let's keep moving! Joshua and Finlay are only getting further away!"

She grabbed onto the rope, prepared to lower herself over the edge. I held up my flashlight to light the way. Ryan just stood there, thun-

derstruck, his eyes not quite in focus. I wasn't quite sure how Meagan
had figured that Ryan should have had enough clues to draw the
conclusions she was suggesting, but she hardly seemed concerned
about that now. If Ryan had turned and departed, I don't think it
would have bothered her. Her determination was set. Mary and Becky
gave Ryan a sympathetic look, but they too had to focus on what was
ahead. Ryan slowly turned to me, still speechless. I shrugged, as if to
say, "Not *my* fault I'm a Roman. I was born that way."

Meagan and Mary climbed down to the ledge below without
much trouble. As Becky prepared to descend, I tied Ryan's rope
around her waist for additional support. Mary caught her and helped
her inside the ledge. I turned to Ryan again.

"Are you coming?"

He still hadn't said a word, nor hardly moved. Yet to my question
he nodded absently and took hold of the rope. I couldn't have said
what he was thinking, but I'm not sure it was quite clear to him
either. Whether prodded by curiosity, pride, or dementia, it didn't
seem to matter. He was determined to stick with us. It was the first
thing I'd observed about his character that seemed mildly worthwhile.
Maybe there was a trace of mettle in him after all.

* * *

It's me, Becky, again. I'll take over for a while.

*After we'd crawled back underneath the shelf that took us into the
deeper level, Mary started shouting Joshua's name. We listened to the
echoes bounce back and forth through the tunnels. Unfortunately, nobody
answered back. Either Joshua and Mr. Finlay were already way ahead of
us, or they weren't even here. I began to wonder how well Joshua really
remembered the way. Maybe he'd gotten lost.*

*I looked around in wonder at all the colors and formations. It had
been so long since I'd been here that it was like I was visiting for the first
time. I had a rush of feelings—memories, really. Things I'd forgotten
came swirling back. Mainly I started to remember how frightened I'd
been the first time we came through here. I was just so little, I guess.*

*For comfort, I reached up and felt the two stones under my shirt. I
even pulled them out and held them up to my eyes. I couldn't look through*

both stones at the same time—the frames must have been designed for somebody with a much larger head. So I looked through with one eye at a time, staring at places where Apollus and Ryan were shining their flashlights. It was so interesting. It wasn't as if I could see directly through the stones. They were too cloudy for that. Nevertheless, they seemed to separate the light beams into different colors. Somehow it sharpened everything. I felt as if I could make out shapes and images even if I stared at a place where it was still dark.

Finally, I put the stones down. I was still so tired and hungry. After calling out Josh's name for another hour and getting no response, everybody was getting discouraged. We really weren't prepared to go much further. At least not as a group. No canteen, no food, no blankets—and according to stories from my dad, it sometimes took two days to get through the cave.

Apollus had taken Mary's advice and remained behind us a little ways. But as we reached the place where the trail became a two-foot-wide ledge along the side of a cliff (with a drop-off so deep that I couldn't see the bottom), Apollus caught up to us and asked the obvious question.

"How far will the rest of you go before turning back?"

Mary and Meagan looked very depressed. I think they'd been hoping to catch up to Mr. Finlay long before now.

"I'm so thirsty," I said again.

"There's a spring not very far from here," said Meagan.

"But after that," reminded Apollus, "there's no water until the passage beyond the Rainbow Room."

"What is this Rainbow Room that everybody keeps talking about?" asked Ryan.

I was surprised at how few questions Ryan had asked. He seemed to be taking it all in stride now. Well, maybe not in stride. He definitely seemed nervous. But he'd stopped trying to argue with anybody. When he asked his question, people sort of shuffled their feet, not quite sure where to begin, so I decided to answer him myself.

"It's this big beautiful room that glows every color in the rainbow, and it has something to do with what makes it possible to go into the ancient worlds. There's this other room called the Galaxy Room, but I've never seen that room. In fact, the Galaxy Room may not exist anymore. Dad said it kinda went weird on them and got discombobulated and the power source went out."

"That's not entirely true, Becky," said Meagan. "The power source did become distorted after Harry and I broke through the floor, and for a while it did look like the nebula was dying out, but the last time we went through it, I swear there was something bright and glowing inside that orb in the ceiling. The energy seemed to be building up again. By now, who knows what it might look like."

Ryan's face appeared almost in pain as he tried to follow what we were saying. I tried to imagine how our words must have sounded. No doubt they sounded like we were insane. Or maybe he thought he was the one going crazy. Mary came to his rescue.

"What they mean, Ryan," she said, "is that there's an energy source in this cavern that nobody quite understands. Somehow it allows a person to visit other lands and times besides the one in which they were born. It's this power that allowed me to come and live in your century for the past two years."

Ryan backed up a step. "You're one of them too?"

I giggled. He was sounding like Mary was one of those pod-people from Invasion of the Body Snatchers.

Meagan took his hand. "No, she's not a Roman, Ryan." He looked mildly relieved until Meagan added, "She's a Jew from the first century A.D."

Ryan pulled another face. "You told me she was a foreign exchange student!"

"Well . . . she is," said Meagan awkwardly. "Sort of. Her parents are both dead, so Jim brought her home to live with us."

"Brought her from the first century A.D.?"

"Yes. Our whole family was there two years ago."

He shut his eyes and joggled his head. "You guys have some weird family vacations."

"It wasn't a vacation," said Meagan. "Harry and I had gone to find—" She put her face in her hands. "This is getting too complicated."

"You really believe this stuff, don't you?" He looked at the rest of us with awe and disbelief. "All of you. You really think Apollus is a Roman and Mary is a Jew from the first-century A.D.?"

"And Marcos is a Nephite," I added, just to get in my own two cents.

Ryan started trembling. He glanced back, possibly to see if there was a way to escape, but Apollus was standing there with his sword. He pressed his temples with the palms of his hands, trying to relieve a headache I think.

"I gotta . . . I gotta sit down."

He leaned against the rocky wall and slid down to the floor.

Meagan knelt beside him. "Maybe you should go back, Ryan. This all must be happening way too fast for you. We're not trying to freak you out—really we're not. I should have never dragged you into this. I didn't think we'd have to go this far. I thought your part would be over long before we reached the cave."

"I'm not leaving you," said Ryan firmly. He took a deep breath. "I can handle this. I just . . . need a second."

Apollus rolled his eyes impatiently.

"That's the problem, Ryan," said Meagan. "We don't have a second. We have to keep moving."

"This is aggravating," said Apollus. "You've all come far enough. I should go on alone from here."

"Just a little further," said Mary. "We should at least go to that room with the candle wax melted into the floor."

"Yes," said Meagan. "That's where we used to camp for the night. It's not very far. Finlay might try to rest there too. If we haven't found any sign of them before we reach that room, I promise we'll turn back."

Apollus frowned and looked like he might object, but he seemed to know better than to argue with Meagan. Ryan came to his feet and we continued on.

At last we reached a tiny fountain of water. It trickled out of the wall and flowed back between some cracks in the rock. I drank and drank. Everybody else drank too. It was only a few minutes later that we reached the room with the candle wax. Still, there was no sign of Joshua.

Everybody sat down tiredly against the wall. The two flashlights were set on the stone floor, the beams pointed upward. We were so exhausted. At least I'd gotten a few hours of sleep, but I don't think anybody else had slept for the last twenty-four hours.

"Well, that's it," said Apollus. "I'll keep one flashlight. The rest of you start making your way back. I'll keep on until I reach the Rainbow Room and the Galaxy Room. If I find nothing else, we'll have to conclude that Finlay and Joshua went another way."

My heart started hurting. Again, I felt guilty for abandoning my brother. Why did I listen to him when he told me to run away? If I'd stayed, at least I would have known where he was. My imagination played this horrible scene of Joshua falling into a bottomless pit. I shivered and shook it off.

"It's not possible," Meagan said to herself. "They couldn't have moved that fast. Not so fast that they wouldn't have heard the echo of our shouts. Joshua would have called out—done something to let us know where he was."

"If Finlay had bound his hands and kept a knife close by, he might've kept very quiet indeed," said Apollus. He turned to Ryan. "You will help these girls to get safely back."

Mary was close to tears. "I don't see how we can give up now. They might be so close. Finlay can't go on forever."

"He may have more energy than you think," said Apollus "He might feel like he's been storing it up for the past twenty-five years."

"Or he might be waiting at the mouth of the cavern just like he said in the note," Ryan suggested. "We might even meet him on the way back."

He stretched out his leg and accidentally kicked over his flashlight. The beam fell across the floor, toward the place where the tunnel kept going deeper. He reached out to set it upright again.

"No! Stop!" I yelled.

Everyone looked at me strangely.

I picked up Ryan's flashlight and carried it over to where the light had pointed. Then I shined it down on something until the beam became a little circle, like a spotlight. Meagan came over by me.

"What are you looking at?" she asked.

I reached down and picked it up. Then I turned around and showed it to everybody else, still shining the flashlight at it.

"It looks like a pebble," said Mary.

"It's a pistachio shell!" I said. "Joshua's pockets were filled with pistachio shells!"

Now everybody was on their feet and coming closer. Sitting there on the ground the shell had looked just like what Mary said—a pale brown pebble. But now they could see that it was a shell.

"Then Joshua was here," said Mary excitedly.

Apollus shined his own flashlight deeper down the tunnel, his sword tightly in his hand. "My guess is they left just moments ago. I suggest that they've heard every one of our shouts. They're trying to keep ahead of us."

"Then we stick to the plan," said Mary. "Even if we have to go all the way to the Rainbow Room."

"How much further is that?" asked Ryan.

"Seven or eight hours," said Mary.

"Seven or eight hours! That's crazy!"

"There will be water there," said Mary. "The air is cool. We won't sweat that much."

"You might get there," said Apollus. "But in your exhausted condition, you'd never get back. The return route is all uphill."

"If we have Joshua, we can rest as long as we want," said Meagan. "We can even stop for a day in the ancient world to get supplies."

"Which ancient world?" asked Apollus.

"Obviously the one I know how to reach," said Meagan. "I've never been to the world of the Nephites."

"It will be no simple thing to find supplies in the wilderness of Judea," said Apollus.

Meagan thought a second. "All right then. The world of the Nephites. I still remember the place where we separated from Jesse and Micah. It shouldn't be that hard to find the right passage. Besides, Becky has something around her neck that I'd like to ask about. It's probably just an ornament of some kind, but I'd like to ask somebody just the same. Maybe we'll find a Nephite bishop."

"If Josh still remembers the way, the Nephite world might be where he'll take Mr. Finlay," I added.

"I can't believe this is a real conversation," said Ryan. "If we're really serious about this, we should go back to Cody, Wyoming, and get the proper supplies."

"But then we may not catch up!" said Mary.

"What about that phone call from Jim?" asked Apollus.

Meagan looked stricken. She seemed to have forgotten all about it. "But we can't go back now!"

"What will Jim and Garth think?" asked Mary. "They'll be very frightened."

Suddenly Meagan seemed confident. "I'll tell you exactly what they'll think. They'll think we did precisely what we did. And they'll come right through here. Anyone have a pen?"

"I think so," said Mary. She still had her purse. She took it from around her shoulder and looked inside.

"What about a piece of paper?" asked Meagan.

"Just Finlay's note," said Mary.

"Give it to me."

Meagan set it down on a stone and began writing on the back. Her message was this:

We have Becky. But Finlay still has Joshua. We
will pursue as far as Galaxy Room. May get help
and supplies from Nephites.
Love Meagan, Mary, Becky, Apollus, Ryan.

She would have written more, but the stupid pen quit about halfway through. She had to shake it and scratch it to write as much as it did. She set the note near the pile of candle wax to make sure it would be found.

"Just in case," she said.

As we prepared to set out again on our journey, I looked back at that little piece of paper and had an eerie feeling. A silly feeling. I wondered if this was the last message from us that anyone would ever read.

CHAPTER 11

We continued our descent from the room where we had left the note. Ever the alert centurion, I remained in the rear as much as possible with my weapon in hand. It was approximately four hours later that I felt a most unusual vibration, quite faint, in the earth. Mary was the first to bring to it the company's attention.

"Did you feel that?" she inquired.

"I didn't feel anything," said Ryan.

"I think I felt something a few minutes ago, too," said Becky.

"Was it a tremor?" asked Meagan.

We stood still an instant longer, but when the vibration did not immediately repeat itself, we shook off the event and recommenced our journey. A few minutes later, however, the event reoccurred.

"Okay, I felt it that time," said Ryan.

"What do you think it is?" asked Becky.

"It reminds me of something I felt several years ago as we were approaching Jerusalem," said Mary. "Even from a great distance we could feel the impact of the Roman battering rams as they tried to breach a hole in the city walls."

"Maybe the vibration is caused by Joshua and Mr. Finlay," suggested Becky. "Something they're doing."

I had my doubts about that. To me the vibration was far more immense in scale, even larger than any impact created by the mighty rams. Its origin seemed somehow interconnected with the earth herself, like a shrug from her utmost depths. As before, the phenomenon did not repeat itself right away, so we went deeper. But then, after a similar interval of time, the vibration struck again.

We were less startled this time and did not pause, but sure enough, after another comparable interval, there was another vibration. The tremor seemed to be increasing in intensity.

"I'm going to time the next one," said Ryan. He pushed a button on his tiny wristclock.

When the next one occurred, Ryan hit the button again and announced, "Seven minutes and thirty-two seconds."

"What could it be?" asked Mary again.

"Is it part of this Rainbow/Galaxy Room thing?" asked Ryan, half facetiously.

"I've never felt anything like it before," said Meagan. "I've felt an earthquake in these tunnels, yes. But nothing quite like this."

Seven minutes and thirty-two seconds later, the vibration hit again. It was definitely growing stronger, as if we were drawing closer to its source.

"That's really weird," said Meagan.

At precise intervals of seven minutes and thirty-two seconds, the vibration continued to repeat over the next several hours, increasing in intensity until it actually became audible. The sheer power of it, resonating as it was from the heart of mother earth, became quite disconcerting for our group.

"I'm frightened," said Becky.

She grasped onto Mary's hand and insisted upon holding it from that time forth. After the next pulse shook the ground, Meagan offered the first rational speculation.

"It must have something to do with the Galaxy Room. We'll be there in less than an hour. The way that it seems to be building, I'd almost guess that the shock wave is centered right where the Galaxy Room is located."

"Why would it quake every seven and a half minutes?" asked Ryan.

"No idea," said Meagan. "But like I told you before, the last time we came through here two years ago, there was something glowing inside that nebula way up in the Galaxy Room's ceiling. All I can think is that it has something to do with that."

I went over in my mind the three separate occasions when I had passed through this mysterious room. The first time I saw it, the place had been a firestorm of colors. There seemed to be no rhyme or reason to the chaos. I felt the most unusual sensations in my flesh as the energy passed through my body. The second time I saw the room, we were making our way back to search for Harry. The room had seemed quite dead, just as Meagan had described. My interpretation of the room upon our final return would have been much the same as Meagan's. Something was definitely alive and pulsing inside that massive orb in the ceiling, but none of us could have guessed what the final state of the room would eventually be. My own opinion had been that the mystical phenomenon that had allowed a person to pass from one world to the next might be dissipating. If Meagan's instincts were accurate, the prospect of what might await us was alarming indeed.

The terrain was becoming familiar to me now. I knew that within a couple hundred yards we would reach the narrow tunnel that arched up to the crystalline cliffs overlooking the Rainbow Room. But for right now we were climbing down into one of the last large chambers—a room filled with many unusual formations, including a ceiling decorated with large, pink-crystal stalactites. The room bent around and climbed up a kind of tilted stone balcony, finally making an egression into a tighter channel at the opposite end. Hanging back as I was, I only caught a brief glimpse of the sight that drew shouts of adulation from the lead members of our group.

"Joshua!" I heard Becky cry.

"Mr. Finlay, stop!" shouted Meagan.

At last, we had caught up to them. They were at the other end of the chamber, just ascending the tilted balcony into the next tunnel. Todd Finlay shined a flashlight back in our direction, then abruptly faced forward, ignoring our presence. Joshua tried to look back at us, but as I had first suspected, his hands were bound together in front. There was a short length of rope between his wrists to allow some flexibility for climbing, but there was another cord secured around his waist. This line was held by Finlay, who yanked on it severely when it appeared that Joshua might hesitate. The two of them disappeared into the next chamber.

"Wait!" cried Mary.

"Let him go, Mr. Finlay!" shouted Meagan. "You don't need him anymore!"

Finlay did not respond. Suddenly he was in a great hurry. Our group had the same idea, but as we started to break into a run, the tremor struck again, nearly knocking us off our feet. As with every other instance, it was just that single jolt. Everyone hastily recovered, and with Meagan and Ryan leading the way, they crossed the chamber and ascended the rocky balcony, desperate to catch their quarry.

As for me, I brought myself up to a halt halfway across the chamber and eyed a pair of obscure passages to my left—both barely large enough for my body. I knew that there was an entire honeycomb of tunnels beyond the Rainbow Room. Perhaps one of these passages would allow me to connect up with one of those tunnels. If I could do that, then maybe . . .

I veered to the right and slipped into the tight passage.

* * *

The chase was on. I was moving so fast now that it was impossible to keep holding Mary's hand. Mary and Meagan kept calling out to Joshua and Mr. Finlay, but they refused to answer. Now and then we could see the reflection of Mr. Finlay's flashlight in the passage ahead, but the tunnels were too twisted and winding for us to get another straight-on look.

"We're almost there," said Meagan at one point. "The Rainbow Room is just up ahead."

The tunnel dropped down and then started to go through a long passage that appeared to be a dead end. But right at the end of the passage, Joshua and Mr. Finlay were climbing up into a thin crawl space that had a breeze blowing out of it.

"Joshua!" Mary cried again.

"Hold it right there!" cried Ryan.

"Get back!" shouted Mr. Finlay. "Get back or I'll kill him!"

We could see that he was carrying a knife. Just a small hunting knife, but it was large enough to control my brother. We screeched to a halt as Mr. Finlay dragged on Joshua's rope, forcing him to climb up into the crawl space ahead of him.

"Mr. Finlay!" said Meagan. "Let Joshua go. We can show you how to get to the ancient worlds from here. I promise if you let him go, we'll tell you anything you want to know!"

"I have all I need!" he growled back. "The boy knows the way!"

"Please!" Meagan begged.

But Mr. Finlay climbed up into the crawl space behind Joshua.

At that instant another one of those terrible tremors hit. We'd been chasing Joshua and Mr. Finlay for exactly seven minutes and thirty-two seconds. This tremor was the most powerful yet. The whole chamber seemed to echo, like with a sonic boom. Mary fell. Ryan and Meagan grabbed onto the sides of the tunnel for support. I grabbed onto Ryan.

As I looked back toward the crawl space where Joshua and Mr. Finlay had disappeared, I swear there was a flash of light. Is that the right way to describe it? It was definitely a flash of something. A big gust of wind swept over the top of us. But it wasn't just wind. It was like a wave of energy. The energy passed right through us and seeped into the rocks. I felt a little like I'd just been electrified. It certainly wasn't a pleasant feeling, but just like every other time, it was only that one single vibration and then everything went still again and became like before. We recovered and stood up straight.

"Did you see *that*?" asked Ryan, indicating the flash of light at the end of the tunnel.

"Yes," said Meagan. "And Joshua climbed right up into it!"

She scrambled as fast as she could to reach the end of the tunnel. The rest of us stayed right on her heel. Whatever had caused the vibration, we knew that we had at least another seven-and-a-half minutes before it hit again.

Somehow Ryan got ahead of Meagan and squirmed up into the crawl space ahead of her. I was climbing up behind Meagan. Mary was behind me. I realized that nobody was behind Mary. Where was Apollus? I knew that he had been lingering back a little, but I wouldn't have thought he was *that* far back. And I felt sure that he'd been with us when we'd started chasing after Joshua. I could only hope he wasn't lost.

I kept my eyes straight ahead, looking right at Meagan's shoes as we continued pulling ourselves through the crawl space. I could tell that Ryan had reached the end and was rising to his feet.

"Oh, my gosh!" I heard him say in awe.

He'd reached the Rainbow Room—that was obvious. But it seemed to me that there was also fear in his voice—much more than I might've expected. A chill ran through me, thinking that any terrible thing that Ryan was looking at could only have to do with Joshua. As Meagan climbed out of the space and stood up, I could see the reflection of the colored lights all around her. Just like Ryan, Meagan had stopped dead in her tracks, which was also a bit nerve-racking, because I knew that Meagan had already seen this room several times before. She was acting like she was seeing it for the first time.

I'd never seen the Rainbow Room personally. When we made our journey back through the cavern from the land of the Nephites, I was told that we'd gone a slightly different route and managed to go around it. But I'd heard so many descriptions throughout my life that I felt like I had a very clear idea of what to expect. However, when I came to my feet and stood there at the edge of those chalky, crystal cliffs, the scene before me was very different than anyone had ever described.

It was Uncle Jim who had said that the Rainbow Room was the size of several football fields. Yet if I had been describing it, I would have said it was even larger than that. My father had said that the walls all around the edges of the room were pouring with waterfalls that all gathered into one fast-moving river that disappeared into a hole at one end. This was the only thing that still seemed to be true. There were waterfalls—dozens of them—at different levels and distances, spilling over the cliffs and splashing into the river, except now there appeared to be two rivers that came together before all the water washed into the hole.

I remembered distinctly that Harry and Meagan had both said that the ceiling of this room was like a glittering sea of crystals, glowing every color in the rainbow. I could still see many of these crystals along the walls, and just like everyone had said, they sparkled and twinkled with hundreds of colors—reds and golds, blues, greens, and purples. But unlike what Harry and Meagan had described, there was no ceiling to this room. At least not the kind of ceiling that I felt like I'd been prepared for. Instead, the ceiling was five hundred feet above us. At the very top was something that resembled the orb or nebula that Meagan had used to describe the Galaxy Room.

But the one thing that nobody had ever described was the shimmering silver pillar. The pillar looked like it shot up from the floor at the place where the two rivers rushed together. And just like that laser beam that came out of the roof of the Luxor Hotel in Las Vegas, the pillar continued in a perfectly straight line until it connected right into the center of the orb in the ceiling. But it wasn't just laser light. There was substance to this pillar—energy. The pillar looked like it was about ten feet across and the energy inside it seemed to swirl upward. Even though its color was a bright, almost metallic-looking silver, if I squinted my eyes or made them just a little bit out of focus, the pillar seemed to be swarming with colors of its own, as if absorbing or reflecting all the colors of the rainbow crystals. It was misty at the top and bottom of the pillar, like at the bottom of a waterfall. Because of this, it was sort of hard to see the place where the pillar went into the ground, but it looked like the base of it was on a very small neck of land between the rivers. On one side of the pillar the water flowed around it and seeped into a crevasse or space at its edge. But no, that wasn't quite true. It was more like the water was pulled into it. It actually became a part of the pillar and swirled upward toward the glowing red orb in the ceiling.

"The two rooms are one now," I heard Meagan say, and her voice made a very strange echo.

"You mean the Galaxy Room and the Rainbow Room?" asked Mary.

"Yes. Harry and I were always convinced that they were right above and below one another. Something has made the floor that separated them disappear."

I suddenly had a strange idea. I took the silver frames with the two seer stones out from under my shirt. Oddly, the color of the stones looked a lot like the color of the pillar—a silvery, pale white. And the way it reflected the colors of the rainbow crystals looked similar too. Recalling the strange effect that the stones had had when I'd looked through them at the flashlight beams, I wanted to see what would happen if I looked into them in the midst of this room. I held them in front of my eyes. As before, I closed one eye and peered through with one stone at a time.

I was looking straight at the shimmering pillar. What I saw surprised me so badly that I dropped the seer stones and let them dangle around my neck again. What had I seen? I'm not sure I can describe it. In fact, I know I can't. It was as if I could see into the energy. Oh, that's a terrible description. Let me try again. It was as if I could see deep into the silvery substance of that pillar—much deeper than just five or ten feet—and I could see . . . time.

Wow, that's even worse than my first description. Of course nobody can see "time." Time isn't something that has any shape or form. It just is. But that's what I felt I saw—voices and feelings and lifetimes and places and . . .

Oh, I give up! I'm not making any sense. I'd have to think about this for a while longer. But it's enough to say that the image startled me. I just didn't understand it.

"There they are!" shouted Mary, her voice also giving off a quivering echo.

She was pointing along the cliff wall to the left of the little shelf where we were standing. It was Joshua and Mr. Finlay! They were making their way up the narrowest of ledges, climbing along the left wall toward . . . I'm not sure. To me it looked like they were headed for a total dead end that would force them to climb back. Maybe if they'd been rock climbers or if Mr. Finlay had been Spiderman they could've made it to some wide tunnel openings about twenty yards beyond them, but if there had ever been ledges that acted as a bridge to those tunnels, the ledges were gone. With his hands tied, Joshua had even less chance of getting over to those tunnels. I wasn't quite sure what Mr. Finlay was thinking. Was he just desperate to get away from us?

"Mr. Finlay!" Meagan shouted. "Come back! You can't make it! There's no place to go!"

He continued on, yanking at the rope that pulled Joshua along. Then I realized there was someplace for them to go. There were several small cave openings above and below them. Neither looked very deep. But maybe Mr. Finlay had a better angle. Whatever the case, getting into these tunnels would be very dangerous. One slip and they'd both fall into the river.

"Mr. Finlay, please," Mary pleaded. "Let Joshua go free. He can't do anymore for you than he already has."

"This boy is my insurance!" Mr. Finlay shouted back.

"No one will try to stop you," said Mary. "Any of those tunnels, if you can reach them, should take you to the ancient worlds."

"Joshua!" I cried out. "Joshua, are you okay?"

"Don't tempt him to speak!" said Mr. Finlay. "He's been told that for every word he utters, I'll cut off one finger!"

"At least untie his hands!" begged Meagan. "He could fall off and drown!"

"Then let him drown!" yelled Mr. Finlay. "It couldn't do him any more harm than what his father did to me! I've been drowning for twenty-five years! This boy is going to repay the debt owed to me by his father and uncle. He will help me to get back that sword!"

I realized then that Mr. Finlay wasn't just cruel or obsessed. Joshua had been right. He was plain crazy. It was no use trying to argue with a man who wasn't right in the head. I felt terrified for Joshua's life.

"Mr. Finlay," said Mary. "I know you don't really want to hurt anyone. Joshua can't help you get back that sword. But I can. Take me instead of him."

I looked at Mary in surprise. Who'd have thought that this girl from 70 A.D. would be so willing to trade her life for my brother's? I didn't know what sword everyone was talking about, but I felt sure that Mary couldn't have done anymore for Joshua than any of the rest of us could've done. She was bluffing.

"How can you help me?" asked Finlay. "Who are you?"

"I come from the ancient worlds," said Mary. "I know how to take you there. I promise that if you come back here and let Joshua go free, I'll show you how to get to wherever you wish to go."

Meagan whispered to Mary harshly. "What are you doing?"

"Bargaining for Joshua's life," she replied.

I felt terrible that I had ever rolled my eyes at Mary for being so uptight. But her bargaining didn't matter. Finlay wasn't buying it.

"I don't believe you," he said. "Now go back and leave us alone, or the boy will die right here and now!"

I shuddered inside. Mary's strategy had backfired. What choice did we have except to do what he said?

But then something flashed—just over Mr. Finlay's head. It was the tip of a sword! It was Apollus! He was crouching down inside the small cave just above them. Joshua and Mr. Finlay were still looking back toward us, so they couldn't see him. But as soon as Mr. Finlay turned around and looked up, Apollus' shadow would have been just as clear to them as it was to us. I heard Mary gasp, so I knew that she had seen him too. She grabbed Meagan's shoulder, and I could tell she wanted desperately to point him out, but that would have given him away to Mr. Finlay.

Apollus edged forward and my heart skipped a beat. What was the Roman going to do? There was no room to attack. To protect himself, all Mr. Finlay had to do was threaten to push Joshua off the edge. One yank on the rope and it would all be over.

Mr. Finlay turned back again, but his eyes were lowered, looking at his hands. He was climbing up to the exact tunnel where Apollus was crouching down. Whatever happened, it was going to happen in the next ten seconds! I said the quickest prayer in my mind that I've ever said: Heavenly Father, protect them! Don't let my brother die!

* * *

I considered shrinking back into the darkness, but it was too late. He would have heard me now. I tried to press myself against the cave wall, but this hardly hid me from view. At best it might have deflected a casual glance by helping me to blend in with the rock—and this was precisely what it seemed to do. Finlay did glance up—more to orient his bearings than anything else. But his gaze immediately went back to his hands as he looked for a place to secure his next grip. The small knife was placed in his teeth where it was more convenient to carry. His other hand was still holding the rope tied to Joshua's waist, while the canvas bag I had seen with him at that cantina in San Andrés, Tuxtla, was draped over his shoulder.

The boy was just a body length below him, still looking unnerved and frightened, and clutching the cliff wall slightly to Finlay's right. But then Joshua saw me and his eyes filled with alarm. The moment of action had arrived. Finlay pushed up with one leg. His face appeared, just overlooking the base of the tunnel where I was poised. He saw my legs first. His eyes scanned up my body until he was staring straight at my clenched teeth, then his eyes widened in horror.

I responded swiftly with the only defense I could manage in this awkward position. I kicked him in the face. The blade flew out of his mouth. Finlay began wheeling his arms as he toppled backwards and started skidding down the face of the cliff. But he was still holding Joshua's rope!

I lunged forward—head first—and dove toward Joshua, dropping my sword and letting it clatter down the cliff wall. A short distance below Joshua the cliff sheered off dramatically. Finlay began to free fall. My shoulder hit a ledge near Joshua's head, and my arm caught around a nub of stone. My other arm shot forward toward Joshua's bound wrists just as the rope went taut.

Joshua yelped as the rope jerked at his waist. He was instantly yanked down the cliff. He would have fallen into the river as surely as Finlay, but I managed to hook my arm through his bound hands. I caught the rope with my elbow and hung on. The force of the jerk whipped the rope out of Finlay's grip. He screamed and dropped into the churning waters, the canvas bag still hanging around his neck.

I'd have wagered that the river would have dragged Finlay toward the dark hole at the far end, but he'd fallen far enough out from the ledge that he was caught in an eddy of current that dragged him toward the place where the water was seeping into a whirlpool on the far side of the silver pillar.

Finlay screamed again as the current whipped him behind the pillar, out of my view. The scream was cut short. I couldn't raise my eyes at that instant—I needed to concentrate on maintaining my grip on Joshua—but I didn't need to see any more to know that Finlay was gone. He was swallowed up by the whirlpool. Joshua was kicking his legs, trying to find a foot hold. The rope that bound his wrists was cutting into my elbow.

"Hang on!" I heard someone call out.

I looked up slightly and saw Meagan and Ryan making their way toward us along a thin crystal shelf. It was undoubtedly the same route that Joshua and Finlay had used to get here. But something about that fragile shelf, and something about the *timing* caused me to draw in my breath in suspense. How many minutes had passed since the last jolt?

"No!" I cried. "Get back onto safer ground!"

But just as the final syllable broke from my lips, I noticed that the silvery pillar had become brighter than ever. But it was the red orb five hundred feet overhead that exhibited the most dramatic change. The crimson light had become almost blinding, and the entire chamber was suddenly filled with an ear-splitting echo, like a whistle of steam, rising quickly in pitch and volume.

And then it struck.

The explosion shook the entire room, and suddenly colors were flying everywhere, as if a billion butterflies had burst into flight. This was followed by a blast of energized wind and brilliant light. All of the crystals on the chamber walls seemed to catch fire—the whole *room* ignited—as if the energy of the blast was absorbed into the stones.

The jolt had been too much. I'd lost my grip. I was sliding down the cliff! What was more, I noticed that the crystal shelf upon which Meagan and Ryan had been standing completely gave way. They, too, were plummeting toward the water.

I heard a dizzying echo of shouts and screams. One scream escaped from the throat of Joshua as we reached the place where the cliff became sheer. We toppled over the edge. The roiling white waters of the river came rushing at our faces. We hit in a foaming splash. As

I threw back my head for a final gulp of air, the end of the rope tied to Joshua's waist slapped my cheek. I seized the rope as the current spun me around and tried to use it to pull myself back to the surface. But this tug had another result. As it turned out, Joshua and I had both been sucked in by two different currents. He was being dragged back behind the pillar toward the same whirlpool that had captured Finlay, whereas I was being pulled toward the gaping hole at the far end of the room. For what it was worth, the weight of my body had yanked Joshua into my own current. We were now being carried toward the same place.

But then fate took another unusual turn. A short distance from the shores of the small neck of ground where the shimmering pillar stood, a short stalagmite protruded up from the river depths. Joshua was being swept around one side while I was being carried around the other. The rope caught! Because of my greater weight, or perhaps because I was being dragged by a stronger current, Joshua was wrenched upstream. He managed to throw his bound arms over the top of the stalagmite and hang on. My own body, however, was caught in a violent undertow. The current whipped me under the water with an unexpected force and the rope was torn from my hands, leaving a red and blistered rope burn.

There were no obstacles to save me now. I belonged to the river. I managed to reach the surface one final time. In that instant I caught sight of Meagan and Ryan, also flailing in the rapids and being drawn steadily toward the gaping hole where the earth swallowed the river. I also heard the echoing screams of Mary and Becky somewhere above, but their voices were cut silent as I gulped for breath and another savage undertow pulled me beneath the surface. An instant later, the glow of the Rainbow Room was snuffed out, and except for the gurgle of bubbles in my ears, I heard no other sounds.

It seemed strange that at this moment the face of my younger sister came into my mind. Albia had died with my mother in a carriage accident on the Felsina Road when I was a boy. She and I had been quite close. I'd heard it said that strange visions often befell a man at the moment of his death, so I assumed that this was no exception. Yet I found it disturbing—and oddly comforting—that my sister was laughing at me. Laughing as gaily as a summer zephyr, a laugh that blended with the bubbles. And then she spoke, and the words penetrated my heart, and faded away.

"*Hold your breath, dear brother,*" she whispered in my ear. "*Your time is not yet. Do you understand? It is not yet . . .*"

CHAPTER 12

The river swept them away! Right before our eyes Meagan and Ryan and Apollus had fallen into the rapids and got sucked down into the hole! It had happened so fast. One second they were there and the next they were gone!

I had no doubt that they were drowning. How could I think anything else? My mind went numb. I was in shock. And yet I couldn't *be in shock! I couldn't allow myself to faint and shrivel away, because Joshua was still alive.*

With his hands still tied, he'd looped them around a rock that was sticking up out of the rapids. We could still see him down there, hanging on, his legs still being knocked around by the current. And yet he'd caught himself pretty good. Unless that rope that tied his hands suddenly broke, he could continue to hang there for as long as he wanted. But the second he let go, he'd be washed away and drowned as surely as the others.

Mary also looked grief-stricken. But like me, she knew that for Joshua's sake she had to keep her wits.

"Joshua!" she cried. "Can you hear us?"

My brother turned his head and looked up. He nodded, but then with a shiver in his voice, he said, "The w-water is so c-cold."

I felt tight in my chest all over again. Sure, Joshua could hang on, but in a few minutes he'd freeze to death!

"We have to get down to him!" I said.

Mary scanned the walls of the Rainbow Room, searching for a way to reach the neck of rocky ground where the rivers came together. It was the same neck of land where the pillar of silver energy swirled up toward the ceiling. There definitely wasn't any way to get there from here. If we could've gotten over to those big tunnel openings that were just beyond the place where Joshua and Apollus had fallen into the water, it looked like there was a ridge to climb down. But how could we get from here to there?

I thought about Apollus. Somehow he'd gotten himself over to that skinny cave where he kicked Todd Finlay in the mouth. I also remembered how it was possible to reach the ancient worlds without going through the Rainbow Room.

"We have to find another way over to those tunnels," I said to Mary.

"Let's get to that small cave where Apollus came out and see if there's another tunnel that will take us over there," Mary suggested.

"But what if the tremor hits again?" I asked fearfully.

"We still have a few minutes. Come on!"

So Mary and I scooted as fast as we could across the narrow ledges where Joshua and Mr. Finlay had been climbing. This was a climb that would've taken all our concentration even if we hadn't been in a hurry. To do it this fast was only asking for disaster. It might've been easier if we could have backtracked and found out where Apollus had first gone in, but we had no flashlight now. We were completely helpless without the light from the Rainbow Room. All we could hope was that this light would reflect throughout all the nearby tunnels and guide us to where we needed to be.

Joshua kept hanging on. We jarred loose some crystals and watched them splash into the water above him. How long had it been since the last time the room had shook? It was certain that any jolt would have knocked Mary—and probably me, too—off into the river. Mary was wearing a watch. She was the one from ancient times, yet she was the only one who had thought about wearing a watch. She glanced at it and announced, "We have about a minute and a half."

We continued to climb along the crystal shelves toward the cave opening where Apollus had come out.

"Thirty seconds," said Mary.

We started climbing the last stretch toward the cave.

"Ten seconds!"

There didn't seem to be any way we could make it. We were just pulling ourselves up the last few feet when Mary announced, "That's it! It will hit any instant!"

Thankfully, Mary's timing was a little off. It was seven more seconds before we reached the hole—just as that high-pitched ringing began to build. Mary pulled me in from the cliff.

We laid down flat against the ground just as the blast of energy struck. The cave filled with light, and wind rushed over the top of us. Five seconds later it was over. I crawled back to look down at the water. Joshua was still there, hanging on. We had no more time to lose. We started the desperate search for another route.

Mary tried to choose tunnels that showed some glimmer of light—some hint that it would work its way back around and come out in another entrance of the Rainbow Room. There were some stretches that were quite dark. But there always seemed to be a dim glow. I considered it a miracle that before the next vibration even hit, Mary and I were both standing at the edge of one of the wide tunnels that overlooked the piece of land closest to Joshua. We'd done it! And without a flashlight! I was about to start climbing down when Mary grabbed my arm. She was looking at her watch.

"Twenty more seconds," she said.

We braced ourselves and waited. The next explosion shook the room, but its force was just the same—no stronger or weaker. Now we were safe to make our way down. As we started down the ridge, we focused on the silver pillar. When we reached Joshua, we'd almost be standing right next to it. The very base of the pillar was still fogged by mist, but the closer we got, the easier it was to see. It looked just like it came to an end right there on that rock, like a laser being fired from a giant alien gun until it went all the way to the center of the earth.

After another minute we reached level ground again, and the silver pillar was less than twenty feet away. Mary and I worked our way around it, trying to keep as far away from its surface as possible without falling into the water. It surprised me that even though I could now see the pillar's back side, I still couldn't tell if the water that flowed around one part of the pillar got sucked up by it or washed down into a crevasse. All I knew was that it had created a whirlpool—the same whirlpool that had sucked Todd Finlay down.

The closer we got to the pillar, the more awesome it appeared. The brightness was almost hypnotizing. I could stare into it and see all sorts of different patterns and colors swirling around inside. I don't know how, but the patterns almost seemed to reflect how I was feeling, like I was looking into a mirror. Not a mirror like a bathroom mirror, but a mirror of my emotions. I turned away. I couldn't think about that right now. I only wanted to focus on saving my brother.

We edged up as close as we could to where Joshua was hanging on. He was only about ten feet out from shore, but it was still too far for us to reach him, and the water looked very fast and deep. He was barely conscious. His lips were blue and I could see him shivering violently. The white water from the current sometimes splashed up right over the top of him.

"Hang on, Joshua," said Mary. "We're going to get you out of there."

The end of the rope tied to Joshua's waist whipped back and forth in the current like the tail of a snake. I went down the bank a couple yards and waited for it to wash closer. I reached out as far I could, but it never seemed to whip over close enough.

"We'll have to work together," said Mary. "You're lighter, so it will probably be better if I act as anchor. I'll hold your wrist and you hold mine. Then you're going to have to try to lean out into the water and grab it."

"Who will be holding you?" I asked, swallowing.

She looked around. There really was nothing for her to grip. She just had to lay down as low as possible and hope the current wouldn't carry us both downstream. Actually, I was the one in real danger, but I'd risk it all for my brother.

My emotions already felt numb, so I hoped my flesh would feel the same and the chill of the water wouldn't affect me. As I stepped off the rock and plunged in up to my waist, I realized how wrong I was. Wow! It was like needles of ice! The cold sank right to my bones. There was nothing I could do to stop a cry of pain from eeking out of my throat.

"I have you!" Mary yelled reassuringly.

I reached out for the rope. Just at that instant, the current washed it closer. I had it!

"Pull me back!" I cried.

Mary dragged me back with all her strength. I hoisted myself from the water, still dripping, but the warm air, seemingly electrified by the glowing orb and the silver pillar, gave me almost instant relief. We carried the rope up the shore, just across from Joshua. He looked at us and smiled weakly.

We dug in our feet, then Mary said, "All right, Joshua. Just raise your arms. Let go of the stalagmite. Don't worry. We won't let you go."

I wondered if Joshua even had the strength to raise his arms. His skin was so white. It didn't look like there was a drop of blood in his face. He nodded, then he dragged himself forward a few inches, as if hugging the stalagmite with his elbows. He raised up his arms.

The river tried to quickly sweep him away from us, but Mary and I had him! We dragged Joshua to shore. When he was close enough, Mary put her hands under his armpits, and pulled him the rest of the way out.

Right away we snuggled around him, rubbing warmth back into his arms and legs. Mary untied the rope from his wrists and waist. It was like cuddling a gallon of ice cream. His teeth started chattering so badly I was afraid some might crack. And yet if his experience was gonna be anything like mine, I felt sure the room's air would warm him up fast.

"Th-th-ank you," Joshua stuttered.

A minute later that awful vibration struck. The force didn't feel any different here than anywhere else. Ground zero seemed to be inside that nebula above us. We watched the crystals on the walls light up again like they were on fire. It was all so spooky and disturbing. I wanted out of here, and I didn't want to ever return. But where could we go?

No flashlight. No food. We were stuck *here! Stuck until somebody came and found us. It might be days or weeks before Dad or Uncle Jim came looking for us. Could we last that long, especially with our nerves being rattled every seven and a half minutes? We'd go crazy! I was* already *crazy. Crazy with grief. Now that Joshua was safe again, my mind flew back to thinking about Meagan, Apollus, and Ryan being washed down that hole. Tears filled my eyes. Then the dam burst and I started sobbing.*

I felt Joshua's cold arm wrap around my waist. "It's-s okay, B-Becky. They'll b-be okay."

I looked at him. Color was starting to come back into his lips, but his thinking obviously wasn't clear. Maybe Joshua hadn't seen what Mary and I had seen. He didn't realize what the river had done to them.

"They're gone, Joshua," I wept. "There was nothing anybody could have done."

"No, they're not," said Joshua. "They d-didn't drown."

"How do you know?" asked Mary.

"'Cause Dad told us," said Joshua. "Don't you r-remember? He told us the river w-was another way back into B-Book of Mormon times."

I remembered now. Joshua was right. But how could anybody survive such a thing? Even Dad had told us that he'd almost drowned. Harry and Meagan had almost drowned too. Still, Joshua's words gave me a glimmer of hope. I wiped off my tears.

We held Joshua till he stopped stuttering, then we focused on our situation.

"We can't stay here," I said to Mary. "I'll wig out if I have to feel that vibration many more times."

She looked around at all the crystal walls. "I wonder if those crystals emit a light on their own, like a candle or a flashlight."

It was an interesting idea. She may have been onto something.

"We'll let Joshua recover a few more minutes," said Mary. "Then I'd like to break a few off and give it a try."

I stood up to let the water drain off my pants a little better. I scanned the room myself, turning in a circle. My eyes stopped on the silver pillar. What a sight it was, especially this close up. I followed it up all the way to the ceiling and got a little dizzy. How had it formed, *I* wondered? *I'd seen geysers and rainbows, and on TV I'd watched tornadoes and volcanoes, but this was still by far the strangest thing in nature that I'd ever seen. The pillar wasn't made of anything but energy. Yet it didn't make sense. Why didn't it burn us to a crisp? I took several steps toward it. Its surface was only ten feet away now. With each step I could see more details. Over the river's roar I could tell it made a kind of humming sound. Eerie in a way, but relaxing in another. Then I thought about the vibration that was coming again in two or three minutes and shuddered.*

Even this close, the base was blurred with mist. I decided to get close enough to see if the pillar went into the ground or ended right there, on the surface of the rock. Another three steps and I still *wasn't sure. The energy seemed to* blend *with the ground, almost like a sponge soaking up water. Mary saw me and came closer.*

"Be careful," she said. "We still don't know what that thing is."

I stopped. "Why do you think we can't feel it? We're only five feet away. Shouldn't we feel heat or cold or an electric shock?"

Mary shook her head and shrugged.

"I almost think . . ." I hesitated, but then I said, ". . . that it's alive.*"*

Mary nodded. "I know what you mean."

"Each time I move closer, I see something different, like it's reacting to me."

I took another step, and just like before, the colors seemed to change a little and swirled in a different pattern. Joshua felt left out, and came over beside us. He looked almost completely recovered.

"*Meagan didn't think it was here before,*" *I said.*

"*I certainly don't remember it,*" *said Mary. She sighed, then sounding like the responsible guardian again, she said, "Let's leave it alone and work on getting out of here.*"

"*Wait,*" *I said to Mary. "I wanna show you one more thing.*" *I pulled out the seer stones. "Something weird happens when I look at the pillar through these. I tried looking at it from the ridge and it almost frightened me. Maybe* you *should try it.*"

I handed them to Mary. She gave me a skeptical look, then put one of the stones up to her eye. She stared into it for a second, then said, "Pretty."

"*Pretty?*" *I repeated. "That's it?*"

"*It sort of makes the lights dance,*" *said Mary.*

"*And that's all you see?*"

She drew her eyebrows together. "What else should *I see?*"

"*I don't know . . . just . . . well,* tons *of things. Did you try staring deep into the pillar?*"

"*Becky,*" *she said, almost scolding. "The stones aren't completely transparent. It's not like you can see all the way through them.*"

"*I can!*" *I insisted.*

"*Let me try,*" *said Joshua.*

He took the stones and held them up to his own eyes. "Cooool!" *he said dreamily.*

"*What do* you *see?*" *I asked.*

"*All the different colors are moving around,*" *he replied. He aimed the stone up toward the crystal walls.*

"*No!*" *I said. "You have to look into the pillar.*"

"*I did!*"

"*And you didn't see anything else?*"

"*Becky, exactly what do you think you see?*"

"*History!*" *I replied. I wasn't quite sure where* that *came from. But I was on a roll. "And time and places and events. It's like I can see* everything!*"

"*Becky, you're exaggerating,*" *said Joshua.*

"*No! I'm not!*"

I grabbed the stones back from Joshua and looked through them a second time. I switched from one eye to the other, looking through both stones. I stared right into the heart of the pillar, and like before, the most unusual and fantastic images began to appear. They weren't images exactly, *but . . .* understandings. *I felt like I had a glimpse of how time itself* worked. *How it moved along from one event to the next. How it really* wasn't *something—what's the word?—intangible! But how it was a very real thing that was actually put in place by God. It didn't always move the same either. It depended on where you stood in the universe and what you were doing. Suddenly I understood how everyone saw it differently—how old people saw it as moving faster, and young people saw it as plodding along like a snail. I felt like I understood time better in those few seconds than I could've understood it from a million math or science classes. But why couldn't Joshua and Mary see it? It was right there! Right before my eyes!*

I was only a few feet away from the pillar now. Close enough that I could've touched it. In fact, I realized that was exactly what I was doing. I was reaching out toward it, holding one seerstone up to my right eye while I kept the other shut. I just wanted to feel it. To feel time. *To smell it and taste it and . . .*

"Becky, don't . . ." said Mary. But her voice wasn't very stern, maybe because she was just as curious as I was. At the last second before my hand touched the surface, I lowered the seer stones. I wanted to watch my hand the normal way first, then compare it later as I looked through the stone. As my fingers made contact, my first sensation was chill. The pillar was very cold. But as I pressed a little deeper, the feeling went away. It became warm and soft—softer than anything I'd ever touched. I turned back to Mary and Josh.

"It feels wonderful!" I said.

But Mary and Josh's eyes were wide with horror.

"Becky, your hand!" Josh reached out toward me.

I turned back quickly and stiffened with awful dread. I couldn't believe what I was seeing! My fingers were gone! *Right where the fingertips were touching, there was a cloudy brown stream! The brown and red was swirling off my hand, like dirt stirred up from the bottom of a creek, or like something caught in a blender. I was sure when I pulled my hand back, my fingers would be completely gone! But I* couldn't *pull it back!*

I yanked with all my might. "Help me!" I screamed. "It won't let me go!"

In fact, it was drawing me in! *It was up to my wrist now and the red and brown stream had circled all the way around the pillar, climbing upward like a stripe on a candy cane!*

Joshua reached out to me. First he only caught the leather string of the seer stones and nearly jerked it out of my hand. But then he and Mary latched on to my waist and legs. Still, it was no use. The pillar pulled me up to my elbow! My blood was swirling all around. It was grinding me up into juice!

I was screaming frantically; my mind was swallowed up in unspeakable terror! It was killing me! *But I felt no pain. No, that wasn't true. I felt* awful *pain as I tried to wrench free! The only relief was to just let it keep drawing me in.* Mary and Joshua were also screaming. "Pull, Becky! Pull!"

It was up to my shoulder. I looked down and realized Joshua's head was touching the silver surface. His whole head at the place where it touched turned into liquid before my eyes, creating a massive swirl of red and brown that striped its way up the pillar. Mary was caught too. It was pulling all *of us in!* Then, an instant later, it was over. The only sensation I felt was spinning, around and around. Except that I could still feel my fist clutched around the seerstone. Then I didn't even feel that. Or the spinning. There was just a blinding whiteness. Then redness. Then black.

Then I felt absolutely nothing at all.

PART II:

THE LAMANITE WHO WOULD BE KING

CHAPTER 13

"Lamanai," came the whisper from the dense brush on my right.

"Over here," I whispered in reply.

It was the nervous voice of my stepbrother, Pacawli-Yak. I was relieved to hear from him, as it had been nearly an hour since we had communicated.

"I found more sign," he whispered. "Another spot of blood. Very moist. She came through here only moments ago."

So we were getting closer. I checked the wind again by watching the feather tied to my wristband. We were still downwind of her, and this was good, because the great Jaguar was wounded, and there was no creature outside the Maw of Xibalba, or another great demon of the Underworld, more ferocious than a wounded she-jaguar.

I had shot an arrow into her ribs at dawn—a clumsy aim—piercing her at least a hand's length below a fatal point. I chided myself harshly, and was now paying the consequences. We had been tracking her now for nearly four hours. At first there were many signs of bleeding and broken branches as she tore a path through the underbrush, but then she began to flee more slowly, licking at her wound and helping it to coagulate. The signs had become more and more scarce. Now it appeared that she had pulled the wound open again. We suspected that she was very close, perhaps hiding in the brush just ahead, waiting for us to draw closer—just near enough so that she might fix her flaming eye on our throats and be the first to strike.

It was well worth the risk. Neither my stepbrother nor myself would have faltered in the challenge. Pacawli and I were prepared to track her into the night if necessary, then lie down to sleep right there in the muddy path, leaving ourselves to the mercy of the mosquitoes, and resume our search at daybreak. A jaguar pelt was worth its weight in jade, to say nothing of the price we might fetch in cacao or shell from the jewelers for its claws and bones, or from the

High Priests of Tikal for its eyes and entrails. No part of the sacred beast would be wasted. It would be the third jaguar that I'd slain in two seasons, and the earnings would feed the family of my stepfather, Kanalha, all through the rainy season, until the time of the first harvest. It was the least I could do to help support the family that had supported and protected me for almost six years. But this wasn't why I hunted them. It was for the sport, the challenge. No creature was more cunning and proud than the Great Cat, the Sacred Balam. And the older I became, the more fiercely my heart beat with the desire to conquer great and proud things.

But even if it was my skillful aim (though on this occasion, *clumsy* aim) that always brought the beasts down, it was the fox-keen eye of Pacawli-Yak whom I depended upon to do the tracking.

"Through there," Pacawli whispered, indicating a trail through the brush and leaves beneath the high canopies of the mahogany and ceiba. His voice was still edgy with anticipation. "There is a deep cenote beyond this ravine, as wide as a small lake. She is surely using it to try and relieve her thirst."

"I could also use it to relieve mine," I replied, thinking of the nearly empty water bag at my hip.

Pacawli and I edged forward through the brush, moving now with greater caution, though perhaps not with as much caution as the situation demanded. I suppose I was thinking too much of our triumphant return—the wide eyes and cheers of the villagers as we arrived with our quarry tied to a pole and resting upon our shoulders.

We were nearing the edge of the cenote. The undergrowth became less dense and a blade of sunlight stabbed through the leafy canopy. I remembered seeing this small lake before, but that was three years ago, when I was fifteen. Its banks were a gentle slope of mud, unlike many sinkholes—or cenotes—that had a steep, limestone cliff. Nevertheless, it was still considered sacred by the wise men of the village. This was because of the spring that bubbled out of its center—a true sign of a secret doorway to Xibalba and the world of the dead. Pacawli continued searching the ground for signs of the wounded she-jaguar.

I took the lead as the trail neared the water's edge. My bow was at the ready as the dark liquid surface appeared, mirroring the mighty trunks of the trees which grew at its banks. There was a space at the water's edge as wide as the width of two men and framed by the trunks of two gangly trees whose serpent-like roots arched and descended into the water to drink. It was exactly here that I would have expected the wounded jaguar to be lying in wait. I'd felt so certain that she would be here that I'd set the shaft of my arrow to the corner of my eye, ready to fire. But to our disappointment, the creature was not to be seen.

Pacawli and I looked at one another, and a feeling of vague presentiment passed between us. The very smell of mystery was in the air. It wafted over the surface of the water, played with the light, and exhaled the breath of the wind. A soft breeze rustled the vines, as if the jaguar had somehow transformed into a ghost and its invisible spirit was moving around us. The wind died and the corner of Pacawli's mouth twitched. He made an uneasy smile, as if his imagination was conjuring the same visions as mine, and such a smile should dismiss them. I approached the water's edge, seeking a glimpse of the beast's orange and black mottling in the shadows of other mahoganies around the lake's edge. Pacawli motioned that he would be moving down the bank toward the west to seek a better angle and search for more sign. I nodded and peered across the dark green water.

Just as I remembered from three years before, the spring out in the center of the cenote gurgled and bubbled lazily from the water's depths, causing small waves to lap against the shore. I watched the place where it bubbled up, pressing back in my mind the images of the fleshless skulls and rotting corpses that the priests used to describe the realities of Xibalba. As a child, these images had haunted my dreams. As I grew older, they left me alone. But then they returned again during that terrible year when I was twelve, and still appeared from time to time on restless nights when the wind was howling. But this was daylight and the air was still. By the blood of Chac, I would not be haunted in daylight. I squatted down in the brush and again scanned the shoreline for any sign of the great jaguar.

Unexpectedly, my eyes were drawn back to the bubbling spring. Was it my imagination again, or had the gurgling sound increased? Were there suddenly more bubbles popping and crackling at the surface, hissing like angry serpents? My muscles clutched more tightly at my bones and I wondered if somehow I had tread upon forbidden ground, angering the spirits of the Underworld gods. I glanced down the bank to see if Pacawli was also watching, but my stepbrother had vanished into the brush.

Suddenly, my eyes bulged from their sockets as some inexplicable creature—a monster of Xibalba—sprang up in the midst of the spring, like a dolphin from the sea depths, sending up a ferocious splash. The creature— now possessing the head and shoulders of a man, though this was certainly not its *real* image—drew a huge gulp of air, coughing and gasping, then disappeared again beneath the surface. I was standing arrow-straight now, one foot poised to flee into the forest—when *another* creature burst forth from the spring, also drawing air in a deep, wheezing gasp!

The first creature began kicking its legs, swimming toward a spot of shore not five canoe lengths away from my chin. The second monster was in the shape of a female, with long, light, water-drenched hair that spread over its face, as if it had no face at all. But then, as if my chest was not already clenched in fright and my heart swollen with blood, a *third* of these terrible monsters erupted from the water's depths with a cry in its throat as it drew air into its inhuman lungs.

My legs were bound to the earth. I couldn't have run now even if I had tried. Nor could I have torn my eyes from the scene. I watched in breathless wonderment as the two male monsters assisted the female, and all three of them swam the remaining distance toward shore. Upon reaching the muddy bank, all of them collapsed on their faces, continuing to cough and spit water from their mouths. At last I could look away, but it was only to search again for Pacawli. Was it possible that he had not seen any of this? That he had missed this incursion from the heart of the dark earth? What was I to think? How was I to interpret this? Was I witnessing the beginning of a new age? A reappearance of the Hero-Twins and the Rainbow Goddess? *Where was Pacawli?*

As one of the creatures rolled onto its back, I crouched again, choosing to keep myself hidden rather than expose myself to certain death at the hands of supernatural powers. Over the beat of my heart, I inclined an ear to try and listen as the demons began to speak.

"Is everyone all right?" asked the larger of the two males, still panting in exhaustion as a result of his journey from the watery realms.

The female nodded, though her eyes were closed, as if she was barely hanging on to consciousness. The other male, whose hair was as white as lightning, forced himself to expel additional liquid from his stomach. It seemed surprising that supernatural creatures should exhibit the mortal symptoms of almost drowning, but perhaps I was viewing just the opposite. Who was I to judge? Perhaps their bodies were making the same adjustments for a world of air and wind that a human being might make when adjusting to the World of the Dead. On such matters I was exquisitely ignorant.

As the eyelids of the white-haired male finally fluttered open to take in his surroundings, he seemed genuinely dismayed.

"Where in Jupiter—? . . .What *is* this?" He coughed. "*Where are we?*"

The larger male acted no less surprised. He appeared to be looking to the female for an opinion or advice, which disturbed me at first. But as I thought about it, it only made sense. If she was, as I suspected, the Mistress of Rainbows, Ix-Chel, she may have been infinitely more familiar with the workings of the Middleworld, considering how often she manifested herself before and after hurricanes, and how she was always near during the birth of a child. But the goddess did not express any opinion at the moment, still recovering her physical strength. The more muscular male, whom I felt drawn to call Hunahpu, the Evening Star of War, assisted Ix-Chel, the Rainbow Mistress, to sit a little more upright. Her eyes also fluttered open, and yet she acted no less entranced by the vision before her eyes than the Hero-Twins.

"Will you be all right?" Hunahpu asked her again.

"Of *course* she's not all right!" answered the white-haired male, whom I felt drawn to call Xbalanque, the Lord of the Sun. "*None* of us are all right! What happened? Where are we?"

Xbalanque collapsed into another fit of coughing. He turned over on his side in the mud, expelling one last swallow of water and wiped the spittle from his mouth with the hem of his unusual cloak—a tight-fitting material the color of white flint, truly a garment of the gods.

Ix-Chel spoke again, though she sounded dizzy and out-of-breath. "This is it," she said. "The world of the Nephites and Lamanites. Oh, I *hate* to travel that way—underwater express!"

My breath stilled in my lungs. She had spoken the ancestral name of the people of the Waterlilies. As well as the ancient name of the people of Kucalcan, the Feathered Serpent, who had been driven out of the land by my father. But to speak both names in the same breath? And to speak the name of the worshippers of Kukulcan before the people of the Waterlilies? It almost sounded blasphemous!

Ix-Chel continued, "I think we got here the same way as Jim and Uncle Garth when they were thirteen years old. They fell into the river too, just like we did."

Xbalanque suddenly became quite agitated, as if he had partaken of the wrong kind of mushroom. "Explain this to me again! What are you *talking* about? Nephites and Lamanites! I'm losing it! I've gotta be totally losing it!"

Hunahpu ignored the rants of his brother, Xbalanque. He spoke again to the Rainbow Mistress. "You mean it's the same world as Marcos and Gidgiddonihah and Jashon?"

"It *must* be," said Ix-Chel, not sounding entirely certain. But then her mind became inflamed with another subject. "*Joshua!* What happened to Joshua! I saw him fall with you into the river!"

"His rope caught onto a stalagmite," said Hunahpu. "I don't think he came with us. His hold looked pretty firm."

"Mary and Becky!" mourned the Mistress. "They must think we're dead!"

"How do you know we're not?" muttered Xbalanque.

"Ryan, please!" said Ix-Chel. "You've got to get a grip! This isn't heaven or hell and we're not dead. I tried to explain to you—the cave leads to other worlds. This is the world of the Nephites. If I remember right from Jim's stories, it's the east wilderness of Zarahemla."

I strained my mind to comprehend. These were very strange words. They were speaking now like cursed spirits from another age. World of the Nephites? Zarahemla? I knew of an abandoned city far to the west called Zarahemla. Indeed, it had once been inhabited by the people of Kukalcan. But if this land had ever been connected to that city, it was from a time long before the memory of priests or kings. And what was this pet name she had given to the Lord of the Sun? *Ryan?* Was she trying to be disrespectful?

"So how do we get back?" asked Xbalanque. "I want to go back. I've got to get back *now!* I'm starting BYU next week and I *will* be there."

"You think I can just wave my magic wand while you tap your ruby slippers?" the Rainbow Mistress replied with extreme impatience. "I don't *know* how we get back. We never reached the place where Jashon and the others descended into the tunnel. I know that tunnel comes out at the base of a volcano in a land called Melek, but I don't have the vaguest idea where that is right now. We've got to find someone who can help us."

Again I rubbed my forehead in consternation. The deities of Rainbow and Sun and Evening Star felt they needed *help?* What did this mean? Again, I had to remind myself that these were matters I did not comprehend. Such understandings were only to be found in the arcane knowledge of shamans and priests. My father might have understood. That is, before he lost his magic and godhood; before the power of my ancestors abandoned him and he was killed by his conquerors. But I was too young to have received any endowment of knowledge. I was only twelve when he was beheaded in the great square of Tikal. Perhaps if I had received that endowment, I would have understood the scene before my eyes, but because of my ignorance, I suddenly felt terribly conspicuous.

At last I took a step backwards, preparing to turn and flee. But regrettably, the string of my bow caught on a leaf and the stem snapped. I became as still as a jaguar, but it made no difference. The noise had been heard, and all three gods turned in my direction.

Hunahpu came to his feet, and I saw at last the fullness of his magnificence. His skin was the color of maize and he stood nearly a head taller than myself. With a thunderous voice, he called out, "Who is there?"

Naturally, I did not reply. Who was I to speak to a god? Terror was scorching my breast. I resolved in my mind that I would likely not live to see the end of this day. The others had come to their feet as well, looking startled and concerned.

"Show yourself!" the voice of Hunahpu commanded, and though my heart pounded like a tunkel drum, I felt I could not disobey.

I stepped forward through the undergrowth, pushing aside the leaves until I stood before them on the bank of the lake, close enough that I felt as if I could taste the lightning of their presence. Again I was awed by their appearance. Xbalanque had even whiter skin than Hunahpu, and his eyes were the color of turquoise stones. Though still dripping from head to toe, and though her brightly colored garments were matted with mud, Ix-Chel was truly as beautiful as the rainbow, with white skin and red lips and hair that glistened like firelight. And yet I did not bow to the earth. Was this an oversight on my part? Yes, it was. I was so overwhelmed that I should find myself standing in presence of deities that I utterly forgot.

To my surprise, Hunahpu, Xbalanque, and Ix-Chel looked just as surprised to see me—even astonished. I could only assume this was because, in their human form, they had also taken on certain human vulnerabilities. This frightened me all the more. A monster who feels vulnerable will usually defend itself, often with fatal results. At last, I displayed the proper obeisance and pressed my forehead to the ground. With my eyes properly averted, I listened as the deities continued to speak, drawing closer.

"A Nephite?" Hunahpu inquired.

"Or a Lamanite," answered Ix-Chel. She called out to me, "Don't be frightened. We're not going to hurt you."

"Us hurt *him?*" Xbalanque protested, his voice low. "*He's* the one with the weapon."

They were looking at the bow and arrow in my grip. I released them and left them beside me on the ground.

"He probably saw us pop up out of that spring," said Ix-Chel. "It likely scared him out of his wits."

I opened one eye and saw Hunahpu quickly recover my bow and arrow, as if he feared I might take them back.

"Who are you?" he said in his commanding voice. "What is your name?"

"Apollus, lighten up," Ix-Chel scolded. She bent down and I felt her hand come to rest on my shoulder. "It's all right. You can stand up. We're not monsters or demons."

"Maybe we *are*," said Xbalanque in protest.

"Stop it," said Ix-Chel. "I'm not gonna play that game."

She touched my cheek and encouraged me to raise my eyes. I did so, and again was held entranced by her countenance.

"Speak for yourself," Xbalanque said. Then he pounded his chest once and roared, "I am Ryan, the Great and Powerful!"

Ix-Chel rolled her eyes. "Ryan, stow it, will ya?" Speaking to me with a tender voice, she said, "Tell us your name. Where are you from? Do you live near here?"

Slowly, I came to my feet. Hunahpu tightened his grip on my bow, expressing that he was perfectly capable of using it. My heart stirred with many emotions. And yet my fear seemed to be subsiding. At last, I opened my mouth.

"I am Lamanai," I said. "I am of the village of Seibalche."

"Where is that?" asked Hunahpu.

"Three hours to the west," I replied.

"What tribe are you from?" asked Ix-Chel.

I narrowed one eye, hesitant to answer. Never in the past six solar years had I revealed my true lineage. Nor had I ever revealed my *paal kaba*, or sacred name. Always I had gone by Lamanai, the pet name of my grand-mother. It had been so since my father's loyal priest, Hapai-Zin, brought me to the forest of Seibalche, near the shrine of Kanalha, the healer. I was told that I should never tell another soul my sacred name and lineage or I would surely be hunted and killed by the warriors of Fire-Born. Fire-Born had cruelly murdered every other member of my family, including my mother, the queen, my brothers and sisters, and even my aunts and uncles. It was only by the cunning of Hapai-Zin that I even survived. Besides Hapai-Zin, only Kanalha, my stepfather, knew the truth. But he had sworn a blood oath never to reveal it. Even the porters who had carried me to the village were poisoned by Hapai-Zin before they ever returned to Tikal. My father's priest had promised that one day he would return for me, but I never saw him again. I suspected he had become part of Fire-Born's royal purging. But since that day, I, along with Kanalha, had kept the oath of secrecy.

But these were supernatural beings, were they not? Could I lie to the gods? Perhaps this was a test—the beginning of the sign that Hapai-Zin had promised would one day be revealed to show that the power of my ances-tors was growing strong again. But if these were gods, they were doing much to confuse me, calling each other strange, foreign names, intimating that they were not divine, and appearing before me in the guise of human beings. Yet I could not deny what I had seen—how they had emerged from the depths of the sacred cenote. I decided that for the first time in six long years, I would finally tell the truth.

Drawing a deep breath, I declared, "I am Eagle-Sky-Jaguar of the lineage of Yax-Chaac-Xok, and the eldest son of the Great Jaguar-Paw of Tikal."

The gods stared at me, but I wasn't certain if the information I had given had inspired reverence or confusion.

"You're a prince?" asked Xbalanque.

He spoke the question with such casualness. I felt my face flush and I looked away, shame curdling in my stomach—a shame that I deserved. For there was no longer any power in these names, and I felt foolish to have spoken in pride.

"No," I replied. "I am not a prince. I am—" I sighed. "—only a hunter. A collector of jaguar pelts."

"I'm sorry," said Xbalanque. "I didn't mean to offend you. I just thought . . ."

Ix-Chel interrupted. "Are you a Lamanite?"

I turned back to her, stymied by the question. It was as if she was asking me if I was human.

Noting my perplexity, she added, "Have you ever heard that word?"

I nodded. "Lamaya, the ancestor. Is that who you mean?"

"I guess so," said Ix-Chel. "Laman and Lemuel: Lamayan."

"We are *all* Lamayan," I said.

"What year is it?" asked Ix-Chel.

"Year?"

"Yes. Do you still reckon your years from the sign of the Savior's birth?"

I stared at her in consternation. If this was a test, I was surely failing, because I hardly understood a word of what she was saying. And yet since the time I was a small child it had been my habit to follow the cycles of years. So I answered, "We reckon it as it has *always* been reckoned, according to the stars. It is the year of 8 Baktun, 17 Katun, 8 Tun, 10 Winal, and 10 Kin."

Hunahpu looked at Ix-Chel, and said, "He's not a Christian."

"That can't be right," said Ix-Chel, seeming vexed of soul. "If this is the world of the Nephites, *everyone* is a Christian."

"What year do *you* think it is?" Xbalanque asked Ix-Chel.

She shook her head. "I'm not sure anymore. Jim and Garth and Marcos all seemed to think it should still be during the time when the Nephites were living in peace and harmony, shortly after everyone was converted to the gospel."

"Well, we already know *that* can't be right," said Xbalanque. "Because if it was during that era, this guy wouldn't be calling himself a Lamanite. Lamanites and Nephites didn't distinguish themselves again by those labels until after about 200 A.D."

"You're right," said Ix-Chel thoughtfully. "And by then it may have had nothing to do with race or skin color. It was just a distinction to separate those who followed the Savior and those who didn't."

I remained attentive to their words, though it must have been apparent by my expression that I was completely lost in a wind of the mind.

"Have you ever heard the term Nephites?" Xbalanque inquired.

I nodded. "Of course. But . . . they are your enemies, are they not? They are the enemies of *all* the gods."

Again, they considered me with faces of grave concern and agitation.

"Are there any Nephites around here?" asked Ix-Chel.

I shook my head. "The Nephites left these forests many years ago, before I was born. They made a treaty with my father and the kings of the north."

"Where are they now?" asked Hunahpu.

"Northward," I replied. "For many years they have made war with my people in Tehuantepec, the land of wild beasts, in the region of the narrow neck. But they are driven further and further north by Fire-Born and his armies. Their battle captives are carried back to Tikal for the Festival of Sacrifices. It is said that the great king of Teotihuacan, Spearthrower Owl, has sworn an oath in blood to drive them into the sea."

"Fire-Born?" repeated Xbalanque. "Spearthrower Owl? What kind of Nephite and Lamanite names are those?"

"They are not Lamaya," I said, my tone boiling with enmity. "But they killed my father and took his throne. They have taken over our armies, using our warriors like dogs."

Ix-Chel released a deep and frustrated sigh. "This is a *mess*. The politics of this land aren't making sense at all."

"Maybe they *shouldn't* make sense," said Xbalanque. "Remember, the Book of Mormon was written from the perspective of the Nephites. They may not have felt the need to get into detail about all the kingdoms and politics of the enemy."

"Book of *Mormon?*" I responded.

Ix-Chel turned to me with interest. "You've heard of it?"

"I have heard of Mormon," I said. "There is no child of the Lamaya who has not heard of the Warrior of Thunder, Mormon."

"Warrior of Thunder? Really?" said Xbalanque. "What have you heard of him?"

"He was the scourge of my father," I replied. "It is said that he was a fierce and courageous man. At least *now* this is what they say. Now that he is dead."

Ix-Chel's face paled. "Mormon is dead?"

I nodded. "So it is said. He died before I was born."

"How old are you?" asked Hunahpu.

"I have seen eighteen cycles of the sun."

"Eighteen? You mean he's been dead for more than eighteen years?" Xbalanque shuddered in disgust.

"That can't be right," said Ix-Chel. "Not if the Nephites still exist as any kind of people."

Their expressions were drawn, and I sensed a keen disappointment. In the face of all this confusion, I found that my courage was growing. At last I was brave enough to ask the most important question of all.

"Why have you come here from the depths of Xibalba? What do you want of me?"

I swallowed as I awaited a reply, concerned that my boldness would finally engender the offense that would turn them against me.

But then the eyes of Ix-Chel softened, and she said, "I'm sorry, Lamanai. We've been very rude. My name is Meagan. This is Apollus and Ryan. We need your help. We need it badly."

"Can you take us to your village?" asked Hunahpu, or as Ix-Chel wished me to call him, Apollus.

"We haven't eaten in a long time," said Ix-Chel, or Meagan. "Did you bring any food?"

I nodded, still taken aback by the events of this day. It was all so strange and extraordinary.

"What about telling us how to get home?" asked Xbalanque, or Ryan. "I mean, back to this place, Xibalba?"

"I will take you to the shaman of my village," I said, "He is my stepfather, Chilan Kanalha. He will understand more of your words. He will be able to help you."

"If your village is three hours away, we'll need to eat long before that," said Meagan Ix-Chel. "I'm already feeling woozy, like I could collapse."

She was eyeing the travel sack on my shoulder and wetting her lips. How much, I wondered, did a god eat? Then suddenly her words reminded me of Pacawli. My eyes anxiously searched the forest.

"What are you looking for?" asked Apollus Hunahpu.

"For my stepbrother, Pacawli-Yak. He came here with me, but we separated to track the jaguar."

Ryan Xbalanque gave a start. "Jaguar?"

"Pacawli is carrying the food—maize cakes and breadnuts. He was going to circle the cenote the other way."

I became deeply troubled by his absence. He should have returned by now. Had he seen the gods emerge from the Underworld and fled through the jungle in fear? Perhaps he had pursued the wounded jaguar around to the other side of the cenote and gotten himself tangled up in the swamp, but I still would have expected to hear from him. Unless, of course, he had found the jaguar . . .

I turned to the gods. "You will come with me."

I said it almost as a question, wondering if I had the right to make such a request. Fortunately, they had no objection. I led the way back toward the animal path that had brought us to the edge of the cenote, checking frequently over my shoulder to see if they were following.

Apollus Hunahpu whispered to Meagan Ix-Chel. His words were faint, but I thought I heard him ask, "If these people are the enemy of the Nephites, are we safe in their company?"

"Shh! I don't know," she whispered back. "I'm not sure yet about *any* of this."

This made two of us, but I did not respond to their private words. My mind was directed now toward finding Pacawli. Until now I had not raised my voice because I didn't want to alert the wounded jaguar, but with everything that was happening, such concerns now seemed a very small thing.

"Pacawli!" I shouted.

We stood still and listened to the silence. He did not reply.

We continued on, moving stealthily through the sun-dappled woods. Meagan and Ryan remained behind me, but Apollus Hunahpu insisted upon walking at my side, my bow and single arrow looking very comfortable in his hands. At last we had reached a dark tunnel of the forest, a place where the sun did not penetrate the overhead canopy. As we started to cross, I heard Ix-Chel make a small gasp in her throat.

I spun to my left and peered into the shadows. All at once my heart clenched in pain. It was Pacawli! His body was lying in a crumpled heap in a low place off to the side of the trail, his eyes wide and staring upward. His throat had been torn and the muddy ground was drenched in blood. His bow was lying near his silent right hand. An arrow was still gripped in the fingers of his left. Whatever had struck, it had given him no time to make a target of it.

"Pacawli!" I cried again, my voice shattered, the grief blackening my mind.

I rushed toward him to lift him into my arms, my steps splattering through the mud, my heart praying that I would hear a final whisper from his lips. But there was no life, no movement, except—

Except for a crouching phantom to my left, nestled in the vines. I heard a single ear-rending roar as the shadow sprang from the darkness in an orange and black blur. I squeezed my fists, as if willing my weapon to return to my hands. Defenseless, I shielded my face with my arms.

Its paws smashed into my chest, crushing out the air in my lungs. I was thrown down into the mud. Its head crashed into my neck, prepared to tear out my throat like Pacawli. But its jaws did not clamp down. Its claws did not rip into my flesh. My eyes were out of focus and my heart was dizzy with confusion. It took several seconds before I realized that the mighty beast was not moving. It was almost as if it had fallen asleep, cuddling on top of me like a faithful dog. But it was not asleep. The animal was dead. As my eyes came into focus I saw the arrow—*my* arrow!—embedded in its skull, directly behind its ear.

In desperation, I hoisted the creature off to the side. The bruises against my ribs throbbed with pain. It rolled off limply, one side of its orange-mottled coat caked in blue mud. I could see my first arrow still protruding from its abdomen, the fur bloody, the wood splintered and chewed from where its teeth had broken off the shaft.

Only then did I raise my chin to see the figure of Apollus Hunahpu standing over me, my empty bow dangling at his side. The other gods came up swiftly behind him. Ryan Xbalanque reached down to help me to my feet. But I could not take my eyes off the Lord of the Evening Star of War. He'd saved my life. A god from the realms of death had saved my life!

Then in a searing instant I understood, like a perfect vision born from the Netherworld of light. It was the sign—the great and sacred sign once mentioned to me in a vague prophecy by the mouth of my father's priest, Hapai-Zin. The prophecy was vague to a boy of twelve, but not to man who had seen eighteen cycles of the sun and was enlightened by the vision quest.

The day had finally come. My "protectors" had arrived: Hunahpu—the Lord of the War Star, Xbalanque—the Lord of the Sun and Eternal Life, and Ix-Chel—the Goddess of Rainbows and New Birth. Each was a symbol of the reemergence of power. Each was a special envoy of the great and sacred mission that lay ahead. With these three deities at my side, how could I fail? How could Spearthrower Owl of Teotihuacan, or his slobbering son, Lord Blue-Crocodile, who sat on the throne of Tikal, defy the will of the gods? And how could the great Fire-Born hope to stand against anyone who would follow me?

No longer would I be Lamanai, the orphan boy who the people of the village spoke of in tones of mystery and presentiment. I would be *Men-Chan-Balam*, the Great Eagle-Sky-Jaguar, King of the Lamaya.

Soon the throne of my ancestors would again be mine.

CHAPTER 14

I felt like I was a living cartoon. Becky Plimpton and Bugs Bunny. We could now relate in a way we never had before. The Wily Coyote had nothin' on me. We'd both been through the wringer—or in my case, the blender—and lived to tell the tale. I'd always wondered how the Wily Coyote straightened himself out after his body was smashed like an accordion, or twisted up like a slinky, or flattened like a pancake. Now I knew.

Well, okay. I didn't really know. But at least I felt like we had something in common.

The first thing I remember when I came to, and after the dizziness started to fade away, was that I was lying face down on a sandbar, a tornado ringing in my ears. As my thoughts started to clear I realized it wasn't a tornado. It was a waterfall.

I pushed myself up a little and started spitting dirt off my tongue. There was a lot of it. What had I been doing? Licking the sandbar like a lollipop? I looked up to make sure it was, in fact, a waterfall that I was hearing and not something more dangerous. It took a few seconds for my eyes to focus. When the colors came together, I could see water pouring out from underneath a lip of rock on the side of a cliff. Not exactly Niagara Falls, but enough that it still made a lot of noise. The sky was bright blue, like a robin's egg. So bright it almost hurt my eyes.

My eyes followed the downward course of the waterfall to see that it emptied into a pool almost as blue as the sky. There were a few scrubby bushes growing around the edge of it, and more bushes along the stream that trickled down into a narrow, desolate looking canyon, but . . .

My thoughts caught up to reality. It was like getting dunked in a barrel of ice water, even though the air around us was so hot that I could feel the skin burning on my back—even through my wet shirt!

In my panic the first thing I did was look every which way for Mary and Joshua. Were they here? Or had that silver pillar sent them to an entirely different world?

No, they were here all right, sitting a little further up the sandbar, near the bottom of the steep ravine that surrounded us on every side, except down the canyon. Mary sat with her eyes closed, her head between her knees, like she was trying to recover her strength. Her yellow dress was a total mess, soaked, splotched with dirt, and torn in several places. Her pantyhose were also snagged and torn. Somehow she'd managed to hang on to her small white Kathy Lee vinyl purse, the strap still hanging around her shoulder and neck.

Joshua was slumped over a rock, almost like it was a bean bag chair. He looked a mess too, but he seemed to have recovered better than Mary or I. He held something in his hand, but I couldn't see what it was. He watched me as I woke up. Mary raised her head too as I pulled myself further out of the water. Despite her tiredness, she came over and put her arms around my shoulders.

"You're awake. Thank goodness," she said. "Your brother saved your life. He pulled you out of the water."

Joshua's mouth curled into a smile.

"Was I . . . drowning?" I asked, still not clear about what had taken place.

"We poured out of that waterfall," said Joshua. "You were barely conscious, gasping like a maniac. I just pulled you over to the side."

"He helped pull me over too," said Mary.

"Aw, shucks," said Josh. "'Twern't nuthin'. I just held my breath longer."

"Held your breath?" I said. "But we didn't fall into the river. We were sucked in by that pillar."

"Somewhere along the way it became an underground river," said Mary, "Or maybe the energy in that pillar was like a river of water all along. I don't know. But it spat us out here just like Josh said."

"Where's 'here?'" I asked, looking around again at the barren, dead-looking cliffs and hills all around us.

"Jerusalem," said Josh. "It's just like the place that Harry and Meagan described. I'll bet if we climb this hill, we'll be able to see the Dead Sea."

Mary thought about this. "It could be Jerusalem. I pray that it is. If this really is the wilderness of Judea, I'll know exactly how to get to the cave that will take us back home."

"But I thought this was your home," said Joshua.

She didn't quite know how to reply to that. As I looked back at Joshua, I realized what was in his hand. It was the seer stones in the silver frame. But then I caught my breath. One of the stones was missing! One of the settings in the frame was empty! I crawled over to Joshua and pulled it out of his hand.

"*What* happened *to it?*" *I demanded.*

"*How should I know?*" *he said defensively.* "*You were still gripping it when you popped up out of the water, gasping for breath. You dropped it when I swam you over to shore. I dove to the bottom of the pool and picked it up. That's how it looked. The other stone must have fallen out in the underground river.*"

I went back to the pool's edge. "*Then it should still be at the bottom.*" *I looked down the canyon.* "*Or else a little ways down this stream.*"

Josh was shaking his head. "*I don't think so. I looked. That milky white stone would have stood out pretty good.*"

Suddenly I remembered that Josh had yanked on the leather string when he tried to pull me away from the pillar.

"*You probably knocked it out when you grabbed me back in the cave. It might be lying on the ground right in front of that pillar.*"

"*Well, don't be mad at* me *for that,*" *said Josh.* "*You were the one who just had to touch it. I was trying to save you.*"

"*How was I supposed to know it would suck me in like a vacuum cleaner?*"

Josh looked up the ravine. "*I'm gonna climb this hill and see where we are.*"

"*I'll go with you,*" *said Mary.*

I wasn't staying here alone, so I retied the string around my neck and struggled up the steep hill behind them. Panting heavily, we reached the top and looked out over the horizon.

What an ugly place. Dead and rocky and desolate. Hardly a plant in sight. Even looking at it made me thirsty—and I still felt waterlogged from my ride in the underground river. But just as Joshua had predicted, there was a long, glistening lake down in the valley, muddy and brown along its shore, and deep blue—almost black—out toward the middle.

"*Ta da!*" *Joshua sang out, like a magician who'd just pulled a rabbit out of a hat.* "*The Dead Sea! I told you it was Jerusalem.*"

"*Judea,*" *Mary corrected.* "*Jerusalem, or what's left of it, would be about five leagues that way. Or as you would say, fifteen miles.*"

I looked at Joshua in amazement, his chest puffed out in pride, then at Mary, sounding like a prim and proper schoolteacher. Was I the only one who realized how insane all this was? How dangerous?

"What do we do now?" I asked Mary. "We'll fry to death before we can walk that far."

Mary's face grew serious again. She glanced around, then back at us. "Do we have anything that will carry water?"

Did she think we had canteens hidden in our pockets? My pockets were completely empty, except for my Warner Bros. key chain with Marvin Martian and two keys—one to the front door of our house and one to my diary.

Josh turned his own pockets inside out, unearthing a bunch of wet pistachio shells. He also came up with a leather wallet—the one he'd inherited from Dad. It had been pretty worn out even before getting drenched in the underground river. Josh examined the contents: a five dollar bill—all that was left from the allowance he'd gotten before Mom and Dad left for Dallas. Plus his lucky two-dollar bill, and sixty-five cents in change. He also pulled out his "Articles of Faith" card with the Provo Temple on the front. That is to say, he pulled out half of his "Articles of Faith" card. It tore apart because it was wet.

"Ah, man!" he said in disgust.

There was also his Junior High identity card, a temple recommend for baptisms for the dead, a smeared piece of paper where he'd written down the combination for his gym locker, and last but not least, an authentic Roman coin that Dad said he got in Ceasarea during his last adventure.

"Hey, this might come in handy," he said.

"Yeah, that'll hold a lot of water," I said sarcastically.

Mary was busy emptying out her purse, but she wasn't having any more luck than the rest of us. There was about seventy-eight dollars in bills, a bunch of change, her brand new driver's license, a bunch of papers and receipts, including our ticket stubs to Lagoon, some dusty-rose-colored lipstick, Maybelline eye makeup with a little mirror, cherry flavored Vaseline Lip Therapy petroleum jelly, an extra pair of Silky Looks Sheer-to-Waist pantyhose, Avon Moisture Therapy hand cream, a nail file, clippers, tweezers, a nifty penlight, a Vidal Sassoon hairbrush, a tiny solar-powered calculator that probably didn't work anymore, a Bic pen that didn't write, a sewing kit, and a half-empty pack of Dentyne Ice sugarless gum—"Arctic Chill" flavored. For someone so recently intro-duced to the modern world, she seemed to have all the necessities of a twenty-first-century girl well in hand.

Nevertheless, she laid all that stuff aside and announced, "We'll try this."

"Your purse?" asked Josh doubtfully. "You want to use your purse as a canteen?"

"Why not?" she replied. "Let's see if it holds water."

Josh looked at all the makeup and money she'd left in the dirt and said, "You can't just leave all this stuff."

"It won't do us much good here," said Mary. "Except perhaps the penlight."

"Are you kidding?" said Josh. "Every single thing here could be worth a fortune! Becky, you have pockets. Help me out."

So Joshua and I began filling our pockets with everything she'd left behind. Mary made her way back down to the pool. As we arrived behind her—our pockets stuffed with hairbrushes, pantyhose, and sewing kits—Mary was lifting the water-filled purse out of the pool. I'll be darned if it didn't hold about five cups of water. The vinyl didn't seem to be leaking. There was even a handy-dandy zipper to hold it all inside.

"This won't last very long," said Mary. "I suggest that we drink as much as we can before we leave."

"I'm already waterlogged," I said.

"Drink some more. I promise in about three hours you'll be glad you did."

"Not if I throw it all back up again."

"Which way are we going?" asked Joshua.

"South, I think," said Mary. "I know that the cave that brought me to your century is south of Jerusalem. I should recognize the terrain when we get there."

"Shouldn't we go to Jerusalem first?" Josh asked. "I mean, just to make sure you have the proper orientation?"

"What about food?" I asked. "I'm starving."

"If we head south it might not be long before we run into some Parthian or Edomite tents," said Mary. "Then we might try Joshua's suggestion of trading some of the things from my purse for food."

"But what about Jerusalem?" said Josh. "There's plenty of food in Jerusalem."

"You're not listening," I said to him. "It's the wrong way."

"*How do we* know *that?*" *he insisted.* "*It'll be a lot worse if we get lost in the desert. At least in Jerusalem we can ask for directions.*"

"*There* are *no directions to this cave,*" *said Mary.* "*Nobody else knows about it. I just have to remember the landmarks. We'll head west until we find the road that runs along the Salt Sea to Engedi, then west to Tekoa. I should be able to find it from there.*"

"*You don't sound so sure,*" *said Joshua.* "*Are you sure it wouldn't be easier to find it from Jerusalem?*"

"*What makes you so anxious to go to Jerusalem?*" *I asked.*

Joshua pursed his lips, almost like he was holding his breath. He looked ready to bust. Finally, he blurted out, "*Because it's* Jerusalem! *Man alive! Don't you girls have any sense of adventure? I can't believe we're right here in ancient Israel and nobody wants to see Jerusalem!*"

"*Jerusalem was destroyed, Joshua,*" *said Mary.* "*There isn't very much to see.*"

"*There must be* something *to see. Meagan and Uncle Jim said it was being rebuilt. We'd be* nuts *to pass this up!*"

"*You're* the only one who's nuts," *I said.* "*We could die out here!*"

Joshua brushed this off. "*Never happen. God wouldn't* let *it happen. If we were 'sposed to die, we'd have died already—drowned in that underground river. We're here for a reason. There's* always *a reason. Don't you guys get it? We're supposed to* do *something. So I suggest we go to Jerusalem and find out what it is before we get all fired up about going home. What do ya say?*"

My brother could sure get some twisted ideas. First, he'd had that bizarre idea about somehow changing history and preventing the Nephites from being destroyed. Now the idea that the Galaxy Room had sent us to ancient Judea for a reason. *But if Josh believed that God automatically put a bubble of protection around time travelers, he needed to have his memory jogged. Had he forgotten about Harry's injury in Jacobugath—the one that had almost made him crippled for life? Okay, so he was healed later. But what about Gidgiddonihah and those other Nephites killed in Athens while they were trying to rescue Harry and Mary? So whatever Joshua may have thought, the danger here was very real. Faith in God's power was one thing. But expecting His protection when you deliberately did stupid things was another.*

And yet . . .

Despite all my doubts and fears, Joshua's idea about going to Jerusalem seemed right *to me. Why would I feel that? I certainly didn't feel it was right for the same reason as Joshua. I'd never been the He-woman/warrior-princess/adventurer-type. Maybe I felt the way I felt because something about this whole* situation *didn't seem right. Or at least, not how it appeared. Maybe in Jerusalem we could get our bearings and make sure that everything was really how it seemed.*

I know, I know. These were really weird thoughts, and I strained to figure out where they were coming from. Then it hit me.

The stone!

It was something I'd seen in the stone. Something just before I'd touched the smoky, silver surface of that pillar. But what had I seen? It was almost as if . . . as if I'd seen exactly where we were going. Exactly where that pillar was going to spit us out. But it was fuzzy now. All I knew for sure was that somehow things were not the way Joshua and Mary thought they were.

"I think I agree with Joshua," I said meekly.

Joshua raised his eyes. "You do?"

"But it's out of our way," Mary argued. "We can't waste any time. It would be like tempting fate. We can't expect God's protection if we deliberately do something foolish. I feel sure I can find that cave, but it's not back toward Jerusalem. Jerusalem is to the northwest. The cave is south."

She was saying the very things I'd been thinking before I remembered the seerstone. My opinion started to waver again. After all, Mary was older. She was from *this land. Wasn't that enough to convince me that she'd know what was the right thing to do? Still . . . I wanted to look into the stone again. The whole idea was a little embarrassing. Mary and Joshua hadn't seen* anything *when they'd looked into it. What would they say if I told them I agreed with Josh because of what I'd seen in the stone?*

Only one way to find out.

"I think we should go to Jerusalem because . . ." There was no good way to put this. I just babbled it out. ". . . because I think that's where the stone wants us to go."

They looked at me a little dumbfounded.

"The stone?" said Mary.

"The seer*stone," I repeated, clutching at the necklace.*

"What are you talking about?" asked Joshua, like I'd said something ridiculous.

"Just before I touched the pillar, I saw something in it."

"Saw what?" he challenged.

I bit my lip, trying to think how best to describe it. "It was like . . . I saw where the pillar would take us."

Mary became interested. "You mean you saw this pool? This waterfall?"

"Yes," I said.

"You saw ancient Jerusalem?" asked Joshua doubtfully.

"Yes," I said, less certain. "But . . . oh, it's so hard to explain."

"Lemme see that," said Joshua.

He reached out and took it off from around my neck. He held the single stone up to his eye again, concentrating hard, even holding it up to the sun, as if the brightness might make the stone seem more transparent.

"I don't see nuthin'," he declared.

Mary continued talking to me with great interest. "I'm not sure I follow you, Becky. What did you see?"

"Just . . . I don't know. Scenes. Images. Or maybe they were thoughts."

"That doesn't make sense," said Josh, one eye still closed as he peered into the stone's pearly white surface. "All I see is . . . just that white, pinkish color."

"Are you sure?" I asked, my voice almost pleading. I did not want to be the only one who saw it. "Concentrate."

"I am concentrating." He finally pulled the stone away. "I feel stupid. There's nothing to see!"

I turned to Mary. "You try again. Please. You have to believe me."

She held it up and tried again, but only for second. It was obvious she still saw nothing, just like Josh. But as she handed it back to me, the look of interest hadn't left her eyes.

"I want you to try again, Becky. And as you look, I want you to tell me what you see."

Now I felt put on the spot. Josh shook his head, acting like the whole thing was nonsense. But Mary seemed very eager to hear what I had to say.

I took a deep breath, closed one eye, and looked. I stared into the blazing white surface. I brought up my other hand to cup around it. For some reason, the images in the stone seemed a little clearer when everything around it was dark or shadowed. Or maybe it just helped me to concentrate.

Just as before, I did see things. But how could I describe it to Mary?

"Well?" she asked.

"I-I don't know! Be more specific."

"Huh?" asked Josh.

"I mean, ask *me something."*

"Explain," said Mary.

"Ask me a question."

"Like what?"

"I don't know. Anything."

"Where are we?" asked Mary.

I concentrated, then I replied, "We're just where you think. We're in Judea. But there's . . ."

"There's what?"

"I'm not sure. Ask me something else."

"This is ridiculous," said Josh.

Mary scolded him. "Quiet, Josh. I don't think it is. Becky may have a gift that you and I don't have."

"You gotta be kidding!"

"No, I'm not," said Mary. "We all have different spiritual gifts. This may be Becky's."

"All right then," said Josh. He still sounded doubtful, but he decided to ask me, "Where's Meagan and Apollus and Ryan? Are they alive?"

I strained to see, trying to focus every thought on what appeared. "Yes," I declared. "They're alive."

Mary gasped with relief. Josh still sounded frustrated.

"How do you know *that?" he demanded. He sounded positively green with envy.*

"Because I see them," I said. "They're . . . covered with shadows . . . a forest . . . a jungle."

Joshua finally started to sound excited. "Book of Mormon times?"

"I-I think so. It's . . . a little blurry."

"This is weird," said Josh. He turned to Mary. "Is this normal? Is it right?"

"It must *be," she answered, almost as if she might start weeping with gratitude.*

"Then tell me this," Josh said to me. "Why do you agree with me that we should go to Jerusalem?"

I continued staring into the stone. The light from inside it started to dance again. My head filled with thoughts. I tried to put the thoughts into words. This wasn't nearly as easy as it seemed. If I let my mind stray even for a second, it was like the whole thing became jumbled and confused.

"Because . . . because we're supposed to learn something there . . . See something," I replied.

"Ah hah!*" said Josh. He slapped Mary's shoulder playfully. "What did I tell ya! I didn't need a seerstone to figure that out."*

Something disturbing came into my mind. I lowered the stone and raised my head. "If we don't go I feel like . . . we may never get home again—ever! No matter what we do, no matter how long we try."

Josh and Mary gaped at me.

"Okey-dokey," said Josh nervously. "I'm convinced. Let's go!"

"What are we supposed to learn, Becky?" asked Mary.

I put the stone back to my eye. I waited and watched. At last, images started to appear and reappear. A wash of colors. A crowd of people. A large *crowd. Holy cow, it was* massive! *Millions—no* billions*—of people. No, it was* angels! *Both people and angels. Rejoicing with more emotion and energy than I'd ever seen anyone rejoice before.*

"What is it?" asked Mary anxiously. "What did you see?"

"I-I'm not sure," I said. I felt myself starting to smile. I couldn't help it. "But it was . . . it was wonderful."

I was tingling all over. I'd never felt anything like it before. For some reason, I couldn't stop smiling. Finally, I lowered the stone again. Tingling waves of warmth continued running up and down through every part of my body, like I was being played like a harp. Then tears came to my eyes. Tears of joy. "Oh, it was wonderful!*" I said with a big exhale.*

"That's it?" said Josh. "Can't you give us anymore than that?"

I wasn't sure what to say. How would I describe it? I decided to give it a try. "It was like . . . all these people. People and angels and . . . There were so many *of them. They were so happy. Celebrating. Like they'd been waiting for something forever and ever. And it finally happened."*

"This is why we're supposed to go to Jerusalem?" asked Josh.

"Yes," I said, my emotions still overwhelmed. Then I thought about it more deeply. "Or at least . . . part of it."

Mary's face was glowing with fascination. "And if we do this, we'll be able to make it home to your century?"

I nodded, suddenly feeling a little uncertain. It was weird how the feelings faded so quickly.

"You don't seem so sure anymore," said Josh.

I braced myself and raised the stone to my eye again to reconfirm what I'd seen before. But the instant I focused on that foggy, white surface, the tingling stopped completely. The whole scene instantly changed. Immediately the stone, my body, the whole world turned into darkness! It was the blackest, most angry darkness I'd ever experienced. The feeling was so horrible that a cry wrenched out of my throat. All my strength drained out of me. Mary and Josh reached out to catch me, but they weren't fast enough, and it caused them to trip too. A second later we were all lying on the sand at the pool's edge. Goose flesh broke out all over my arms. I started shivering.

"What is it?" Mary asked frantically. "What's the matter?"

*"It was h-*horrible*!" was all I managed to say.*

Josh propped me up and put his arm around me. "What did you see, Becky?"

"It's here too! It's gathering from everywhere!"

"What's here? What?"

But rather than answer my brother, my eyes turned toward the top of the ravine. I hadn't heard anything, and I hadn't yet seen a shadow, but I knew that someone was there. Someone dangerous. And I was right.

Crouching on one knee at the top of the ravine, staring down at us with coal-black eyes, was a bearded man in a large scarlet cloak and a kind of puffy red hat with a shawl rolled around it. He was holding something long and steel in his hands. A sword? No, it wasn't a sword, although I did see a sword hanging on his back. The object in his hands was held up to his eye while the other end was pointed at our hearts. Joshua and I wrenched backwards. Mary gasped in terror.

The man was aiming a rifle.

CHAPTER 15

Okay, time for some sanity.

It's me, Meagan Sorenson. My turn to take the baton for a while. This was probably the most unique situation that I'd ever been in. Not only because we were deep in Lamanite territory in a time period toward the end of the Book of Mormon, but I had just become a goddess! One look at the face of Lamanai—or as he apparently preferred to be called, Eagle-Sky-Jaguar—and it was clear that he thought we were supernatural beings. But it was also unique because I'd never before found myself in the company of two guys so determined to compete for my attention.

I know everyone is *dying* to know how I was handling this—the guy part, that is. After all, it's every girl's fantasy to think she's an object of desire for multiple guys at once, right? WRONG! When you honestly care about *both* guys, it's unspeakably frustrating, and I wouldn't wish such a mess on anyone.

At first when I realized that Lamanai (I'm gonna keep calling him Lamanai; it's just easier to say) was a Lamanite, or "Lamayan," and that he hardly recognized many aspects of the Lamanite or Nephite culture that we knew from the Book of Mormon—and furthermore when he said that the great general Mormon was dead—I definitely started freaking out. We'd fully expected that the land of the Nephites would be a land of peace and plenty, completely devoted to the gospel of Jesus Christ. Apparently things had fast-forwarded a little more than we might have expected. But if Mormon was dead, then it meant we might not find a single friend in this world who would help us. Thankfully, Lamanai had also mentioned that Nephites were still around, just not nearby. I knew that if the Nephites existed in any shape or form as a people, then Mormon was still alive too. So was his son, Moroni. Maybe other Christians as well. Therefore, Lamanai's information about Mormon's death eighteen years before had to be false.

I seemed to remember that there was a period of time when Mormon had refused to lead the Nephite armies. I wasn't quite sure how long this period had lasted, but if it was a good ten or fifteen years, a rumor of his death might have been spread among the Lamanites. After all, Mormon was the Nephite's best general. If he was no longer leading the Nephite army, he *must* be dead!

Now the question was, where *were* Mormon and Moroni? How far away were the Nephite tribes? Or perhaps more importantly, where was the land of Melek with the volcano that could supposedly take us back to our world? Was Melek even *called* Melek anymore? Would there be anyone among the Nephites who even remembered where it was located?

I suppose I ought to have asked the Lamanites that question first. But just as such an idea popped into my mind, we'd made the awful discovery of Lamanai's stepbrother in the jungle. Then the jaguar leaped, Apollus took aim, and after the "smoke" had cleared, Lamanai believed we were gods more than ever. How can I describe the look on his face? It was adoration, pure and simple—exactly the way my face might have looked if I was gazing at the face of an angel. This whole thing made me totally uncomfortable. But Ryan seemed to like it. He was feeling over-whelmed anyway, and I think he wanted to feel he had some kind of edge on these strange, unfamiliar people in this intimidating place.

But there was something else in Lamanai's eyes. A kind of euphoric excitement, as if by saving his life we'd proven something to him. Or convinced him of something. I wasn't sure what it was, but it only added to my discomfort.

Lamanai was a remarkable-looking person. Not handsome, exactly. At least not "Brad Pitt" handsome. Or even "Apollus" hand-some. But definitely exotic looking. In a way, almost Cro-Magnon. I guess that doesn't sound very flattering, but with him it actually was. His forehead looked like it had been artificially flattened, almost to the point that the slope of his nose continued all the way up to the crown of his head. I'd read somewhere that the Mayans—especially *royal* Mayans—would often bind a baby's head between two boards, one at the back of the head and one against the forehead. These were left in place for several days, until the cranial bones had set. When I'd first laid eyes on Lamanai the feature was so different looking that I almost thought it repulsive. But after staring at it for a while, I began to see why the ancients might have found it compelling. Undoubtedly if Lamanai was a prince he'd had the procedure done by experts. The way it made the ridges of his eyebrows so pronounced gave him a fierce, almost feline look. His eyes emphasized this even more—large and dark with long brown lashes.

He wore a cotton loincloth that went between the legs and wrapped around his waist. His chest was bare and rippled with muscles, almost as well-defined as Apollus. (Though I must confess, it had been several years since I'd seen Apollus bare-chested.) Ancient men could sure carve some nice bods, I decided. Refined sugars and office cubicles weren't helping our generation at all. But I digress.

He also wore some kind of cape that covered his shoulders and hung nearly to the ground. His sandals were a thick hide of some kind, bound to his feet by two thongs that passed between his toes. He was totally decked out in jewelry. Hanging across his throat were two different necklaces: one of animal claws—probably jaguar—and another of jade beads with a pendant that looked like a small figurine with blue-green eyes. I learned later it was his animal spirit or guardian, a sort of good-luck charm, fashioned to represent (surprise, surprise) a jaguar. He also had wristbands, armbands, anklebands, and two separate piercings in both ears that supported what appeared to be seashells. A small black bead was also pierced into one nostril and another in the nub between his lower lip and chin. And tattoos! This guy was covered with them! The tattoos were black mostly, with a little red. The abstract patterns consisted of dotted lines and square angles fanning out from the corners of his eyes, then running down each side of his neck, over his shoulders and down his arms. Other patterns appeared on his hips and down the sides of his legs, running all the way to his ankles. More tattoos "fountained" up from his navel and outlined the creases in his chest muscles. President Hinckley and other prophets would not have approved of these fashion choices one little bit.

He also wore a bone-handled knife with a brown-mottled flint blade, and a quiver with four arrows. It would have been six, but two of those arrows were now embedded in the dead jaguar. Lastly, he wore a kind of sack or bag made of leather and cords and decorated with more beads and feathers. The sack strapped around his waist and hung at the small of his back, sort of like a backward fanny pack. It looked stuffed to capacity, but I couldn't have guessed what was inside.

My emotions remained on edge for quite some time after what had happened, and I was trembling like a leaf. I glanced at the dead body in the mud, then turned into Apollus' shoulder, leaning on him for support.

Lamanai took in the scene around us one more time, then declared with renewed sadness and regret, "I must carry my stepbrother and the jaguar back to the village."

"The jaguar?" I said, wondering why that was even a concern any longer.

But Lamanai became quite animated and emphatic. "Yes. They must know how it happened. They must see for themselves. Then they, too, will recognize the signs."

"What signs?" I inquired.

He seemed surprised that I would ask. "The signs that define why you are here. The signs that reveal how this people will rise against the oppressors from the north, the conquerors from Teotihuacan, and bring our ancestors back from the ninth abyss."

My eyes widened. We were here to inspire all *that?* There was so much energy and passion in Lamanai's voice that I wasn't sure what to say. But this was ridiculous. How could we carry on such a charade? I shook my head and was about to make some sort of protest when Apollus spoke first, as if he sensed what I was about to do and wanted to beat me to the punch.

"*We* will carry the jaguar," he declared.

Lamanai shook his head vigorously. "It cannot be done. I will not allow you to burden yourself in your earthly form with such undignified labor."

"Don't worry about it," said Ryan. "Our 'earthly form' will be just fine."

Before he could argue with them any further, Apollus took some rope from Pacawli's belt and proceeded to tie the jaguar's paws together. Ryan obtained a long branch and threaded it through both paws, then he and Apollus balanced the creature on their shoulders. Lamanai wrapped Pacawli's body in his own cape, as well as the cape that had been around Pacawli's neck. Then he hoisted the dead body over his shoulders and carried it fireman style.

We set off for Lamanai's village, weaving our way through the thick undergrowth along a trail that could only have been made by the wild things of the jungle. We crossed streams with slippery moss-covered stones, and listened to the noisy chatter of colorfully plumed parrots—sometimes flying over our heads in flocks that numbered in the hundreds—and listened to the mocking hoots and howls of red-bearded monkeys with long curly tails. The jungle smelled spicy, musky, ripe-sweet and rotten: all the odors of rampant growth rooted in old decay. The sweat was pouring off Apollus and Ryan, but when I asked if I could take a turn at helping to carry the carcass, they both brushed me off with typical masculine curtness, neither wanting to confess in the presence of the other that they might need a rest. Lamanai showed no signs of strain whatsoever and kept up a steady and deliberate pace. Blood soaked through the capes wrapping his stepbrother's body and drizzled down Lamanai's chest. I shuddered at the sight of it.

But despite my loss of appetite from all that had happened, I simply couldn't continue without something to eat. Lamanai gave each of us some cornmeal cakes and dried fish from his stepbrother's travel bag, both of which tasted horrible.

"I am sorry that your first meal as human beings is so cold and plain," said Lamanai. "There is manatee back at the village."

"Manatee?" I asked.

"Yes. Your arrival will be cause for a great feast."

If he meant what I thought he meant, I lost my appetite all over again. Could he really mean those wonderful, harmless sea cows that were so endangered in Florida? They *ate* those things?

We spoke very little as we walked, despite the fact that my mind was bristling with questions. Lamanai had gotten a little ahead of us and out of hearing when I whispered to Apollus, "I don't feel good about this. I want to clear this up and explain to him that we are not gods."

"For now, I think it is better if we remain silent," said Apollus.

"I agree," said Ryan.

"Why?" I asked.

Ryan answered, "Because if he thinks we're gods, he'll be more likely to help us."

"But it's *wrong!*" I insisted. "He's bound to figure it out on his own. What happens then?"

"Until then we should do all we can to be what he wants us to be," said Apollus. "In the far east they also believed Alexander the Great was a god, and he conquered whole empires without bloodshed. But when Alexander died, they slaughtered his armies like pigs."

"Your point?" I asked.

"He means," said Ryan, "if they find out the truth, they'll likely string us up like this jaguar and barbecue our livers."

I scoffed at that. I suppose I should have taken a picture—Apollus and Ryan agreeing with each other? That was a first. But I still couldn't feel comfortable about this. It was bound to blow up in our faces. That's what always happened in the movies. Nobody ever pretended to be a god without bringing down the wrath of the *real* God.

It was very late in the afternoon when we finally arrived at Lamanai's village. We passed through a grove of trees where a scattering of men was just finishing their labors of harvesting some kind of nut. They stopped and stared at us with eyes of wonder. Obviously they'd never seen people like us before. Many of them would have surely known the identity of the young man wrapped in the cloaks, yet they hardly seemed to notice to him. We took center stage.

The air was thick with smoke. It hung low to the ground and made nearby people and buildings seem ghostlike and surreal. I realized this was also how we looked to them—like ghosts coming out of the dark woods. Numerous campfires were burning in preparation for the coming night, but the main source of smoke came from fields and gardens encircling every hut. Piles of old dry weeds and stalks lay smoldering. The people were busily working the ashes into the soil. That is, until they saw us, at which point all work ceased.

Before we had arrived, the village had been echoing with the sound of women pounding tortillas onto flat stones, but even these patting hands went silent as we passed. If it had just been Lamanai and Pacawli, I think the villagers would have greeted them with cheers. No doubt it was a beautiful prize jaguar. Our presence and the body on Lamanai's shoulders dampened any mood of celebration. A gathering was steadily forming behind us as we approached the center of the village. At first it consisted of mostly children and their pets. For every third child there seemed be an accompanying pet, whether dog or monkey, parrot or iguana. I also saw several anteater-looking things with raccoon faces—called coatimundis—that I remembered from some book that I'd read as a kid. But there was another kind of pet that I'd never seen before in my life. It was a cuddly-looking thing with a luxurious yellow-brown coat, the face of a teddy bear, the body of a cat, and the prehensile tail of a monkey. I later learned that they were called kinkajous.

As we reached the central square (only a couple hundred people lived here at most) a young woman of sixteen or seventeen broke away from a group of five or six other girls and rushed up to us. She stopped squarely in front of Lamanai, forcing him to halt. With her face stricken in despair and horror, she took in the cloth-wrapped body, then stared pleadingly into Lamanai's eyes.

"Pacawli?" she asked breathlessly, somehow hoping beyond all hope that he might deny it.

Lamanai looked at the ground. The girl started to wail. Her elbows folded in front of her chest and her knees buckled. Several of her girlfriends lunged to catch her. The wails alerted everyone who hadn't witnessed our arrival. Adults emerged from leaf-thatched huts. Within thirty seconds every inhabitant of the village surrounded us.

But unlike the girl, their eyes were riveted on us. I'd never felt so much like a freak attraction in my life. Several men helped Lamanai lay the body carefully upon the ground. Apollus and Ryan also set down the jaguar, then adopted a wary posture. But no one was threatening us. Lamanai started to raise his hands to speak, but suddenly another man began pushing his way through to the front.

He was in his mid-twenties, I guessed, with a flattened forehead like Lamanai, although the procedure appeared to have been done with somewhat less skill. His forehead had an uneven, concave shape, as if the board tied in place at birth had been slightly rounded. Unlike the feline look of Lamanai, it had given this man an unbalanced, rodent-like appearance, turning his large and sloping nose into a shrewish beak.

Without glancing at either Lamanai or us, he fell onto his knees at the head of the shrouded corpse. He unwrapped the face until it was visible to everyone present and stared at it for a long time. At last his shoulders started trembling, like a mountain before an eruption. He stood quickly, his eyes hot with tears, and demanded of Lamanai, "What happened to my brother?"

"His soul was taken by the sacred Balam," said Lamanai solemnly, then his eyes lit up and he indicated us. "But see what his sacrifice has brought, Kux-Wach! These three powerful deities have come to take his place. I witnessed their emergence from the depths of Xibalba with my very own eyes!"

The crowd backed off several steps, muttering among themselves in astonishment. I might have thought somebody would express doubt—demand to see some identification or something before they swallowed the whole god thing. Were we really so different in appearance? We were taller, I'll grant that. Even *I* stood half a head taller than most of their men. Our hair and skin color also stood out. But gods? I guessed it was mostly our clothing—Ryan's tan trousers and white Polo shirt, Apollus's denim jeans and Mexican button-up, and my own lavender blouse and hip-hugging Calvin Kleins. To them, the styles and patterns might have looked as different as alien uniforms from a Fifties science-fiction movie would have looked to us. I saw a flash of skepticism on the face of the dead man's brother, Kux-Wach. Or maybe it was just confusion.

"Why?" he asked. "I don't understand. Why would Pacawli's death have evoked the powers of Xibalba?"

"Because he has the blood of a shaman," said Lamanai. "His sacrifice opened the doorway between the realms."

"Is this what they have said?" asked Kux-Wach, pointing at us.

A hush swept over the gathering. They waited eagerly for our response—the first words they'd ever heard from the lips of a god.

It was Ryan who finally replied. "Sure. Sounds good."

"Then what is your purpose here?" demanded Kux-Wach, his face still grief-stricken. "Why have you come among us?"

We squirmed a little. We couldn't just say we'd taken a wrong turn at Albuquerque. But before we could say anything, Lamanai interrupted.

"Before they reveal the reason, Kux-Wach, we must first speak with your father, Chilan Kanalha."

Kux-Wach looked offended at this. His brother was dead. He wanted an explanation now. I got the feeling that Kux-Wach didn't much like Lamanai. Obviously this relationship between stepbrothers wasn't as close as the one between Lamanai and Pacawli.

"My father is still in the forest," said Kux-Wach impatiently, as if Lamanai should have already known this. "He is preparing for the Festival of Sacrifice. He may be gone for several more days—"

"I am here, my sons," said a voice.

I turned to see an old man holding a staff and standing beside a hut that had been thatched with cornhusks. In his other hand was a woven sack filled with leaves of some sort, a few of them poking out the top.

I wasn't sure about his age—mid-sixties, perhaps. He may have been even younger, but his physical appearance made him look more decrepit. It was almost frightening, yet I felt more sympathy than fear. Unlike the other men in the village who tied their hair into a tight ponytail at the top of their heads, his hair hung loose, wild, and uncombed. He had on only the barest of loincloths and a pair of well-worn sandals. His body was dotted with the same style of tattoos as Lamanai and other Lamanite men (and women, for that matter) but in his skinny, wizened condition, the designs looked shrunken and distorted. There was hardly a tooth in this man's head, and the corners of his eyes were almost completely glossed over with milky-white cataracts. There was a terrible scar on his hip, as if something had once taken a bite out of him.

Balancing himself with the staff, Kanalha ambled forward with small, limping steps. The crowd watched in hushed reverence. This man was apparently very well respected. From the sack of leaves he carried, I guessed he was a medicine man or witch doctor. Perhaps the leaves were used to make some kind of potion. But what did I know? Maybe they were food for a pet iguana.

Only as he reached us did he finally look down upon the face of his dead son. He shuddered a little, but that was the only hint of inner anguish that I perceived. He raised his eyes again to look at us. Or more specifically, he was looking at Ryan. Maybe it was that blonde-haired, blue-eyed, all-American look that made him stand out. Then again, if these people represented the first Americans, Ryan looked about as *un*-American as a person could possibly look.

"So you have returned," the old man declared.

I cocked an eyebrow. Ryan looked baffled as well.

Kanalha turned to the gathering and said with reproof, "Why do you stand and gawk, you children of the Lamaya? Do you not bow to the earth to honor the arrival of the long-awaited Kukalcan?"

Another gasp gripped the crowd. Many of them seemed genuinely alarmed. In a flurry of surprised exclamations, all two hundred men, women, and children began dropping to their hands and knees and bowing their heads low to the earth. Lamanai acted no less astonished than everyone else, as if even *he* had underestimated the full breadth and importance of who we were.

"Kukalcan?" he said in perplexed surprise. "But how can that be? He is Xbalanque, the Hero Twin. The Sun God who . . ."

Kanalha bowed with everyone else, his hands stretched forward, his staff and his sack of leaves now lying at his side. After studying Ryan one last time with an expression that appeared to be a combination of embarrassment, fear, and sincere apology, Lamanai also dropped to his knees. He must have decided that Kanalha was much more qualified to interpret our true identity.

It took me a minute to process the information, and when I did, I too was reeling in astonishment. Kukalcan. Lamanai had used that word to describe the Nephites—"the people of Kukulcan." That's when it hit me. *Of course!* I'd had the Aztec word for Feathered Serpent—Quetzalcoatl—so ingrained in my mind, that I'd entirely forgotten that Kukalcan meant exactly the same thing in Mayan.

Oh my heavens! They thought Ryan was the *Savior!* Blue eyes, white shirt—it was obvious! The only thing missing might have been the beard, but who knew how specific some of these traditions were in the fourth century? A thousand years from now wouldn't Cortez and Pizarro and Columbus be mistaken for the same person?

I also understood the shock in Lamanai's voice when he'd said, "*But how can that be?*" To the Lamanites, Kukalcan was a *Nephite* god. A *Nephite* tradition—one that most Lamanites had apparently rejected almost two centuries ago. By making this proclamation, the old man was essentially confessing that at least *this* Nephite tradition might have been dead on. No wonder there was so much alarm on the villagers' faces. It would have been like introducing Jesus Christ to a Buddhist, and forcing him to rethink everything he'd been taught all of his life because of what he was seeing with his own eyes!

This was unacceptable. I was not going to stand here and let these people think something so ridiculous.

"Please," I said to everyone. "Don't do this. Don't bow down to us. You don't under—"

Apollus grabbed my wrist and squeezed. I looked into his face. It was full of warning. He shook his head ever so subtly, jaw clenched, pleading for me to keep my mouth shut.

Ryan looked bewildered and uncertain. Then he saw the expression on Apollus's face and made a decision. He had no more idea what Kukalcan meant than the man in the moon, so he collected his wits and said, "Yes, do as she says and rise to your feet. You don't need to bow before us."

"He will destroy us," I heard a woman whimper.

"The god of our enemies will curse us," said someone else.

Ryan waved this off. "No, no. Have no fear. There'll be no cursing or destroying, I promise. We are here to serve and help. All we ask for is your . . . your kindness and hospitality."

"If you are Kukalcan," asked Kux-Wach, "then who are the others?"

Ryan looked befuddled by the question for an instant, then he stood up straight. "I'm glad you asked. This," he put a hand on Apollus's shoulder, "is my faithful servant, Apollus. He does whatever I tell him to do. Day or night."

Apollus's eyes glinted like flame-throwers.

"And this," he gestured toward me, "is the lovely Meagan, exemplar of all that is beautiful and harmonious. It's her job to—"

I interrupted quickly. "—To make sure that Kukalcan doesn't make any mistakes or say anything foolish, so that lightning does not strike him down from heaven and roast him to a crisp." I gave him a tight smile.

Lamanai spoke to his stepfather, Kanalha. "But the Nephites always say that Kukalcan will come down from the clouds. These gods emerged from the bubbling cenote in the Mosquito Forest."

It was finally dawning on Ryan who they thought he really was. He started to look *very* uncomfortable.

Kanalha replied, "Only the Nephites speak of a white god with features such as this. My eyes may be dim, but not so dim that I cannot perceive his likeness to the Nephite prophecies. Nor so dim that I cannot learn from my pride and errors. For I saw the coming of

Kukalcan and his companions last night in my dreams with the Vision Serpent. That is why I have returned from the forest."

Now I *was* bedazzled. He'd seen us coming in a dream? The villagers spoke anxiously among themselves again, trying hard to interpret what all of this meant. Lamanai approached Ryan tentatively. He spoke to him in an aside that only Ryan, Apollus, and I could hear.

"But you are still here to bring glory again to our ancestors, are you not?" he asked.

Ryan nodded. "Yes. Certainly. We're here to do whatever we can."

Aagh! I could have *beaten* him! Ryan had no idea what he was saying. How could he possibly understand the ramifications of the promise he had just made? Lamanai's face was veritably glowing.

"Then we must go to my stepfather's house," he said. "Tonight we must decide our strategy. Tomorrow you must announce to the people that I am to be their king."

Ryan's eyes flew wide. Finally it dawned on him what a donkey's hind end he was making of himself. Rule number one: Before pretending to be a god, know what god you're pretending to be, and what the people might expect you to do.

* * *

The sun was just setting behind the three-tiered jungle canopy as Ryan, Apollus, and I were led to the home of Kanalha, the village shaman, atop a grassy hill at the western end of the settlement. We were accompanied by the old man and his son, Kux-Wach, as well as by his stepson, Lamanai. Also in attendance were three men who were introduced to us as "elders of the village." The mayor (so to speak—I think his official title was Master of the Skulls) was named Ajul-Jolom, or just Jolom. He was followed by his counselors, Quillkiah and Riki-Kool. (Yeah, I know. It might seem cool to find a Lamanite named Ricky Kool. But the pronunciation was more like "Reekee-Koh-owl.") Many of the villagers followed us a good part of the distance, rarely taking their eyes off Ryan, and some chanting a song. They weren't exactly singing in unison, and many were singing in different keys, but the song appeared to be a hymn.

The words went something like this:

Sovereign Kukalcan,
Luminous Feathered Snake,
Shaper of the earth,
Framer of the sky,
Of darkness and of light,
The great sages knew,
They were knowers of your essence.
In darkness and in light,
You shaped and framed the sky,
You shaped and framed the earth,
Luminous Quetzal Serpent,
Sovereign Kukalcan.

Ryan would nod to them and wave, like a movie star in a parade, but the expression on his face was uneasy. He looked like he desperately wanted to find a moment to speak to us alone to figure out what we ought to do. But it didn't appear that we were going to get such a moment anytime soon. I could only cross my fingers and hope that he wouldn't say something else to make the situation worse.

The body of Pacawli was being taken by several women to be prepared for burial. I could have sworn that I heard Kanalha mention to the elders that the body would be interred under the floor of his own house. I must have been mistaken. Who in their right mind would want a corpse buried underneath their bed? Forget about the smell—just the creepiness of the idea made me cringe.

Kanalha's house was one of the only structures in the village built of stone. It was actually rather elaborate, despite its small size, with complicated designs painted in bright reds, yellows, and greens. Around the doorway the stone had been carved into shapes that resembled an animal mask of some sort, with wide-rimmed eyes and abstract-looking fangs, as if Kanalha lived inside the jaws of a jaguar. A stone hearth was emitting great puffs of white smoke about five yards in front of the door. It was tended by four women, who I guessed were also servants to the shaman. Or maybe they were his wives, but none of them looked old enough to be the mother of Kux-Wach and

Pacawli. One was even nursing a small child. All of them, including the nursing mother, stood up straight to reverence our arrival.

The feeble Kanalha led the way to the top of the hill, balancing himself with his staff and moving at a steady pace, assisted at certain points by the mayor's two counselors, Quillkiah and Riki-Kool. He was still ahead of us as we approached the doorway of his house. That's when something appeared from around the building's far side. It was just a head at first—a sleek, black head with shining yellow eyes. My heart stopped. I let out a screeching gasp and latched onto the closest person near me, who happened to be the mayor, Jolom. Apollus, still armed with Lamanai's bow, tried to push Ryan out of the way so he could get a clear shot. The massive-sized jaguar, or panther, or whatever it was, stepped out into the open. Its eyes were fixed right on Ryan, ready to pounce.

Kanalha turned aside from the doorway and went toward it. He was stepping *in front* of it! Then I heard Lamanai's voice call out, "It's all right. She will not attack us."

Not attack us? How could he be so certain? His own stepbrother had just had his throat torn out by this same species of animal less than five hours ago! Kanalha reached his hand toward its face. It could have bit the limb right off, but instead it stood stock still, its eyes burning a hole into the three of us.

Kanalha touched its neck. He began to pat it. He was patting it like a house cat. A tame jaguar? Impossible! How could anyone have possibly raised a pet jaguar? Unlike the specimen that Apollus and Ryan had carried to the village, this one had a much darker coat. The front half of its body was almost pitch black, but toward its hind end the typical patterns and colors of other jaguars were revealed, although the orange was quite subdued. The brightest thing about its coat was the tail. The orange tip looked like a torch flame—a flame that danced like a serpent as the creature made it undulate in the waning light. It was slightly larger than the one Apollus had killed, although not quite as stocky. This animal looked as if it could move through the forest with the stealth of a soft breeze.

Kanalha continued to scratch the top of its head and announced, "This is Huracan. She is my companion and guardian in the forest. I see that she has been hunting." Kanalha slid his hand along the underside of the beast's chin. When it came away, his palm was moist with blood. "She has killed a monkey and brought it here."

That's when I saw the lump of fur and flesh lying by the corner of the building. The jaguar had carried a dead monkey from the jungle and left it beside the shaman's house.

Kanalha continued, "She has paid Kukalcan a great honor to bring him his evening meal. This gift was meant to reveal to all who may doubt, that the great Feathered Serpent has returned."

He was saying this to Kux-Wach.

I continued to gawk at the creature, utterly speechless. I half wondered if this was a dream. A jaguar that was trained to hunt? Only in a Tarzan movie. Not in real life. And the suggestion that it had done this to honor Ryan?—I wasn't even ready to deal with that. How could anybody still believe we were gods considering how we had just reacted? The great Kukalcan had nearly had a heart attack. Our hearts were still buzzing like lawnmowers, our faces drained of blood. But the people seemed to be taking our reaction for granted. Some were even giggling, pleased to see that even gods could be surprised.

Surprised? We'd nearly peed our pants!

"Come," Kanalha said, inviting Ryan forward. "You must meet your sacred guardian spirit. Tell her what you think of her gift."

Ryan looked like he might shake his head and refuse. But Apollus put his hand on Ryan's shoulder and gave him a mild nudge. Ryan began walking toward it, glancing back once uncertainly. He nodded to everyone present to reassure them that he wasn't afraid, and continued forward. All the while the great jaguar watched Ryan the way a cat watches a dancing string. Kanalha remained at the animal's side, caressing its dark coat.

Ryan got to within three feet of its nose, then straightened himself. Licking his lips for courage, he looked the cat straight in the eye and said, "Thank you, Huracan, for the monkey."

The jaguar stared back. I swear I heard a low growl in its throat. I swore it was about to attack. But it just stood there, almost as if it was listening.

Ryan cleared his throat and continued, "You have done me a great honor." He looked at the dead monkey and swallowed painfully, then added, "In fact, it's *too* great an honor."

I stiffened. What was Ryan doing?

"I'd like you to have it for yourself, Huracan. You look like you might be hungry. Sooo—it's all yours. *Bon appetite!*"

I wanted to crawl under a rock. How could he do that? A gift from a sacred guardian spirit! How could he reject it? Was there anything more insulting?

Then the most incredible, insane thing happened. The jaguar stepped forward, causing Ryan to start a little. But he kept his ground, and Huracan began *licking his hand!* Suddenly she turned off to one side, lifted the dead monkey back into her jaws, and dashed off down the hill, disappearing into the undergrowth. That was it. Now I'd seen it all. I could go to heaven knowing I'd seen every bizarre thing a person could possibly see. To top it off, the people were *clapping!* The women, the elders, the onlookers—they were all applauding as if Ryan had just done the most heroic, benevolent thing imaginable. Then Ryan, after shaking off the initial shock, held up a hand as if to say, "Ah, nuthin' to it."

Apollus grinned and shook his head in disbelief. It was like we could do nothing wrong. How much more of this could Ryan handle before he started to believe he really *was* a god?

A few minutes later we found ourselves seated in the middle of the shaman's house. The floor was covered with several beautiful woven mats. Ryan was invited to sit on the largest mat with the most elaborate designs. But the rest of us also sat upon mats, as if the idea of sitting on the bare stone floor would have been uncouth. Ryan was facing the doorway where the light of the hearth illuminated his face. Apollus and I were placed on either side, while Kanalha and his sons, along with the three village elders, faced us in a semicircle.

Lamanai could hardly contain himself. "Elders of Siebalche," he began. "I have called everyone together this night for a glorious purpose. With the arrival of the Great Ones, and the death of Pacawli-Yak, the time has come for me to make a sacred announcement." Lamanai made eye contact with his stepfather, as if seeking his approval for what he was about to say.

Kanalha shut his eyes and nodded. "Yes, the time has finally come."

The suspense in the air was thick, and there was also an air of heaviness. The mayor, Jolom, felt he ought to break the tension.

"Then we must smoke," he said.

The mayor's two assistants began passing out cigars. Real cigars! They were about seven inches long, and frankly I saw very little difference between them and the kind of cigars for sale at any grocery store or smokeshop, except that there was no paper ring. Everyone placed the cigars in their mouths and began passing around a burning taper. The mayor lit one end and took a long drag, afterwards blowing the smoke out of his lungs. Within seconds the room was saturated with the most awful, obnoxious tobacco cloud. They were *all* smoking—all but the three of us—who looked down at the cigar in our fingers with distaste. That is, all but Apollus. When the burning taper was passed to him, it appeared as if he was actually going to light it. I was shocked!

But then I wondered: Had Apollus ever really been taught the Word of Wisdom? After all, he'd joined the Church in the ancient city of Ephesus. The Word of Wisdom wasn't exactly part of the baptismal interview in 73 A.D. For the life of me I couldn't recall if anyone had ever explained it to him during the time he'd lived with us in Salt Lake. I guess I'd just *assumed*.

I whispered his name sharply and shook my head. He looked up innocently, surprised by my reaction. But he immediately removed the cigar from his mouth. He glanced over at the villagers, then back at me, clearly worried that I was about to commit another grave offense.

"Will you not smoke with us?" Jolom asked Ryan.

Ryan amazed even me with his quick and clever reply. "I'm afraid not. A god cannot defile his body with tobacco. We must remain pure and unpolluted while we reside in the flesh to keep our minds in harmony with the universe around us."

After thinking about this a moment, Kanalha and the elders nodded with complete understanding, even admiration. I was pretty impressed myself.

"Will it offend you, Great One, if the rest of us indulge?" asked Jolom.

At this same instant I started coughing. Oh, those cigars were foul-smelling! My hand began waving desperately in front of my face to try and clear the air.

Ryan answered the mayor without missing a beat. With all the smoothness of a Public Service Announcement, he replied, "Actually, second-hand smoke can be as harmful as smoking itself. For the health of everyone present, why don't we hold off on the stogies for the time being, shall we?"

No need to ask twice. The Great Kukalcan had spoken. Cigars were summarily crushed out. I was reminded again that a god could do no wrong. If only the Surgeon General could get such a prompt response!

For the first time I noticed that Kux-Wach looked somewhat irritated. As he crushed out his cigar I could feel a definite vibe of resentment. At first I attributed this to the grief and pain he no doubt still felt over his brother's death. But it was more than that. Was it possible that at least one resident of this village wasn't buying the god act?

Lamanai started speaking again. "It is time that I revealed the truth about who I am, and how I came to be among you."

The elders glanced at one another. "We already know this," said Quillkiah. "Over the past six years Chilan Kanalha has related the story to us many times. You were an orphan whose family was killed in the siege of Tikal when the armies of Fire-Born burned the villages outside the city wall. When he found you in the forest it was revealed to Kanalha that you should be brought up as the son of a Chilan. Is this not true?"

"It *is* true," said Kanalha. "All but the part about raising him to be a Chilan. Lamanai is much greater than a mere village shaman. For he has the blood of Ahmen."

Eyes widened. It was another surprise in a day of surprises.

"Ahmen?" said Kux-Wach. "You mean Lamanai is a high priest? That's outrageous!"

"Six years ago," Kanalha continued, "while I was communing with the Vision Serpent in the forest, the King's First Priest, Hapai-Zin, brought me a twelve-year-old boy. After he told me the boy's identity, we shed blood together and I swore an oath that I would not reveal his true identity until the time was fully ripe and the gods gave us a sign. There can be no greater sign than the appearance of Kukalcan. So now the oath can finally be broken."

"Then who is he?" Kux-Wach asked his father.

Kanalha turned to Lamanai. He would allow his stepson to answer this question for himself. Lamanai started to rise, but then stopped himself and looked at us, waiting. I realized that he didn't feel right about standing to make this announcement unless we, too, were standing. As if anything else would have been inappropriate.

I almost refused to move. This whole thing had gone on long enough. How could we allow them to break such oaths on account of us? More than ever I wished we could just slink off into the forest, let them go on about their lives as if we'd never appeared. But it was too late. Besides, Apollus and Ryan were already on their feet. They waited for me. Reluctantly, I arose.

Lamanai looked down at the elders and declared with a brassy voice, "I am Eagle-Sky-Jaguar, eldest son of Great Jaguar-Paw."

The shock that gripped the room was at least as great as when Kanalha had announced that Ryan was Kukalcan.

"You are a prince of Tikal?" said Riki-Kool in astonishment.

"Unbelievable!" said Jolom.

"It cannot be!" said Quillkiah.

Kux-Wach just sat there, his jaw dangling.

"How is it possible?" said Jolom. "How did he survive the purges of Fire-Born?"

"By the will of the gods," said Kanalha, nodding toward us.

"Wait," said Kux-Wach. "Just wait a moment. How do we really know that this is the son of Jaguar-Paw? By the word of an old High Priest, who by now has undoubtedly been executed along with everyone else of noble blood?"

The village elders were hardly listening.

"It all makes sense," said Jolom.

"I always suspected that there was something more to be known about this boy," said Riki-Kool.

"Honorable elders!" Kux-Wach exclaimed, slapping his hand to the floor. "Listen to yourselves! Even if my adopted brother—whom I have known and watched for six years—is truly a prince of Tikal, what difference does it make?"

"What *difference?*" said Quillkiah. "If he is the son of the Great Jaguar-Paw, it means that the lineage of Yax-Chaac-Xok is not dead. The true heir of the throne of Tikal still lives!"

"But there is no more power in this lineage!" Kux-Wach declared. "The magic has gone out of the descendants of Yax-Chaac-Xok. If this were not true, the warriors of Fire-Born would not have conquered the kingdom and placed Blue-Crocodile, the son of Spearthrower Owl, on the throne of Tikal."

"But the kingdom is *not* conquered!" declared Riki-Kool. "Not while a son of the Great Jaguar-Paw walks and breathes!"

"And what now?" asked Kux-Wach, addressing Lamanai, trying to appear amused. "Will you personally challenge the armies of Fire-Born? Bring upon us the wrath of Spearthrower Owl? Just you and the old men of Seibalche?"

"Not just the old men," said Lamanai. "Me and the mighty Lord Kukalcan. With these gods as my protectors, I will be invincible!"

"That's it!" I interrupted. "Cut. Rewind. Go back. Guys, this is getting *way* out of hand. Listen, we'd love to stick around and help you to reconquer your kingdom and all, but to be quite honest, we're just passing through. I think there's been a major misunderstanding here."

Talk about taking the wind out of people's sails. Everyone gawked at me with ultimate confusion, including Apollus and Ryan.

Lamanai turned to Ryan. "What does she mean?"

Apollus said sternly, "She means nothing. She does not speak for Kukalcan. She is, after all, the goddess of love and harmony."

"Ah," said Jolom, as if this explained why I might have been squeamish about reconquering kingdoms.

But Lamanai wanted to set the record straight once and for all. With his eyes full of insistence, he said to Ryan, "Was this not the reason that you came forth from the Underworld? To help me reclaim the throne of my father? For what other purpose would you have come?"

"To make a fool of you, Lamanai," said Kux-Wach. "These are not gods from the realms of power. They are demons from the place of darkness. Jesters from the fecund loins of the Dark Maw himself, here to taunt us all, and entice us to destroy ourselves, charging headlong into the spears of the lightning warriors of Fire-Born. *Kukalcan indeed!*"

"Kux-Wach!" snapped the old shaman. "Silence your blasphemies! He *is* Kukalcan!—just as it was revealed to me by the Vision Serpent."

"Father," said Kux-Wach, his tone now pleading, "I have never questioned your wisdom or your visions. But listen to reason. Your mind is weary. Your eyes are dim. The Nephite deliverer is a myth and a lie. The memory of such lies should be annihilated, just as the Nephites themselves are being annihilated. Just as the Nephite prisoners will be annihilated on the Day of Sacrifice. Do not allow yourself to be deceived, or to deceive and confuse the people of the Lamaya . . ."

Kux-Wach said something else. Something about urging his father to step aside and allow him to assume the duties of village shaman, but I wasn't listening anymore. My ears were still ringing with the statement about Nephite prisoners and sacrifice. Ryan had picked up on it too.

"Nephite prisoners?" he asked. "What are you talking about? What prisoners?"

"The captives from Tehuantepec," said Jolom. "They are said to be spies. Fire-Born brought them to Tikal bound and naked four moons ago. They are to be beheaded in the Royal Square at the Festival of Sacrifice. Fire-Born himself will drink the blood of the Nephite commander."

"Commander?" I asked. "What is his name?"

The elders shrugged.

"A captured enemy has no name," said Quillkiah.

Then Riki-Kool added, "But he is said to be the son of the Thunder Warrior, the same man who struck such fear into the hearts of all the Lamaya in the days of my youth."

Thunder Warrior. I'd heard that term. It was the term that Lamanai had used to describe—

"You mean Mormon?" I asked. "One of the captured commanders is the son of Mormon?"

I could feel my heart pounding against my ribs. For a split second, like a camera flash, I had a glimpse of something that I couldn't quite define. As if everything that was happening was starting to seem part of some grand cosmic design.

"Yes," Riki-Kool confirmed. "He is said to be the son of Mormon."

"What is his name?" I asked urgently. "Has anyone ever mentioned his name?"

Again the elders were looking around at one another and shaking their heads. But then a light seemed to flash on in the weary mind of the old shaman, Kanalha. He remembered the name.

"Moroni-Iqui-Mahucatah," he said. "His name is Moroni the Wind Traveler."

CHAPTER 16

The man in the scarlet cloak with the puffy red turban continued to point the rifle at our hearts. Nobody had to tell me he was an Arab. It was the rifle *that had me so confused. When were rifles invented? Wasn't it at least a thousand years after Mary had lived in Israel? Or was it a thousand and* five hundred *years? And yet it wasn't like any rifle I'd ever seen. More like ones I'd seen in pictures of George Washington crossing the Delaware. He had pistols at his waist too, and a long curved sword in a scabbard on his back. But the rifle was his favorite weapon at the moment.*

"Don't shoot!" Joshua shouted. "We're just kids!"

The man got a really strange look, as if he was seeing us for the first time. Maybe he was surprised to hear Joshua talk in his own language.

"Who are you?" he demanded. "Are you English?"

"We're from America," I said.

That seemed to baffle him even more. He lowered his rifle, but kept the scowl on his face.

"Where-you-learn-speak-Arabic?" he asked.

I could tell he was talking in broken English, even though to us it all sounded the same. Josh wasn't quite sure how to answer.

Mary took over. "Please. We're lost. We need food and shelter."

"You are not American," said the man, pointing a grubby-looking finger. "You speak Arabic too well."

It looked like Mary had the gift of tongues too, even though this was her native land. There was only one way to explain this: it was a different century. But when?

"I am Jewish," said Mary. "I am from Jerusalem."

I wasn't sure if she should've said that. I knew Arabs and Jews didn't get along a lot of the time. But were they always enemies?

"What are you doing here in the desert?" he asked fiercely. "This is the land of Sheik al-Farabi of Wadi Musa. Why are you drinking from his spring?"

"We didn't know it belonged to anyone," said Mary. "I'm sorry if we've offended somebody."

"Women are never *allowed to drink from this spring. Now it is polluted." He spat on the ground to show us what he now thought of this water. How awful, I thought. So if a woman got lost in the desert, what was she supposed to do? Just die of thirst?*

"We can pay you," said Mary, recalling what Joshua had said about the stuff from her purse.

A change came over the Arab's face. At first I felt relieved, because instead of a scowl he now looked quite interested. But a second later I realized it was much worse. It was a hungry *look. A savage look. He began climbing down the ravine in his red boots. We just stood there dumbly, watching him reach the bottom where the pool drained into the stream. He dropped his rifle on the bank and continued walking toward us, his teeth clenched.*

We started backing away. It occurred to me that he didn't need to wait for us to pay him. He could just take what he wanted. In a flash the man reached over his shoulder and drew out his sword. Fear, like little bolts of lightning, exploded in my head. He was going to kill us!

The seerstone had been right. Darkness was closing in. Mary and I shrieked at the same time. Where could we run? The hill behind us was so steep that we'd be cut down before we ever climbed it.   I clutched the seerstone, fell against the hillside, and closed into a ball. The Arab raised his sword high.

A horse whinnied.

"Hazim!" shouted a voice above us. "Stop! What are you doing?"

I opened my eyes and saw a man on the canyon rim riding a beautiful black steed with white ankles. He looked almost as strange and surprising to me as the Arab. He was old and wore a long, black cloak with white stripes. The top of his head was bald. He looked like a monk—just like a picture I had in my head of Elmer Fudd in some Bugs Bunny cartoon when he'd been dressed like a monk—except that he also had a long gray beard. Unlike the Arab, he wasn't wearing any weapons. Just his striped cloak with a belt tied around the middle, and a pair of shoes that looked more like slippers. Oh, and a beanie on top of his head, sort of like the cap I'd seen Jewish men wearing, but it was white with a tassel. I guessed it was to protect his bald head, but the rest of his face was pink and peeling from sunburn. His skin was lighter than the Arab's. I decided they couldn't possibly be related, yet at the sound of his voice the Arab lowered his sword and became humble. Well, not humble *exactly, because he still acted eager to do us some kind of harm, but guilty-looking and embarrassed, like he'd been caught in the act.*

"They are trespassers!" he told the monk. "They should not be drinking from al-Farabi's water."

"They are children," *the monk replied. "And women. You are the sheik of al-Arabah. Why should you care about property of the sheik of Wadi Musa?"*

"We are brothers."

"Nonsense. Your tribes have been feuding for four hundred years. You are in my *service now—the service of the Brotherhood of Mount Sinai, and if you harm a hair on their heads, you and your men will not be paid and I will find another escort at Jerusalem to take us back."*

Hazim was still for a moment, as if wondering if he ought to kill us anyway. Then his face broke into a wide grin. "I was not going to harm them, Holy Excellency. Just put the fear of Allah into them."

I glared at the Arab. Frighten us? Was that really all he was going to do? I felt sure if the man in the striped cloak hadn't shown up, he'd have cut us to ribbons and stolen everything we owned.

"I think the fear of God is in them already," said the monk. "Have you spoken to them?"

"Yes, Holy Excellency. They speak some Bedouin. The children say they are Americans, and the girl says she is a Jew from Jerusalem." He said this as if he had some doubts.

"Americans? Truly?" said the monk, or priest, or whatever he was. "What are they doing here in the desert?"

"We're lost," Mary repeated.

"That is for certain," the monk chuckled. "But how did you get here? And are you truly Americans?"

"Yes," said Joshua quickly, sensing that this title carried some weight. "Do you know America?"

"There is no son of Greece who does not know and love Americans. The generosity of your people during the struggles of my countrymen saved many lives."

"Oh? Which struggle was that?" asked Josh. He was fishing to find out what year it was.

"Our struggle with the Sultan, of course. Come out of there. All of you. Let me get a better look at you."

We climbed out of the ravine. Hazim followed us closely, holding his rifle sideways to urge us to walk faster. The sheik watched with great interest as I retied the seerstone around my neck, probably wondering if it might be valuable.

As we reached the top, I looked down into the valley toward the Dead Sea and now saw several men and camels. I also saw Hazim's horse down in a gully. This one was chocolate colored with a fancy black and red saddle and saddlebags. There was also a spear of some sort with steel tips on both ends.

The monk dismounted and bowed to us slightly, his hands held in front and hidden beneath his sleeves. "I am Brother Nicholas. This is Sheik Hazim Haggai. He and his men are our guides to Jerusalem."

Hazim made a loud "Hmmph!" to show his dislike of us, then he went to fetch his horse.

We introduced ourselves, and then Joshua asked Nicholas, "Are you a monk?"

"Yes," he replied with a smile. "I belong to the Holy Brotherhood of the Fathers at the Convent of Mount Sinai."

"I've never seen a real monk before."

"It's been a long time since I've seen a real boy as well. At least one who was not of the tribes of the Bedouins. But in truth you are the second, third, and fourth Americans I have met in recent days."

"Who was the first?" I asked.

"An explorer. He was visiting Petra under the guidance of the sheik who Hazim believes to be the owner of that spring. This man was also headed to Jerusalem, but he took the higher road through Hebron."

"What was his name?" asked Josh.

He thought a second. "Stephens. John Loyd Stephens. We may see him again at the monastery of St. Elias. It is one of the only convents that will show hospitality to the desert Arabs. My only worry is that a scuffle may erupt between the men of al-Arabah and al-Farabi. Their tribes are bitter enemies."

Josh whispered to me, "You ever heard of a famous American explorer named John Lloyd Stephens?"

I shook my head.

"Did you say you were going to Jerusalem?" asked Mary.

Nicholas nodded. "We are on our way to get supplies. And also to pick up a novice from St. Elias and take him back with us to the holy mountain."

"Is it possible . . . I mean, can we go along?"

"Of course," said Nicholas. "If you hadn't asked, I would have insisted. Are your families in Jerusalem?"

I started to say, "Well, not really—"

But Josh cut me off and said, "Yes. They're waiting for us there. Probably worried."

He looked us over again. I don't think he believed Joshua, but he didn't want to push the subject. "Then we should get you there as quickly as possible. You two climb aboard my horse."

"Really?" I asked.

"Of course. I will lead him."

Mary helped me and Joshua climb into the saddle. Nicholas might've insisted that Mary ride too, but she was in a dress—a very dirty dress, but still a dress—and on this rough ground it was impossible to ride sidesaddle. She walked at Nicholas's side as we started down toward the others who were waiting by the roadside. Hazim was already galloping back to them, his scarlet cloak streaming in the wind. His men, about ten as far as I could tell, shouted questions at him, asking who we were and what he'd found. It looked like there was at least one other monk besides Nicholas. He was riding a camel, and as we got closer, I wondered about what Nicholas had said about not seeing a boy in a long time who wasn't Bedouin. This monk looked very small compared to the Arabs around him. I saw that he was smoking a pipe. Either monks started smoking very young, or he was very short.

"I have never seen clothes like yours," said Nicholas. "Is this what they are wearing in America?"

"Yeah," said Josh. "Everybody I know owns at least one pair of blue jeans."

"Blue jeans?"

"Yeah. My pants. They're an American invention, I think."

"Where did you learn such fluent Greek?"

"Oh, we've been around," Josh said awkwardly. "So have you ever met the Pope?"

Nicholas gave Josh a weird look, seeming a little put out. "I told you I was Greek.*"*

"So?"

"We have no pope."

"No pope? I thought all monks believed in a pope."

"I am Orthodox," said Nicholas.

"And you don't have a pope?"

"Josh," I scolded. "It's a whole different Church." I wasn't sure about that, but I hoped it would save Josh from sticking his foot in any deeper.

"We have bishops, and we have a Patriarch in Constantinople. But we do not believe that men should be lifted one above another."

Josh tried again to learn the year. "So this struggle with the Sultan that you mentioned back there—is it over?"

"I think so," said Nicholas. "For some years now."

"What year did it end?"

He seemed to be thinking hard about the answer, then said, "I'm not sure."

"What year did it start?"

"I couldn't say for certain."

"Can you make a guess?"

Now he seemed a little embarrassed. "I'm afraid I couldn't. I've been at Mount Sinai now for over forty years. This is my first trip outside its walls in five."

"Five years! Holy mackerel!" said Josh. "Then how do you even know there was *a struggle, or that Americans were so generous?"*

"We hear about it," he replied simply.

Josh decided to try a different tack. "So what year did you become a monk?"

"That would have been at the turn of the century," said Nicholas. "Long, long ago."

I could tell Josh was getting frustrated. He couldn't very well ask, "What century was that?" At least not without looking like an idiot.

We arrived back at the road. I could tell now that the other monk was definitely not a small boy. He was a midget! *A dwarf! I never would have thought I'd see a midget monk, or even a midget riding a camel. He puffed away on his pipe, watching us closely.*

"What have you found, Brother Nicholas?" he asked.

"This is Mary, and Joshua, and . . ." He'd forgotten my name already.

"*Rebecca,*" *I reminded him.*

"*Ah, yes. Rebecca. They are Americans.*"

"*Ohhhh,*" *sang the dwarf excitedly.*

"*This is Brother Paolo,*" *said Nicholas.*

Nicholas helped us down from the horse. The Arabs started sniffing about us. I'm not kidding. One of the younger ones, a man with close-set eyes and a squashed nose, was actually sniffing Mary's hair. Another one felt the material of my shirt, and even touched my pants. I moved closer to Nicholas.

"*Can they not do that?*" *I asked.*

"*Enough!*" *snapped Hazim, still riding his chocolate-colored stallion.* "*We ride!*"

The men backed away.

Nicholas told Hazim, "*These children will be coming with us.*"

Hazim looked irritated. "*What will they ride? They cannot all ride your horse.*"

"*One or two of them can ride with me,*" *said Paolo.*

"*And the other with me,*" *said Nicholas.*

"*No!*" *said Hazim sharply.* "*They must ride the spare camels.*"

I was confused. Was he suddenly being generous?

"*But they must pay.*"

Ah, there was a catch.

"*I will pay for them,*" *said Nicholas.*

"*No!*" *said Hazim again.* "*They have money. They must pay for themselves.*"

I wasn't sure why it mattered who paid for whom. I think Hazim just wanted to know how much money we had.

"*How much would it cost?*" *asked Josh. He reached into his pocket and pulled out some dollar bills and change.*

Hazim spurred his horse and rode up beside him. Josh was trying to straighten out the money and count it, but Hazim snatched away his five-dollar bill and held it up to the sky.

"*What is this?*"

"*It's five dollars. Cool looking, eh?*"

"*Who is this man?*"

"*It's, uh, Abraham Lincoln. He was our president. Or is our president. Or will be our president.*"

"*This is no good,*" *he said.* "*I will see your coins.*"

He handed him some change—two quarters, a dime, and a nickel. "The guy on the big one is George Washington. Have you heard of George Washington?"

"Ah, George Washington," said Nicholas, nodding.

But Hazim couldn't have cared less. "No good! These are neither gold nor silver. They are worthless!*"*

He tossed them back. Josh dropped a few, but he didn't bother to pick them up. Two of Hazim's men stepped forward and collected the fallen coins for themselves.

"Perhaps we can make a trade," said Mary.

Hazim leaned down to look into her eyes. "What will you trade, young girl?"

Mary looked uncomfortable. Hazim seemed to enjoy that, but he turned back to us, looking at the seerstone around my neck.

"What is that?" he asked, pointing.

I closed my hand around it and shook my head. "It's not for trade."

Joshua reached into his pocket again, this time pulling out the hairbrush, the nail clippers, and the half empty pack of Dentyne Ice *gum. "How about one of these?"*

The Sheik reached out snatched all three things from Joshua's hand, then he rode out of reach. He looked closely at the hairbrush and started laughing. He held it up for his men to see, and they started laughing too. Everybody seemed to think it was the funniest thing they'd ever seen.

He held the nail clippers up for Joshua and asked sharply, "What is this?"

"Here, I'll show you."

Hazim reluctantly handed it back and Joshua gave him a little demonstration. By the look of Hazim's nails, he definitely needed this gift the most. Afterwards, he took it back from Joshua and again held it up for his men.

"A little knife for clipping fingernails!" Again his men roared with laughter. He held up the last item. "And this?"

"Chewing gum," I said.

He grunted to indicate that he didn't understand.

"You break the pieces out of the aluminum thing and chew them," I explained.

He began fiddling with the little foil package, bending it back and forth, but not getting any gum.

"Lemme see it," said Joshua.

Josh tried to grab it back, but Hazim's grip was firm, so Josh popped out the little piece of gum while he was still holding the package. The gum got away from them. As Hazim tried to catch it, it flipped out toward some of his men and landed in the dirt. The men leaped off their horses and started scratching in the dirt like dogs over a bone. One of them had it in his fist, but three or four other fists were grabbing that fist. Hazim yanked his rifle from the gun holder on his horse, rode over to where they were fighting, and whacked several men with the rifle butt. I mean he really clobbered *them! I was sickened inside. For goodness sake! It was just a piece of gum! At least two men were knocked to the ground, including the one with the gum in his fist.*

Hazim demanded that he give it back. The man got to his feet, one hand holding his bruised ear, and dropped the gum into the sheik's palm. Then he backed off swiftly to avoid being hit again.

Hazim eyed the gum very closely, fighting to steady his horse.

"You chew it," Josh explained. "But don't swallow it, or it'll take seven years to digest."

"Is that true?" I whispered.

Josh shrugged.

The sheik put it into his mouth and chewed. After a few seconds his eyes bugged out. He spit the gum back into his hand.

"Lightning of Allah!" he exclaimed. "It tastes like fire!*"*

All of his men were cracking up again. Hazim finally broke into a smile, his eyes still wide. He popped the gum back into his mouth and continued to chew.

"I will spit fire like a dragon tonight!" He turned back to Josh and me. "You may ride my camels!" It looked like he was gonna take all three *things for payment.*

We did our best to climb aboard the camels. This was an experience I wouldn't soon forget. The saddle, or basket, looked so high I thought I might get a nosebleed. My camel got completely down onto its belly before I could climb aboard. As I was about to pull myself into the basket, it made an awful honking sound. I scrambled out of the way in a hurry.

"It's fine," said Nicholas. "She always makes that sound."

Josh and I climbed into the basket together. It stood up first with its back legs, nearly tossing me up over its head, then brought us up evenly again. I clung onto Josh's waist the whole time. A rope connected us to Paolo's camel. Mary rode by herself, her camel tied to the saddle of the man who'd been sniffing her, which I don't think she appreciated.

Nicholas rode his horse beside Mary. "So did I hear Hazim correctly before? Are you a daughter of Israel?"

"Yes," she replied. "But I'm a Christian."

"I see!" said Nicholas, quite pleased. "Have you always lived in Jerusalem?"

"Only when I was very young. For much of my life I lived in Pella in the Decapolis."

He nodded, but said nothing.

"Does Pella . . . still exist?" Mary asked.

"Pella? Yes, I think so," he answered.

He obviously hadn't heard of the place, but Mary didn't seem to mind. "What's it like living at Mount Sinai? It must be very hard."

"Our convent has stood for more than a thousand years," said Nicholas. "We grow oranges and dates, grapes and figs."

Mary seemed surprised. "Is there enough soil and water?"

"Of course. And there are always miracles." He started to tell a story. "Once there was a poor cobbler who was trying to reach the holy mountain, but he weakened too soon and was forced to take shade under a hanging rock. He would have died there of thirst, but instead he took out his cobbler's tools and began to make a new pair of shoes. Then and there he resolved that if God would spare his life, he would leave the world forever and live out his days in prayer and meditation right under that rock. He then put on his new pair of shoes and kicked the stone. Water gushed forth and a living fountain has been there ever since."

"Nuh-uh," said Josh. "You don't really believe that, do you?"

Nicholas raised his eyebrows. I don't think anybody had ever questioned the story before. "I have seen the fountain with my own eyes. And the shoes."

"I think the story is wonderful," I said.

Nicholas sent me the sweetest smile. I was really starting to like him. I looked toward the front of our little caravan and saw Hazim still riding his horse. I thought about what I had seen in the stone. The memory of that dark feeling made me shiver all over again. Hazim was part of that darkness. I felt sure of it. Maybe others were too. But what could I do about it now? I could only hope that after we reached Jerusalem I'd never see him again.

Joshua whispered to me. "Becky, look in the stone one more time. Find out what year it is."

"I tried that before," I said.

"Try it again!"

Heaving a sigh, I closed my eyes. I tried to clear my mind. This wasn't going to be easy with the rocking of the camel, but I held it up to my eyes and sealed out the light. Then I sort of thought about Josh's question and let my mind go wherever it wanted to go.

"Well?" asked Josh impatiently.

"Hold on a minute," I said.

Just like before, I felt like I could see light dancing inside the milky white surface. But I still wasn't sure if I was seeing pictures in the stone or in my brain. I rattled off each image exactly as it appeared.

"I see . . . a house . . . a cabin *. . . and a plough."*

"You mean like for farming?"

"Yes. It's near . . . a hill. A hill with trees and grass. And a stone. A man is lifting the stone. Lifting it with . . . a lever. He's lifting it with a branch." I drew a sharp breath. "I know who it is! It's the prophet!"

"Becky—" Josh's voice sounded nervous, but I was too caught up in what I was looking at.

"It's Joseph! *Under the stone is . . . a box!"*

"Becky!" His whisper was stern, but I just had to keep looking.

"It is!" I declared. "It's the plates! The gold plates! Oh, they shine! More shiny than I ever—"

Josh squeezed my leg, digging in his fingers. I jerked. He knew how ticklish I was there. I quickly lowered my hands. When my vision cleared I saw Hazim less than four feet away. He'd ridden over to us, probably as soon as he saw me looking into the stone.

"What are you doing?" he demanded.

"Nothing, I'm just—It's nothing."

"What is that you are holding?"

"Just a stone," I said innocently.

"Is it a jewel?"

"No. It's a stone."

"Why were you looking into it? Why did you say 'gold?'"

"Gold? Oh, I didn't mean—"

"You can see gold in the stone?"

"Of course not. It's just a plain white stone."

"Ah, it is a diviner's stone. Is it not?"

"A what?"

"To find treasure! Did you see treasure in this stone?"

"No! It's not what you think—"

"You will let me see it," Hazim insisted.

"Like heck!" said Joshua. "It's Becky's. Don't touch it!"

Nicholas galloped his horse back to us to see what was going on. "Is there a problem, Hazim?"

"He's trying to steal Becky's stone!" accused Joshua.

Hazim pulled back his hand, scowling angrily.

"Is this true?" asked Nicholas.

"She has a witch's charm!" Hazim blurted out. "A diviner's stone! Allah will curse the sorcerer!"

"Nonsense," said Nicholas. "You're too superstitious, Hazim. Now leave this girl alone with her child's trinket."

The whole caravan had stopped to watch us. Hazim's eyes were thin and mean. Finally he kicked his horse and galloped back toward the front. When he got there, he turned back again, still giving us a dirty look. He leaned over to one of his men. The two of them started talking, constantly throwing us glances.

Nicholas was also looking at the stone. "May I see it?"

Joshua shook his head at me. But as I studied Nicholas's eyes, I felt it would be okay. I took it off from around my neck. The old monk studied it closely.

"Very interesting," he said. "How did you come to obtain it?"

"We found it," I said.

He looked it over a few seconds longer, then gave it back. "It's quite unique. Do you use it for magic, as Hazim has said?"

I started to shake my head, but then I decided it probably wasn't necessary to lie. "Not really for magic. But I can see things in it."

"What kind of things?"

I bit the inside of my cheek. "I'm not sure yet. I'm still kinda practicing."

"Ah," he said, smiling at me the way all grown-ups smile when a young girl says something cute or silly. "The Bedouins are very curious about such things. Despite what he said, they are easily taken in by charms and amulets and foolish legends."

I thought of his story about the shoemaker and had to chuckle inside.

"If it is a holy relic," he continued, "it can only bless your life. But if it is evil, it can only curse you. My advice is that you keep it hidden until we are safely in Jerusalem."

"Thank you," I said. "I will."

He kicked his horse back to ride beside Mary. I tucked the seerstone inside my shirt. Not that it made any difference now. They all knew I had it. Every Arab in the caravan was looking over at us from time to time, and my ears were burning from all the whispering. If Paolo hadn't said we would be in Jerusalem soon, I think I'd have been very afraid to go to sleep that night.

Later, as we began to pass the first little villages at the side of the road, I thought about what I had seen.

"1830!" I suddenly blurted out.

"Huh?" asked Josh.

I lowered my voice. "I think that's what year it is. That's why I saw those things in the stone. It's just about the time when Joseph Smith is finding the gold plates and bringing back the gospel."

"Seriously?" said Josh.

I could tell he found the idea very bizarre. I guess a person never thought about Arabs and camels at the time of the Restoration.

Finally he let out a sad sigh.

"What's wrong?" I wondered.

"I don't know. I guess it's kind of a let down. To think we're all the way over here at the same time that Joseph Smith is about to translate the Book of Mormon. Why couldn't we have been sent to Palmyra, New York, instead of the opposite side of the world?"

"I don't know," I said.

"Still, I guess it explains what you saw before. The stuff about angels and people celebrating. They were celebrating because the gospel was about to be restored."

I thought about this. I supposed it made sense. But somehow I felt it wasn't quite right. Maybe part of it. But not all. I was dying to look into the stone again. But maybe that wouldn't be necessary. An hour later we came up over a rise and the walls of Jerusalem appeared below us.

We were still several miles away, but it was nevertheless an enchanted-looking city. Mary in particular seemed fascinated by all the changes that had taken place. High walls surrounded it on every side, and inside were hundreds of little white buildings, as well as towers and steeples that looked right out of the Middle Ages. On the far right I could see a building with a huge metal dome. I swore I'd seen pictures of this building before. It was called . . . the Dome of the Rock! *But in the pictures I'd seen, this dome was bright gold, not such a dull greenish copper.*

Actually, the whole area looked a lot more desolate than I might've expected. Except for a few tall, thin trees outside the walls, and some other trees and bushes growing in rows on a hill to the east, there really wasn't a whole lot of growth.

Then our caravan did something I wasn't expecting. We reached a fork in the road and to my surprise the caravan started going south, away from the city.

"Aren't we going to Jerusalem?" I asked.

"We're here," Nicholas announced. "Our novice is waiting for us at the monastery of St. Elias. Tomorrow we'll go into the city for supplies."

He pointed south toward a large stone building on a small hill.

"I thought we were going into the city," said Joshua.

"If you'd like, I could have Hazim's men take you to the gate."

"No," I said quickly. "I guess we'll walk."

"Where did you hope to meet up with your guardians?" he asked.

We stood there looking kinda dumb, and I think by our silence that he drew his own conclusions.

"There are *no guardians waiting for you in Jerusalem, are there?"*

"No," Mary admitted.

"Then why did you wish to go there?"

Again, we weren't sure how to answer.

Nicholas's eyes filled with sympathy, and he said, "Perhaps for tonight you should stay with us at the monastery. You may eat a nutritious meal, regain your strength, and perhaps tomorrow we will find someone who will take care of you."

Mary and Josh were both looking to me. I was the one with the seer-stone. They must have figured I'd know what was best. I was so tired. Honestly, I didn't think we were going to get any better offers.

Mary must have read my thoughts, because she turned to Nicholas and said, "Thank you. If you'll have us, we'll come with you to the monastery."

Hazim was close enough that he'd heard every word, and I think he was disappointed.

* * *

For dinner we ate black olives, white beans, a salad with vinegar and oil, dates, and a strange black bread with a crust so hard I thought I might crack a tooth. Still, as hungry as I was, it all tasted wonderful.

The Arabs stayed outside and fended for themselves. I don't think they'd have been caught dead in a Christian monastery anyway. We ate with about sixty other monks in a big, dark room lit only by a few candles. On the wall were smoky-looking murals of the baby Jesus with a halo, Joseph and Mary at the manger, and winged angels above the shepherds. There was also a scene showing the killing of the little babies in Bethlehem that was too gruesome to describe. The whole time there was a man at one end of the room reading from the scriptures by candlelight in a very boring voice.

The monks watched Josh and I with great interest as we gobbled down our food, but I noticed that many of them felt very awkward about looking at Mary. A few were bold enough to gawk at her for minutes on end, but most turned away in shame, or they tried to avoid looking at her altogether. She was very beautiful after all, and I don't think some of these guys had been around girls in a long time. The "Superior" of the monastery, or Papa as everyone called him, actually seemed irritated at Nicholas for bringing us inside.

Honestly, I found it just as interesting to watch the monks eating as they found it to watch us. Nearly all of them had such wild jungles of beard on their faces that I was surprised that their spoons were able to find their mouths. The only one without a beard was the novice who would be traveling back to Mount Sinai with Nicholas and Paolo. It wasn't that he was a young man. He was in his thirties, I guessed, but his face and cheeks were pocked with scars and for some reason a beard just wouldn't grow. This man looked weird for other reasons too. He was bald like the others, but with big ears and beady little eyes. His front teeth stuck forward a little and his skin was as pale as cream. In his monk's robe he reminded me of Dracula. Not the Dracula from old American movies, but the German Dracula—the one I'd seen on the Movie Channel late one Halloween night. Nosferatu, I believe. His name was Shika and he talked to us at supper.

"*Brother Nicholas says you are from the New World,*" *he said.*

"*Yup,*" *said Josh, eager to stuff in another mouthful of beans.*

"*How did you come to be in the East?*"

"*We're lost,*" *I said, sticking with the line that Mary had told Nicholas.*

"*Lost children. How fascinating.*" *He said it in a way that sounded sort of creepy.*

I wondered a little what might cause somebody to want to become a monk—especially a monk who would live so far out in the desert. Whatever the usual reason, I had a feeling that it wasn't the same one Shika had.

"*So what'd you do before you became a monk?*" *asked Joshua.*

"*I was a smith,*" *he replied.*

"*Smith?*"

"*Blacksmith,*" *he explained. "And a soldier.*"

"*Really?*" *said Joshua. "Did you fight in the same war that Nicholas talks about where Americans were so generous?*"

"*I'm not a Greek,*" *he said. "I'm a Syrian. But I've fought in other wars.*"

"*Against who?*" *asked Josh.*

Nicholas broke in. "Joshua, it's not proper to ask a novice why he has elected to leave the world and lead a life of piety and devotion. Sometimes a man must be allowed to forget his past."

Something told me that Shika was doing more than trying to forget. He was trying to hide.

"*Rebecca,*" *said Paolo the dwarf. "You must show Papa your stone.*"

The Papa was a chubby-faced man with a snow-white beard longer than anyone else's. After the way the Arabs had reacted to the stone, I didn't really feel like being put on the spot. But the Papa was sitting just two people away, so I pulled it out of my shirt and showed it to him. He reached inside his cloak, looking for something. But then he gave up and leaned forward, squinting.

"*Very nice,*" *he said.*

"*It's a sacred relic,*" *Paolo went on. "She sees visions in it.*"

"*Oh?*" *said the Papa. "What kind of visions?*"

I tried to go back to eating, but Shika said, "Yes, Rebecca, tell us what you see in the stone."

"*Just things,*" *I shrugged. "It's not that interesting.*"

"*The men of Hazim al-Arabah seem to think it might be used to locate lost treasure,*" *said Nicholas with a wink.*

Shika raised his blonde eyebrows. "It that so? Perhaps she could give us a demonstration."

I looked at Mary and Josh, who seemed to think this was a very bad idea. But then Nicholas said, "Yes, Rebecca. A small demonstration shouldn't hurt."

If it had been anyone besides Nicholas, I'm sure I would have refused. But his kind smile convinced me that I was safe.

"Well," I said, "it's better if somebody asks me a question."

"What kind of question?" asked another of the monks.

I shrugged. "I don't know. Anything."

"I have it," said the Papa. "I lost my spectacles today. Perhaps you could help me to find them."

There was a laugh in his voice, as if this was all very childish. But Nicholas nodded, so I slowly raised the stone, closed my palms around it, and peered into the center.

What happened next amazed even me. I knew the answer! I couldn't believe it came so fast.

"In the garden," I said.

The Papa chuckled a little. But he was the only one. All sixty of the other monks looked stunned.

I continued, "It's sitting under the third orange tree, right underneath the stool that you stood on this morning when you picked oranges."

The room became very quiet. Now even Nicholas looked amazed.

"Brother Gregorio," said Papa to a monk near the end of the table. "Go and see."

Gregorio took a lamp near the door, lit it with a candle, and left quickly.

"How did you know I was in the garden this morning?" asked Papa.

I looked at all the faces, feeling a little embarrassed. "It was . . . I saw it in the stone."

"You are in the garden every day, Papa," said another monk.

"But not picking oranges."

A moment later Gregorio returned. He held the spectacles high in his hand. "I have them, Papa!"

The monks all gasped in delight.

"A miracle!" someone announced.

"The child is blessed!"

"A miracle child!"

I felt a little sick inside. I wasn't sure why.

"What else will this stone tell you?" asked Shika.

"Will it truly reveal the location of lost treasure?" asked Paolo.

Nicholas must have seen the nauseous look on my face. He turned to the Superior. "I think the girl needs to rest now."

"What about a man?" Shika persisted. "Will it tell you his past? Or his future?" Those beady little eyes were looking right into me.

"It tells me whatever I seem to ask," I replied shyly.

"Incredible," someone whispered.

The sickness in my stomach was worse than ever.

"I think you're right," said Papa to Nicholas. "They all must be very tired. Brother Jerome, please show our guests to their room."

* * *

"It's because you were showing off," said Joshua.

I was still a little sick, but as I curled up on the many mats and pillows that covered the floor of our sleeping room, I started feeling a little better.

"Remember what Dad told us?" Josh continued. "When you have a spiritual gift, you have to treat it with respect, or the Lord can take it away. I'll betcha anything that's why you feel sick."

"I wasn't showing off," I said. "I was just doing what they asked."

"But I think Josh has a good point," said Mary. "The Savior taught us not to cast our pearls before swine."

"But they're monks," *I said.*

"That doesn't mean some of them aren't swine," added Joshua.

"From now on," said Mary, "I think you should avoid looking into the stone at all in the presence of strangers."

"Okay," I said, closing my eyes. "I won't."

"But what about what the stone told us earlier?" said Josh. "You said our only chance of getting home was to come to Jerusalem. Well, we're here. What do we do now?"

I heard the question, but I still didn't open my eyes. And I certainly wasn't going to look into the stone again today. I felt like it was part of the reason I was so tired. It seemed to take so much energy. Then again, there were so many things today that had drained my energy that I couldn't put all of the blame on the stone.

"We'll just have to hope that we find out more tomorrow," said Mary. "Until then, we should all get some rest."

A few minutes later all my memories of Arabs and monks and camels quickly faded away. But I felt like I'd only been asleep for a few hours when something woke me up. I opened my eyes, but the room was totally dark. This surprised me. I knew there'd been a candle on the wall near the door. It had sort of acted like a night-light. I wasn't sure why anybody would have doused it. But then I sniffed the air. There was a hint of smoke—the kind of smoke that you smell after a candle has been blown out.

My heart started beating faster. Someone else was in this room. I was sure of it. I heard a noise—and it wasn't Mary or Joshua rolling over. Someone was walking across the room—walking toward me. I sensed the outline of someone leaning over my face, a hand reaching toward my mouth—no doubt to silence me so I couldn't scream.

But they were too slow. I screamed at the top of my lungs—so loud that the whole monastery echoed. The shadow jerked back. I think the intruder stepped on Mary, because she started screaming too. The shadow fled across the room. Our door was thrown open. But it was just as dark in the hallway. A few seconds later lanterns started coming down the hall from both directions. The first one to enter our room was Gregorio, the monk who had gone after the Superior's spectacles. The next person was Nicholas.

"What is it?" he asked desperately. "What happened?"

"Someone was in our room!" Mary replied.

"Who?"

"I don't know!" I said. "It was too dark!"

Nicholas turned to Gregorio. "Did you see someone in the hall before you came?"

"No, Brother Nicholas."

"They were trying to take the stone," Mary said.

More monks arrived, including the Papa, all dressed in white gowns and nightcaps and rubbing their eyes.

"It's all right," said Nicholas. "Someone frightened the children, but everything is fine now."

It took about five minutes for them to ask all of their questions. Then one by one each of the monks started going back to their rooms.

"I'll sleep in the hallway the rest of the night if it makes you feel safer," said Nicholas.

"No, Brother Nicholas," said the Papa. "It wouldn't be proper. Whoever it was, they are certainly too frightened to try again tonight. Tomorrow we will assemble all the monks for confession and keep them there until we find out who attempted this vile act."

"But there are also other guests in the convent," said Gregorio.

"Then we'll question them in the morning too," said Papa.

Nicholas was the last to leave. As he stood in the doorway he told us, "I intend to sleep with one eye open for the rest of the night. Do not hesitate to call out again, if necessary."

We thanked him, then found ourselves alone with our hearts still beating fast.

"The Papa is probably right," said Joshua. "I don't think anyone would be brave enough to try it again."

"I don't care," I said firmly. "I want to leave here tonight. Now!"

"Are you sure?" asked Mary.

I was still so shaken up I wasn't sure I was thinking straight. When Nicholas had invited us to stay here I'd felt sure that we'd be safe. Now I didn't feel safe anywhere. "I'll look in the stone."

"All right," said Mary. "But I think we should also pray."

The prayer came first. When Mary was done saying it, I almost didn't feel it would be necessary to look in the stone. We all felt confident that leaving here was the right thing. Nevertheless, I held the stone up to my eye and peered inside it. What I saw only confirmed the prayer. Only I was surer than ever. There was something very wrong in this monastery. Something evil. More evil than I'd ever encountered before. I suddenly felt that there was no way we could've gotten out of there fast enough.

"We'll wait a little while for everyone to settle down again," said Mary. "Is that all right?"

"No waiting," I said. "There's something wrong here, Mary. We have to go now."

Mary hesitated. She knew that there hadn't been enough time for the monks to fall asleep again. Yet she nodded. "All right. But we should walk as quietly as we can."

The three of us crept into the hallway and began making our way silently toward the front entrance of the monastery. We kept our eyes peeled for any movement. A few oil lamps burned at the end of the hallways, and in the main corridor, but no one came out of the shadows to try *and stop us. The smoky paintings on the walls made me feel creepier than ever, like the eyes were all watching us.*

Only after we'd slipped through the tall wooden doors and passed by the fountain in the courtyard did I begin to feel a shred of relief. We exited through the front gate and entered the road that would take us to Jerusalem. But three seconds later, we stopped. The moon was almost full and we could make out the outlines of tents on both sides of the road. When we realized what we'd walked into, it was too late to turn back. That's when I smelled the tobacco.

"Well, well," said a voice behind us.

We spun around. A man was standing right outside the gate, leaning against the wall where we couldn't see him. In his fingers glowed the ash of a cigarette.

"Look who couldn't sleep," said the dark silhouette, tossing the cigarette away and reaching for the sword that hung on his back.

We'd walked right into the camp of the men of Hazim al-Arabah.

CHAPTER 17

At last Apollus, Ryan, and I had a moment to ourselves. The elders of the village, along with Lamanai and Kux-Wach, and even the old shaman, Kanalha, had all departed for the night and left us to sleep in the place of honor, the shaman's house at the top of the hill. Despite the whirlwind events of the last forty-eight hours, we were still determined to stave off sleep for a few more minutes. Our minds were still reeling with the revelation that had come out of our meeting that evening—the casual mention of a Nephite commander slated for sacrifice in four short days in the central square of Tikal, one of whom was said to be named Moroni-Iqui-Mahucatah, the son of Mormon.

I thought about the names Kanalha had attached on the end: Iqui-Mahucatah, or Wind Traveler. No such names had ever been mentioned in the Book of Mormon. Then again, why would they have been? The prophets were always saying how they avoided talking about history and tried to focus on spiritual themes. Surely there were millions of things about the Nephites that Mormon never explained. The more I thought about it, the more the name made sense. At first I might have thought it meant that Moroni ran very swiftly. Although this may have been true, I sensed that it meant something more. That Moroni's *way of life* was like the wind. In other words, that he never stayed for long in the same place. This not only would have described his life as a child, when upheavals and wars constantly kept his family moving about, but it would also describe his life until the day he died.

That is, it *would* describe his life if he weren't beheaded in four days in the city of Tikal.

"Do you really think it's the same Moroni?" asked Ryan.

"It *has* to be," I said. "How many people named Moroni could possibly be the son of a great Nephite war general named Mormon?"

"But they said this man was slated to die," said Apollus.

"He *can't* die," I declared. "One day this man is going to deposit the gold plates of the Book of Mormon in the Hill Cumorah in New York. He's going to appear as an angel at the bedside of Joseph Smith and show him where it's hidden."

"Then somehow something is going to happen that will prevent that ritual in Tikal from taking place," said Ryan. "We don't need to worry about it."

"*Don't need to worry about it?*" I was nearly hysterical. "What do you mean we don't need to worry about it? Don't you guys realize what might be happening here? Why we might have been brought to this very place and time? Why the people of this village may think that we're gods? *We might have been put here to* rescue *him!*"

Ryan let this statement reverberate and he turned a little pale. "That's crazy! We're just tourists here. Just passing through. We don't have the ability to change history. With or without us, things will go on exactly the way that they're supposed to." His expression changed. "Won't they?"

"Are you willing to take that chance?" I asked.

That put ice down his back. Even as I asked the question, it seemed to send a ripple of urgency throughout my soul. It had the same effect on Apollus.

"If I have learned anything as a Christian," Apollus said, "it is that nothing happens without a purpose. How far is this place, Tikal?"

"Wait, wait, wait!" said Ryan. "Let me get this straight. You think we may have been put here at this place and time to stage a rescue of Moroni and the other Nephite prisoners?"

"Yes," I said. Then less boldly, "Maybe. I don't know."

"Just how do you propose that we do that?"

I suddenly felt befuddled. "I don't know that either. But I think we have to try."

It was time for the Roman to chime in. "I'll tell you how we do it. They believe we're *gods*. We can ask these people to help us with almost anything. Tomorrow when Lamanai makes his announcement about being the heir to the Lamanite throne, we will declare that his first act as king should be to organize a rescue party."

"I think Ryan should declare it," I said. "He's the one they seem to respect the most."

"But I'm not Kukalcan!" he exclaimed. "In fact, I think Kukalcan is another name for the Savior."

"I think you're right," I confirmed. "But it's a name whose meaning has obviously been changed and corrupted by the Lamanites over the last two hundred years. If Lamanai and the elders think you're Kukalcan, it may help us to get everyone to rally around the idea of rescuing the Nephite prisoners."

"I can't believe you're saying this," said Ryan. "Wasn't it you who only a few hours ago had a major problem with pretending to be gods?"

I pondered this. He had a point. This whole thing still didn't sit well with my conscience. Then an idea flashed in my head. A wonderful, enlightening idea!

"Then we'll use all of this to point these people back to the *real* Kukalcan. We'll teach them about Jesus Christ! Oh, this is perfect! *Inspired* even! For all I care they can go on calling you Kukalcan. Hey, it's just a name. But tomorrow you'll tell them that you're only a servant of Jesus Christ. You've come to bring them back into the fold like lost sheep. Don't you see it? This whole thing might be the greatest opportunity we could ever imagine!"

"I don't know," said Ryan nervously. "We'd be doing it under false pretenses. This is sacred stuff. They think I'm a *real god!*"

"We will let that perception diminish," said Apollus. "I think it will diminish anyway, whether we want it to or not."

"I think Apollus is right," I agreed. "It's just a matter of time before they figure out how human we really are. And as the idea of our godhood fades, we'll be able to replace it with something far more glorious—a testimony of the Savior! Oh, this is wonderful!"

At last we doused the torches and settled ourselves upon our mats and under our soft cotton blankets to sleep. But in the darkness of the ancient night, the more intimidating all of my aspirations began to seem. Did I really think that we could convert these people and convince them to rescue Moroni? It's not like it was the first impetuous idea I'd ever had. Hadn't it been my idea to save the gospel of Matthew? Still, this objective seemed more ambitious than all the rest. It could only be done with God's help, I decided. But as I'd said before, succeed or fail, I felt we had to try.

A part of me just wanted to go home. What if we were stuck here? What if going home was impossible now? Then I scolded myself. Hadn't I learned anything from our other adventures? God was in control. Nothing could change that fact.   As this idea settled over my mind, I was soon fast asleep.

Sometime in the night, my eyes popped open wide. I felt someone's body snuggling up against my back. At first I thought either Ryan or Apollus was getting way too fresh. But then I heard both of them breathing in front of me. The alternative suddenly seemed much more disturbing. Could it be Kanalha or one of the other villagers?

The only light that entered the room was that of the stars and the dim glow of the coals from the hearth outside. Cautiously I reached back and felt the person's body. But my fingers clutched a handful of fur. It was an *animal* lying against me!

My touch caused it to release a low snarl. I stiffened. It was a *jaguar!* Was it the same black-furred beast that had licked Ryan's hand? If it wasn't the tame jaguar we'd met that afternoon, the next thing I was going to feel was its claws ripping off my head! What was a girl supposed to do upon finding an uninvited jaguar lying next to her? That was easy. *Absolutely nothing.* I lay there without moving another muscle, my heart pounding.

"Meagan, are you all right?"

It was Apollus. I guess I shouldn't have been surprised that the low growl had awakened the Roman Centurion.

"Yes," I whispered. "I'm okay. It's just Huracan."

"The *jaguar?*"

"Shhh! It's all right. I'm okay." Which was the same thing as saying, *please don't make any sudden moves.*

But Apollus arose and came over beside me. He looked down at the reclining jaguar. I rolled over as well, and the beast's shiny black coat seemed to draw in the light from the hearth fire and stars. So did its eyes, open now to watch us. Apollus knelt by its head. Slowly, he reached out to touch it.

As his hand began to scratch the back of its ear, the jaguar immediately closed its eyes in pleasure. I reached out as well and carefully began to stroke its fur. The creature rolled onto its back, its legs sticking up in the air like a great big pussycat. It started *purring!* And if you've never heard a jaguar purr I'll just compare it to an idling motorcycle. I was surprised. I'd heard that big cats didn't purr. Maybe it was more like a continuous low growl. I laughed softly, still awestruck that such a ferocious predator could be acting like this. I smiled at Apollus and shook my head.

"It must make it a habit to come in here and sleep with Kanalha every night," I speculated.

"I've only seen one other animal behave like this," said Apollus. "When I was a child my father took me to the estate of a senator at Puteoli. He had a whole menagerie of wild and dangerous animals. But the gem of his collection was a leopard that he had raised since it was a kitten. The animal had been born to a fighting leopard at the circus in Rome."

"Extraordinary," I said as I rubbed its belly.

"Yes," Apollus agreed.

We continued to pet the jaguar in silence, practically lulling it off to sleep. At one point I met Apollus's eyes. The thought struck me that he was sort of like this jaguar. Ferocious and lethal, yet under the right circumstances, as tame as a kitten. It was an odd thought and I broke my gaze abruptly. I was grateful for the dimness of the light or Apollus would have seen me blushing.

It occurred to me that this was actually the first time that we'd been alone together since his return. Ryan was still present, of course, but he was sleeping the sleep of the dead, so it was just *like* being alone.

"So," said Apollus, "are you betrothed to this young man, Ryan Champion?"

"Of course not," I said. "We've only been dating for a couple of months."

"Dating," Apollus repeated, as if this idea was still quite foreign to him. "But are you in love with him?"

Apollus certainly hadn't lost his ability to shoot questions right between the eyes. At first it took me off guard. Just the sound of it coming from the lips of Apollus struck me as completely absurd. A familiar pain welled up in my chest. How could he have asked me that? After all we'd been through. After all that we had shared.

I continued to scratch Huracan's belly and replied, "I care about Ryan a great deal. Just like I care for you."

"I see," he said succinctly, as if I'd resolved the matter for him. "Well . . . I'm glad for you."

I couldn't believe it. Was he really so willing to give up? Did he feel nothing for me? I suppose he'd already proven that by how long he'd been gone. Anger began percolating inside me—anger that I'd repressed for two years. It was all I could do to keep it from exploding.

But I couldn't stop myself from saying bluntly, "No. I *don't* think you see, Apollus. I don't think you see at all."

"Don't I?" he asked. "Then why don't you enlighten me?"

Unexpectedly my anger melted and I felt vulnerable. "Why did you go away for so long, Apollus? Didn't you . . . think about me?"

"I thought about you all the time. But . . ."

"Yes?"

Unexpectedly, his hand stopped scratching Huracan. It slid down and softly laid itself over my wrist. He gazed into my eyes. Then, as if he was speaking to a child, he said, "I felt it wasn't appropriate for me to return."

"That was a stupid thing to think." I'd wanted to say it with a punch in my voice, but it came off sounding a little breathless. This was the first time he'd really touched me since his return. I was afraid he'd feel how strongly my heart was beating in the pulse of my hand.

"I suppose I felt it would be unfair to intrude into your life," he added.

"Don't you think I should be the one to decide about that?"

"You were very young when we last met. I felt I was making the best decision for us."

"That's still how you see me, isn't it? A foolish young girl who can't make up her mind about what she wants or what's right."

"Not foolish," Apollus said. "Never foolish. But . . . young."

"Well, in case you haven't noticed, I'm almost as old now as you were when we first met. And my feelings for you haven't changed."

"What feelings are those?" Almost aimlessly, his hand moved up my arm until he touched my shoulder.

I could have yanked his tongue out. "Man, you can be dense! What do you *think* my feelings are?"

"I think . . . you still may not see things as they are."

"And how is that?"

His eyes saddened, and he touched my cheek with the back of his hand. I closed my eyes to relish the feeling. Then I reached up and grasped that hand, pressing it even closer.

"We come from different worlds, Meagan," he continued. "I could never give to you what someone like Ryan could give you."

"So we're from different centuries! What would that matter in the eternal scheme of things?"

He drew back his hand. "I can see that another thing about you hasn't changed. You still don't think very practically."

"And you do? Don't you believe in love, Apollus? Don't you think that if two people hold the same values and beliefs and are really and truly in love, that everything will work out?"

He couldn't seem to stop looking at me. Then, acting on an impulse that he couldn't contain, he leaned in and kissed me. I was shocked! Apollus was *kissing me!* He held my head in the palms of his hands. But just as I was about to become lost to all reality, he pulled back, released me, and moved away.

He looked at the ground and snorted mockingly, "Everything will work out. Those are women's thoughts. Women are often blind to the truth of things."

I felt utterly embarrassed and resentful. "Well, excuse me for being a woman. I happen to think my way of looking at it is the only *clear* perspective that there is. You could *use* some of that clarity, Apollus. *You're* the one who's hopelessly blind if you can't figure out how simple things really are."

He huffed. "Simple? How is it simple?"

No, no, no. He wasn't going to make me say it. I was not going to let him off that easy. "You're just gonna have to go back to school, Centurion. Start over with two plus two."

He smiled slightly, his eyes glistening in the starlight. "I fear I'm not very good at math. But I suppose . . . as long as you are the teacher."

He was making fun of me! He knew how attracted I was to him and he found it hilarious! "Don't count on it," I said curtly. "You may have to deal with a grouchy old substitute."

He laughed a little, and then sighed longingly, as if this little parlay of words hadn't changed his perspective one bit. "In case you couldn't tell, little one, the most difficult part for me is that my feelings for you haven't changed either." It almost sounded like a warning.

"You haven't been listening," I said. "It's not that difficult. It's not difficult at all."

"I'm afraid it's you who hasn't been listening. But I forgive that. It's the weakness of your sex."

My head came up, my eyes like Medusa, desperately wishing this man would turn to granite so I could beat on him with a hammer. "You really are a stupid man. But that's the weakness of *your* sex!"

Ryan stirred. Huracan snarled. I decided I'd better lower my voice. In fact, I decided this conversation should end. I turned away from him, draping my arm across the jaguar's black neck, and shut my eyes.

"Meagan, wait—"

"Go back to bed, Apollus."

"Please. I'm sorry. What I said was . . . rude. The truth, if you really must know, is that I—"

"Forget it. Not interested. Conversation over. Good night."

Oh, what a meathead he was! Why did I have to give my heart to such a cretin? Still, as I fell back to sleep with Huracan's purr buzzing in my ears, I felt a sense of satisfaction. At least I'd finally admitted to myself how I still felt—the same way I'd felt for two long years. But why did such feelings have to be coupled with such pain? That was love, I guessed, whether I liked it or not. A part of me must have still liked it, because as I drifted off into slumber, I heard Apollus finish his sentence in my dreams: *The truth, if you really must know, is that I love you, Meagan, more than I could ever love anyone else in this world or a million other worlds. And I could never let you go again.*

* * *

When I awakened the next morning, Huracan was gone. But outside the stone house we could hear dozens of mumbling voices. Some were groaning, as if in pain.

"What's going on?" asked Ryan, only half awake.

Apollus was already up and standing over by the doorway. After he took in the scene outside, he turned back to us and said, "I think we're in trouble."

I took a look myself. There must have been a hundred people—all of them lined up in a long row down the pathway of the hill. The sick, the lame, the infirm. The first one in line was a mother with a little girl who was propped up by a feeble makeshift crutch. Behind her was a blind man, helped along by his teenage son. Apollus was right. We were in *big* trouble.

The three of us stood at the side of the doorway, peeking out just enough to keep from being seen. Ryan's mouth was gaping. His hair was going in all directions from having slept on it. He looked about as much like a god as a hobo in a train yard. And he also looked scared to death.

"What do they all want?" he asked, dreading the answer.

"Isn't it obvious?" said Apollus, offering no comfort.

I'd never seen a person break out in a cold sweat as suddenly as Ryan at that instant. "They want me to *heal them? I can't!* What are we going to do?"

"You're the great Kukalcan," said Apollus. "You better think of something fast."

This was it, I thought. The moment we'd all been dreading. The jig was up. We were about to be revealed for the charlatans that we were. I guess this scene shouldn't have shocked me. Undoubtedly the best known legend about Kukalcan would have been how he had healed the sick, given sight to the blind, and caused the lame to walk. Was it any wonder that they had all gone home last night to gather up their sick children? Or that they had spread the word to their relatives that the great healer had returned? Some of these people had probably been traveling half the night to get here.

Ryan backed into the corner. "They're going to kill us. There's no getting around it. When they realize I can't do anything for them, they'll tear us apart!"

"I knew this whole thing was going to blow up in our faces," I ranted. "Didn't I tell you?"

"Okay! Fine!" cried Ryan. "So what are we going to do *now?*"

"Why *can't* we heal them?" asked Apollus innocently.

"*What?*" Ryan was beside himself. "Are you serious? In case you haven't noticed, Apollus, I am not a god!"

"But we have been given the Savior's power, haven't we?" Apollus turned to me. "Have we not been given His power?"

It took me a moment to recover and see what Apollus was driving at. I knew that Apollus had been ordained an Elder back in Ephesus.

It had been kind of a whirlwind thing a few days after his baptism. In modern times such an ordination wouldn't have occurred. They'd have waited until he was a member for at least a year. But in 73 A.D. things had worked a little differently. I think there was a feeling in the Church at Ephesus that the days of having the priesthood among them were numbered. Thus, converts were moved along faster than normal. The fact that Apollus was a Roman Centurion might have influenced them as well. Apollus did in fact hold the Melchizedek Priesthood. I felt sure Ryan did too. I'd seen the oil vial on his key chain. But I thought I better ask.

"Are you an Elder, Ryan?"

"Huh?" he asked, still a little flustered. "Yeah. Sure. Dad—my father—ordained me this spring. But Meagan, get a grip! We're talking about performing *miracles* here! I can't perform miracles!"

"Why not?" I asked.

"*Why not?* Meagan, do you even know what you're saying—?"

"Okay, okay," I interrupted. "I'm just trying be rational here. I understand our doubts and fears. But Apollus is right. You have His power. The Savior healed the sick by using the same priesthood that your father gave to you."

"But I don't have His—! I couldn't even *begin* to—"

"Have you ever performed a blessing?"

"Not really. No."

"But there's a vial on your key chain."

"My little brother gave me that. I've never used it."

"You've never given a priesthood blessing?"

"Give me a break! I've only been an Elder for five months! I'm not even sure how it goes."

"*I* know how it goes," I said. "Is there oil in that vial?"

"I think so. But not enough for all these people."

"It doesn't take much. Apollus can assist you."

Apollus raised his eyebrows. "I can?"

"I can't believe this!" I gruffed. "I'm here with two guys and I'm the only one who knows anything about the Priesthood!"

"I *know* about the Priesthood," said Ryan. "I know enough to know that if we go out there and try to bless these people when they think I'm a god, it would be the most sacrilegious thing we could possibly do.

They're supposed to put their faith in Jesus Christ, not in me."

"Then I suggest you do what we talked about last night," I declared. "Their faith is going to be like the faith of a child. You have to tell them that your power comes from Jesus Christ and Heavenly Father."

"How do I do that?"

"How? There's only one way. You just do it."

Ryan pursed his lips in determination. But then he seemed overwhelmed again. He closed his eyes and shook his head. "I can't do this. I have no . . . no . . . I'm *nobody!* I'm an eighteen-year-old kid from Provo, Utah! *I can't do this.*"

Suddenly I was overcome with sympathy. For all my bravado, I was sure if I'd been in Ryan's position, I'd have felt just as terrified. "Before we go out there, I suggest we kneel down and say a prayer."

There were no objections. The three of us knelt down in the corner of the stone building. Instead of just one of us saying it, all *three* of us said it. The prayer began with me, and then Ryan, and finally Apollus, but I think the spirit of the words that were expressed by Apollus summed it up best.

In all humility, the Roman warrior drew a deep breath and began, "Father in Heaven, grant us, your servants, the greatness of your power. I am not a perfect man. I am weak and I've made many errors. I have been angry with the gods—with *You*—as when I lost my mother, and Allia, and finally, my father. But I know that You love me." His voice broke slightly, but he was determined to go on. "And I know you're there, and I'm sure that you hear us. And I also know that you know how much these people need your blessing. If you let us bless these people, I promise we will do everything we can do to give you the glory, and tell them all about you. I make this pledge with my life. In the holy name of your Son, Jesus Christ. Amen."

We opened our eyes and studied each other's faces. I could tell our hearts were still beating fast, but there was also a calmness in the room. If that calming Spirit hadn't been present, I'm sure I couldn't have gone through with this.

"All right," said Ryan. "Let's go."

The moment that we emerged from the stone house, everyone all the way down the hillside began bowing all the way to the ground, like a long line of dominos. There were more people now. It appeared that the whole village had gathered on the hill. I saw Lamanai, and Kanalha, and the village mayor, Jolom. I also saw Kux-Wach sitting off to the side, one knee drawn up to his chest, looking as cocky as a rooster. He seemed to fully anticipate that our charade was about to be exposed.

Ryan waved his arms and reminded the people, "No, no! Don't kneel to us. It's like we told you yesterday. It's not necessary to kneel."

Slowly, the people started to rise.

Jolom approached. "Great Kukalcan, many of our sick and injured have gathered to seek healing at your hand. Our shaman, Chilan Kanalha, has done all that he can for them. They require the power of Kukalcan."

Ryan looked over at me, as if for encouragement. I nodded to him. He turned again and faced the gathering. "The kind of power that you're looking for this morning is a power that I don't possess. At least not of myself."

That caused a stir among them. Kux-Wach got a smug grin.

"If I have any power at all, it's because that power was given to me."

The murmuring stopped.

"It was given to me by the God that I worship. The true God of this world. His name is Jesus Christ. He's the God of *all* of us. Without Him, I don't have any power at all."

I could hear the people testing the name on their tongues—"Jesus Christ." Some of them looked confused, including the mayor, Jolom.

"But you are Kukalcan," Jolom said. "There is no power greater than Kukalcan."

Ryan shook his head. "No. That's not true. I'm not a god. We're not supernatural beings. At least not how you think. Yes, it was a miracle that brought us here. But we're flesh and blood, just like you. You can call me whatever you like. But I am a servant of Jesus Christ. I know that many of you have come here seeking a blessing. And I'd be honored to give you one. That is, *Apollus* and I would be honored. But it's very important that everyone here realize that if you are healed . . . or helped, or made more comfortable in any way, it won't be my power that causes it to happen. It will be the power of Christ. He was born into the world in a land far away, and when He died, His sacrifice healed the world of all sin. He was resurrected from the dead and by His resurrection He made it possible for all of us, if we repent of our mistakes, to live with Him in heaven. If you are healed, it won't be from anything I do. It will be because of your faith and belief in *Him*."

The people continued staring up at Ryan, a little perplexed, but nevertheless with faces full of solemn reverence. Suddenly I wondered to myself if I had ever seen a gathering of people with so much faith in their eyes.

"Can you do that?" Ryan asked the people again. "Can you put your faith in Jesus Christ?"

They looked at one another, seeming to agree among themselves that they would be willing to do this.

At that moment the old shaman, Kanalha, spoke up. "If Kukalcan says that his power comes from this God, Jesus Christ, we will believe it. We will believe it because Kukalcan has said it."

Ryan smiled. I was smiling as well, but I confess that inside I was a bundle of nerves. Only Apollus looked perfectly calm, his chin erect and confident. I could see Ryan's hand shaking as he reached into his pocket to find the vial of olive oil on his key chain. He came over to me and asked again quietly, "You know how it goes?"

I nodded, running it through my mind to be sure. I'd listened to Jim and Uncle Garth give numerous blessings over the last year. I'd received one myself when I had the flu last winter. "First you state the person's name. Then you state your authority. Then you say the blessing. No, wait. First you *anoint* and seal the anointing—let's just do one and I'll walk you through it word for word."

We looked across the anxious crowd one last time. My eyes took in the first person in line—the little girl with the homemade crutch under her arm. There was a bandage on her leg. It appeared that she had cut it open somehow, and by the looks of it, the cut had become infected. The poor thing was flush with fever. I thought about how hard it must have been for her to make this climb. I thought of telling Ryan to say something to everyone about how they shouldn't expect immediate miracles. I felt he should tell them that it might take time for the blessing to have any effect. I kept my mouth shut. There really was nothing more to add. What happened now was in God's hands.

The three of us approached the little girl. Her large brown eyes looked up at Ryan in awe, and a little fear. She was clearly in a lot of pain.

Ryan took the oil vial off of his keychain and unscrewed the tiny lid. He turned to Apollus. "You want to . . . anoint?"

At last the tough Roman betrayed a twinge of nervousness. "What do I—?"

"Don't worry," I assured him. "I'll tell you what to say."

So Apollus took the vial. I had the little girl seat herself upon a stone. The girl's mother backed away, as if to give the miracle a little more room to occur.

"Anoint her right on the crown of her head," I told Apollus.

"Just a drop," said Ryan. "In fact, *less* than a drop. We have a lot of people to bless."

That was an understatement. The amount that Apollus actually used was hardly visible, but it was there. He placed both hands upon the child's head."

I knelt down to her eye level. "What's your name, honey?"

"Copal'in," she replied.

"Copal'in?" I repeated. "That's a beautiful name."

She tried to smile, but it was feeble.

I told Apollus to state her name, and he did. I told him to say: "By the authority of the Holy Melchizedek Priesthood which I hold, I anoint you with this oil which has been consecrated for the healing of the sick, in the name of Jesus Christ, Amen."

He repeated each phrase after I pronounced it, and then Ryan stepped in. The blessing began.

After Ryan had repeated her name, stated his authority, and sealed the blessing, he paused for a long time. I cracked open one eye to steal a peek. His expression looked intense, utterly absorbed, trying so hard to be in tune with the Bestower of miracles. Just by that intensity I realized that Ryan was no longer thinking about himself. He was no longer concerned about his own fate or the response of the crowd. At this moment he was there for that little girl in pain, and nothing else.

Finally he blessed her. I don't remember the words exactly. But I remember how humble it sounded. How sincere. And I remember distinctly that he blessed her to be healed. No mincing of words. No mention of any conditions. "Be healed," was what he said. "By the power of Jesus Christ, be healed."

When the hands of the two Priesthood holders came away from her head, the gathering was dead silent. Ryan's eyes were sparkling with moisture. I watched the little girl's face. I wasn't sure what I expected to see. I don't think I expected her to leap up and run into her mother's arms. But I expected something. And I was not disappointed.

She smiled. Copal'in rolled her head back. She rolled it back so far that Ryan and Apollus would have been upside down—and she smiled. This time it wasn't feeble, and most significant of all, it wasn't full of pain.

Apparently her expression hadn't disappointed the crowd either. I heard murmurs of delight and I saw tears—particularly in the eyes of her sweet mother. She came forward and wrapped the little girl in her arms, but she couldn't take her eyes off Apollus and Ryan. Neither could the young girl.

"Thank you," the mother whispered.

Ryan shook his head. "Remember not to thank me. You must thank Jesus Christ."

"Will you thank Him for me?" she asked.

"He should hear it from you," said Ryan. "I promise you that He will listen."

The little girl finally stood. Should I have felt suspense? Would she really walk? For some reason this was hardly a concern in my mind. Whether she walked or not almost didn't matter. A miracle had taken place here—*was* taking place here. And it seemed to me that it went much deeper than a little girl's wounded leg. Suddenly I felt more honored to be here—right here, right now, on this very spot—than any other place I'd ever been. It hardly seemed important whether the little girl walked without her crutch or not.

But she did.

And as she and her mother began descending the hill, I didn't see any hint of pain. My heart lifted, expanded, and swelled over with gratitude.

Next in line was the blind man. He was so excited that he could hardly stand still as his son held his hand. He kept asking his son questions—wanting a blow-by-blow description of all that was taking place. I'd felt sure that when it became this man's turn my heart would sink. An infected leg was one thing, but blindness?

To my surprise, my heart *didn't* sink. I only felt anticipation. Apollus and Ryan looked as if they felt exactly the same. As they laid their hands upon the blind man's head, they hardly needed me to help them with the words—only on the part where the anointing had to be sealed. As Ryan began this second blessing, there was hardly a pause in his voice.

Here again, I had no idea what to expect. I think if I'd had a chance to think about it too long, I might have hinted to Ryan that he should search the Spirit for different words. That perhaps he should bless this man only with greater understanding of the handicap that he had been given. That the Spirit might simply grant him a surer knowledge of how this infirmity had actually *blessed* his life in ways he couldn't comprehend. How it had given him insights and strengths that he couldn't have gained any other way. But those were not Ryan's words.

"Be healed," he said. "In the name of Jesus Christ, be healed."

As to what happened next, I can hardly speak of it even now. All I can testify is this: It wasn't us. It wasn't Ryan. It wasn't Apollus, and it certainly wasn't me. It was *them*. And it was *Him*, our Savior. The *people* brought about the miracle. Their unquestioning faith. So meek. So childlike. So perfect. It was a kind of faith that I don't think I could have summoned for myself. At least not before this day. I knew too much. That is, I *thought* I knew too much. That is, I *know* I thought I knew too much. But not these villagers. They didn't seem to carry any of that kind of pride. All of their lives they had been brought up to trust what they couldn't see. All they needed was someone to point them to the right source of power. Of course this person had to be someone they could believe and trust. Today that was Ryan and Apollus. And only God can understand why the miracles were allowed to happen.

All I knew was that after the blessing that man could see. For the first time in I don't know how many years, those optic nerves filled with light and began to register shapes, shadows, and colors. He let out a whoop of joy, embraced his son, and danced a cloud of dust around his feet. Like everyone else, my own eyes overflowed. Unstoppable. Ryan's reaction was the same. That eighteen-year-old kid from Provo, Utah. That newly ordained holder of the Melchizedek Priesthood—by the grace and power of Jesus Christ, he'd been an instrument in God's hands. It occurred to me that back home there were a million others like him. Oh, the power of the youth of Zion! If only they knew it. If only they could grasp it.

Tears came for Apollus too, that unconquerable Roman. He held it back as long as he could, but in the end he was utterly defenseless.

One by one the people were blessed. But I'll say it right now, not everyone was healed. At least not right away. Sometimes Ryan and Apollus did *not* declare the words, "In the name of Jesus Christ, be healed." Sometimes there were conditions. Sometimes they said the healing would take time. But in every case the words pierced deeply into the villagers' hearts. Whether or not Ryan or Apollus understood why they gave the blessing that they gave, the *person* seemed to understand, and that was all that mattered. In every case they nodded and wept, and appeared to know without a shadow of a doubt that the message was from the Holy Spirit.

I'm not sure how many miracles I witnessed that day. At least a dozen that were as direct and wonderful as the little girl and the blind man. For the others, only time would tell. The most common ailment was actually some kind of fever that caused the person to sweat and shake. If I ventured a guess, I'd have said it was malaria, but I wouldn't have known for sure. In every case the blessing stopped the convulsions, but many of them still had to be carried back down the hill on the stretchers that had brought them. Still, there was always an expression of gratitude toward Ryan, and frequently a shout of praise to Jesus Christ. This brought us the most satisfaction of all.

The Spirit was so powerful, so all-encompassing, that I couldn't have conceived how anyone would not have been affected. But there was one. Throughout the entire event, Kux-Wach observed the proceedings from his place on the hill without comment. His face was often filled with wonder, but never with faith. Or at least, not faith in Christ. I can't really explain how I knew that. Maybe it was the hint of disapproval that I caught in his eyes from time to time. It occurred to me that Kux-Wach had never stated that he didn't believe we were gods. He'd never questioned Lamanai's word that we had emerged from the Underworld. What Kux-Wach doubted—what he had *always* doubted—was the source of our power. The purpose of our visit. To him, there was nothing good that could come from it.

But who could deny all the goodness that we were accomplishing that day? It took my breath away! Was this how it had felt to Peter, and Paul, and Ammon, and the Sons of Helaman, and Joseph Smith, and John Taylor, and Wilford Woodruff and all the other great missionaries of history? I felt like we'd been given a sacred glimpse into the all-encompassing power of God, and I never wanted to forget this day as long as I lived.

Toward the end of the morning, with the blessings concluded, the people were called into the village square where Lamanai would make his announcement. Apollus, Ryan, and I sat in the grass behind him, surrounded by dozens of little children. They couldn't seem to get enough of us, especially Ryan and Apollus. If nothing else, I considered it a great feat to have convinced these people that we were not untouchable gods, but that we were real and personable and that we could give and receive hugs. I don't think we'd completely dispelled the notion that we were supernatural beings. I tried to look at it more as the kind of reverence and respect that one might give a prophet, or even a missionary. In that light I had no problem with their adoration, but I realized that we'd probably have to remind them a hundred more times that we were just flesh and blood, as fragile and vulnerable as any other living thing.

When Lamanai and Jolom took their places in the center of the gathering, the mood was already one of celebration. I don't think any of them could have imagined that something might happen to make this day even better, but they were about to find out.

"People of Seibalche," Jolom began, "there is more to celebrate this day than the arrival of Kukalcan and his companions. With their arrival the time has come to make the most extraordinary announcement. Many of you know young Lamanai, and you know the story of how he came to be a part of the family of Chilan Kanalha. But there is something that you do not know—a great secret that has been kept hidden for six years. After all we have witnessed, how can anyone deny that the time has not fully come to reveal this sacred truth? Men and women of Seibalche, I present to you Eagle-Sky-Jaguar, son of Great Jaguar-Paw!"

Expressions changed throughout the square. At first it was shock. Everyone knew these names and they knew what they meant. A low murmur swept through the people, hastily rising in volume.

"Lamanai is Men-Chan-Balam?" I heard them whisper. "How can it be? A descendant of Yax-Chaac-Xok survived?"

But in no time flat the shock and surprise was replaced by excitement. "Eagle-Sky-Jaguar! It's true! He lives! He's one of us!"

I was afraid the square might turn into a free-for-all. The pitch of jubilation looked like it might erupt into a riot. Only as Lamanai held up his hands and cried, "People! People!" did order begin to be restored.

But with the words he spoke next, the passions of the villagers were inflamed all over again.

"Jolom has spoken the truth. I *am* the son of Jaguar-Paw. I was present when the warriors of Fire-Born marched into the city of Tikal. I watched as the barbarians of Teotihuacan raped and killed my mother and sisters. Today is a new dawn for the people of the Waterlilies. Spread the word far and wide to all the scattered and downtrodden of the Lamaya in all the forests and hills of the earth! Tell them to prepare for their liberation from the oppressors of the north. Let those who will fight gather as quietly as the midnight Jaguar to this place in the forest and here we will build an army that will contend with the murderers of Spearthrower Owl and his son, Blue-Crocodile. An army that will restore to the throne of Tikal the righteous descendants of Yax-Chaac-Xok for now and many generations to come! The people of the Waterlilies will again rule earth and sky! The Sun has decreed it! The Moon has foretold it! And the wisdom of Kukalcan and his noble companions will guarantee our victory!"

Wow, I thought. Now there was an orator. A natural leader. Even at his young age, he had the soul of a king. But what was that last part again? Kukalcan and his noble companions would guarantee *what?* With all of the wild cheering and chanting I hardly heard it. Did he say we would guarantee *"victory?"* Talk about a change of spirit! Yet it seemed totally natural to these people to blend both emotions into one—a love of God and a love of heritage. A passion for religious devotion and a passion for war. There were only about four hundred people in that square—just the populace of the village along with the visitors who'd brought their sick and infirm. Yet they made the place sound like Times Square on New Year's Eve. Lamanai had made an announcement that people had obviously been hoping and praying for ever since the death of Jaguar-Paw—ever since the invaders from Teotihuacan had captured the throne. There was no way to tell it now, but I sensed that the ripple effect of Lamanai's words was going to turn the Lamanite world upside down. And we were here to see it. Was this a good thing or a bad thing?

Whatever it was, it was clear that Ryan, Apollus, and I had been the catalyst that had brought it about. I didn't like that feeling at all.

But as I looked into Apollus's eyes, I saw a burning flame. This was a nation in bondage, a people who had been abused and enslaved. Nothing stirred the righteous indignation of a man like Apollus more than an oppressed people who had been conquered by a tyrant king. The cry of freedom had aroused feelings in him that had lain dormant now for over two years. As for myself, I'd never wanted so badly to go home.

But then I remembered Moroni—Moroni the Nephite commander. Moroni, the man who was marked for sacrifice in four days.

I turned to Ryan. "You have to tell them now. You have ask them to help us rescue the Nephite captives. There may never come a better time. You have to do it now!"

Ryan nodded, his eyes swimming in uncertainty. With an unexpected burst of energy, he leaped to his feet, almost as if he decided that if he waited any longer he might change his mind. Apollus stood as well. If a military action was to be discussed, he wanted to be in the thick of it. As he and Ryan stood beside Lamanai, the effect was an awesome thing to observe. In three seconds the place was perfectly silent. What would the servants of this god, Jesus Christ, have to say about Lamanai's announcement? They waited with bated breath.

Ryan looked nervous. Far more nervous than when he was dispensing the blessings of the Priesthood.

He began, "Listen to me. Listen to both of us. We . . . didn't expect all of this. If the time has come for all that Lamanai has described, then he's right. It *is* a great day. A great time for all your people. But there's something we have to say. Maybe there's a way . . . a way that your cause can receive the approval . . . I mean, the *sanction* of God." He pointed upward, as if the people might have forgotten whom he was talking about. "Actually, I shouldn't say that. I don't know for sure. But I *do* know that right now the Lord needs your warriors for an important mission. He needs you to help us rescue one of His great men.

One of His prophets. A man who will one day became an instrument in God's hands to bring about a marvelous work and a wonder. One day he will change the history of the world . . . and bring salvation to the people of the earth . . ."

He paused, groping about for the right words.

"Who is this man?" asked Riki-Kool on the front row.

Apollus perceived that Ryan might need some help. So he stepped up and said, "This man is a Nephite."

The gathering came alive with urgent whispers.

Apollus continued, "He is a prisoner in the city called Tikal. A man who is to be killed in three days. His name is . . ."

He looked at me. He didn't want to pronounce it incorrectly. I took the cue and stood.

"His name is Moroni the Wind Traveler," I proclaimed.

"The captives from Tehuantepec!" someone whispered loudly.

Lamanai gave Apollus and Ryan a puzzled look. "The son of Mormon? Our old enemy?"

"Yes," said Ryan. "But he's *not* your enemy. Not if you believe in Jesus Christ. Not if you have faith in the priesthood that healed so many of your people. Moroni is a prophet. A servant of Jesus Christ who is far greater than I am. He may even help you in your quest to drive out the invaders."

That caught Lamanai's attention. His eyes brightened. The village elders also began ruminating upon the possibilities.

Jolom said to Lamanai, "If the Nephites were to become our allies . . ."

Quillkiah exclaimed, "The Nephites control the narrow pass to the lands northward!"

"But they are our *enemies!*" cried a new voice. As I might have expected, it was Kux-Wach. "Our fathers swore an oath in blood to destroy them!"

"Those were different times!" declared the old shaman, Kanalha, in a feeble voice. Once again, he stood at odds with his son. "They were different days. In our quest to drive out the armies of Fire-Born and Spearthrower Owl, the Nephites and the son of Mormon may become our closest friends."

Kux-Wach stood defeated. There was nothing more for him to say. The enthusiasm of the crowd was increasing. It was working.

They were going for it. On the other hand, I was very confused. What could all of this mean? I knew full well the ultimate destiny of the Nephites. I knew that in the battle at Cumorah they would fight the Lamanites, and if I remembered right, also the robbers of Gadianton. For all I knew, the Gadiantons and the invaders from Teotihuacan were one and the same. But even if this were true, how did it all fit? How could an alliance between Nephites and the followers of Lamanai make sense in the overall scheme?

All at once I had a chilling recollection of a recent conversation I'd had with eleven-year-old Joshua Plimpton. He'd spoken of changing history, saving the Nephites from their ultimate destruction at Cumorah. Good gracious! Was it possible that Apollus, Ryan, and I were bringing to pass exactly what Joshua had described? It was inconceivable. It was *insane*. Yet here we were witnessing events that might bring about this very conclusion. But what about Moroni? If he were to die in three days, wouldn't *that* change history as well? This whole thing was nuts! Yet even if I'd tried to turn things back to the way they were, I think my voice would have been drowned out in the tide of emotion. It was the tide of destiny.

"We will do as Kukalcan has asked!" shouted Lamanai. "We will gather our warriors and march to Tikal! Moroni and the Nephite captives shall be delivered! Let this be the beginning of our campaign to reclaim our sacred lands! *Let the battle of freedom begin!*"

The cheering elevated to a fever pitch. Apollus and Ryan had their fists in the air along with everyone else. It appeared that my two potential suitors had become united in a noble cause.

Out of curiosity, I searched the crowd for Kux-Wach. I wanted to see his reaction. But Kux-Wach had disappeared. Somehow he'd slipped away. Later I realized that he'd left the village. Where he was headed and what he would do wasn't entirely clear. But it didn't take Lieutenant Columbo to figure out that it wouldn't be good.

The next time I laid eyes on Kux-Wach, he was definitely our enemy.

CHAPTER 18

"Give me the stone," said the darkened figure of Hazim. *"The one around your neck. Give it to me."*

One of his hands was reaching out toward me while the other finished drawing out the long, curved sword off his back.

"Run!" cried Joshua.

My brother didn't wait for me to react. Instead he practically pulled my arm out of its socket. He and Mary decided to run left. I couldn't see why this was any better than running right, but I was glad for their quick action, because my legs had been petrified stiff. Only now they were tripping over each other to keep up.

"Wake up you lazy brutes!" Hazim called to his men. *"The children with the stone are escaping!"*

We were passing right through the middle of six or seven tents. I was sure that everybody inside was fast asleep and couldn't have possibly had enough time to stop us. My problem was that I still hadn't gotten back my balance. Joshua dragged me right through a campfire that wasn't totally burned out. My feet sent up a blizzard of little pink sparks. It was this that finally caused me to sprawl forward onto my face. My hand was torn from Joshua's grip. I fell right smack into the middle of one of the tents.

The tent collapsed and the camel hair canvas folded up around me. Underneath me was the squirming body of a very surprised Bedouin. He must have figured out somehow that I was the prize that Hazim wanted to catch, because he tried to close his arms around me from inside like a Venus Flytrap.

I felt Mary's hands grab under my shoulders, trying to drag me out of the mess. At the same time Joshua was pulling her. With both of them *pulling I managed to free myself, but not before Hazim caught up. The whoosh of his sword cut the air just inches from my head.*

Fortunately, as the man in the tent flopped around, it ended up tripping Hazim. He spilled over, blurting out a terrible curse, his sword clattering on the stones. Joshua, Mary, and I jumped a low stone fence, crossed a vineyard of grapes belonging to the monastery, and fled like wildfire into the night. Glancing back, I thought I saw someone come out of the monastery's front gate, but I couldn't tell who it was. A minute later, as I realized that nobody was pursuing us, I decided it must have been Nicholas. Only Nicholas could've stopped Hazim from coming after us.

We ran down a hill, dodging all the rocks and boulders as best we could in the dark. (It seemed like this land was nothing but rocks and boulders!) At the bottom I smashed through some kind of thorn bush. When I came out the other side, I could still feel slivers in my legs. Still, I kept running with the others. Mary led the way, and using the light of the moon, we met up with the roadway leading to Jerusalem.

We stopped, gasping great gulps of breath. I figured we'd run almost a mile. There were dim fires burning a couple hundred yards off to either side of the road, but I had no desire to check out who was sleeping around them.

"Where . . . do we go . . . now?" I asked breathlessly.

Mary looked toward the walls of Jerusalem. If it wasn't for the moon, I doubt I would've even known there was a city there. A couple of the towers were burning lamps; otherwise it looked as dark as the mountains.

"There," she said. "That's where the stone told us to go. From now on we better follow such instructions exactly."

From here I guessed the walls were still a good mile away. We started marching down the road. I didn't think too much about how special it was to be visiting the city where Jesus had taught, eaten His last supper, and been crucified. I just wanted a soft place to lie down again. But it didn't look like we'd get that anytime soon. A half hour later I think I'd have been just as happy lying on the roadside with a rock under my head, but our fear of Hazim kept us going all the way to the city gate.

But then, to my extreme annoyance, the gate was shut. Jerusalem was closed! *How could anyone close a whole city? The thick swinging doors were bolted from the other side. A lamp was burning in the gate tower. Above it a red flag was flapping in the wind, but that was the only thing stirring.*

We weren't the only ones locked out. On both sides of the road leading up to the gate there must have been fifty people with their camels and donkeys. They all looked fast asleep, their cloaks pulled around them as blankets. Some were even curled up against the stone cliffs that made up that part of the wall. There were a few tents and campfires still burning. I also saw the glowing ash of several cigarettes, so I knew some of them were awake and watching us. No way was I going to sleep out here. How could it have been any less dangerous than at the monastery?

"Hey!" I called up at the tower.

Mary became concerned. "Becky, don't! The city is shut for the night."

"We need to get in there," I said. "It's not safe out here."

Sleeping bodies started moving around and mumbling unkind things.

"There's nothing we can do until morning," Mary whispered.

"I'm with Becky," said Joshua. "I'm not gonna sleep out here."

"Hey!!" Joshua and I both cried at the same time.

Mary put her arms over her head, pacing around in a tizzy. Even though she'd been born a good eighteen hundred years before now, she still felt she had a much better grasp of how things here were supposed to work.

Finally, a voice called down sharply, "Who is it?"

We looked at each other, unsure of what to say. Josh felt he had the perfect response. "We're Americans. And we demand entrance!"

There was no reply.

"Hey!" Josh shouted again. "Did you hear m—!"

Something flashed in the tower, like the reflection of a bowl or pot. Two seconds later the most foul, gross stuff imaginable splashed in my face. It splattered over all of us.

"Ohhhh yuckkkkk!" said Joshua in disgust.

"Shut up Christian dogs!" yelled the man in the tower.

I wiped my face with the back of my hand and smelled it. There was no mistaking what it was. I started to cry. Mary led me away from the gate and down along the city wall.

"Jerks!" Joshua shouted up at the tower. "You guys are jerks!"

"Joshua!" Mary scolded. "Be quiet! Do you want them to come out here with soldiers and weapons?"

I was still sobbing when we found an open place where nobody was sleeping. Mary tried to comfort me. Josh went on and on about their rudeness.

"*There must be a mayor or governor of this town,*" he said. "*Tomorrow I want to lodge a complaint.*"

"*I doubt it would do you any good,*" said Mary. "*I have a feeling this is no longer a land of Christians. Or Jews. They worship the god called Allah.*"

"*That wouldn't make them so mean,*" I said. "*In third grade my best friend was a girl from Pakistan. Her family was Moslem, and they were the nicest people I knew.*"

"*Moslem?*" asked Mary.

"*It's a religion,*" said Joshua. "*They believe in this guy named Mohammed and every year they have to visit this city called Mecca.*"

"*Not every year,*" I said.

"*Well, I don't like them,*" said Joshua. "*They're always throwing rocks and blowing themselves up with bombs.*"

"What? " said Mary.

"*Don't listen to him,*" I told her. "*He doesn't know what he's talking about.*"

Mary turned to Joshua. "*Don't hate people for their beliefs. In Pella I learned what it's like to be hated for that reason.*"

"*Sorry,*" said Josh, scraping his shirt against the wall to wipe off more gunk. "*I just can't believe they wouldn't let us in.*"

"*I'm frightened,*" I whispered.

I snuggled up closer to Mary and my brother. We leaned back against the wall and held each other in the darkness.

"*Maybe you should look in the stone,*" Mary suggested.

"*Yeah, right,*" said Josh sarcastically. "*Maybe it'll tell us how we can run into Hazim again.*"

"*You don't mean that,*" said Mary.

"*How come it told Becky that we should leave the monastery? We nearly got ourselves killed!*"

"*That's not fair,*" said Mary. "*We all prayed about it, and we all got the same answer. I'm sure it would have been far worse if we'd stayed.*"

"*Well then why couldn't the stone have at least told us to take a different escape route?*" asked Josh. "*A way where we wouldn't run smack into Hazim? And how come it keeps telling us to come to Jerusalem? What are we supposed to find here?*"

"*As I remember it,*" said Mary, "*you were the one who was so anxious to come to Jerusalem.*"

"*That was yesterday,*" *said Josh.* "*Now I just wanna go home. It's like the stone won't give us the whole picture. Or else Becky can't quite see all the information.*"

"*You're right,*" *I said.*

"*I am?*" *said Joshua in surprise.* "*Which part?*"

"*The part about the stone not giving us the whole picture,*" *I said.* "*I don't think it's me. I mean, maybe it's me, but I don't think so. The stone tells us a lot, but sometimes it isn't very clear.*"

"*What do you mean?*" *said Josh, sounding angry that we'd ever followed the stone's advice in the first place.*

"*I don't understand,*" *said Mary.* "*Is it just a matter of experience and practice?*"

"*Partly,*" *I said.* "*But it seems like when we were in the cave, and both stones were together in the frames, I could see things a lot clearer.*"

"*I don't get it,*" *said Josh.*

"*It's like things were more in* focus. *As if one of the stones gave me the picture and the other one made the image sharper. Sort of like the difference between using one eye or using both.*"

"*That's just great,*" *said Josh.* "*The other stone is gone forever.*"

"*One eye is still better than being blind,*" *said Mary.*

"*I'm not so sure,*" *said Josh.*

"*No, she's right,*" *I said.* "*I'm* sure *we were supposed to come here. I'm just not sure why. But I'm convinced it has something to do with finding a way home.*"

"*You mean finding a cave that will take us back to the Galaxy Room?*" *asked Mary.*

"*Yeah, sort of.*"

"*But Mary already knows where a cave like that is,*" *said Joshua.*

I shook my head. "*That's just it. One thing I felt sure about when I looked into the stone back at the spring was that Mary's cave doesn't exist anymore.*"

"*Doesn't exist? How can it not exist?*"

"*It was destroyed. Or at least the main tunnel was. An earthquake or something. It happened centuries ago.*"

"*How do you know that?*" *asked Josh.*

"*I saw it. That's all I can tell you. I saw it.*"

"*But you said everything was out of focus.*"

Mary grew impatient. "Joshua, I'm sure she was just giving an analogy. Since you and I don't possess the gift, we should just listen."

"Then I'll try to explain what I know," I began. "Something is supposed to happen here. It's going to happen very soon. I don't know what it is, but it's going to be wonderful. Somehow, while this thing is taking place, the visions in the stone will be crystal clear. That's when I'll know exactly where to go and what to do to get home."

"You still don't have any idea what this event is?" asked Mary.

"Not exactly. But I know if we're not here when it happens—or if I lose this stone—we may never get another chance again. We'll be stuck here forever."

Joshua let out a groan. "Why does it have to be so complicated? It was never this complicated for Dad and Uncle Jim. They just found the cave and it took them home again. Cut and dried."

"It's not the same as it used to be," I said. "The Rainbow Room and the Galaxy Room are one now. Somehow that orb in the ceiling along with the pillar of energy controls it all. It's like living time. Living and breathing. That pillar can send a person to any century or place. But it's all a matter of timing."

"Time is a matter of timing," Josh said sarcastically. "That makes sense."

"Don't tease me," I begged. "I'm serious. Think about what's happened to us. We were sent here. Meagan and Ryan and Apollus were sent somewhere else. And Todd Finlay was sent someplace different altogether. When I touched that pillar yesterday, I knew exactly where it was going to send us. I just wasn't sure what I was looking at until I got here and looked in the stone again."

"But that was only with one stone," Josh reminded me. "Are you really sure it's 1830?"

"Pretty sure," I said hesitantly. "It's very close to that."

"Well, doggone it. That's it," said Joshua. "Tomorrow I'm going to find out exactly what year it is or tear this city apart trying."

"Let me see if I understand," said Mary. "While this important event is happening, you'll look into the stone and receive a clear picture of where we have to go in order to get back?"

"Not just where," I said. "It's also a matter of when. Timing!"

"Right, right," said Mary. "Timing. So you're saying that the stone will tell us where we need to go and when we need to jump in?"

"Exactly," I said. "Jump in. That's it. Otherwise we might end up anywhere during the whole history of the world."

I felt relieved that I was finally able to explain it. But Mary and Joshua looked anything but relieved. They both kind of slumped into themselves, totally overwhelmed by what I'd said. I guess I couldn't blame them. It all sounded very difficult and frightening. Mary especially seemed to look depressed.

"One week," I heard her say very quietly. "Harry was coming home in one week."

It almost surprised me. It was the first time she'd ever mentioned Harry's name, or given some hint of the pain she was feeling. I guess it would have been foolish to think he was ever very far from her thoughts. It made my heart hurt to hear her say it. I wished there was something I could have said to assure them that as long as we stayed here and didn't lose the stone, it was going to be okay, but that wouldn't have been totally truthful. Honestly, I was just as scared as they were.

"Look in the stone again," said Mary. "Please, Becky. Find out if there's anything else we need to know. Any other important details."

I sighed exhaustedly. Of course I would do it—for Mary if nothing else. I was just so tired and I knew the stone would take every extra ounce of energy I had. Still, I put it up to my eye. The night was so dark that I hardly needed to use my hands to block out the light. I just focused on the stone and thought about what Mary had asked me to ask it.

For an instant, I actually felt energized. Right before my eyes began a replay of the magnificent things I'd seen yesterday afternoon—an echo of all those rejoicing people and angels. It was so beautiful, but in addition I gained a little better idea on how soon *this event was going to take place. It was close. Very close. But again, my focus was a little foggy. Only one new piece of information really came to me strongly. So strong that I lowered the stone to think and make sure it made sense.*

"What's wrong?" asked Mary.

"We need to move," I declared.

"Are we in danger?" asked Josh.

"I'm not so sure it's that. It's just that we're in the wrong place. If we don't move, we're going to miss it all."

"Move where?" asked Mary, her voice a little panicky.

I got to my feet and gazed up and down the wall of Jerusalem. One last time I looked into the stone. My eye was still focused on the pearly white surface when I raised my hand and pointed east.

"*That way,*" *I said.*

Without waiting for Joshua and Mary, I began walking eastward along the wall. They caught up quickly. We couldn't walk directly beside the wall the whole way. We started to climb down into a valley. The moon was our only light. We did our best to follow a thin pathway that took us around some very old tombs. Finally we reached a stone-lined pool of water. We washed the rest of the gunk from our faces and clothes as best we could. Then we continued on.

We followed around the wall until we were on the east side of the city, passing through another large cemetery where, even at this late hour, people were still visiting by candlelight. Lanterns lit up another city gate. As with the first gate, there were plenty of sleeping people and camels along both sides of the road. I led Josh and Mary as close to the gate as I felt was necessary. We finally stopped on the left side of the gate, beside a large boulder.

"*This is it,*" *I said.* "*This is where we're supposed to be.*"

"*I don't get it,*" *said Joshua.* "*It's just another city gate.*"

"*But it's the* right *gate. This is where we'll wait.*"

"*How long?*" *asked Mary.*

"*I'm not sure,*" *I said.* "*Not very long.*"

"*What are we waiting for?*" *asked Joshua.*

"*I don't know that either,*" *I said in frustration,* "*but when it happens, I'll know it.*"

I was driving Mary and Josh crazy, but I didn't know what else to do. We huddled close together on the ground like before.

"*Do I have to stay awake?*" *Joshua grumbled.*

"*No,*" *I said.* "*We can all go to sleep now.*"

I wasn't certain about that, but I didn't think I had much choice but to say it. I already felt like I was still walking in a dream. It wouldn't have surprised me if I went to sleep and woke up to find that we'd never left the monastery. We did our best to use each other's arms and shoulders as pillows.

But even though I'd told Mary and Joshua that they could sleep, I wasn't sure I wanted to take this advice for myself. What if I slept too long? What if I missed what was going to happen? I thought of finding some twigs and propping them under the lids of my eyes to keep me awake. But I don't even think that would have worked. One minute I was staring up at the Mount of Olives, and the next my head had drooped and I was dreaming about the roller coasters and Ferris wheels at Lagoon.

Sometime during the night those dreams changed. I started dreaming about something that I hadn't dreamed about since I was a very little girl. It was the Savior. I dreamed about His face, the same way it had been that day in Bountiful when I was three. Details came back to me that I'd entirely forgotten. I remembered how the sky had looked, how the breeze had felt. Most interestingly, I remembered Jesus' prayer on the temple steps just before the angels came down and surrounded Josh and me in a ribbon of fire. Every single word came back. I relived the whole thing. Strangely, when I finally did wake up, I forgot much of it again. But the feeling stayed with me, and it was no less powerful than the feeling I'd had looking into the stone and hearing the angels rejoice. I realized something else. Jesus' prayer was directly related to what was about to occur.

The thing that finally woke me up was somebody chanting out of a bullhorn or something from the top of one of those high, skinny towers inside the city, saying, "Allah is greatest," and calling people to pray. I opened my eyes. It was just before sunrise. I looked toward the Mount of Olives and could barely make out the colors of the trees and rocks and the dark outline of some buildings at the very top.

"Who's yelling?" Joshua mumbled, his eyes still closed, half asleep. I think if he'd had a pillow he would have put it over his head. Eventually he rolled over and konked out again. Mary's eyelids fluttered open too, but after briefly looking around she closed them back up.

Many of the people waiting outside the gate were washing their hands or laying out little square rugs. Some were already standing with their faces pointing south toward Mecca, putting their hands up to their ears and repeating, "Allah is greatest," and praising Allah's name and then kneeling down toward Mecca. I'd never actually seen the Moslems praying before, but I felt sort of rude to be staring.

A few minutes later I heard the squeak of the city gate. A man and a woman were standing just outside it. They led a donkey by the reins and waited as a soldier with a big, curly moustache and wearing an army uniform finished pushing open the two heavy sides. Most of the people finished praying. They put more sticks on the fires that they'd let burn out during the night. The morning air was warm and I smelled coffee.

For some reason my eyes continued to be drawn toward the newly opened gate. I watched the man and woman with their donkey enter beneath the tunnel-like stone arch and disappear into the city. And then I saw someone come out.

It was a man wearing a blue waistcoat and brown trousers. He was a little portly with a square face and hair as red as a fox's tail. I guessed he was thirty-five or so, but what struck me right away was that he was not an Arab. Nor was he a Greek or a Jew like most everybody else around here. Actually, he looked like an American. Or an Englishman. In his hands he carried some sort of case. Something about him completely captivated me. Maybe it was just the way he carried himself. His eyes were bright and he had lots of energy in his step. Not that he was in a great hurry. As he came out of the gate he seemed to breathe in the morning as if it was the most beautiful morning he'd ever seen. But then his eyes locked onto the Mount of Olives and his steps became more determined. The man walked right by me, close enough that I could see his blue eyes. Then he went on down the road without even noticing that we were there.

"Orson," I whispered to myself.

I knew the man's name! It had popped into my head like a camera flash, as if some bit of information that I'd seen in the stone the night before suddenly clicked.

"Orson . . . Hyde."

My whisper wasn't loud enough for the man to hear me, so he didn't turn around. But it was *loud enough to awaken Mary.*

"Did you say something?" she asked.

"That man," I said, pointing. "He's . . . an Apostle!"

Mary turned sharply to see who I was pointing at. He was already quite a ways down the road. I realized that in less than a minute he'd be out of sight. I shook Joshua briskly.

"Joshua, wake up! It's time! We have to go!"

He sat up and joggled his head. "What's wrong? Go where?"

"We have to follow that man!"

Still half groggy, Mary and Joshua got to their feet. Urgently, we started after the red-haired man with the case. As we walked I found myself clutching tightly onto the seerstone in its frame, partly to comfort myself that I hadn't lost it and partly because I felt that I might need it at any instant.

The man walked south, leading us over a small bridge with a gurgling brook underneath it. The road was starting to become busy with people—merchants and farmers who were headed into Jerusalem to sell or trade. Women in long white veils were carrying flowers to the cemetery. We did our best to keep far enough away from the man with the case, and yet I desperately didn't want to lose sight of him.

"Who is he?" Joshua asked. "Where is he going?"

"His name is Orson Hyde," I said, "and he's an apostle of Jesus Christ."

"You know his name?*" he asked in amazement.*

"Yes," I said impatiently. "Hurry!"

He finally left the road and started up a little footpath on the slope of the Mount of Olives. We kept on following. Everywhere we looked were tombs and shrines and little flower gardens. We passed through a grove of some very old, gnarled-looking trees whose branches twisted around at all sorts of odd angles. Some women in colorful shawls and boys in bright, big-buttoned shirts were carefully pruning back the branches. Sometimes there were even caves dug into the sides of the hill with a thick wooden door over the entrance. Elder Hyde paused a short distance up the path and went inside a small gate in a stone wall. After he'd entered, the three of us gathered at the gate and watched. Elder Hyde had gone into a kind of courtyard or garden with several of the same ancient trees.

"Are those olive trees?" whispered Joshua.

Mary nodded. "I've still never seen any tree so beautiful."

I realized there was a sign on the wall. Part of it was written in English. It was light enough now that I could actually read it: Garden of Gethsemane.

My heart went pitter-patter at that. I couldn't say for sure if it was the real *Garden of Gethsemane where Jesus took the sins of the world on Himself, but just reading that sign and thinking about how close I really was sent tingles up and down my back. I tried to imagine the Savior there, kneeling down and praying while his disciples slept outside. For a second I almost thought I could feel the touch of His hand, just like when I was a little girl, and I caught just a hint of that overwhelming feeling of love. Tears came to my eyes and I grabbed my brother's hand. I think he was remembering too. But Mary seemed to be affected the most.*

"So much has changed," I heard her whisper as she wiped a tear. She looked around at the hills and gardens. "And yet so much is just the same."

We watched as Elder Hyde plucked a tiny branch off one of the trees. He looked over his surroundings one more time and shut his eyes. When he opened them again, they were filled with tears too, and I could tell he was thinking a lot of the same thoughts that we were. He didn't seem to want to leave. Nevertheless, he started back toward the gate.

"He's coming right toward us," whispered Joshua.

We looked around anxiously. There was no place to hide. But then I thought, so what? Why should we hide? We couldn't change history by just standing here, could we? The three of us stood off to the side of the gate. Mary hopelessly brushed some of the dirt off her dress and we all stood a little straighter. Elder Hyde came out of the garden. He did a double take as he saw us. We smiled stupidly.

"Good morning," said Elder Hyde, smiling back.

"Good morning," we replied.

His gaze stayed on us another second. I had no idea what he was thinking. No doubt he found it a little weird to see two children and a girl in such peculiar clothing just standing there gawking, but his mind was obviously a long ways away with other thoughts. He nodded good-bye and continued up the side of the hill. We just watched him go.

As soon as he was out of hearing, Joshua asked, "Is he really an apostle?"

I nodded. "He's one of the first apostles ever called. In the latter days, I mean."

"So he knows Joseph Smith?"

"Yup."

"What's he doing all the way over here?"

"I think we're about to find out."

We kept following him up the little path, still keeping our distance.

"Is it time yet?" asked Joshua. "Can you look into the stone?"

"Not yet," I said.

He passed by several shrines and ancient church buildings that were supposedly built over exact spots where this or that event had occurred, or where one or another holy prophet was buried. There was the Sepulchre of the Virgin, the Grotto of the Twelve Apostles, and the tombs of Jacob and Absolom and Jehosophat. I would have loved to have seen them all, but Elder Hyde didn't even pause. Wherever he was going, he seemed determined that nothing else was going to distract him.

The land was spreading out below us in all directions. I turned back once to see the old city. It looked like it was glowing in the first rays of the rising sun. I could even see far to the west a thin blue stripe that could only have been the Mediterranean Sea. When at last we reached the top I even saw the waters of the Dead Sea to the east. It was a gorgeous blue sky. I doubted if Heavenly Father could've created a more perfect day for what was about to take place.

But what was it? What was really about to happen this morning? Elder Hyde made his way along the low stone wall of an old cemetery and found a little hidden grove surrounded by shrubs and bushes. We crept as close as we dared so as not to disturb him. He sat down on a stone and laid his case upon another block of stone in front of him. He opened the case and took out some paper and what looked like a bottle of ink and a feather pen. Then he balanced his elbow on the stone and started to write.

All at once the air seemed calmer. The light breeze that had been blowing through the olive leaves went still. All I was aware of was the sound of my own breathing and the beat of my heart.

We remained there, crouched in the bushes, watching the Lord's Apostle at work. All of us could feel that something tremendous was about to take place, but not until some time later did we begin to realize what it was. Perhaps twenty or thirty minutes passed before Elder Hyde set down his feather pen and gathered up the papers that he'd been writing on. At last the apostle knelt on the stony ground. With no witnesses except God, the Holy Land, and the three of us, he started to pray.

"O Thou! who art from everlasting to everlasting, eternally and unchangeably the same, even the God who rules in the heavens above, and controls the destinies of men on the earth, wilt Thou not condescend, through Thine infinite goodness and royal favour, to listen to the prayer of Thy servant which he this day offers up unto Thee in the name of Thy holy child, Jesus . . ."

The prayer was amazing. He spoke of how he had come to this land out of obedience to a vision. This I understood a little. In fact I could almost feel part of this vision again. Those things that I had seen and felt yesterday as I peered into the stone were coming to pass. Although it may have seemed like we were all alone on top of that hill, I began to sense that there was an audience pressing in all around us. Bigger than I could have possibly imagined.

He continued, "Under the shadow of Thine outstretched arm I have safely arrived in this place to dedicate and consecrate this land unto Thee, for the gathering together of Judah's scattered remnants, according to the predictions of the holy prophets—for the building up of Jerusalem again . . ."

So that was it! He was here to call God's people home! I turned to look at Mary. Her eyes were filled with wonder. She of all people seemed to appreciate what was happening more than Josh and I ever could.

Elder Hyde spoke of the covenant—the promise that the Lord had made to the children of Abraham to make this land an everlasting inheritance, and he said how it was time for that promise to be fulfilled.

". . . Grant therefore, O Lord, in the name of Thy well-beloved Son, Jesus Christ, to remove the barrenness and sterility of this land, and let springs of living water break forth to water its thirsty soil . . . Let the land become abundantly fruitful when possessed by its rightful heirs; let it again flow with plenty to feed the returning prodigals . . . Let Thy great kindness conquer and subdue the unbelief of Thy people. Do Thou take from them their stony heart, and give them a heart of flesh, and may the Sun of Thy favour dispel the cold mists of darkness which have beclouded their atmosphere. . . . Incline them to gather in upon this land according to Thy word. Let them come like clouds and like doves to their windows. Let the large ships of the nations bring them from the distant isles; and let kings become their nursing fathers, and queens with motherly fondness wipe the tear of sorrow from their eye.

That's exactly what Mary did. In fact she wiped both eyes. In her time she'd seen this place ravaged by both war and hunger. She'd watched the Roman soldiers kill her people by the thousands. She may not have been around to see them scattered to all the ends of the earth, but yesterday and last night she'd seen the result, and how this land was now almost barren of trees, and how it was ruled by those who didn't know Jesus or His gospel, or anything her people had stood for.

Then Elder Hyde said something very interesting, and sort of scary. That is, it sounded wonderful for those who did what he said, and scary for those who didn't.

"Do Thou now also be pleased to inspire the hearts of kings and the powers of the earth to look with a friendly eye towards this place, and with a desire to see Thy righteous purposes executed . . . Let that nation or that people who shall take an active part in behalf of Abraham's children, and in the raising up of Jerusalem, find favour in Thy sight. Let not their enemies prevail against them, neither let pestilence or famine overcome them, but let the glory of Israel overshadow them, and the power of the highest protect them; while that nation or kingdom that will not serve Thee in this glorious work must perish, according to Thy word—'Yea, those nations shall be utterly wasted.'"

He then asked the Lord to bless all those who had helped him to come here, including a "stranger" from Philadelphia whom he never met, but who gave him enough gold that he could afford to make this trip. He then asked the Lord to especially bless the newly born Church and to remember Zion, and to give a special blessing to the prophet and Twelve Apostles.

"Give us, therefore, strength according to our day, and help us to bear a faithful testimony of Jesus and His gospel, and to finish with fidelity and honour the work which Thou hast given us to do, and then give us a place in Thy glorious kingdom. And let this blessing rest upon every faithful officer and member in Thy Church. And all the glory and honour we will ascribe unto God and the Lamb forever and ever. AMEN!"

It was starting. The thunderous rejoicing. Though to anybody else this little grove was so quiet you couldn't even hear the rustle of the breeze, I knew that on the other side of the veil there was cheering and celebration and happiness beyond anything I'd ever heard. It was the shouting of angels and people from all ages and times. It was greater than the cheers of a thousand stadiums. I felt it all as I gripped that little stone. Mary felt it too. At least her cheeks were streaked with tears. Joshua's face was beaming with wonder and excitement. All of us were overwhelmed with the magnificence of it all, and I felt as if my heart was about to burst with joy.

Elder Hyde got to his feet with a look of eternal satisfaction. After he'd neatly folded the paper and put it back into the case with the ink bottle and feather pen, he began gathering stones and arranging them in a careful pile. Without anyone having to explain it to me I knew that it was a witness, and it was an ancient custom, and it was meant to show that something holy had taken place here. The celebration in heaven continued with more fervor than ever.

"Is it time?" whispered Joshua. "Are you supposed to look in the stone now?"

It was time. I couldn't have explained it, but I knew that because of the power and joy that was present all around me at this very moment, I could look into that seerstone and see things as clearly as if both stones were side by side in those silver frames. It was as if the veil between heaven and earth was as thin as a thread. I blocked out the light with my hands and gazed into the glowing surface. I made the question burn in my mind: Where do we have to go and what do we have to do to go home?

All at once I saw the answer so brightly that I felt certain I'd know it perfectly when I saw it again. I saw the place, but just as importantly, I saw the moment. Even if my memory of it got a little fuzzy with time, all I had to do was look into the stone again and everything would come back.

"Do you see it?" asked Josh.

"Yes, I see it," I confirmed. I took my hands away and turned my head in the exact direction.

"It's south and a little east."

"But we just came from there," said Josh.

"It's further," I said. "It's a city—an ancient city."

"You mean ruins?" asked Mary.

"Yes, ruins."

"Exactly how far?" asked Josh.

"Not too far. A few days. But we can't waste much time. We have to leave as soon as possible."

"You really saw everything that clearly?" asked Josh. "Do we even need the stone anymore?"

"Of course," I said. "When you look at a map do you remember it all perfectly or do you have to look again sometimes? In this case even if the map isn't quite as clear, I'll know what I'm looking at because I saw it so clearly once."

"To the south and east the desert is very dry and desolate," said Mary. "At least that's how it used to be. We'll need camels and supplies."

"We'll buy them in Jerusalem," I added. "If we trade the rest of the things that we brought with us from our century, we ought to get everything that we need."

"The stone told you that too?" asked Josh.

"No," I confessed, "But . . . I'm hoping."

This was sounding more and more expensive. Would our silly trinkets from the twenty-first century really buy all of this stuff?

Elder Hyde had finished building his pile of stones. He was starting to leave. I realized he was taking a little different route than he had in *coming, around the other side of the ancient cemetery, perhaps to see some slightly different scenery going down.*

"Let's follow him," said Josh. "Maybe he can tell us where to find people who will sell us camels and things."

"Then let's wait till he gets back to Jerusalem," I said. "I don't want him thinking we were spying on him all this time."

We followed him down the path, past the old olive trees of the Garden of Gethsemane, and back out onto the road that led to Jerusalem. But Elder Hyde didn't turn toward the city. Instead he walked down into the valley below the southeast wall. He was acting very much like a tourist now, passing by the tombs on the hillside and poking his head into a small, dark tunnel that appeared to go back underneath the city. At last he went across to the pool where we'd washed ourselves the night before. It appeared that he wanted to do the same. He took off his shoes and started rolling up his pants. We continued to watch him, hiding behind one of the stone slabs of a tomb.

"Should we go talk to him now?" asked Josh.

"It would be rude to disturb someone while bathing," said Mary.

We settled back to wait until he finished, but a moment later something startling appeared on the hill to the south of us. There were five camels and a chocolate brown horse coming down the road. I'd have known that horse anywhere, but more especially I'd have known the rider in the red robe and boots. It was Hazim and several of his men. Were they going to Jerusalem? All I could guess was that they were on their way into the city to get supplies for the journey back into the desert. Either that or they were looking for us.

When I heard Mary gasp I realized that she had seen them too. We crouched down a little further behind the tomb.

"What are they doing?" asked Joshua.

"Just riding toward the gate," Mary replied.

But almost the instant she said that, Hazim pulled his horse to a halt. He was looking down into the valley toward the lone figure of Elder Hyde as he continued to rinse himself off at the pool. Hazim's horse suddenly veered off to ride down into the valley. The camels of his men began trotting behind him. A sick feeling began to curdle in my stomach. I realized that Elder Hyde was completely defenseless down there. He was far enough away from the traffic on the roads that anybody could've taken advantage of him. I couldn't think of any other reason why Hazim would feel the reason to approach.

But wait a minute, *I thought. He'd be okay, wouldn't he? I mean, was there anything in the history of the Church about Elder Hyde getting attacked by robbers? Maybe there was. I really didn't know. But even so, he'd still get to America with the copy of the prayer he'd given on the Mount of Olives, right? In a way I felt like I was watching an episode of one of those old Westerns on TV—the kind where the bad guy rides into town, but you know that by the end the hero will be perfectly fine. Maybe I shouldn't have even felt any suspense. And yet I was trembling like a bowl of Jell-O.*

Elder Hyde had noticed the riders now. He must have sensed how defenseless he was because he started making his way back through the water toward his shoes. Hazim's horse arrived at the pool just as the apostle began unrolling his stockings to pull them back onto his wet feet.

"Why are you bathing in this pool?" *Hazim started railing.* "Now this water is polluted."

Oh brother! *I thought. The water thing again! Harassing people at springs seemed to be one of Hazim's favorite things. The other camels arrived around him. Several of his men were climbing off the humps.*

"I apologize," *said Orson.* "I wasn't aware that anyone would be offended. I'll be on my way."

"It's too late," *said Hazim.* "I am offended."

"Now see here," *said Orson.* "I'm a visitor here. An American citizen. I have a letter of recommendation from the consul at Jaffa."

One of Hazim's men started taking special interest in the case that Elder Hyde had been carrying—the same case that had the prayer inside. Elder Hyde snatched it up to keep him from taking it, but I didn't think this was going to make much difference. Hazim's men had started taunting him, just like bullies on a playground. Another one grabbed Orson's shoe.

"You must pay to bathe here," *said Hazim, leaping down from his horse.*

"I most certainly will not," *said Orson.* "Get your hands off that!"

They were trying to take away the case! What was going on here? Was this really going to turn out like the old Western? Something about this whole thing seemed terribly wrong. Another of the men grabbed Elder Hyde from behind. They pushed him to the ground, rummaging through his clothes. But as they tried to take away the case, he started to fight back. Oh, this was horrible! How could this be happening?

"I know what it is," Mary suddenly gasped. "I know why we're here—what we're supposed to do!"

She was looking right at me. In that instant I understood too.

"We have to stop them!" Josh said desperately. "They're going to kill him!"

One of Hazim's men had drawn a knife. I waited no longer.

"Wait!" I cried, leaping to my feet. "Don't hurt him! I'll give you what you want! I'll give it to you! Just let him go!"

The fighting stopped. All eyes—including those of Orson Hyde—focused on the three of us rising to our feet. I was gripping the stone so tightly that it might've crumbled to dust. But it didn't. And it wouldn't. With Mary's words I'd understood it all. Yes, we were supposed to come to Jerusalem. But it wasn't for the prayer. And it wasn't so much for any vision of how to get home. It was for this moment. Yet it seemed that we'd be giving up everything that we'd been trying to gain. By handing these villains the stone, we'd be saving the life of Elder Hyde, but we'd also be giving up our only window to understanding this strange world.

We'd be giving up the only tool we had to help us get home.

PART III:

THE CURSE
OF THE JAREDITE

CHAPTER 19

"I am Apollus Brutus Severillus, and by my word you will not accompany us to Tikal!"

Meagan nearly went into a conniption, but I would not have her endanger her life because of her stubborn pride. My, but she was a vocal child! Equipped with the lungs of an elephant when it came to expressing her mind. This she continued to do in the relative privacy of the shaman's house on the hill while Lamanai and his warriors waited below for my signal to depart. Ryan was just outside, somewhat offended that Meagan had requested to speak with me alone.

She continued her ranting. "Don't think for a minute that I intend to stay here and wait. Jolom has sent out word for warriors loyal to the son of Jaguar-Paw to gather here from all over. If they arrive here and wish to catch up with you and the sixty men who've volunteered to march to Tikal, you can bet that I'll be with them."

"Which is why I have instructed Jolom that if you attempt to follow us, he is to tie you to a tree until we return."

"He wouldn't dare."

"Perhaps not on my word," I said. "But Ryan concurred, and the elders wouldn't dare go against the great Kukalcan."

Meagan made a frustrated screech similar to one of those infernal monkeys in the jungle. "I want to be there! Why am I any more of a liability than Ryan?"

"You think we need *two* liabilities?"

She had a point about Ryan. Honestly, I would have preferred it if he had remained in the village as well. He was no warrior. He had no training whatsoever in essential weapons—bows, stone-edged swords, battle axes or a spear-throwing weapon called an atlatl. But he was Kukalcan, and despite all of our efforts to convince these people that we were not supernatural beings and possessed no power beyond the strength of a man, they nevertheless looked upon us as deities. Or if not as deities, as men who could claim the special *favor* of deities. This would have been difficult to refute considering the miracles that they had witnessed for themselves. In *their* minds, Ryan was still the central instrument of heavenly authority. They would have happily carried him upon their shoulders the entire distance through the jungle if he had requested it. Though I feared greatly for his well-being in the face of an actual military confrontation, I was somewhat comforted knowing that any of these men would have sacrificed their lives to defend him.

Meagan changed her tactics and adopted a more pleading tone. "Please, Apollus. Don't make me wait here alone in this strange place. I'll go crazy with worry. I can't stand the idea of being separated from . . ."

I raised an eyebrow. "Yes?"

"Oh, you're *awful*, Apollus! You know exactly what I mean! From *you!* Are you satisfied?"

My face softened. "And if we're both killed while I'm trying to defend your life, what good will that do either of us?"

She sat heavily upon the bench. "In all the years that I've known you, I've never had to worry about what might happen if you went off into battle. At least not since that day on Mount Gerizim."

"If I have my way there will not *be* a battle. We'll be back here in four days with the Prophet Moroni and his fellow captives."

She went on as if she hadn't been listening. "And now I have to worry about Ryan too."

That ruffled my feathers a bit. I was rather enjoying being the sole object of female angst. I had nearly forgotten my competition. Not that I felt I was competing. "You'll do best to give your worries to him," I said.

"That's not what I meant," Meagan snarled. "And you know it. Forty thousand warriors. They said Fire-Born has forty thousand warriors in and around Tikal. And that's not even a *tenth* of his—"

"I don't need to be reminded of the obstacles. Lamanai says most of those warriors are Lamanites—men whose loyalties might be turned the instant they discover who he is. The morning is growing late. The men are waiting."

"Hold on!" She arose from the bench and came to me, her eyes full of insistence. "Aren't you going to say anything to me?"

I thought a moment. "Farewell, Meagan."

"Anything *else?*" Her teeth were clenched.

"I need your prayers."

She continued standing there, her frustration mounting. Suddenly her hands reached out and clasped around the back of my head. She yanked me down until our lips met violently. She kissed me hard until I actually stopped resisting. But the instant I began to truly relish the sensation, she gripped onto the hair on the back of my head and thrust me away with equal violence. Then she faced the opposite direction. Without looking at me again, she commanded, "Just leave."

I stood there in befuddlement for several seconds. This had obviously been a taunting replay of my actions the night before. Still she would not turn back, so with a wave of my hand that signified the insanity of all women everywhere—and this one in particular—I did as she commanded and departed the shaman's house.

Ryan joined me as I began descending the hill. "What happened?"

"She's—uh—she's going to miss us very much."

I ran my tongue along the inside of my lip. It felt bruised and swollen. A moment later I laughed out loud. What a girl she was! The more I thought about it, the more hard-pressed I was to think of anything about her that I didn't admire.

Ryan acted as if he would have liked more details, but I refused, and within the hour we were marching to Tikal.

* * *

Lamanai and his warriors were in high spirits as we passed through the dappled shadows of the trees that the Lamanites called ceibas. The scheduled execution of the Nephite named Moroni was only three days away, on a festival day of the Lamaya known as the Day of Sacrifice, when every tribe sought favor from the gods as the first crop of the season was planted in the earth. Lamanai reported that two of those days would be required to travel to the city where Moroni was imprisoned, the Lamaya capital at Tikal.

In all, sixty-two men had accompanied Ryan and me on our expedition—virtually the entire population of military-aged males who had been present on the day of the blessings. Several were actually people who had been healed. They believed we were embarking upon a sacred mission ordained by heaven, and therefore we could not fail. Though I would not have said it so boldly, I did feel an unconquerable spirit pulsing in my veins.

The jungle air was dense and humid. I was constantly bombarded with stimulating odors and overpowering colors and images. Strangely contorted trees, giant-leafed plants, towering and feathery ferns, monstrous and spongy fungus pressed in and hemmed us about to the point of suffocation. The canopy overhead was like a green cloud cover and even at midday we were marching in an emerald twilight. Every growing thing, even the petals of flowers, seemed to exude a warm, moist stickiness.

Birds of every conceivable hue and design flashed back and forth like warning arrows. The air about us was hung with hummingbirds no bigger than bees and fanned by butterflies the size of bats. Around our feet, creatures stirring or fleeing rustled the underbrush. Perhaps some were deadly snakes, but most were harmless things: lizards, which ran on their hind legs, big-fingered frogs that climbed the tree trunks, and glossy, brown-furred creatures that were neither cats nor rodents, but a warped hybrid of the two. These would scamper a short distance ahead and then stare back at us with black, beady eyes.

Monkeys continued to bark and howl at us from the treetops. Those of us who carried javelins were instructed to walk with our spear points directed skyward, as it was a favorite hunting technique of jaguars to loll on a tree branch and wait to drop on unwary victims passing below.

That afternoon the clouds delivered quite a downpour that ceased toward evening. I was used to this weather pattern after living for more than a year in San Andrés, Tuxtla. In fact I felt I understood this climate rather well. During my sojourn in Mexico I'd also had occasion to visit the Yucatan cities of Campeche and Merida, whose locations in the future century I determined to be somewhere to the north. I think most of my comrades in the old Fighting Fifth Legion would have shriveled away in this oppressive heat and humidity, but I felt that my own body had already adjusted. In truth, I rather liked it. Nothing like a good sweat to invigorate the mind and cleanse the body of all its poisons. Unfortunately, Ryan did not share my enthusiasm. The poor fellow acted as if he could hardly breathe. Perspiration matted his hair and stained every part of his garments. A permanent drop of sweat seemed to dangle off the end of his nose. To his good fortune, the warriors of Seibalche had insisted that he carry no burden other than a wooden sword with razor-sharp volcanic blades and a battle-ax of marbled flint. In truth the weapons were appallingly primitive, even by Roman standards, but they looked doubly ridiculous bouncing off the rustic form of Ryan Champion—as ridiculous as a garland of daffodils might have looked festooned around the neck of Emperor Vespasian.

Two of the village elders had also accompanied us on our expedition—Quillkiah and Riki-Kool. Age had forced Jolom and Chilan Kanalha to remain behind. I was fast learning to respect the young Eagle-Sky-Jaguar. Virtually overnight he'd taken on the persona of a true leader. His men were naturally drawn to him, and I was convinced that it was for more than his lineage. The lad had real charisma. The level of ambition that had sprung up within him was almost intimidating. He fully expected to have this entire country rising up in revolution in an extraordinarily short period of time. The liberation of Moroni-Iqui-Mahucatah was only the first in a long list of campaigns that I could see him carefully working out in his mind.

We bivouacked that night some distance off the main highway in a region of smelly swamps to avoid drawing attention. Apparently sixty-four men armed to the teeth was not a familiar sight on these trails, particularly without the feathered shields that bore the atlatl and owl insignia of Fire-Born and Teotihuacan. Lamanai was still convinced that as soon as his identity became known, a mass mutiny would erupt among the Lamanite soldiers in Fire-Born's ranks. Our challenge now was to remain alive until word of his identity could filter through to the general populace.

For bedding, each of us was issued a net of slender rope woven into a kind of beanpod shape which could be slung between any two close-set trees. These, we were assured, would keep us out of reach of most snakes. I found the innovation so convenient that I might have introduced the idea to the Roman legions, particularly in the muddy woods of Britannia and Germania. We also received a mantle of light and delicately woven mosquito netting that we were to drape over ourselves as we slept. Without this I doubt we would have survived the night, so pestilent were the flying insects.

"The netting will also discourage scorpions and blood-sucker bats," added Riki-Kool.

That evening as the blood-red sun was setting in the west, Ryan found me sitting alone near my fire eating a sample of the greasy snails that had been collected from the swamp. In his hands was one of the curious spearthrowing devices called an atlatl.

"This is the one I want to learn how to use," he said. "Can you teach me?"

I gave him a look of mild amusement. Did he really think that proficiency with such a weapon could be accomplished in a day? But even if this were possible, I had to confess to him, "I'm not familiar with that weapon. You may wish to ask Riki-Kool. It appears that he has used it for hunting all of his life."

"The Romans really had nothing like this?"

"We didn't. But the mechanics of it certainly seem simple enough. I'm sure I could master it in a week or two."

"Well, what *could* you teach me? I want to stand my own ground when we reach Tikal. No one should have to defend me."

"Ryan," I said, my voice patronizing, "I recommend that you stay in the rear as much as possible. Start to see your presence among us as symbolic, like a battle standard. Otherwise you're going to get yourself butchered."

He sat back, chewing on this. Then he said testily, "You really don't think much of me, do you Apollus?"

"I think you're a noble bearer of God's Priesthood," I replied. "But you're not a soldier. And the sooner you accept that truth, the better."

He glowered at me. Suddenly he stood up on his feet and cocked his fists.

"Come on."

I raised an eyebrow. "Come on and what?"

"You need to ask? On your feet." He adopted an unusual fighting posture, one fist back and the other forward. "Ever done any kick boxing? I took three years. I think you need to learn that I'm not completely defenseless."

I stood reluctantly. "Why are you doing this?"

"If you need to ask, maybe you need to go back to boot camp, Centurion. Come on! I won't hurt you. Here, watch."

In an instant he brought up his leg and kicked sharply toward my head, retracting his foot just before it impacted my ear. I flinched. I'd never seen a move quite like it. Now that I had, however, it caused me no concern.

"Careful now!" he gloated. "I coulda tagged ya! Better watch it!"

He threw a quick punch hoping, I think, to flick my nose. In response I snatched his wrist, bent it around, and tossed him flat on his back in the dirt. He expelled a grunt of wind.

"Aaagh!" he moaned. "What was *that?*"

"I thought I was defending myself."

Ryan rose unsteadily. His eyes were more full of caution. We'd drawn the attention of several warriors. Quillkiah and two other men came over to us, their faces clouded with concern.

"All right," he said, shrugging it off.

He got back in his fighting stance, moving around me, looking for an opening. I stood my ground, hardly moving more than my eyes. All at once that leg came up again, only this time I reacted swiftly. I kicked his other leg out from under him, came up from underneath, caused him to do a full flip, and brought him down upon his stomach.

"What are you doing to Kukalcan!" raged Quillkiah.

I raised my hands in innocence. "Nothing. I swear it by Jupiter. Just reacting."

I realized that the other two men were prepared to draw weapons in Ryan's defense. Meagan's boyfriend panted on the ground several more seconds, then sat up on his haunches. There were a dozen Lamanites around us now.

Quillkiah faced me. "You will not hurt Kukalcan again."

I nodded and turned to my defeated adversary, "You hear? No more."

He appeared as if he might defy this, despite all that had happened. Then he succumbed to reason and let his head sink between his knees. That got to me. If there was anything I couldn't stand it was seeing a man wallowing in humiliation.

"I'll show you some things in the morning," I agreed.

He looked up slowly, then nodded. I helped him to his feet. After brushing himself off, he told the gathering, "Show's over. You can go back to your hammocks."

"I think I will remain," said a burly young Lamanite named Jacobah. I'd been noticing all day how this man had assumed for himself the role of Ryan's personal bodyguard.

Ryan assured him, "Relax. It's under control. I promise."

Jacobah retreated, but not without giving me a threatening stare. Ryan sat over by the fire. I settled down across from him.

"Not bad," I said.

"Excuse me?"

"Your moves. I was impressed."

He laughed mirthlessly, then said with sarcasm, "Yeah, I could tell how impressed you were."

"I met a Persian once in Athens who fought with his legs. Your style is much like his—only better. But this Persian also taught me how to defend against kicks to the head."

"I see," said Ryan.

I snorted in frustration. "Why do you wish to fight at all?" I indicated Jacobah and the rest. "You have every weapon in this company at your disposal."

Ryan looked up sharply. "You think I don't know the difference between sixty-four and forty thousand? If you want to keep me from getting 'butchered'—as you say—you'd better teach me something about weapons."

"Fine," I said succinctly. "We'll rise an hour before we march. I'll show you a few moves with the obsidian-edged sword. Except for a good forward thrust the basic principals should be the same."

"Excellent," said Ryan. "'Cause I'd hate to have to humiliate you again with my kickboxing."

I tried to snicker to be polite.

Ryan looked away again and sighed drearily. "Boxing isn't the only contest I'm going to lose, is it?"

"What do you mean?"

"You know what I mean. I'm talking about Meagan."

I frowned and faced forward, gazing off at the first star of night. "No," I said. "That one you're going to win."

He raised his eyebrows. "You plan to give up that easily, eh?"

I added more sticks to the fire. "Meagan is a fine woman, but . . . she needs someone from her own time. Someone who understands . . . computers and . . . credit cards and . . . how to program the V-C-R."

"Did you tell Meagan all that?"

"Not with those words, but she understood."

"I'll bet. Well, that cinches it. You *are* as dumb as you look."

My eyes widened. "Pardon me?"

"You don't see it, do you? Well I saw it. I saw it the moment that we met. The instant that she set eyes on you out on her front porch. I happen to think that Meagan is the most extraordinary girl I've ever known. But she's never looked at me the way that she looks at you."

"You're overstating it."

"I don't think so. I wish I were. Nope. I know when I'm licked."

I scoffed, recalling his determination from a few moments before. "I think you underestimate yourself."

"Not this time, hombre. Or as you so deftly put it, the sooner I accept the truth, the better."

This conversation was making me uncomfortable. Fortunately, Lamanai showed up at our fire a moment later to discuss the rescue of the Prophet Moroni. He began by describing the layout of the city, then he revealed Moroni's location.

"If they still follow the practice of my father, they will keep all of the prisoners of noble rank in a prison beneath the Temple of the Morning and Evening Star. Their remains would be entombed in a different part of these same chambers after they are sacrificed. There will be eighty of the king's elite lightning warriors guarding this temple at all times, but perhaps only seven or ten near the prison entrance."

"What if we created a diversion?" I suggested. "Something to draw the warriors away?"

Lamanai shook his head, "They know they will be executed if they desert their post. The only way to defeat them is a direct attack. But if, as Kukalcan has stated, the God Jesus Christ will protect us, then we will be victorious."

"Whoa, whoa," said Ryan. "That may be true, but that doesn't mean we just barge in like we own the place. If we act arrogant or foolish we could easily get ourselves mowed down like a bed of dandelions. God will expect us to do everything we can. Even my personal hero, *Captain* Moroni, felt it was justified to use stratagem."

Neither Lamanai nor I knew who that was, but the point was taken.

"I might just know a little about stratagem," said Ryan. "You guys familiar with *Sun Tzu and the Art of War?*"

He got the expected blank looks.

"I didn't think so. 'Clamor in the East, Attack in the West'—that's the principle. I'd still like to explore Apollus's idea of a diversion. We just might have to narrow the playing field. How large is this temple?"

I was beginning to find the Great Kukalcan somewhat tiresome. However, as Lamanai began painting some dimensions, I suddenly began to see what Ryan was getting at. We realized that it might be possible to create a disturbance on one side of the temple and at least draw away any guards at the prison's entrance. *Not bad*, I thought to myself. Maybe the Great Kukalcan could be of some use after all.

"But what about the prisoners?" Ryan asked further. "I got the impression that they'd been in there several months. Will they be strong enough to make a break for it?"

Lamanai nodded. "When they first arrived they would have been abused and humiliated in every way. But for the last ten days they will have been treated like kings. Fed the finest foods and given every other luxury. Lord Crocodile and Fire-Born will not want to consume the flesh of the sick and debilitated. They will want to take inside themselves the spirits of strong and vigorous men."

"You mean they actually plan to eat their flesh?" asked Ryan squeamishly.

Lamanai seemed surprised that he found this so appalling. "It is expected that a king will consume a portion of the hearts and brains of his captives, especially if such enemies are deemed great. He will hope that it may enhance these characteristics of greatness within himself. My father always claimed that his prowess in war was due to consuming the flesh of the great Commander Gideon when he was young. Gideon was the leader of the Nephite armies before Mormon."

Ryan looked pale. "But you know that isn't true, right? You can't gain the characteristics of *anyone* by . . . by cannibalism."

Lamanai tilted his head, as if such an idea had never occurred to him. To me it wasn't such an inexplicable notion. Our enemies in the north were said to have eaten the flesh of their captives. Of course to any educated Roman such an idea was barbaric, but it was rumored that certain Roman commanders had mimicked the practice out of revenge, or to make sacrilege of the tribesmen's rituals.

"We have learned many new and strange things from you, Kukalcan," said Lamanai. "It may be that some things will take more time to understand than others."

* * *

The following morning, surrounded by the ground mists that seemed always prevalent in this region at sunrise, I fulfilled my promise and taught Ryan a few defensive moves with the Lamanite sword. I was impressed at how well he adopted my style and gestures, but every soldier knew that there was no substitute for actual experience on the battlefield.

Because it was expected that around midday we would enter the environs of Tikal, we decided that to retain anonymity we would converge on the capital in separate groups of three or four men each. Ryan and I finally discarded our twenty-first century apparel in favor of the loincloth, leggings, armbands, and chest coverings of the Lamanites. Ryan was a bit reluctant about the loincloth since it covered very little, but after an extra wrapping between the legs he appeared satisfied that his modesty was preserved. Still, I wondered how well we could ever blend in without the tattoos that bespeckled every other Lamanite citizen. My hair was considerably longer than would have been allowable in Roman ranks, but it was hardly long enough for a traditional Lamanite topknot. Nevertheless, a crude attempt was made to imitate the style, which undoubtedly would have drawn much laughter from my old comrades in the Fighting Fifth. Ryan's shorter hair was wrapped in a colorful head cloth and his body was slathered in a brown paste that darkened the pigment of his skin. The time to unveil him as the great Kukalcan would soon come, but not today. My own complexion was lighter than the copper-skinned Lamanites, but not nearly as pink as Ryan, so I got away with a considerably less-generous slathering.

Ryan and I would march with Lamanai as well as Ryan's body-guard, Jacobah. The attack would take place tonight, or rather tomorrow morning during the stillest hour of darkness when, as Lamanai put it, "only the jaguar and the owl are stirring." Since the prince considered this in essence a contest between himself (the jaguar) and the ruler at Teotihuacan (Spearthrower Owl) he spoke this with an air of auspiciousness. We were all to enter the city at random times this evening through the various city gates. Lamanai reported to us that all of these gates would be shut for the night at the setting of the sun—that is, all but one. This he called the Gate of the Priests since the king's shamans often used it as they went to and from their sacred places in the forest at all hours, and also by runners who brought important midnight messages to Lord Blue-Crocodile. This was to be our escape route. Lamanai said that in his father's day it was always heavily guarded, but he had heard that the new Lords of Tikal were not so judicious.

The rendezvous point was the north end of a structure known as the Portico of the Dead that sat only a short distance from the Temple of the Morning and Evening Star—or as I preferred to call it, the Temple of Venus. Ryan's plan of a diversion was accepted. A company of twenty men under the leadership of Quillkiah was to set fire to a shrine that had been erected by Lord Crocodile in honor of his father. They were to attack any guard who opposed them, and then flee in the confusion. The instant we saw the flames, we would storm the prison entrance, kill the guards, free Moroni and anyone else well enough to run, and make our escape toward the Gate of the Priests. We would then be on our own until we arrived back at the first night's encampment. There we would assess our success, or lack thereof, and make the final march back to Seibalche. It was an impressive strategy, but considering our meager numbers, it would still take a miracle to pull it off.

The day was even hotter than the day before, and it began to seem as if the cooling rains would never come. But at last, toward late afternoon, just as the long fortifications of Tikal appeared in the distance, the promised rains arrived. The farmers, busily working the ash from the spring burn-off into the soil, seemed to appreciate the moisture as well. No doubt directly after the ceremonies of the Festival of Sacrifice they would begin planting their seeds of corn, squash, and beans. These were three crops that I'd come to know very well during my tenure in Mexico, though I still preferred Italian wheat over any of them.

Other food crops were grown on narrow strips of land between vast networks of irrigation ditches and canals. On the east these canals must have extended for great distances indeed, since there were many lagoons with dock areas that supported long, dugout canoes. I watched one such canoe being unloaded of baskets filled with colorful and spiny seashells, so I could only conclude that such networks tied into river systems that flowed all the way to the ocean.

"Most of these farmers and traders are the soldiers who might have otherwise opposed us," said Lamanai. "There will be no war or campaigns now that the rains have begun. War is a business that is only undertaken during the dry seasons."

"How long is the rainy season?" asked Ryan.

"Half of the year," he replied.

"And wars are *never* fought during this time of year?"

Lamanai shrugged. "Everyone must eat. Including our enemies."

Curiously, I watched a certain man with an official look cross one of the farmer's fields, say something to the farmer, and then move on. This farmer dropped his farming tools and departed for destinations unknown. I saw one or two other farmers doing the same. I could only assume it had to do with the upcoming festival.

The defensive works of Tikal consisted of a wide ditch or waterless moat deeper than the height of a man. By the appearance of it, these fortifications extended around the city for several leagues, except for a space on the east flanked by the natural barrier of a swamp. The dirt from the ditch had been piled up along the inside bank. At the top of this bank of earth stood a timber palisade, complete with catwalks and towers. Proud soldiers, wearing feathers and shields and other implements, stood upon the causeways and above the city gates. Their helmets were designed to represent various animals—crocodiles, eagles, pumas, wolves, and jaguars—with the soldier's face visible inside the animal's jaws. Its appearance was menacing enough, but I wagered that it was far too bulky to be practical. Their spears were heavily ornamented and feathered as well. The volcanic stone tip would certainly have killed a man, but again it looked cumbersome and awkward, undoubtedly designed to intimidate rather than actually defend. And yet there was something else about these warriors. I'd seen countless sentries in my day, from the Praetorian Guard on the Palatine Hill to the provincial grunts at the barracks of Neopolis. I'd come to know the boredom and laziness in such men's eyes—a glazed-over look that vanished only as a commanding officer wandered by. That was not the look that I was seeing now. These men were restless. Expectant. As if at any moment they might be called forth to use those bulky weapons to defend their city to the death. This bothered me. For the first time since our march had begun I felt a surge of warm blood through my heart—the warning sign of impending danger.

We walked across a bridge along the central causeway and entered the city gate behind a stream of men toting burdens of some sort of edible root. Many of the citizens—particularly the old-timers—were watching us with intense curiosity. Especially Lamanai. Was it possible that some of them saw a hint of his father's features in Lamanai? Eagle-Sky-Jaguar hadn't stepped foot in this city since the day he'd been carried off into the jungle. It may have been that some citizens still remembered the young prince, now aged into a striking young man. But if anyone believed it, no one was saying a word, either to each other or to us. Perhaps they dismissed it as too incredible.

The sun was going down. We passed through the various market plazas only to find the merchants hastily closing their final sales. Many were packing their wares into baskets and covering them with rough tarps. We saw several of our number among the milling customers, including Quillkiah and Riki-Kool, but we tried not to make eye contact and we did not speak.

Lamanai took us across the city nearly to the foot of the lofty Temple of Venus. It was a colorful edifice, rather Babylonian-looking in my judgement, with steep stairways on all four sides, bright green walls, black and red porches and platforms, and blood-colored steps. Every stone facing was decorated with detailed designs. In this respect it was nothing like the Babylonians. Indeed like nothing I'd ever seen in the Roman world. At best I might have compared it to the artwork of the Jews, since the representations of people and objects were so stylized and abstract. It generally took a second glance to begin to see the designs: faces and feathers, weapons of war, processions of captives, and depictions of human sacrifice. Partway up each stairway we could see giant stone and sculptured animal masks—jaguars, from what I could determine—in the open-mouthed posture of attack. The whole purpose of this temple seemed to be to glorify war and violence. Not so different from many of the monuments of Rome, I had to admit. In light of this, it only seemed fitting that Tikal's most notorious captives would be housed in its subterranean chambers. We took note of the shrine erected to Spearthrower Owl at the very base of its steps—a kind of gazebo with a large depiction of the owl and spearthrower insignia with a closed fist, and an even larger stylized sculpture that may have been a facial representation of the great king himself on his throne in the faraway city of Teotihuacan. Casually, we wandered around to the back side of the Temple of Venus.

Lamanai pointed out the entrance to the prison, presently guarded by a contingent of thirty warriors. This was over twice the estimate Lamanai had given us earlier, but he shrugged it off.

"There should be a change of the guards after sunset. Then we will have a truer count of our adversaries."

I was alarmed by the whole appearance of the temple. I counted nearly three hundred warriors on its platforms. These men were not wielding the bulky ceremonial weapons of the sentries at the gates. They had light javelins, bows, and atlatls. These men were ready for action. What was more, their faces were virtually a black mask of tattoos. Lamanai identified them as the lightning warriors of Fire-Born, the last remnant of the professional soldiers from Teotihuacan who had remained to defend their kingdom's new realm.

"Tomorrow is the Festival of Sacrifice," Lamanai continued. "During the day they will have doubled the guard in anticipation of the coming events, but after dark it should return to normal. Today and tomorrow merchants from all over my father's kingdom will arrive to peddle their wares in the marketplace."

I chuckled at Lamanai's presumptiveness, calling this his father's kingdom even while it was still in the hands of its conquerors.

"So the Prophet Moroni is really in there," said Ryan contempla-tively, as if the reality of such a thing affected him deeply. "I can't believe I'm this close to the man who . . . who made the Book of Mormon possible . . ." His voice trailed off. I realized again the rever-ence that his generation felt for this prophet.

But to remind us of Moroni's tentative future, Lamanai said, "The rituals to appease the god Chac of rain and Kinich of sky will begin tomorrow when the sun reaches its zenith. The sacrifices will continue until the setting of the sun."

As today's sun disappeared beyond the jungle canopy, we wandered between two reservoirs where many of the city dwellers received their water supply and on toward the royal palace complex. Again, it was a beehive of activity. Priests were reciting prayers and burning incense at the base of every stairway to bid farewell to the setting sun, and to welcome the rising moon. Soldiers, slaves, and dignitaries were arriving and departing from a central building—the headquarters of Lord Blue-Crocodile.

Spearthrower Owl's son was said to be a young man, not much older than Lamanai. He'd been put on Tikal's throne by the military commander, Fire-Born, and kept in power by his armies. In the beginning, the warriors had been from Teotihuacan, but a good portion of those warriors had gone home now. Fire-Born's army consisted primarily of Lamanites who had offered themselves as loyal subjects in the face of an inevitable shift in power. I finally asked Lamanai a question that had vexed me for some time.

"Why would your people be so quick to give their loyalties to a conqueror?"

"Because he *is* a conqueror," Lamanai replied simply. "My people believe a king may only be defeated by the will of the gods. If the gods have chosen a new king, they would not alienate the powers of the divine by refusing to become the king's subjects."

"Then why would you expect the people to give their loyalties back to you?" asked Ryan.

"Because a king is not defeated if his sons live. When it is learned that I am the heir of Jaguar-Paw—and that I am supported by Kukalcan—the people will know that Fire-Born and Lord Crocodile are not their rightful kings."

I sensed the turmoil inside Lamanai as a thousand memories of how this city had once been passed through his thoughts. But then he stiffened his jaw and gave a subtle, but malevolent smile. For him the day of reckoning had arrived.

Darkness soon fell across the Lamanite capital, and the smell of cookfires and the sounds of drums and flutes from another temple across the plaza began to fill the air. Some sort of minor ceremony was underway in that direction, which had drawn the attention of many of the city's inhabitants.

The four of us began to make our way over to the Portico of the Dead for the scheduled rendezvous with the other warriors of Seibalche. I soon recognized that this was one of the seedier districts of Tikal where alehouses served a favorite alcoholic beverage distilled, as far as I could ascertain, from some kind of cactus, and where houses of prostitution shamelessly advertised their services. Every city in the world seemed to have such establishments, and Tikal was no exception.

Upon arriving at the Portico of the Dead I noticed that this patch of ground was also a favorite gathering place for the city's beggars and vagrants. I assumed that some of the sleeping mats being laid out also belonged to the poorer class of visitors from the surrounding region who couldn't afford the price of an inn, if indeed such places weren't already filled to capacity. It was festival time in Tikal, and the main event was the sacrifice of a prophet named Moroni and the ceremonial drinking of his blood and devouring of his flesh by a presiding war commander named Fire-Born.

We joined several other warriors of Seibalche assembling in the portico's far-north corner. The rest filtered in over the next hour. Our neighbors may have wondered at the sudden appearance of so many armed men, but few made comment. The people were probably a little better behaved than normal.

"Are you police?" inquired one old beggar.

"Yes," replied Quillkiah. "For the festival."

The beggar returned to his place, satisfied at this answer.

We laid out our mats like the others, but no one slept. Anticipation was burning warmer and warmer in my breast. I was ready. And yet I couldn't shake the feeling that something was wrong. The city was not right somehow. But I couldn't pinpoint any particular reason. I only knew that I wanted to get this operation over with and escape this city as quickly as possible.

Soon the drumbeat from the temple across the plaza went silent. A blanket of calm overshadowed Tikal, broken only by the occasional bark of a dog, the cough of a vagrant, or the ill-tuned song of a drunk staggering home from an alehouse. Finally, even these sounds vanished. Except for some faint stirrings near the city wall to the south, Tikal was asleep.

We waited another hour, then at last Lamanai and Quillkiah rose to their feet. The whisper was passed from one man to another. The time for the assault had come.

For such a large city I was surprised at how few torches or wick lamps were left burning throughout the night. Only the palace and the summits of a few of the temples were left aglow. Most of the torches actually seemed reserved for the Temple of Venus, as if competing with the stars of night.

We watched the temple from a distance in the murky gloom for several minutes. Just as Lamanai had predicted, there appeared to be fewer warriors guarding it than there had been in daylight, but it was too dark to know precisely how many. At last I made a signal to Quillkiah and departed with my company while the twenty men who would create the disturbance at the Shrine of Spearthrower Owl remained behind.

We moved as stealthily as leopards. I was afraid that the foul moon overhead would betray our presence before we ever got in place. To our good fortune we found an avenue whose lofty walls hid us entirely from the peering eyes of the warriors atop the temple until we managed to position ourselves behind the canopy of a butcher shop directly across from the prison entrance.

We waited. The smell of fresh blood and rancid meat filled my nostrils. This brought back vividly to my mind the odors of death that I recalled from the regions of Judea.

I met Ryan's eyes, but he did not endure my gaze for long. I felt I could hear the thump of his heart above my own. He looked as eager as any green legionnaire, full of reckless vigor. I was comforted to see his bodyguard, Jacobah, near at hand.

We had been there all of twenty minutes when the first shrieks of confusion filled the city. As anticipated, the disturbance was coming from the opposite side of the temple. I watched several guards from the prison entrance abandon their posts to find out what was happening. The strategy was working.

At last we perceived the glow of flames—the shrine had been ignited. The moment had come.

"Attack!" shouted Lamanai.

The forty-four remaining warriors of Seibalche began charging en masse toward the prison entrance. As the sentries who had retained their posts heard our cries and saw us rushing toward them, their faces filled with surprise. Weapons were brought to the ready.

Several of our number paused to fire arrows and fling spear-darts from their atlatls. I saw one of the sentries grab at his stomach and crumble. One of our warriors collapsed as well. I leaped over his body. The guards were returning fire, but the barrage hardly seemed of consequence as our forces met face to face at the base of the temple. The warriors of Seibalche swung down with their saw-bladed swords onto the hoisted shields of the sentries, pounding them to their knees. I was the first to reach the prison doors, met by a pair of muscle-bound Lamanites whose features betrayed no hint of fear. A javelin sailed toward me through the air. I dodged it easily and let its stone tip shatter against a stone monument to my left. I discovered that Lamanai was right behind me. As he saw the men who stood as the final barrier between the prison entrance and us, his voice thundered, "I am Eagle-Sky-Jaguar, son of Jaguar-Paw!"

The brawny Lamanites hesitated at this, more perplexed than believing. Suddenly, right between myself and Lamanai stormed Ryan Champion, heaving his sword high overhead and screaming like a gladiator. His head covering had fallen off and his blonde hair was streaming. This seemed to shake the fortitude of the guards more than Lamanai's proclamation. Yet as Ryan's sword swung down, it took very little effort for the first guard to parry the blow. Ryan tripped, landing on his ear, leaving his sword embedded in the guard's shield. For an instant the guard gawked at Kukalcan in bedazzlement. When at last he raised his spear, ready to thrust it into Ryan's chest, Jacabah finally entered the fray and plunged his own javelin into the Lamanite's belly.

My own sword came down upon the shield of the second guard, splitting the plate of wood, leather, and feather in two. As I finished the job with my dagger, Lamanai and several other men were already removing the barricades on the prison door. As the door was flung open, a volley of atlatl shafts whistled around us. The darts leveled the men standing on either side of Lamanai, but Lamanai raised his bow and fired into the opening. Riki-Kool and several other men flung missiles of their own into the tunnel. At least a half dozen men had been waiting in the antechamber between the prison's outer door and the inner door where the captives were housed, but they had no shields to protect them. By the time I entered the tunnel, all of them were either dead or writhing upon the ground.

Ryan was right beside me as I reached the inner door. He'd also had the foresight to bring one of the torches that had been burning at the entrance. I had no further doubt of his tenacity; yet a part of me wanted to grab him by the seat of the pants and fling him back outside. But there was no point to that now. All resistance had been subdued. Nothing stood between the captives and us.

The inner door was pried open. The familiar prison stench of foulness and defecation wafted over us. Ryan was the first to enter the dusty chamber. The eyeshines of six men, and surprisingly, one woman, peered back from the gloom.

"Moroni!" Ryan cried. "Which one of you is Moroni, the Son of Mormon?"

Almost immediately one of the men stepped forward. He stood at least my own height, perhaps a finger taller, which by Lamanite standards was commanding. I was struck right away at the mildness of his chiseled features. He wasn't at all the austere presence that I might have expected from the son of a great war general, but he was right in line with my expectations for a prophet. I'd have sworn by the shape of his nose that his mother was a Roman, but the rest of his features—eyes and complexion—were comparable to any Lamanite, except that he lacked the customary tattoos and flattened forehead. But if I were to be specific, I'd have to confess that his complexion was actually rather pale and his eyes red and worn from what had undoubtedly been months of physical and mental abuse. But as Lamanai had assured us, the Nephites were all wearing fresh mantles and carried themselves with reasonable stamina.

Moroni's voice was clear and resonant as he inquired with a note of urgency, "How many are you?"

I might have expected his first question to be "*Who* are you?" rather than "How many?" I had the odd impression that he already knew who we were.

"Sixty," I replied. "At least that's how many we were at the start."

"*Sixty!*" he repeated with alarm. "You attacked the prison with sixty men?"

"Yes," I said. "But now I advise that we leave here as swiftly as possible."

"But by now the city is surrounded," declared another Nephite, a man who might have been just under Moroni in rank.

Lamanai was taken aback. "What? By who?"

"By the armies of Fire-Born," said Moroni. "A messenger arrived this morning to warn Lord Crocodile that someone claiming to be the son of Jaguar-Paw was organizing a revolt."

Kux-Wach, I thought bitterly. The stepbrother of Lamanai had reached the capital before us.

"Fire-Born himself was here this afternoon to tell me that my sacrifice had been postponed another three days," said Moroni. "He is already marching with a portion of his army toward your village. The rest of the warriors have been assembling north of the city all afternoon."

That explained the farmers whom I saw leaving their fields.

The Nephite of lesser rank continued, "They were instructed to be in position at every gate and along every rampart of the city wall by sunrise to prevent you from entering. But with the disturbance that you created outside the temple, they will know that you are already here."

"You mean," said Ryan, swallowing, "they were expecting us?"

"No," said Moroni. "They were expecting a rescue effort much *larger*. Certainly greater than sixty men. The entire army of Tikal has been put on alert—forty thousand warriors. Twenty thousand here in the city."

My heart stopped in the cavity of my chest.

"They'll be waiting for us," one of our warriors muttered.

"We'll be slaughtered!" another declared.

A cascade of liquid fire and ice crept down my spine. One moment from now, as we emerged from this prison, we would be marching straight into the jaws of a dragon.

CHAPTER 20

Orson Hyde looked hardly the worse for wear after what had happened. He was on his feet again, brushing the thick coat of dust off his clothes after the scuffle. The case with the prayer inside was still safely in his hands. The Arab who'd pulled the knife tucked it back inside his cloak. Elder Hyde looked over at us with utter amazement. We'd just saved his life—"But why?" he seemed to be asking. "Who are you?"

There was no less amazement on the face of Hazim. His eyes were now filled with greed. It surprised even me how quickly he and his men had given up the idea of robbing Elder Hyde. It's not that I didn't think the stone was worth the trade. I guess I just would've expected them to think about it for a few seconds longer—the old thing of, "A bird in the hand is worth two in the bush." Who was to say that the minute they let Elder Hyde go, we wouldn't all make a run for it and that they'd end up with nothing?

They immediately climbed back on their animals and began riding toward us, eyes burning with determination. Then it struck me—they had been looking for us. Attacking Elder Hyde was just an after-thought—maybe just their way of venting off anger at all people from Europe or America. Now they must've thought they were the luckiest villains on earth. Who'd have thought that by attacking a stranger they'd end up flushing out exactly the prize they were after?

I took off the seerstone and the silver frame from around my neck.

"Don't do it, Becky," said Josh. "Don't give it to them."

"She has to," said Mary. "It's the only way."

"Then how will we get home?" asked Josh.

"We'll have to have faith," said Mary. "Becky saw the place once. We'll have to pray that she remembers."

There was a strange look on Hazim's face. His eyes seemed fixed on me just as much as the stone. He didn't slow down his horse one bit as he drew close. Mary also sensed that something was wrong.

"Becky," she said, her voice full of warning. "Just drop it. Drop the stone and come over here. Hurry!"

I was standing apart from the others so that Hazim could take the necklace out of my hand. I just wanted to be done with it, but I was unprepared for what happened next. The sheik leaned off to the side of his horse, arm outstretched. Then suddenly, instead of grabbing the stone, he grabbed me! *He scooped me right off the ground!*

I started screaming. The stone dropped from my hand. He laid me on my stomach over the saddle, his arm pressing me down.

"Becky!" yelled Josh.

Mary lunged at the horse. "What are you doing?"

Hazim called to one of his men. "Haggai! The stone!"

Haggai didn't wait for his camel to kneel. He leaped down and snatched up the seerstone from the dirt. The sheik turned his horse and began riding swiftly away. Mary couldn't catch him, so she did the next best thing. She leaped onto the back of Haggai, laying into him with all her fury, pounding and scratching. Joshua, still screaming my name, chased after us. Even Orson Hyde was running toward Hazim's horse. The chocolate-brown stallion was galloping at full speed as I continued to fight and struggle.

"Let me go!" I cried. "Why are you doing this?"

"My new employer wants not only the stone. He wants you!*"*

New employer? What was he talking about? I caught a glimpse of Mary being tossed off the man's back and landing on the rocky ground. Haggai climbed back onto his camel, the stone in his hand. The other riders were following us as swiftly as their animals could carry them.

I bit Hazim's arm. He grabbed me by the hair and yanked me back hard. He almost lost a bite of flesh.

"Do that again and I'll break your neck! Do you hear?"

I started crying uncontrollably. Mary and Joshua were fading into the distance! "Please!" I begged. "Don't take me away from them!"

"Silence! Be still!"

"Where are we going?!"

"You'll know soon enough."

We rode for over an hour into the desert following no particular trail. Hazim yanked me upright in the saddle, but it was for his own comfort, not mine. His arm continued to pin me to his chest. My mind was spinning out of control. What was happening to me? Was I to become a desert slave? Who was this new employer Hazim had mentioned? The last I knew he was still working for Brother Nicholas and the monks from Mt. Sinai.

"Where is Brother Nicholas?" I demanded.

"Let that foul monk be cursed!" he barked. "Cursed be all his friends and kin to the end of his days! He dismissed us, the old goat! Right after the three of you fled the monastery. He blamed us for your leaving! Then he went right over and hired that son of a cobra, Sheik al-Farabi."

I'd heard that name before. It was the sheik that Hazim had a four-hundred-year-old feud with—the one guiding that American explorer named Stephens. Apparently that job was finished. Brother Nicholas had hired those guys as a replacement for the treacherous Hazim. But who had hired Hazim?

"Who wanted you to kidnap me?" I asked.

"Enough questions! By the winds of Allah, will you stop your chattering?"

"'Winds of Allah,'" I mocked. "You don't even know what that means. You keep saying stuff like that and you're gonna get 'lightning-ed.' You're the worst Moslem there ever was!"

"Silence!"

That one thundered in my ear. I did as I was told.

I didn't even have the comfort of my seerstone. It was still in the grimy hands of the man named Haggai. Our horse and camels kept traveling deeper into the desert. I could see the Dead Sea again off in the distance. By coincidence Hazim seemed to be taking me in almost the exact direction that the seerstone had told us to go. Not that it made much difference. I still needed to look in the stone to make sure of the details. Somewhere beyond the Dead Sea was a ruined city that held the key for our getting home. But even if they took me right to the ruins' front door, I could've never gone home without Mary and my brother. Without me and without the stone they had zero chance of ever catching up. Even if I escaped, what chance did I have of finding them? Would they have remained in Jerusalem? Stayed with Elder Hyde? Gone back to the monastery? I didn't know. I was living a nightmare—the worst nightmare I could have dreamed.

I was all cried out by the time Hazim starting going up a steep hill. Now I was just curious. And angry. Who was this rotten, miserable jerk who'd hired Hazim? Whatever he wanted from me, I was determined that I was not going to give it to him. No matter what he said or what he did. But in spite of all that, the suspense was killing me.

The ruins of what looked like an old church appeared ahead of us. Part of the roof had fallen in, but the walls were still standing. It looked like it had been destroyed by a fire a long time ago, maybe in a war. There were black scars around the window spaces. The wooden front door was also blistered and scorched. The rest of Hazim's men were gathered outside, lazily waiting. They perked up when they saw us. Several fired their rifles into the air, congratulating Hazim for having captured me. Each of those rifle shots rattled my nerves.

Seeing that burnt-out church made me think that I knew who the villain was who'd hired Hazim. I'd met him last night in the monastery of St. Elias. It was that Syrian novice whom Nicholas had been taking back to Mount Sinai—the one named Shika who looked like a vampire. I'd suspected all along that he was running away from a terrible crime that he'd committed in his home country. I could only guess that when he saw me use the seerstone to find the Superior's glasses, he'd decided to go back to a life of crime.

Hazim climbed down from the horse, then pulled me down behind him. He kept a strong grip on my arm, determined that I was not going to get away.

We approached the door of the church. Even before we got there, someone came out to greet us from behind that blistered door. At first as I laid eyes on him, I was confused by what I saw. It took me a good two or three seconds to take it all in. The man was dressed in a long red silk gown with a blue sash tied around the middle. Around his head was a green and yellow striped turban, and on his feet were a pair of pointy red shoes with yellow tops. Stuck in his sash was a pair of pistols with big, ivory handles that he seemed particularly proud to be carrying.

Unlike everyone else that I'd seen in such costumes, this man had no beard on his long, sagging face. There was some gray stubble on his chin, but it was only two or three days old. However, this wasn't the most baffling thing about him. The most surprising thing—the thing that took my breath away and nearly sent me into a state of shock—was what he was wearing over his eyes.

Sunglasses! *If I hadn't been looking straight at him, I might've thought it was a desert mirage. He had on sunglasses with shiny gold rims. After he sucked back his lips and made a toothy grin, there was no longer any doubt. The brown and broken tooth looked as ugly as ever. Even from this far away I could still smell his rotten breath.*

Todd Finlay had found me.

* * *

Several minutes passed and I still couldn't believe my eyes. I was standing in the center of the burnt-out church. The Arabs were all outside. Todd Finlay was sitting on part of a rafter that had fallen in from the roof. He was fiddling with the seerstone in the silver frames, cutting off the leather strings that I'd had tied around my neck and replacing them with some kind of chain. My breath was still coming in short pants. I wasn't getting enough air. I couldn't believe I didn't faint, considering the fear I felt inside.

"What happened to the other one?" Mr. Finlay demanded.

"Huh?"

"The other stone? What happened to it?"

"It . . . fell out," I said.

"Where?"

"In the cave, I think."

He curled the remaining stone into his fist. "The cave, huh?"

He said it as if it was a long-ago memory. It seemed that way to me too.

"Well, it doesn't matter," he said. "That sheik outside—Hazim—says that you have quite a unique talent when it comes to this stone. Very special. Is it true?"

"How . . . how did you find us?"

He acted amused. "Good question. Luck, I think. Yes, I'm sure it was just good luck. Although I do have a few talents of my own, young lady. A few charms that I've learned over the years. Things that come in handy in a pinch."

Finlay had finished attaching the new chain to the seerstone. He looked over his work with a smile. There was some kind of a small black gemstone on the chain, and a hook that made it attach together more like a necklace. But something was weird about it. It was as if . . . yes, I was sure of it. He seemed to admire the little black gem almost as much as the seerstone itself.

He noticed me looking and lowered it, perhaps thinking I was paying a little more attention than he wanted me to.

He continued, "And boy, let me tell ya, I was sure in a pinch three days ago. I woke up to find myself flat on my back in some sort of ancient crypt. I didn't have the foggiest idea where I was except that it was a ruined city with caverns and rooms and facades carved right out of the cliffs."

My goodness! He was describing the place that I'd seen in the stone. Now I understood. Todd Finlay had come out *at the very place that we were supposed to go* in. *Somehow he'd arrived a few days before we did. I guessed that made sense considering how he'd been sucked into the pillar twenty minutes earlier. Oh, who was I kidding? I didn't know* what *made sense anymore!*

"They call the city Petra. Ever heard of it? No? Well, it's an interesting place. Trouble is, the Arabs of Wadi Musa don't much like outsiders visiting there. Even other Arabs. If they catch you they'll do you the honor of removing your head with one of those fancy curved swords. Unfortunately, I got caught. I was able to talk my way out of execution by showing the sheik a few items from my bag of tricks."

He pointed toward a gym bag at his feet—the same bag that I'd seen him carrying over his shoulder in the cave. I remembered it was still hanging over his shoulder when he fell into the river.

"I planned for this trip pretty well. Since I knew that I'd likely be visiting the past I brought only items that I felt I could use as trade goods. They were well waterproofed, of course. I was able to save my own life at the cost of a couple butane lighters and a bag of Tootsie rolls. Not bad, eh? Then came the grand *prize—a digital wristwatch with an alarm buzzer. Only $9.95 at Wal-Mart, but here it got me these fine clothes, a pair of Turkish pistols, and a guided tour back to civilization."*

"You're the explorer," I said, awestruck.

"That's right," he replied. "That's how I introduced myself to them—as an American explorer."

"But they said your name was . . ." I stopped myself. Had I forgotten? Todd Finlay changed names as often as most people changed underwear.

"John Lloyd Stephens?" said Finlay. "Yes, I heard that name once in a college history class. I thought it might come in handy. The real *Stephens came through here only five or six years ago. But alas, nobody I've met has even heard of him. I had to tell them something. I assure you, if I'd told*

them that I'd popped into that crypt from a different century, I wouldn't be here to tell the tale. Muslims are as inclined to kill witches as Christians. Or at least as inclined as Christians used to be. It may be 1841 in the rest of the world, but here in the Middle East it's still very much the Middle Ages."

"It was you last night, wasn't it?" I asked. "You were the one who came into our room at the monastery."

"Yes," he admitted slyly. "And if I'd gotten my hand over your mouth before you started to scream, I'd have dragged you out of there then. It would have saved me a considerable amount of time and trouble."

It made sense to me now—the evil that I'd felt last night when I looked into the stone. That was why the stone, along with our prayers, had told us to leave the monastery. We were being warned about Todd Finlay. But why couldn't the stone have warned us about the dangers that we would face this morning? I was feeling some of the same frustration that Josh had mentioned last night.

"What do you want from me?" I asked.

"Isn't that obvious?" Finlay got up from where he was sitting and walked toward me.

I backed away, not sure if he was gonna hit me or slap me or—

He stopped. "It's all right. I'm not going to hurt you. That wouldn't be in the best interest of either one of us. Not now. I just wanted to give this back to you." He held out the seerstone. "Take it."

Carefully, I put my hand forward. He set it in my palm.

"Should be a little easier to hook around your neck now. Beautiful, isn't it? I'll be perfectly honest with you, Rebecca Plimpton. I think it would be best if you and I learned to work together. Maybe even became friends."

I glared at him. "I think you're a horrible man. I don't want anything to do with you."

He smiled crookedly and waved this off. "Ah, don't be like that. I think you and I got off on the wrong foot, that's all."

I nodded and said sarcastically, "Kidnapping can do that sometimes."

Unexpectedly, his temper flared. "I did that because I was desperate, you little wench! I had no choice! Don't you understand?"

His burst of anger startled me. My eyes widened and my heart skipped a beat. Had I forgotten that I was dealing with a man who was a few bricks shy of a load? He wasn't right in the head and I realized I'd better be a little more careful about what I said.

He calmed himself down with great effort. "I've waited for twenty-five years, Rebecca. Twenty-five years for the opportunity that stands before me now. And the only thing preventing me from getting what I want . . . is you.*"*

"Me?"

"Yes," he said soothingly, trying to be nice now. "You hold the secret, Rebecca. You're holding it right there in your hand. That stone. But if it were just the stone, I'd have simply taken it from you last night and been on my way. You see, I had *that stone. It was in my possession for a long time. I knew that it had great power. I pride myself in being able to tell the difference between a fake and the genuine article with such things. But the stone won't* talk *to me!"*

He spat it out with a weird shudder, like a pop bottle getting ready to blow. But he was looking at it all wrong. Even I *knew that it wasn't the* stone *that had power. It was the Spirit that spoke through it, the same Heavenly power that bound the whole universe together. It was the goodness of God.*

Todd continued. "But it will *talk to* you *apparently. For some reason it likes* you. *That's all they could talk about in the Arab camps when I arrived last night at the monastery—the little girl and the stone. I knew right away that they were describing you. It seems that I still have a bit of luck on my side. So I'm asking you, Rebecca. Will you use the stone to help me?"*

I already knew the answer to that question, but just out of curiosity I asked, "What is it that you want the stone to tell you?"

"I need it to help me find a sword."

That sword again! I remembered him talking about it in the cave. I must have given him a very strange look, because he felt he had to declare loudly:

"Coriantumr's sword! The Sword of Akish! The talisman of Gadianton!"

"But I don't understand how—"

"In our day the sword doesn't exist. Only in the past. That's where you come in. I know you can help me, Rebecca. You can help me to find the pathway. You can help me to discover the window that will lead me to a place and time when the sword still exists."

"You kidnapped me and Josh—you caused all this pain and confusion—over a stupid *sword?"*

I obviously hadn't learned my lesson, because Todd Finlay flew into a rage. "The Sword of Akish is the most powerful charm in the whole *history of the world! It can conquer nations! Fill every dream that a man could ever dream!* Don't you ever call it that again!*"

"Okay, I'm sorry. I'm really sorry. I won't do it again. I promise."

His face was beet red with anger. Again he fought to get his composure back. Finally he said, "All right. Then you'll help me? You'll use the stone to help me find the Sword of Akish?"

After what I'd just seen I was scared to death to say no. And yet there was no way I could say yes. It was all so crazy. All this for a sword? What harm would it really be to help an old man find a silly sword?

Silly sword. Suddenly it occurred to me that I didn't know what I was talking about. Wouldn't it be just as easy to call this thing in my hand a silly stone? But there was one thing I knew for sure. If this sword was really all that Todd said it was, there was no way it was something good. It was something terribly evil.

A lightbulb came on in my head. I realized the opportunity that I had—the power that he was giving to me.

"What if I did *help you find the sword? What would you do for me? Would you let me go free? Would you help me to find Mary and Joshua? Would you let us go home?"*

His shoulders slumped a little. His eyes blinked. Instead of looking into my eyes, he glanced at the ground and answered, "Certainly."

I made my eyes go thin. "I don't believe you. You find Mary and my brother now or I won't help you at all."

The redness starting coming back into Todd's face. Swelling and burning. I swallowed, feeling very sorry that I'd sounded so forceful.

"Sheik al-Arabah!" *Finlay yelled.*

Hazim came through the door. "I am here."

"Do you think you can find the other girl and this child's brother again?"

"I found them once, didn't I? Yes, I could find them again."

"Good. Would you find them *and* kill them?"

I nearly choked. "What?"

Hazim grinned. "With pleasure. Is the flasher still mine?"

"Of course," *Finlay replied.*

"And when it is over, will I still receive the stone?"

"Yes."

Hazim started to leave.

"Wait!" *I cried.*

Finlay roared into my face. "I make the bargains, girl! No one threatens me! Understand? Least of all a snotty little nit like you! Not after all I've been through! Not after twenty-five years!"

I was fooling myself. I didn't have any power at all. Finlay still had all the power.

"Okay," I wept. "I'll help you. Don't hurt them. Please don't hurt anyone else."

Finlay calmed himself yet again. Hazim actually looked disappointed.

"Good," said Finlay with relish. He turned to Hazim. "Tell everyone to mount up! Tonight we ride for Petra!"

"First, the flasher," said Hazim.

Begrudgingly, Finlay reached into his gym bag and pulled out a Fuji disposable camera. Obviously it wasn't the film that Hazim was interested in. It was the tiny flash bulb.

"Remember," Finlay explained. "Push here. Wait for the red light. Then push here."

"And the curse?" asked Hazim.

"Yes," said Finlay tiredly. "Anyone you flash will receive the curse of death. But there are only twenty-three curses left. We wasted one, of course, on your old rival, Sheik al-Farabi."

Hazim grinned wickedly. He pointed the camera teasingly at me, pretending that he might actually give me the curse. I didn't flinch, of course. Instead I shook my head and thought, "How pathetic."

Hazim gave off a big-bellied, slobbery laugh and exited through the door with his camera. It was just Finlay's style, I thought, to attach evil curses to such stupid things.

Finlay shrugged his shoulders at me. "Don't be surprised if those he flashes with that camera really do die on the spot. A curse, of course, is all in the mind." He grinned crookedly.

"Then I hope he accidentally flashes his own face," I said bitterly.

Finlay just laughed.

* * *

An hour later I was sitting on a camel again, only now I was by myself and my hands were tied together in front. I'd never felt so tired and hot and dirty. My camel was tied to Haggai's camel. He'd been put in charge of me. I don't think he liked the idea of being my baby-sitter. He was a beanpole-looking man with one of his ears mangled from some long-ago injury.

By dark we were south of the spring where Mary, Joshua, and I had been spit out. Hazim asked several times if we might stop and make camp, but Finlay refused. Hazim rode ahead, grumbling. We finally camped at a well very close to the shore of the Dead Sea. The well water tasted horrible, but they promised me it was drinkable. They fed me some dried, sticky fruit and a bowl of rice with sand in it. Still, I was so grateful to get rid of the rumbling in my stomach. I slept in a ragged tent—basically just a camel-hair tarp that they stretched over two boulders. They left my hands tied, which made it harder to scratch when I was bitten by fleas. I studied the knot on my hands. I was sure I could've easily picked it loose with my teeth, but I didn't dare to do it now. I was afraid that if they found out that I could escape, they'd tie it again with a better knot. I decided to wait.

At least I had the stone. I put it up to my eye. You can probably guess the question I asked it: Where are Joshua and Mary? Are they okay? I didn't really see an image, but I felt calmer in my heart. I was sure they were okay. My next question was: How can I get away from these slime-balls? To my frustration the stone was blank. It didn't have anything to say about that. No opinion one way or another. So I resorted to the old-fashioned method—praying. I spent much of the night praying and crying and praying some more while the wind whipped at my blanket and the air felt almost as cold as mid-winter.

By morning it was already hot again, and growing hotter. We continued south along a trail that showed the Dead Sea on one side and wild, rugged-looking mountains on the other. It rained a little, which I think was rare for that country because the Arabs got excited about it. Some took off their turbans and let it wet their hair.

By afternoon I couldn't see the Dead Sea anymore. I'd fallen asleep for a couple of hours (not an easy feat on a camel, let me tell ya!) and when I next looked up there was no water to be seen. I wouldn't have thought that anything could live out here, but twice we spooked some sort of gazelle that scampered off into the hills. The Arabs took potshots at them with their rifles, but the buffoons couldn't hit the side of a barn, which made me glad.

I could tell that the Arabs were getting mad at Finlay. He wasn't letting anybody stop and rest. Finlay had already given away several more lighters, some Sour Head candies (which he called aff-ro-dis-iacs, whatever that means), a bunch of Sharpie permanent markers, some Pepcid-AC and a couple dozen single packets of Motrin-IB, most of which the Arabs instantly swallowed to see if they really were magic "pain-pills" like Finlay had said (whether they were feeling any pain or not!)

But still they wanted more. Because of Finlay's obsession to keep moving he'd given away almost all of the stuff in his gym bag. Finally even Finlay needed to rest. The camels were halted and the Arabs threw up a canopy for shade. A small fire was made using camel dung, and water was heated up to make coffee. Why anyone would want to drink something hot on this blistering day was beyond me. After he'd gotten everyone's attention, Finlay brought out his best prizes yet—two used Gameboys with old "Pokemon Silver" and "Worms Armageddon" game cartridges. I could just hear Hazim now, riding across the lonely desert with a Gameboy in his hands and cursing, "Confound that wicked Charzard! I will *have him!"*

While everybody was watching Finlay's demonstration, I tugged on Haggai's sleeve.

Irritated, he said, "What is it?"

"I have to go," I said.

"Go where?"

"To the bathroom."

"Bathroom? What is that?"

"To the potty? The toilet?"

"Then go! Why tell me?"

He stepped forward to see if he could catch a glimpse of the little screen that everybody was looking at. There was a boulder a little ways up the hill that I decided ought to hide me good enough. But as I started walking away, another idea flashed in my head. They were all so busy watching Finlay that nobody noticed as I slipped a goatskin canteen off one of the camels. I carried it in front of me to keep it hidden and made my way around to the other side of the boulder.

Suddenly I no longer had to go to the bathroom. I began anxiously picking at the knot on my hands with my teeth. I could hear them laughing back at the canopy. Finlay was giving them quite a show, and telling them that when we reached Petra, the Gameboys would be theirs.

I had it! The knot came loose! My heart was pounding hard. Maybe I should've asked the seerstone if what I was doing was right. But there wasn't time. A chance like this might never come again. Any second they'd be looking for me. I began walking backwards, careful to be sure that the boulder stayed between me and the Arabs.

Finally, I got brave and started running, still careful to keep the boulder in the line of sight. But in a few seconds it wasn't going to matter. I'd be at the top of the hill; I'd be higher *than the boulder. It suddenly hit me how stupid I was acting. As soon as I was caught I was sure that Finlay would find some terrible way to punish me. I could never run faster than Hazim's horse. Then something surprising happened. A little fox with great big ears darted out from under my feet. It was sandy colored and no bigger than my arm, including its black-tipped tail. It bounded over to a bush straight ahead that grew out from the base of another small boulder. Then it disappeared! It scurried right under the bush and was gone. I raised up part of the stickery branches and saw a hole. A pretty* big *hole. Just big enough to . . .*

"Where is the girl?" I heard Finlay snap.

"Making her toilet," said the voice of Haggai.

I felt sure the little fox had dug a whole bunch of tunnels with lots of other exits, so I didn't think I'd be bothering him. As fast as I could, scratching my arms and neck and getting my hair caught in the stickery bush, I slipped into the hole.

"Find her!" Finlay barked.

My heart was still thudding. I peered back through the tangled bush. The boulder was still blocking my view of the canopy. It still seemed that nobody was panicking yet. At that instant a weird feeling came over me. It was the seerstone. It suddenly felt really uncomfortable hanging around my neck. It was totally strange. I almost felt like . . . like I should take it off and throw *it away! I couldn't believe it. The feeling made no sense. Nevertheless, I pulled it off from around my neck. Just then my eye settled on the little black gemstone that Todd Finlay had attached to the chain. For the first time it hit me—that stone was shaped like an eye. I didn't like it. Silly or not, I didn't want it on here anymore. I realized by breaking it off it would no longer hook around my neck, but I didn't care. I bent it until it made a small snap. Then I reached my hand out of the hole and threw that little black gem as far I could.*

I didn't see where it landed, but just as I pulled my hand back in, Haggai appeared from around the other side of the first boulder. He looked right; he looked left. He looked up; he looked down. Now it was time for him to panic.

In fact, everybody *started to panic.*

"You idiot!" cried Finlay. "I said find *her!"*

The Arabs began scurrying all over the place.

Next I heard Finlay's voice calling out to me. He was almost singing, like this was a game of hide and seek. "Rebecca? Rebecca, I know you hear me. Come out now. Come out and I won't hurt you, but if you give me any more grief I'm afraid you'll have to be punished."

Several of the Arabs were dashing toward me. I scooted into the hole a little deeper. I started to worry—did I leave my footprints in the sand? Had I made it obvious where I was hiding? But the panicking Arabs ran right past my hiding place and up toward the top of the hill to see if I'd gone over the other side.

I was still sure that they would find me. How far could I really have gotten in four minutes? They'd have to believe I was hiding somewhere. Hazim and another Arab got back on their horses to ride around and check a bigger area. But Finlay still seemed convinced that I was close by. I saw him appear from around the same boulder as Haggai.

"Rebecca," he said, his voice still calm. "Come out, Rebecca. You should know by now, you can't hide from me. I can find you now, no matter where you are."

I realized he was holding something. It was hard to see it through the bush but . . . it looked like . . . a head? It was like a sculpture or something—silver colored. Finlay was holding it with both hands and looking at its face. He was looking at its face more than he was looking around for me.

"I'm getting closer. Aren't I, Rebecca?" he said.

I swallowed hard. He was *getting closer. He was walking right toward me! Slowly. Surely. "You're not very far now. I'm getting very close. You might as well reveal yourself. Still, I* am *going to have to punish you. We can't have you doing this every day, now can we?"*

I held my breath. He kept coming closer. Ten more feet and he'd be right on top of me!

"Yes, I'm just about . . ."

He stopped. He was still staring at the statue, but his face had changed. He looked . . . confused?

At that instant I felt a nip on my shoe. Then another one. Goodness! It was the fox! After everything else, the fox was biting me! I guessed there wasn't another way out. I was blocking its only escape. I kicked at it. The biting stopped. I was glad that I was wearing shoes or I'd have probably lost a toe. But just as I thought that, the fox nipped again. This time it got my ankle above the rim of my shoe. Its teeth went right through my sock. Ouch! My eyes watered as I fought to keep from crying out.

Finlay crouched down and looked at the dirt. Then he reached out and picked up something. It was the little black gemstone. For the first time I saw the front of the statue. In one of the eyes I saw another stone that looked almost exactly like the one I'd thrown away. But the other eye space . . . was empty. Finlay took the gem in his hand and placed it in the empty socket.

I kicked at the fox again, but the nasty little thing was growing more determined. Mostly it bit at my shoes, but a second time it got my ankle. Then it tried to make a run up my back. I arched my back and pinched it off. It ran back down my legs. If the fox escaped now, Finlay would find out my hiding place for sure. Yet if I kicked at that creature any harder he would hear me.

Finlay's face turned red. He started shaking with anger. He sprang to his feet, his voice no longer calm. "REBECCA!"

He started cursing up a storm, yelling at all the Arabs who were searching, calling them imbeciles and morons and other things much worse.

He shouted to me one more time. "We could leave you here, Rebecca! Would you like that!? If we leave you, you'll die! Do you hear me!? You'll die out here!"

The fox tried to bite me again. I kicked it a good one right in the head. Finlay started to walk back down the hill, still yelling out threats.

"I'll kill you, you little wench! I'll kill you and Mary and your brother before the next setting of the sun! I promise it! I'll give you one last chance!"

Finally that awful fox caught me off guard, scuttled up my back, pushed off my face with its hind legs, and blasted out of the hole. But by then there was no one close by to see it.

I stayed in that hole for another hour. Eventually the Arabs all made their way back to camp, angry and frustrated beyond belief. But no one was more frustrated than Todd Finlay. Moments later I heard the bang of a gun. It sounded different from a rifle. Maybe a pistol. The sound made me stiffen, but it was the only other sound I heard.

After that I heard the grunt of the camels as the men remounted. I still refused to come out of that hole. Maybe they were only pretending *to leave. Maybe it was a trick. What if Hazim or someone else had stayed behind, thinking as soon as I heard the camels go away that I'd come out of hiding? Then* wham! *Somebody would pop out from behind a rock and nab me.*

I stayed in there two more hours. Three more hours. Every now and then I'd take a small drink from the goatskin; otherwise I hardly moved. The fox didn't return. My ankles were stinging and throbbing. I knew that terrible fox had made them bleed, but I didn't dare to climb out and look. I couldn't say for sure how long I was in there. All I know is that by the time I got brave enough to crawl out of that hole, the sun was almost down.

I finally got a good look at my ankles. There were at least three bites marks and some dried blood. Just perfect, *I thought sarcastically. If I didn't die of sunstroke or thirst, I'd die of rabies. I moved quietly and carefully back toward the boulder where I'd untied my hands, then peered out from behind it. Sure enough, the canopy was gone.* Everything *was gone.*

No, that wasn't true. There was something *down there, partly hidden by weeds and rocks. I went down to see, but just before I reached it, I stopped and gasped in fright.* A body! *Oh, it was* terrible! *They'd killed Haggai—the Arab who'd been assigned to watch me! They'd killed him because I ran away. The gunshot must have been one of Finlay's pistols. He'd shot Haggai in cold blood.*

His people didn't even bury him. Just left him for the vultures and foxes and whatever else was out here. I started running back up the hill, then fell to my knees. I started gulping out sobs, hardly able to breathe. I was alone in the middle of nothing. The middle of nowhere. And I wasn't sure which way to go.

I remembered the stone. All this time I had never let it out of my hand. I put it up to my eye again, but I was too panicked to concentrate.

"Where should I go?" I said out loud.

What I saw was fuzzy and confusing. But it wasn't the stone that was fuzzy. It was me. Somehow I had to calm down.

"Please, Heavenly Father!" I said aloud again. "Please help me!"

After a while I did calm down, and then I looked into the stone one more time. My question was a little more specific: Which direction should I go?

To that question I got an answer. Though I had no idea what I might find or how far I would have to travel, I turned south—at least I think *it was south. That is, if the sun was still setting directly in the west. It was almost gone now. I took the chain and tied it into a knot, then I slipped it back over my head and around my neck. I thought about last night's cold and I was already shivering. But there was nothing I could do. I just started walking as the blanket of night was quickly pulled over the desert.*

CHAPTER 21

The panic we all felt in that dungeon below the Temple of Venus was becoming palpable. Never in my military exploits or confrontations had I found myself so exponentially outnumbered. Even fighting three men at once, as I did on that rooftop in Judea with Meagan and Steffanie looking on, or six at once as I had that night in the cane fields of Domingo Guzman, couldn't compare with the prospect of twenty thousand warriors versus sixty. But it wasn't Lamanai who became the calm voice of reason and sensibility. It was the experienced voice of the Prophet Moroni.

"Listen to me," he said, directing his remarks primarily to his fellow captives. "These men have already surmounted incredible odds to make it this far. This is our opportunity at escape—our *only* opportunity. And by God's might, we'll take it."

"And die like warriors!" cried another Nephite. "Not squirming like peccaries under a Gadianton's blade!"

"No, Gilgal," said Moroni. "*Live* like warriors. We'll make for the east end of the city and take refuge in the swamps."

That was more like it. Finally, a definitive plan. Yet for some, this idea sounded more daunting than facing Tikal's twenty thousand warriors. Earlier that evening I'd noticed that there was a large segment of Tikal's eastern boundary with no fortification wall. But in the light of the setting sun I could also see the golden reflection of mangrove swamps as far as the eye could see. I hadn't even considered this as a possible path of escape. No one in their right mind *would* have—not if there were other options. The lords and kings of Tikal had left it undefended for a reason. The natural barrier was far superior to anything that might have been created by men.

"We'll drown," said Gilgal in protest.

"Or become a feast for crocodiles," said another Nephite.

"We'll worry about that if we make it that far," I said.

"What about the Gate of the Priests?" asked Lamanai.

"The army will be at *every* gate," proclaimed an unexpected voice.

It was the lone female captive. She stepped forward into the light of Ryan's torch. I couldn't quite tell if she was a Nephite or a Lamanite, but at least she'd been spared the multiple tattoos and flattened forehead. She was also young. Eighteen or nineteen. Pretty as well. Or at least she *might* have been. It was difficult to tell under that hard exterior. Her raw and callused appearance wasn't just the result of her imprisonment. One look and it was apparent that she'd led a rough life. She practically *exuded* hostility. I'd never met her and I felt sure that she had a firm dislike for me and every other soul in this room.

I turned to Moroni. "I'm with you."

"I'm with you too," said Ryan, still awestruck to be in this man's presence. Frankly, if Moroni had suggested that we run headlong into the enemy's spears, I think Ryan would have been agreeable.

Kukalcan's declaration was all that the men of Seibalche needed to hear. Whereas Ryan was prepared to follow Moroni into the jaws of a dragon, the warriors of Seibalche were prepared to follow Ryan. Moroni gazed at Ryan as if for the first time, marveling at his appearance, but there was no time for inquiries now.

"What about weapons?" asked Gilgal.

"Here!" barked Riki-Kool. He'd brought several of the spears and swords from men who had fallen at the entrance.

The woman staked the first claim, selecting for herself an atlatl with one of its flexible javelin "darts" that were a little more than twice the length of my arm. Moroni took up a saw-edged sword, while Gilgal chose a regular full-length javelin. Many of the warriors of Seibalche gave up hatchets and knives. Ryan noted that his hands were fully occupied with his sword and decided to give the spear-dart for his own atlatl to the woman.

"Here. You might make better use of this," he said.

The woman took it with an ungrateful scowl, then ignored him and started for the exit.

One of the Nephites chuckled to Ryan, "Don't expect to make friends with her. Tz'ikin is fighting her own private war."

"Let's go!" I cried.

But this declaration was suddenly mingled with shrieks from the tunnel. The warriors of Tikal were at the entrance. Had we really been discussing our strategy once we reached the swamp? It would be a miracle just to get beyond the temple plaza! As we entered the tunnel our warriors were fighting hand to hand just outside the doorway.

"We'll have to break through!" Moroni shouted at us all. "Don't stop to fight unless you're forced to! Just follow me!"

Nevertheless, the girl, Tz'ikin, loaded her atlatl dart and flung it with all her might toward the doorway. A Lamanite was standing right in the center, prepared to launch a spear of his own. But Tz'ikin's spear-dart struck first, piercing right through the warrior's feather and bone breastplate and sinking deep into his chest. As the man fell, the rest of us charged the entrance. Tz'ikin paused only to yank her dart from the fallen warrior's ribs. Ryan had been right to suspect that she would make good use of her weapons. This girl could take care of herself.

As I burst outside, I came upon a scene of horror unlike any I'd ever witnessed. At least a hundred warriors from the temple ramparts had converged on the prison's entrance while more warriors were pouring into the plaza from all directions. Among the fighters I noticed Quillkiah and one or two of his men who'd apparently fought their way through to our position from the opposite side of the temple.

Immediately a fierce-looking Lamanite to the side of the entrance attacked me. I blocked the swing of his blade just before it bit into the flesh of my neck, and thrust him back. As his weapon swung at me again he overstepped his footing and tripped. I seized the opportunity and thrust my own weapon upward with lethal results. But then I caught his body before it fell and hoisted it over my head to protect myself from a storm of arrows raining down from the temple platforms above. It was in this hail of fury that I saw Riki-Kool fall, pierced by an arrow in the throat. There was no time to grieve. The body that I held was hit in three places before I discarded it and continued my flight across the plaza. I looked around for Ryan, fearing that he'd been cut down. But then I saw him charging ahead, miraculously unscathed. His bodyguard, Jacobah, was just ahead of him, clearing the path with wide swipes of his blade. I noticed that Quillkiah was bleeding from a gash at his waist, yet he continued running with all his strength.

Our numbers had been cut in half—and in less than fifteen seconds! At least twenty of our men lay dead or dying. Two of the Nephites were also dead. And now the barrage of arrows and atlatl darts was coming not only from the temple, but also from the warriors flooding into the plaza. In seconds we'd be surrounded and consumed by a raging torrent of men.

"Keep going!" cried Moroni, his voice only slightly louder than the whistle of arrows and the screech of hostile voices throughout the city. The din of twenty thousand converging warriors was rising in volume like a forest fire.

Moroni directed our flight eastward, which was also the region least congested by the enemy since it led to no city gate. I saw Quillkiah falter. He was about to collapse. I caught him and supported him with my arm.

"I have you."

"I won't make it," he panted.

"You will while I'm holding you. Where are the men who were with you? Did they go another way?"

"Dead," was his reply. "All dead."

I stood corrected. We were only a *third* of the force that we had been. Already forty men had sacrificed their lives to save the Nephite prophet. And he was still a long way from being saved.

We bounded up a short stairway to a platform surrounded by a complex of small buildings. At the far edge of this platform was a steep drop-off to the muddy banks of a city reservoir, but it was impossible to run another way. Several companies of soldiers had spotted us and were streaming around the platform on either side. Another company of ten or fifteen men appeared in front of us from between the small buildings. They'd climbed the platform from another angle. Moroni clashed swords with the first man to reach us. Moroni was a remarkable fighter, even after enduring the hardships of that prison. His foe was defeated in a matter of seconds.

I had no choice but to release Quillkiah, realizing that a large

Lamanite with battle-axes in both hands had set his sights on me. He rushed forward, the axes twirling like a fire-eater's batons. I ducked to avoid the first blow and blocked the second axe with my sword. I then spun and managed to heave my blade into his back. But such a deft move on my part went unrewarded. I heard the sound of a hollow thunk on a piece of wood. The Lamanite was wearing a shield on his back that deflected my blow. His axe swung around and connected with my sword. The saw-blade shattered. Suddenly my weapon was half its original length.

He grinned savagely and raised his other axe. I dove headlong into the man's stomach. His breath expelled; he fell back against the platform. I rolled away, but before I could retrieve my broken weapon Lamanai had appeared and finished him with his javelin. I nodded to him in gratitude, then I returned to Quillkiah. The elder of Seibalche was lying flat on his back, heaving for oxygen and bleeding profusely from his side.

As I reached down to lift him, he said adamantly, "I can't go on."

"You *will* go on," I commanded.

"No!" croaked Quillkiah. "Take my sword, Master Apollus. I'm going to meet . . . your God."

His body went limp and his chin dropped. My heart was heavy, but several hundred more Lamanites were bounding up the platform steps. They began launching a succession of atlatl spear-darts.

Ryan gripped my shoulder. "Come on!"

There were only sixteen of us now who leaped over the edge of the platform, landing on the reservoir's muddy bank. Tz'ikin landed awkwardly and crumpled. Ryan helped her to her feet, but as soon as she was upright, she shoved him away and continued on her own strength. The water was only ankle-deep, but the yellow mud was thick and our legs soon became encrusted with it. We struggled through to the opposite bank amidst a volley of missiles launched from the platform.

But the darkness was now working to our advantage. We entered a residential district with no burning lamps and only the light of the moon. Yet the clamor of pursuing warriors continued to resound behind us and on either side.

"Through here!" shouted Moroni, directing us down an avenue that ran directly east.

But ten seconds later the street ahead filled with warriors. They pointed at us and shouted. We veered south, through a narrow defile between several buildings that were still under construction, then through a refuse pile of pottery and bones. Our feet crashed through a flower garden. Suddenly four warriors waiting in ambush sprang up behind a garden wall, their bows loaded and firing. Two more of our number crumpled. Moroni struck one down. Another had his arrow aimed at Ryan. Jacobah dove into Ryan's back, but the missile had already fired. I knew it had struck something, but in the darkness I couldn't tell who or what it had hit. Tz'ikin launched another atlatl spear-dart and killed the offender while the Nephite named Gilgal thrust his javelin into the chest of the last remaining attacker.

As Jacobah arose, I realized the arrow had not struck him. I held my breath as Ryan was pulled to his feet. The arrow was protruding from Ryan's shoulder!

"You're hit!" I gasped.

Yet he didn't seem to realize it. Jacobah grabbed the arrow's stone point. Ryan snatched at the other end, which was sticking forward, out under his chin. With relief I realized it had not pierced his flesh— merely gotten itself tangled up in Ryan's chest armor.

Glancing back, I saw warriors streaming through the narrow defiles between at least a dozen buildings, like bees angrily bursting forth from a dozen hives. We leaped several more garden walls until at last we could see the reflection of the moon in the channels and marshes of the eastern swamp.

"That's it!" Lamanai cried.

The waters were just over a stone's throw away. My lungs burned with exhaustion, but I kept running. A kind of trench or channel had been cleared right at the swamp's edge that had created a wide waterway to the first strip of mangroves. It was meant to give canoes easy access along the city's shoreline, but it also meant that we'd have to swim a short distance before we arrived at the safety of the brush. Beyond the first mangroves stretched more muddy channels and marshes that went on *ad infinitum*. The logical course for us would have been to continue groping eastward through the marshes, and at some point turn south, but it was impossible to know if or when the swamps would recede and we'd find ourselves on dry land again.

My heart sank as I saw the silhouettes of more warriors converging from the north and south along the banks of the channel. I judged that we'd intersect at the same moment. Several had paused to arm their atlatls. Some of our number were faltering in confusion.

"Don't slow down!" I cried. "Keep moving!"

I could tell by the black tattoos on their faces that these were the elite of Fire-Born's army—the lightning warriors from Teotihuacan. Javelins and atlatl darts were flying. One of the Nephites running beside Moroni was hit. He crumbled. Several more of our company cried out and fell. As I reached the shore of the channel my sword was already high overhead, my mind caught in a tornado of fury. I started swinging wildly at any black-faced figure. I caught a glimpse of Tz'ikin down the bank. She was trying to commandeer a canoe. Ryan and Jacobah were right behind her. Jacobah swung his battle-ax at an attacking warrior, still furiously defending Kukalcan. But another attacker broke through and charged straight at Ryan, his sword hoisted and ready to strike. In the next instant I watched Ryan successfully deliver the kickboxing move that he'd attempted on me earlier. His lightning-fast kick laid his attacker out flat in the mud. Moroni and Gilgal—the last two surviving Nephites—splashed into the water. Lamanai fought furiously to drive back the warriors who were trying to get at them.

I'd already killed three of Teotihuacan's finest, but a fresh dozen was right behind them. Fighting anymore was useless. I drew a deep breath and dove into the waters of the channel. Instantly, the silence and blackness surrounded me. The contrast was jarring and deceptive, for I knew that the demons of hell were raging just above the surface. I swam through the blackness as far as my breath would allow. My obsidian-edged sword caught on something. It had become too cumbersome, so I let it sink to the bottom of the channel. Then I kept on swimming until at last I collided with the roots of a mangrove tree.

My head broke the surface. I gasped a revitalizing breath, then gripped the slick roots of the mangroves and pulled myself out of the water. I turned back to see who God in his mercy had allowed to survive. Moroni and Gilgal were just down the line of trees, pulling themselves through the mud and into the protection of the brush.

Back on shore the warriors of Tikal were gathering by the hundreds, now igniting flaming arrows and propelling them into the mangroves. Suddenly, just an arm's length away from my face, the surface of the water exploded. Lamanai emerged and gasped a life-giving breath. The heir to Tikal's throne had reached the mangroves alive.

I looked southward and saw Tz'ikin's canoe out in the middle of the channel, its bow pointed slightly upstream. She was kneeling inside it, paddling furiously with her back bent low. Two other persons were clinging to the canoe's outside edge, trying to swim it across the channel while keeping themselves hidden on the sheltered side. Though I couldn't see their faces I could only conclude that it was Jacobah and Ryan. Two other shadows emerged from the water to the north and entered the mangroves. These were the only other survivors that I could see. Eight souls. Was that really all? Eight out of sixty-four? I reeled in devastation. Yet that number was by no means a final count. If I didn't concentrate I could easily become victim number fifty-seven.

The flame-tipped spears and arrows were fired primarily at the canoe. It was the only target still visible in the darkness. Tz'ikin was encompassed by a meteor storm of projectiles that whizzed over her head and around her shoulders. Some of the fire bolts bounced off the hard wood of the canoe. Others sizzled into the surface of the water. By heaven's inexplicable will none had yet pierced her flesh. I realized Tz'ikin was paddling toward an opening in the mangroves—a canal for irrigation and travel.

Lamanai pointed back toward shore. "They're boarding dugouts to pursue her!"

I cringed as three other canoes were launched. Didn't Tz'ikin realize that this would happen? Her canoe idea was useless. Our only hope of escape was to crawl through the thickest, most impenetrable stretches of swampland where no one would pursue.

"Abandon the canoe!" I shouted.

But my voice only brought arrows and spears hurling in our direction. As branches around us began to take fire, Lamanai and I dragged ourselves deeper into the mangroves, half swimming, half crawling through the mud and water, perpetually dodging the gnarled roots of the swamp vines. We scrambled southward to head off the canoe. Along the way Moroni, Gilgal, and the other two surviving warriors of Seibalche joined us. As we reached the irrigation canal, I could hear Ryan's voice.

"Jump out, Tz'ikin!" he pleaded with her.

"No! I need it!"

"You have to! They're gaining on us!"

The lead canoe, filled with Fire-Born's elite warriors, was only about twenty canoe lengths behind them. They had six paddles in the water while she only had one. They'd overtake her in seconds!

"Sink it!" shouted Moroni. "Just overturn it and swim to us!"

This was directed at Ryan and Jacobah, who immediately complied, rising up out of the water with their hands on the rim. Tz'ikin spilled into the drink. The five of us waded out into the canal to pull them into the trees. The lead canoe began launching missiles. A full-length spear with flaming feathers imbedded in the brambles to my right. Thinking twice, I retrieved the weapon, leaned back, and hurled it at the enemy's dugout. It pierced the chest of the front warrior and created a chain-reaction of disarray that caused the remaining warriors to overturn their own boat.

Ryan and Jacobah were holding Tz'ikin by the armpits, forcing her to stay with us as we sloshed through the mud. They rightfully feared that if they let her go she'd return to bail out the canoe. This girl was becoming a serious detriment. If it had been me I'd have left her behind. But Ryan was considerably more patient.

"Get your filthy hands off me!" she scowled, still struggling.

Ryan gave her a stiff, well-deserved slap. "Stop it! You're staying with us!"

For now the angry voices of Tikal's warriors were falling farther and farther behind. But ahead of us stretched a vast concourse of marsh-covered forest that threatened to swallow us whole. We continued almost blindly into the darkness, swimming and sloshing ever eastward. It was conceivable that by the first light of day we'd find ourselves lost forever in the swamp's tentacles.

I couldn't have said how far we traveled before the smoky haze of dawn appeared in the east. The fetid swamp filled our nostrils with the noxious, rotten-egg odors of decay. As the light increased, the air thickened with mist. The fog became no less blinding than the darkness. My companions had become unrecognizable masses of mud and slime, broken only by the whites of their eyes.

Ryan and Jacabah had long since released Tz'ikin. To my surprise, she remained with us, perhaps convinced that the likelihood of her survival increased if she was part of a larger group. Or perhaps she felt that at least one of us had to know where we were going. Lamanai took the initiative to lead the way; however, I was sure that he knew as little about this ground as the rest of us.

For weapons I still had my stone blade and battle-ax, though the latter continually picked up so much moss and debris that I seriously considered abandoning it. The last two surviving warriors of Seibalche were named Antionum and Cancun. Antionum had tenaciously retained a long javelin, but Cancun, Tz'ikin, and Gilgal had all lost their weapons while crossing the channel. Moroni had somehow retained his obsidian sword, while Jacobah still had a short blade.

As the light increased, exhaustion settled over our muscles like drying plaster. We dragged ourselves on by pure force of will. I tried to estimate in my mind how many hours of sleep I'd managed over the last week or so and came up with an appallingly low number. I was driving my body beyond the limits of human endurance.

The goal became to find some island of ground—anything that might accommodate eight human beings. As I emerged from a particularly dense stretch of swamp vines, I peered though the fog at what may have been just such an island. I stepped forward onto a submerged log, hoping for a better view. But two seconds later, the log moved.

I tripped backwards. The surface erupted and the gaping jaws of a crocodile twisted around and snapped at my face. The creature pursued as I armed myself with a weapon. It backed me up against a stand of mangroves and lunged forward. Just as it was about to sink its teeth into my hip I swung my battle-ax crossways like a scythe and split its lower jaw. Hardly deterred, the crocodile kept coming, but by then Antionum and his javelin had sprung into action. He stabbed downward into its skull. The beast convulsed and settled back beneath the surface of the water. Antionum gave me that "you're-lucky-to-be-alive" look and yanked his javelin free.

The worst injury I'd received from all that was a gash to my arm from the tree that I'd backed against. Otherwise I appreciated the fresh burst of stamina that the incident had unexpectedly provided. I had just enough energy to forge the rest of the way to the island.

Just as we pulled ourselves from the water, the first rays of the sun turned the mist into a froth of liquid gold. We stretched out upon a billowing lawn of grass. No one spoke a word. We simply collapsed and lost consciousness for several hours.

When I awakened the mist had burned away. Every living thing as far as the eye could see was covered in a feathery green moss—even the surface of the water, except for a black swath leading up to the island that had been created by us. Everyone else was still asleep. All except Moroni, who was seated at the water's edge. He was still hardly recognizable for the coating of mud.

I joined him and asked, "How are you feeling, Prophet?"

"Prophet?" he chuckled. "You must mean my father. Who told you that I was a prophet?"

I pointed at Ryan.

He concentrated on Ryan's appearance for a moment as he lay there with his mouth open, then Moroni said, "Never in my life have I seen hair of such color. Some Nephite women will blanch their hair, but the result is more silver than gold. Who is he?" He turned back to me. "For that matter, who are you?"

For all our exploits of the past night, I realized that we'd never been introduced. "I am Apollus Brutus. The one with golden hair is Ryan Champion. And over there is Eagle-Sky-Jaguar, heir to the throne of Tikal."

Moroni finally had to ask, "Why did you rescue us? So many warriors lost. If that truly is Eagle-Sky-Jaguar, then he is the son of a man who was an enemy to my people all of his life. I just don't understand."

"You don't need to understand," I replied. "At least not now."

"Where are you from, Apollus Brutus?"

I paused to consider my answer, then said, "From a land very far away. A place where I believe your ancestors are from."

"Nephi? You're from the land of Nephi?"

"I think even a few generations further back than that."

His eyes widened. "Jerusalem? You're from the homelands of Father Lehi?"

"Not precisely. But I am from a place on that side of the world. A city called Rome."

He'd never heard of it, so there was no sense boasting. "But," I continued, "if you ask the people of the Lamaya, they will say that we are here by a miracle. And they will say that Ryan is the Great Kukalcan."

"Nonsense!" Moroni proclaimed. "Kukalcan is the corrupted name that the Lamanites have given to the God of my fathers, Jesus Christ."

"I know," I said. "But they still insist on calling him that. We have told the people of Seibalche a few things about the Savior. Many of them were healed by His power."

Moroni looked astonished. "There are Christians among the Lamanites?"

"Not officially," I said, "but—"

"Is this why you staged the rescue? Because you felt you might be saving fellow Christians?"

"Partly. And partly because Eagle-Sky-Jaguar wishes to form an alliance with you against the conquerors from Teotihuacan."

Moroni scoffed. "I don't believe it."

"Believe it," I said.

He studied my eyes and saw that I was perfectly serious. He pondered this, then he became almost overcome with emotion. "I never thought I'd see the day when the Lamanites would seek an alliance with the Nephites. If what you say is true, it will fill my people with greater hope than they have felt in thirty years. For four years now my people have been gathering into the land of Desolation to defend themselves against the armies of Fire-Born. Even my father is convinced that the Nephites are doomed. This will breathe new life into the hearts of every man, woman, and child in Desolation."

"First we have to get there," said Gilgal. He and several others were starting to awaken, including Lamanai.

Moroni looked at me squarely. "You saved my life, Apollus Brutus. For that, and for this news that you have brought me, I am eternally in your debt."

"Will you do it?" asked Lamanai. "Will your people join with mine to form an alliance?"

"I can't speak for my father and our Presiding Judge. But I feel strongly that they will consider such an alliance heaven-sent."

Lamanai was beaming. "Then our efforts have been worth it. The warriors of Seibalche did not die in vain. The gods—I mean the one God, Jesus Christ, has allowed us all to survive to fulfill this destiny."

Lamanai's rejoicing stirred me to a startling remembrance of Moroni's words from the previous night. Fire-Born was still marching for Seibalche with twenty thousand additional warriors. He was marching straight for Meagan!

"We have to keep moving," I said, "or we won't reach Seibalche in time to warn them. There will be nothing left but a smoldering ruin."

Lamanai shook his head. "It's impossible. The speed of Fire-Born is legendary. If his army has been marching since yesterday, they may arrive tonight."

"It *can't* be impossible," I said. "There must be a way."

We turned south, although what we would find in this direction was unclear. As it turned out, the waters were considerably deeper, forcing us to waste an aggravating amount of time swimming. Ryan removed from his armpit a wriggling black leech. We all had them. It hardly seemed worth it to remove them now. We'd pick up a lot more before this day was over. There was hardly a change in Ryan's expression as he tossed it away. Now *that* was the sign of a seasoned soldier, I thought. The boy had come a long way. The flesh of our hands and feet were becoming swollen and pruned, as if they might start rotting away. All of us recognized that we had to get out of this environment as soon as possible.

Twice we had to pull each other out of quicksand and twice we saw more crocodiles, although this time they kept their distance. Serpents were constantly fleeing through the water. Lamanai said that many of them were deadly poisonous. We also spooked a large, odd-looking creature with a pendulous snout that could have either been a small cow or a large pig.

"A tapir," Jacobah identified.

We crossed a major waterway that had been dug for canoes, but at present there was no traffic going in either direction. Our confidence surged as we spotted cultivated fields to the west. But at just about that time tragedy struck again.

"Where's Cancun?" Antionum asked in alarm.

He'd disappeared somewhere behind us. None of us were certain how long he'd been missing.

"I'll go back and look," I said.

"I'll go with you," said Moroni.

"No," I insisted. "Continue southward. I'll catch up to you."

I didn't have to go far before I found Cancun's body. He was face down in the water, already dead. As I turned him over I saw the fang marks clearly on his upper arm. Why hadn't he cried out? Was he even aware that he'd been bitten? His tongue was swollen so large it hung grotesquely out of his mouth. Perhaps by the time he'd realized that he was dying, he wasn't *able* to cry out. Only a priesthood blessing might have saved him, but an opportunity to provide it had never been granted.

When I caught up to the others they had finally reached dry ground. The jungle remained thick, but there was a narrow trail that Jacobah said had been created by tapirs. I reported Cancun's death, which reminded us all again of our own mortality and the fact that unless we kept moving we'd find ourselves in the same predicament. All I could think about was Meagan. We halted only long enough to remove each other's blood-sucking leeches and let our cracked and bleeding feet dry a little in the sun. Tz'ikin found some roots in the earth which she called wild sweet potatoes. After eating a few of these, we continued on.

"So where are you from?" Ryan asked Tz'ikin.

She looked over at him. I thought sure that she would repulse him, but her spirit seemed to have softened a little.

"Lachoneous," she answered.

"Where is that?"

"West. In the mountains."

"Is it far?"

"Yes."

"What brought you to Tikal?"

"Revenge," she said coldly.

"I see. Against who?"

Tz'ikin hesitated. I didn't think Ryan was going to get anymore out of her. Gilgal, however, decided to fill in the blanks.

"Didn't you know? Tz'ikin here is an assassin." Gilgal had a mocking grin. "She came all the way to Tikal to kill the great commander Fire-Born all by herself. Didn't get that far unfortunately. In fact, she didn't get beyond the palace compound before she was arrested. They found in her maguay sack a yellow-chin viper that she intended to put in the general's bed."

"That was only my second choice," said Tz'ikin. "I would have preferred to give him the dagger."

"Why?" asked Ryan, "would you attempt something so dangerous?"

Tz'ikin clammed up.

"Don't bother," said Gilgal. "We've all tried to get her to tell us that. It's a secret. But I can tell you this. The valley of Lacandone sits right between here and the lands of the Nephites. Fire-Born has marched through with his armies more than once. I have a feeling he took some . . . liberties."

Tz'ikin swung at Gilgal. He caught her hand.

Moroni came between them immediately. "Stop it!" he said to Gilgal. "Leave the girl alone."

"She attacked *me!*"

"You have an offensive mouth."

"Fine, Captain. I'll be quiet."

It was the first time I realized that not all Nephites were like Moroni.

It was approaching midday when we came upon a small village with several palm-thatched huts. At the far end, however, stood a large stone house, the architecture as elaborate as any estate in Tikal.

"I know this place," whispered Lamanai, trying to keep his voice down so as not to attract the attention of several women weaving at the loom and working in small gardens. "It was the estate of Calak-Tun, one of my father's noblemen."

"*Was?*" asked Moroni.

Lamanai nodded. "Calak-Tun was murdered by Fire-Born on the same day as my father. There. You see?"

He pointed toward the central building where the owl-spearthrower glyph had been placed above the stone doorway. This estate was now the property of a loyalist of Lord Blue-Crocodile and Fire-Born.

"I came here once as a child," Lamanai continued. "Calak-Tun was an extraordinary man. He raised and bred very unusual animals."

At that instant I heard one of the most musical sounds in all the world—the whinny of a *horse*. We stared beyond the estate complex to the confines of a stone corral. There *were* horses! *Six* of them! Five were grazing while another was running the perimeter of the fence.

"Are those real horses?" asked Moroni. "I've never seen one before."

"You haven't?" asked Ryan.

"No. My father tried to describe them to me once. He's never seen one either, but he read of them in the ancient records. Once there were many horses among the Nephites and Lamanites. Most of them died out even before the coming of the Savior. There are said to be a few in the land of Lachoneous where Tz'ikin is from, but I have never searched for them."

"We need them," I said plainly.

"What for?" asked Gilgal.

I looked at him strangely. "To ride, of course."

"I'm not getting on one of those things," said Tz'ikin.

"Can horses be ridden?" asked Antionum.

I couldn't believe what I was hearing. "*Absolutely* horses can be ridden. What did you *think* horses are used for?"

"For food," said Gilgal.

"*Food!*" I said in disgust. "You don't eat horseflesh! Not unless you're a barbarian who'd as soon eat his own shoe leather."

I motioned for them to follow. We tried to conceal ourselves in the trees, but it was impossible. As the women caught a glimpse of us making our way around to the horse corral, mud smeared and covered with insect welts, one of them screamed. The next thing I knew they were all fleeing from us like we had the plague—but not into the compound. They were running down the trail, away from the village. This told me all that I needed to know.

"There are no men here," I said confidently. "The horses are not being defended."

"The new owner is likely an army commander from Teotihuacan," said Lamanai. "He is either marching to Seibalche or defending Tikal."

"How far are we from the city?" asked Ryan.

"Not far. Less than a quarter day's journey."

"Let's keep moving," I said. "They may have gone to alert a local garrison."

But to our surprise the horses *were* defended. A wrinkled old man appeared at the gate of the horse enclosure. In his hands was an atlatl with a spear-dart ready to launch. I'd come to learn that this was weapon was deadly in the hands of anyone, regardless of age. We stopped in our tracks.

"Don't come any closer," the old man ordered.

Despite the warning, Lamanai took one careful step forward. "Cocao, do you remember me?"

"No," he replied. "I don't know any of you."

"I was here as a boy," Lamanai continued, "with my father."

He squinted his dim-sighted eyes, thinking hard. Lamanai took another careful step.

"Stay back!" he said again, ready to launch the atlatl dart.

"I am Eagle-Sky-Jaguar," said Lamanai calmly, "son of Great Jaguar-Paw."

Fear entered the old man's eyes, followed by amazement, then reverence. His old limbs started to quake and the weapon was lowered. Tears filled his eyes as he started to kneel. "Prince Sky? Can it really be you?"

It was another example of how quickly the loyalties of this people would change once word got out of Lamanai's identity. Old Cocao had apparently been the caretaker of these animals for much of his life, maintaining his position even after the estate's change of ownership.

Lamanai went to him, bidding him to rise. "Where is your new master, Cocao?"

"He was summoned to march with Fire-Born. There are strange rumors being whispered. Now that I see your face, I know that these rumors are true. Fire-Born and Lord Crocodile are said to be quite agitated. Never before have they alerted the armies at the beginning of planting. And never has the Festival of Sacrifice been postponed. But now I understand." He hesitated. "You are not a ghost, are you, revered prince?"

He took the old man's hands into his own and said, "No, Cocao. Not a ghost. A new day is dawning. The dynasty of my father will again sit on Tikal's mat of honor, and again we will rule all the lands of the Lamaya. The usurpers will be driven back to the lands of green obsidian. The Lamaya will again become a free and powerful people. But the ancestors of Yax-Chaac-Xoc require your help."

"Anything, Lord Prince," he said enthusiastically. "Anything to know that I was able to serve the memory of your father."

"First, you shall let the people know that you have seen me. And second—" Lamanai turned to me to explain it.

"We must have these horses," I said. "We must ride with swiftness to warn those whom Fire-Born would destroy."

"You may take them," he said without hesitation.

Though I couldn't see it, I knew this had to be a heart-rending decision for the old man. He certainly loved these animals very much.

"They can be ridden, can't they?" asked Ryan.

"Certainly!" said Cocao with pride. "I have broken and trained them myself."

But despite these words, I soon discovered that they had been trained in a manner entirely different from what I was accustomed to. There was no bit or stirrup. They were controlled with mildly spoken words and modest tugs on the mane, not kicks. This would take some getting used to; otherwise I'd find myself bucked off into the mud every other moment.

Cacao offered a short riding lesson to Lamanai, Moroni, and the others. But all of his careful instructions of subtle pulls and tugs and words hardly seemed necessary after he indicated the larger stallion and said, "They will all follow the lead male."

I'd like to have said that these horses were fine-looking animals, but it wouldn't have been true. Actually, they were the sorriest-looking creatures I'd ever laid eyes on, with protruding ribs and a musculature that almost made them appear to be a different species. I'd always prided myself on being a good judge of horseflesh, but here I was entirely at a loss. As I intimated, they were far more inclined to obey a gentle hand rather than the brusque manner of the Romans, which drove me quite mad. At first I'd have thought myself to be the natural choice to ride the stallion, but the horse spurned me entirely, deciding that I was unworthy to sit upon its back. The task of riding the lead stallion fell to Moroni, who seemed to have a natural gift with these animals.

The only horse that would tolerate my manner was the smaller male—a red-coated rogue who I think decided that it might be fun to teach me a lesson. I'd have preferred the company of a mule. More than once as I indicated a command it would stop dead in its steps, as if to inform me that if I expected it to obey, I had better learn to "say it nicer." I might have named it "Meagan" if it had not already received a suitable name of its own—Chac Koshtok, or Red Devil.

Tz'ikin still refused to ride.

"Then ride with me," said Ryan. "We're one horse short anyway."

Tz'ikin shook her head. "I cannot go with you."

"Maybe you better rethink that," said Ryan. "Without fresh supplies and weapons, you don't stand a chance."

"I still have not completed what I came here to do," she said.

Ryan rolled his eyes. "Ah, yes. I almost forgot. Your mission of assassination. In case you weren't listening, Fire-Born is now headed to the same place that *we're* headed. My, you do give the term *femme fatale* a whole new meaning."

I'm not quite sure how that term translated in the mind of Tz'ikin. To my Latin mind it meant a beautiful woman who leads men into dangerous situations. Was that a blush I saw on Tz'ikin's face? For a second I swore that I saw a glint of femininity in this girl's granite exterior. The idea that she was beautiful might not have occurred to her for a long, long time. She might have been flattered by the "dangerous" part as well. Or perhaps it was strictly Ryan's statement that the object of her vengeance would be closer to where we were headed that caused her to give him a hesitant, even shy, nod.

Ryan hoisted her up to sit behind him on the thick saddle blanket. The horse was skittish for a moment, but as Tz'ikin gripped her arms around Ryan's waist, it settled down.

Within minutes we were riding toward Seibalche. A painful foreboding entered my heart. I shut my eyes and whispered a prayer, though I wondered what right I had to plead for one life over all the others that might yet be lost. I uttered it nonetheless. Even if I felt myself unworthy of her love, the notion that there might be a world without her was unbearable.

"*Chanim!*" I shouted in my horse's ear. Cacao had said that this word would make the horse move more quickly. But still, it would not go faster than the lead stallion.

"*Chanim!*" shouted Moroni, but the best he could get out of it was a modest trot—still faster than the pace of a man, but hardly the swift gallop that I felt we required.

It was already noon. Would Fire-Born really have marched all night? Would he really be arriving at Seibalche with twenty thousand men this evening? I wouldn't allow myself to think about it, yet it seemed the only word I uttered for the next several hours was "*Chanim!*"

CHAPTER 22

I couldn't understand it.

It made no sense to me how it could get so scaldingly hot during the day and so miserably cold during the night. And here I was with the icy stars all around me and no coat, no tent, and no blanket to keep me warm. So what did I do? I did the same thing that any other desert rugrat might do. I found a sandy place protected from the wind and buried myself.

That's right. I just lay there and threw handful after handful of sand over my legs and chest until I finally just dug in my arms. I won't say it was warm, but it was a lot warmer than it would have been. If I hadn't done this, I think I would have truly started to freeze.

As it was, the next morning my teeth were all chattered out and my brain felt numb. Just like a lizard, I waited there until the sun came up and started to thaw out my limbs and make me warmer. But then the heat took over. It wasn't long though before I started to miss *the cold. I completely forgot what I'd found so awful about it and thought to myself, "Oh, if only I could feel it again—just for a few minutes!"*

I tried not to stop walking. I told myself that resting wasn't allowed. I just kept going south across the miserable, dry, sunburned landscape. I told myself crying wasn't allowed either. I couldn't spare the water. You know, I think it's possible for a person to get so frightened that they're not *frightened anymore. Maybe that doesn't make much sense. It's like you just keep saying to yourself, "What's the worst that could happen?" Sure, I could die. But what else? Others could die too. We could* all *die and nobody would ever know.* That *was the very worst. And at some point you just say to yourself, "I can deal with that."*

I learned something else that day. Death isn't really as frightening as it seems. What's frightening is waiting *for death—thinking about all that pain*

and suffering that you might have to go through. In other words, the fright-
ening part is all created in the mind. It's only made worse by worrying and
tormenting over it. So I just decided not to. I even told myself that being here
was kinda cool. I was out in the middle of the deserts of Arabia. Wasn't this the
most cliché way in the whole world for a person to die? Out walking in the
desert with the scorching sun overhead and moaning, "Water, water?" It was
kinda funny as I thought about it. Besides, I had *water. A little bit anyway. I*
figured there were at least three or four cups left in my goatskin canteen.

And you know what? The country around me was beautiful. *I don't care*
what anybody says. I thought it was so interesting. Nothing grew but a few
scraggly thorn bushes. Still, everything was so wild and rugged. Rocks were
broken; mountains were cracked and torn. This was how it looked, I decided,
before God had ever made the first plants or animals—just after all the
earthquakes stopped rumbling and the volcanoes stopped grumbling. It just
looked so old. I wondered if I'd ever seen a place so old and fragile. I'll bet if
I could've gotten my hands around all these jagged peaks and given them a
little shake, the whole thing would have crumbled into a puff of dust. I never
knew rocks could have so many colors—purples and reds and oranges and
even blues—every color constantly changing in the sun like the skin of a
chameleon. I pretended I could hear the peaks talking to each other:

"So whatcha doin' today, Vern?"

"Nuthin' much. How 'bout you?"

"Oh, same as yesterday. Same as the last billion days. But hey,
what've we got here?"

"Well, wouldya look at that! Why, that there's a *girl* walkin'
through here! Now, that ain't somethin' we see ever'day."

"No, 'taint. Whacha 'spose she's doin' way out here?"

"Don't rightly know. Should we ask 'er?"

"Nah. Then she'd think she was goin' plum crazy. 'Cause ever'-
body knows that rocks don't talk."

Okay, so I was feeling a little light-headed. The sun was just so hot.
And boy, was I sweating! I gotta admit, it was a bit of a surprise when I
held up that goatskin and only a few drops trickled out. Oh, that nasty
thing! It had fooled me! But one thing about a goat skin. It's not like a
canteen. 'Cause you can squeeeeze it. You can squeeze it and squish it and
twist it and it seems like there's always just a few more drops. Just a little
more to get your tongue wet and—

I couldn't believe it. I tripped. Staring up at that sun and trying to get out those last few drops had made me dizzy. The feeling was still there. Whoa. This was weird. You know how people who get dizzy always talk about how everything keeps spinning? Well, that's not quite true. It doesn't spin. It just sort of floats. But it's not the world that spins. It's you.

I really wasn't sure if I could get up. What was I saying? Of course I could get up. And I'd prove it too. I wasn't real steady, but I did it. There, I said to myself. That proves it. I'm just fine. I can keep walking like this forever.

I think I reached a road. Nice and smooth and paved, just like one of those sidewalks that you jog on with green grass and trees and birds singing. All of it went off toward the sun. Right up into it. But no sir—I wasn't going in that *direction. Wasn't it hot enough down here on earth? I turned the other way. There, that was better. Or what about this way? Sure, that was a good way. I could go this way and find everything I needed. Eeeverything I needed.*

And what do ya know? There were camels *this way. How weird, I thought! And people. Oh, they were good people too. I could tell. Nice and . . . and friendly and . . . Did I say they were nice? And hey! Who was that? Oh, my goodness!* Mary *was with them. She had on a halo like an angel. And Joshua too. They were floating above me just like the camels. Floating right out of the sun. They wanted to talk to me. I could tell, because they floated down real close to my face.*

"Becky?" they said. That is, Joshua said it. The angel *Joshua. Or whoever it was. "Becky are you okay?"*

"Uh-huh," I answered. "Fine. How're you?"

"She's delirious," said Mary, which I thought was kind of a rude thing to say.

"Give her water," said Joshua.

Oh, now that sounded good. Water. Yes, I could drink lots and lots and lots of water.

"Get her out of the sun," said another voice. "Sheik al-Farabi! We're camping here tonight."

Hey, that was Brother Nicholas's voice! Was he here in heaven too? Oh, how nice. How wonderful. The more the merrier. But camping? I didn't think that was a good idea at all.

"No camping," I said. "Bed. I want my own bed. And Lolly."

Lolly was my penguin. Yeah, I know. Kinda childish to have kept my little stuffed penguin. But I'd just had her for so, so long . . .

"You'll be all right, Becky," said Mary, *her voice like an echo, echo, echo. "Everything will be all right . . ."*

* * *

I don't think I fainted. I think I was awake every single minute. But there was definitely a moment when I "woke up."

I was lying face up in the shade of a tent. Mary was holding my hand and Joshua was laying a wet rag across my forehead. There were more wet rags on my shoulders and arms. The light was orange-ish outside. It was evening. I started to get up.

"Don't even think about it," said Joshua, *putting his hand on my shoulder. "Brother Nicholas says you shouldn't move for the rest of the day and night."*

"Joshua!" I whispered excitedly, *as if seeing him for the very first time. "Mary!"*

I realized they were dressed now like real Bedouins, with puffy head cloths wrapped around their brows and everything. The outfit looked totally natural on Mary, like she'd worn this kinda stuff before, but Joshua looked silly.

"We're here, Becky," Mary answered. *"Do you know who we are now?"*

"Sure I know."

"Really?" said Josh. *"'Cause you've been calling me everything from Dad, to Harry, to Todd Finlay."*

"I have?"

"Drink some more of this," said Mary. *She gave me a drink from a goatskin."*

"Uck!" I said. *"Salty!"*

"That's exactly what the Arabs said you need. You were sweating way too much. You got overheated. You're pretty badly sunburned too. You're lucky we found you when we did. I don't want to think about what might have happened if we'd found you just a few hours later."

"But how did you get here?"

"We were looking for you," said Joshua.

"How could you have known where to look?"

"Talk to her,*"* said Joshua, *pointing at Mary. "She's the Sherlock."*

"It wasn't that difficult," said Mary, smiling. "We went back to the monastery. The Bedouins from Wadi Musa were still there. That's how we found out about Todd Finlay, or as he called himself, 'Mr. Stephens.' Sheik al-Farabi had found him in the ruins at Petra and brought him to Jerusalem. He told al-Farabi all about this magical sword that he'd been searching for all of his life. He also desribed the rotten tooth. After that it didn't take us long to figure out who he was. Finlay tried to hire al-Farabi to kidnap you, but the sheik refused. Believe me, he's much nicer than Hazim. In fact, the Arabs of Wadi Musa and those of al-Arabah are bitter enemies. Even more so now after Nicholas fired Hazim and hired al-Farabi instead. Basically, the two sheiks switched jobs. Sheik al-Farabi is guiding Brother Nicholas and the other monks back to Mount Sinai."

"But how did you know to look for me here?" I asked.

"That was plain luck," said Joshua.

"A plain miracle," Mary corrected. "But we knew that you'd be headed to Petra."

"You did?"

"We knew from your vision on the Mount of Olives. You told us that the stone said in order to find a time bridge we had to travel to the ruins of an ancient city to the south."

"Elementary, Dr. Watson," said Joshua.

"How did you escape from Todd Finlay?" asked Mary.

"Never mind that," I said. "What happened to Orson Hyde?"

"He's still in Jerusalem," said Joshua. "He tried to do everything he could to help us. He even went to the Turkish Governor of Jerusalem on our behalf to try and raise an armed posse to go after you. But that was before we figured out the Petra thing and found out about Todd Finlay. Elder Hyde couldn't get the governor excited about helping us at all. That's when we went back to the monastery."

"But what's Elder Hyde going to say?" I asked. "What about history? He's sure to tell everybody what happened."

"I don't think so," said Joshua. "At least he promised that he wouldn't."

"He did? Why would he make a promise like that?"

"Because we asked him to," said Mary simply. "He knew that you had saved his life. We told him that the best way that he could show his gratitude was by not saying a single word—just keeping the memory in his heart."

"You really think he'll keep his promise?"

"Well, yeah," said Joshua as if I'd said something stupid. *"He's an* apostle!*"*

"He gave us some gold, too," said Mary. *"Not very much. But enough to convince al-Farabi to take us to Petra to find you. The sheik is, uh, I think hoping for a little more after we get there."*

"A little more?*"*

Josh took over. *"Well, see, he thinks Todd Finlay, or Mr. Stephens as he calls him, kidnapped you to make you use your stone to reveal the location of a secret hidden treasure somewhere in the ruins. He's willing to protect us and help us get to Petra and all, but I think he hopes that maybe you'll give the treasure to him instead of Hazim al-Arabah."*

"What treasure?"

Josh shrugged. *"We didn't think that far ahead."*

"All we wanted to do was get to Petra," said Mary. *"That's where the stone told us to go, right?"*

"Yes, but . . ."

My head was still a little dizzy. This was all starting to seem very dangerous. I knew that Todd Finlay and Sheik Hazim were going to Petra too. But would they still go there without me? What would have been the point? Without me, Finlay had no way of finding his mysterious sword, or at least that's what he thought. I was still convinced that Finlay was out there in the desert somewhere looking for me. Of course, without his mega-weird statue and eye-stones he'd have to do it the old-fashioned way, but he'd still be looking.

Then again . . .

Todd might've gone on to Petra simply because he felt sure that we'd have to show up there sooner or later. Maybe he knew it was the closest place around that could be used as a time tunnel to get us back to Frost Cave in the twenty-first century.

I started to sit up again.

"Becky," Josh scolded, *"you're supposed to lie still, remember?"*

"I have to look in the stone."

They gave me no objections to that. I took a deep breath, put the stone up to my eye, and gazed into the surface.

"What are you asking it?" Joshua wondered.

"I have to see it again. I have to know exactly when we're supposed to be in Petra."

I still had a bit of a headache, and my sunburn was starting to hurt, but I concentrated hard. When the answer came to me, it wasn't quite as clear as it had been on the Mount of Olives, but it was clear enough.

"Day after tomorrow," I told Joshua and Mary. "Right before sunset."

"But Nicholas told al-Farabi that we should wait here another day for you to recover," said Joshua.

"Never mind that," I growled. "I'm fine. We have no choice!"

I continued staring into the stone. Something new appeared. Something unexpected. I tried one more time to clear my mind.

"There's something else," I said.

"Something else?" said Mary. She sounded terribly uneasy, as if the last thing she wanted to hear about right now was "something else."

"Something . . . we have to . . . deliver."

"Huh?" asked Josh.

It was so hard to see. My head was throbbing. I finally gave up. I couldn't look anymore. I didn't have the energy.

Josh became impatient. "What do we have to deliver?"

"I don't know," I said.

"Deliver where? Deliver to whom?" asked Mary.

I shook my head. "I'm sorry. I'm just so tired. I'll look again later." I started to lie back down.

"I don't want to do anything else," Josh whined. "Tell the stone we quit."

Mary settled him down. "We won't worry about it right now. Just let her sleep."

I closed my eyes and drifted off. The last words I heard were from Josh: "When this is all over, if I never hear another riddle again, it will be too soon."

* * *

The next morning I felt much better. Not perfect. I still could've slept another eight hours. The worst thing was the sunburn on my face and arms. It was burning and itching like crazy. Paolo the dwarf provided me some chalky cream that helped a little, but not much. Nevertheless, I definitely felt strong enough to ride a camel. I finally got my own Bedouin shawl too, which made me feel like . . . What would be the "girl" name for it? How 'bout "Lorraine of Arabia?" I even got some pouches to tie on my

*belt and carry all the stuff that had been in my pockets. Mary had told
Sheik al-Farabi that I wanted to leave, so everything was all ready to go.*

Nicholas asked me several more times if I really felt well enough to travel.

"I'm okay," I insisted. "We have to get to Petra before tomorrow night."

*Nicholas made a frown that looked very much like a father. If he'd
had kids of his own, I think he would have been a very good one. "If this
treasure that you've seen in your stone has been waiting there for over a
thousand years, it can certainly wait another day. Don't set your heart
upon the things of this world, my child. One day you will pass on, look
around with wonder, and say 'Where is my treasure?' Then you will use
your spyglass and peek down at the earth and see that your children are
only squabbling and bickering about it."*

*I smiled at him warmly. "I promise you, my heart isn't set on those
things. And I really do feel better."*

*He shrugged and shook his head. But before he walked away he sent
me the same warm smile.*

*Surprisingly, not a single person—Arab or monk—had any doubts
about the fact that I really could find this treasure. They just had different
opinions about how important it was. Nicholas didn't seem to care about
the treasure at all, although I did see a glint of adventure in his eye, like it
might still be fun to find one. Paolo didn't seem to care about it either, or
at least I didn't sense that he did. He brought me a cold leg of lamb for my
breakfast and said, "No treasure could ever replace a good tobacco pipe."*

*Sheik al-Farabi acted like he didn't care either, but I knew better than
to believe that. Mary and Joshua were right about him. He was nicer than
Hazim. Then again, maybe "nicer" wasn't the right word. Truthfully, he
looked ferocious. The desert sun had burnt his skin almost to blackness and
his eyes were always on fire. The very best thing about him may have been
that he totally disliked Hazim and the Arabs of al-Arabah. No, that wasn't
true. He seemed to love his religion a great deal. No matter how anxious
everyone was to reach Petra, he still insisted on stopping the caravan several
times a day so he and his men could say their prayers toward Mecca. While
he and his thirty Bedouins knelt on their rugs in the sand, the rest of us said
prayers of our own. One thing we could never get too much of was prayers.*

*I was going to feel a little sad when Mary, Joshua, and I walked into
that tomb at Petra while the others waited outside. Soon they would
realize that we were never coming out again. I really wished there was*

some sort of treasure that I could've given them.

As far as the last member of our caravan, I honestly couldn't figure out what he cared about. This was Shika, the bald, pock-faced guy with the teeth that stuck a little forward. At first when I realized that Mr. Nosferatu was with us, I nearly freaked out. I guess I should've expected it. After all, the whole reason that Nicholas and Paolo had gone to Jerusalem was to pick him up and take him back to Mount Sinai. But it disturbed me all the same.

Maybe it was just the way he looked. Or the way he acted. Or the things he said. The man just gave me the heebie-jeebies for some reason. But even if he didn't show any particular interest in the treasure, he still seemed to have a very strange curiosity about the stone.

He rode his camel beside me that afternoon and asked several unusual questions. "What was it that you said the other night about how this stone came to be in your possession? Or how you learned to see things inside it?"

"I didn't *say*," I replied, hoping he'd get the hint.

He smiled tightly and faced forward. "Ah, so these things are secrets."

"No, I just . . . don't wanna talk about it right now."

"Perfectly fine," he said. "Quite understandable. All men should have secrets. Little girls too. It leaves others with a pang of curiosity that helps them to remember you."

This guy was making me squirm. Why couldn't he ride next to somebody else? Maybe I was being totally unfair. Sure, he was creepy, but hey, he was a monk, right? He'd given his life over to God. How dangerous could he really be?

For some bizarre reason, he decided to reveal one of his secrets to me.

"Do you know what I have here?" He touched something tied to his camel. It was about a yard long and wrapped tightly in cloth and rope. He took a look around to make sure that no one else was listening, then said, "It's a fine Damascus sword."

"A sword?"

"Shhhh! *Not so loudly.* It's very valuable. Our guides have been very gracious so far, but I'm afraid something like this might prove a little too tempting."

"Why would a monk have a sword?" I asked accusingly. "I thought you guys were supposed to give up all worldly property and stuff."

"It's a gift."

"A gift? Who for?"

"For Mohammed Ali."

"The boxer?"

"The pasha in Egypt. I have heard that he is a great admirer of fine swords. I'm delivering it to his agents at Mount Sinai who will then carry it to Cairo."

"I see," I said. *"So why tell me?"*

"I don't know. I guess I wanted to tell someone. *You're so good at keeping your own secrets. I felt you might also be good at keeping mine."*

I thought about Todd Finlay and how he'd been willing to kill my whole family for a sword. *"That's okay,"* I said. *"I don't need to know anyone else's secrets."*

"I wish I could show it to you," he continued. *"I have studied fine swords from all over the world. The sharpness of the Samurai edge, the durability of the Incan copper, and the flexibility and strength of Damascus steel."*

"You've been to all those places?"

"No," he said quickly. *"But I've been to the museums of Spain and Italy. I've melted down samples in my blacksmith shop in Syria. When this sword is finished, it will be my finest work."*

"It's not finished?"

"It needs one more firing. One more plating."

"If it's not done, why are you giving it away?"

"It is my hope and prayer that the Superior at Mt. Sinai will allow me to finish it. But if not . . . I suppose it is God's will."

"Maybe you should have waited until you were done before you became a monk."

"I suppose," he sighed. Then he got a strange look in his eye and added, *"Do you know what the secret is to making the strongest, most flexible sword in all the world?"*

"No," I said.

"Blood. Human blood. Smelted with the ore. Tempered with the steel. The metal must be heated to a bright orange, then dipped into the blood while the blood is still warm. The makers at Damascus have known this for thousands of years."

Okay, that was it. My "creep alert" was buzzing off the scale. Time to change the scenery. He noticed the change in my face.

"I'm sorry. Have I said something to upset you?"

"*I just have to speak to Mary,*" *I answered.* "*Nice talkin' to ya.*"

I made my camel trot ahead until I'd left him well behind. As I caught up to the camels Mary and Nicholas were riding, I glanced back to look at Shika one more time. Vampire-man was busy petting the bundle of blankets hanging next to him on the camel.

"*Something wrong?*" *asked Mary.*

"*I'm fine,*" *I said.*

"*I see that you were talking to Shika,*" *said Nicholas.* "*He's a good fellow. He was very concerned when he heard that you'd been kidnapped. And very attentive when we found you on the desert.*"

"*He was?*" *I asked.*

"*Yeah,*" *said Mary.* "*He gave you his water and built the tent so that you could be in the shade.*"

"*I don't like him,*" *I said softly.*

Their eyebrows went up.

Nicholas waved this off. "*Don't let his manner disturb you. All novices are a little rough around the edges. In five years, if you come back to see us again, you'll find a man as harmless as a butterfly.*"

"*What do you know about him?*" *I asked.*

"*Only that he was recommended to us by the Bishop at Damascus. Very few questions are asked when a man decides to give his life to the Lord.*"

"*Why did he want to go to Mount Sinai?*"

"*Mount Sinai is known throughout our faith as one of the most isolated and peaceful places to serve.*"

"*Did you know he has . . .*" *I hesitated.*

"*A sword?*" *Nicholas finished.*

"*You* know *about it?*"

"*Yes,*" *Nicholas whispered.* "*But it's not something that ought to be spoken of loudly in this company. You know that Shika was a master swordmaker before he decided to become a monk.*"

"*Why would he bring such a thing with him?*"

"*The sword is his penance,*" *said Nicholas.* "*I haven't seen it, but I'm told that it's very beautiful. As you may be aware, our existence at Mount Sinai is by the grace of God and the tolerance of the Pasha of Egypt, Mohammed Ali. Shika's gift may bring us peace and support for many years to come. You can't fault a man for wanting to give up the most valuable thing he has ever created for the benefit of God.*"

"Sorry,"I said. "I guess . . . I didn't look at it that way."

But even knowing this still didn't make me feel any better. What kind of a jerk would come out and tell a young girl about making swords with human blood? I felt like there was only one place I could go to find out more about this man. I had to ask the stone. I just wanted to get a feeling. But every time I thought about holding it up to my eye and asking the question, I'd glance around and there would be Shika, watching me. Always he'd smile and nod. I couldn't very well ask such a question with him gawking at me all the time.

It wasn't until that night, just a day before we reached Petra, that I finally found a quiet moment to put the stone up to my eye. Mary and Joshua were asleep beside me in the tent. I could hear Paulo in the tent across the ravine. For a dwarf he sure had a loud snore. I knew that Nicholas was in the same tent. Shika had insisted on putting his tent further up the hill. There in the darkness I finally put the stone to my eye and asked the all-burning question: Who is this mysterious sword-maker from Damascus?

"Rebecca?"

I nearly jumped out of my socks. Shika was right outside my tent!

"Rebecca, are you asleep?"

I hesitated. I almost didn't answer. I probably should've kept quiet, but stupidly I whispered, "What do you want?"

He spoke so close to the tent that I could smell his breath through the canvas. It was spiced with something sickly sweet. "I just wanted you to know that I'm sleeping out here tonight. Right outside your tent—to protect you."

I felt like something sour was curdling inside my stomach. "That's . . . not necessary."

"It's no bother," he said. "In case that man returns—Mr. Todd Finlay."

He knew Todd Finlay's real name. That seemed strange. I assumed that Mary had told him. But oh, this was so gross! How was I supposed to sleep knowing that Count Dracula was right outside my tent? How was I supposed to concentrate on the stone?

"I don't want *you to sleep there," I said.*

I must not have said it firmly enough, because he replied, "Don't worry. I have my sword."

His voice had moved away a bit. I waited. I didn't hear anything else. Was he still out there? Or was he keeping watch a little ways off? Finally, I said very softly, "Shika?"

He didn't answer. I didn't say anything else. A few minutes later I got brave enough to pull back the tent flap and look outside. No one was there. Okay, could this get any creepier? I went back inside and tried one more time to look into the stone. I was so shaken up that I couldn't see anything. Why was it that inspiration and fear never seemed to mix? I did get a feeling, but I truly didn't know if it was from the stone or from my own frightened thoughts. Whatever the case, it wasn't good, and despite being so exhausted, I hardly slept a single wink all night long.

* * *

It was late afternoon when Sheik al-Farabi announced that we had almost reached the ancient city of Petra. All afternoon we'd been climbing a long and difficult trail. Even the tough Arabian horses of al-Farabi's men slipped once or twice on the steep path. On one side of us were some wild and barren mountains while on other side was a dreary valley that the Arab's called El Ghor. Looming above us was an oddly shaped mountain with tombs carved all around the base and some kind of a building on top which we were told was the burial shrine of Aaron, the brother of Moses. We passed by a stone that was blackened with smoke and surrounded by bits of bone. Paolo told us that this was where the Arabs sacrificed sheep to the Prophet Aaron.

It was a strange, mystical-looking land, and it gave me an uncomfortable feeling, but it wasn't quite as desolate as the rest of the desert had been. There were patches of green grass and several gushing streams. As we approached the largest and "greenest" of these valleys I could see many large tents. It was the village (if any Bedouin camp can be called a "village") of the Arabs of Wadi Musa.

Several boys ran up to our camels and greeted us shouting, "Salaam! Salaam!" Standing beside the large "home" tents were many women with black head coverings and veils that could be quickly pulled over their faces. These were the wives and daughters and sisters of the tribe.

"I don't understand," said Joshua. "Where's the ruined city?"

"Through there," said one of al-Farabi's men, pointing toward a gap between some cliffs that led into another valley.

The tribe of Wadi Musa had a lot more than just the thirty men who'd ridden to Jerusalem. Many more men had stayed here with the rest of the tribe. The first question that Sheik al-Farabi asked a tribal leader as we rode up was, "Has there been any sign of that son of a mongrel dog, Hazim al-Arabah or his men?"

The old man shook his head. "There has been no report of travelers for many days."

"Do Yusuf and Abu-Walid still watch the entrance on the west?"

"They do. I saw Abu-Walid just this morning. He went back at noon." The sheik turned to me. "Do you wish to go there now?"

I looked at the sun. It would set in two hours or less. I nodded eagerly.

"Then we will go there now," said the sheik.

I soon realized that every male with a camel, donkey, or horse that could be ridden was coming with us. The rumor had spread quickly that I was going to discover a hidden treasure, but the treasure seemed to get grander every time I heard someone whispering about it. At first it was just a chest of treasure, then it was a whole room filled with treasure, then it became "the treasure of the Angel Gabriel himself, greater than the heart can fathom." I couldn't believe it when I heard that.

Mary, Joshua, and I didn't say a word, just let the imaginations of these people run wild. It seemed so silly to think that they would believe I could just stroll into a place that they'd been exploring almost every day of their lives and suddenly find a treasure that they'd somehow missed.

I soon learned, though, that at least two people were not coming with us. The two noble monks from Mount Sinai, Brother Nicholas and Brother Paolo, were staying in the camp.

"Go and find your treasure, little one," said Nicholas. "Just remember, the only treasure worth keeping is the one you can fit in here."

He tapped two fingers on his heart. Then he looked at me with another bright smile, although his eyes still seemed far, far away, like he was remembering something from his boyhood, and I thought to myself, He knows that he's not going to see us anymore. Somehow he knows.

I leaned over toward him. It was a little too awkward to give him the kind of hug that he deserved while we were both sitting on top of our camels, but I tried anyway, and I also tried to give him a kiss on the cheek. What I got in return was a mouthful of beard.

"You're staying too?" Joshua asked Paolo.

"Yes," he said, his camel already kneeling. "But if you can spare a gold coin for old Paolo and toss it into some well somewhere with a blessing, I'd be most grateful."

"So it's only us and the Arabs?" Mary asked.

"And me."

We turned and there was Shika, still seated atop his camel, his sword still in the bundle.

"It's been a long time since I've seen a treasure. And I promise, Brother Nicholas, I will watch out for the children."

This seemed to comfort Nicholas, but in no way did it comfort me. Yet I realized that with Sheik al-Farabi and a hundred other Arabs around us there wasn't a whole lot that Shika could do to us. Actually, if al-Farabi found out this was all a hoax and that there really wasn't any treasure, I realized that he might become more angry and dangerous than Shika could ever dream of being.

We started for Petra. Shortly, our camels entered what looked like a stadium two or three miles around. It sat almost perfectly surrounded by rugged mountains and cliffs five or six hundred feet high. The whole area was a waste of ruins, dwelling houses, palaces, and temples—all of it mingled together in confusion. It was awesome to think that thousands, maybe tens of thousands, of people had once lived in this lonely place. The sides of the mountains were cut smooth and carved into the most beautiful building fronts—columns and windows and arches. And all of it had been scraped out of solid rock!

"I've seen this before," said Joshua.

"You have?" I replied.

"Yeah. In that "Indiana Jones" movie. The third one, I think. I swear this place was in that movie."

There were so many caves and tunnels and tombs that it almost boggled the mind. And yet I knew that one of those holes—one of those tombs—led to a secret place that would take us home. Mary was watching me as my eyes scanned over all of the cliffs and I could tell that she was waiting for me to recognize it—somehow pinpoint the exact location of the time tunnel. I realized that many of the Arabs were watching me too.

I thought something might've looked familiar toward a canyon at the other end of the valley, but I really needed to look into the stone to be sure. I pulled it out of my shirt and got ready to put it up to my eye. Before I did, I glanced up at all of the faces. That was a mistake. Boy, talk about pressure! There wasn't a single eye in all those hundreds that wasn't looking straight at me. Most of the Arabs had never seen the stone before *and were whispering excitedly. Even the camels and horses seemed to be looking at me, as if saying in their minds, "Well? You made us walk all this way on the hot sand, Miss Wonder-Worker. So work your wonders!"*

I was sure as I put the stone up to my eye that I wasn't going to see anything at all. The stone just didn't work like this. It wasn't a trick that a magician took on stage to entertain people. Nevertheless, I held my breath, blocked out the light, and stared.

Two seconds! *Man, I wouldn't even be surprised if it was* less *than two seconds! The whole scene flashed into my mind as clearly as it had that morning on the Mount of Olives. As I made a little gasp and pulled down the stone, every man, horse, donkey, and camel seemed to gasp with me. Then nobody breathed at all. They waited for me to say something.*

A little sheepishly, I raised my hand toward the narrow canyon at the other end of the valley. "Over there."

The place instantly burst into excitement. "Over there!" people shouted. "She said over there!"

Horses started galloping. Camels were whipped into action. Half of the people present bolted toward the place where I'd pointed, I guess thinking that if they got there first they might see the treasure before anybody else. I shook my head. They undoubtedly had been over that ground a hundred times. But one pointed finger from a little girl and the gold rush was on.

I turned and saw Shika. He was the only one who didn't seem affected by my announcement. He had a little smile. I even thought I might've seen him nod. A bizarre thought passed through my head, like he was saying to me, "Nicely done"—almost like I was rediscovering something that he already knew.

Shaking off that totally illogical, nonsensical feeling, I urged my camel to keep walking. Mary and Joshua remained close by my side. As we reached the mouth of the canyon, Sheik al-Farabi started calling out, "Abu-Walid! Yusuf al-Sa'id!"

His voice bounced and echoed three or four times. He was calling the two men who'd been set up as lookouts. But nobody answered the sheik's calls. As we gathered in with the rest, the Arabs seemed torn between scurrying about, poking their heads in holes and looking under rocks, or watching me to see if and when I was going to reveal the next clue.

The cliffs were covering us over with heavy shadows. I realized it was very close to sunset. I trembled a little. Was it possible that we were too late? But just as my eye settled on the very tomb that I felt sure was the entrance to our time tunnel, an Arab voice began shouting frantically.

"Al-Farabi! Al-Farabi! They're dead! Yusuf and Abu! Their bodies are here!"

The Arab man was a little further up the canyon, dashing toward us along the banks of the muddy stream. Long before the echo of his cries died out, all heck broke loose. A gun fired. Then another. Then a whole host of guns. With all of the echoes it almost sounded like machine-gun fire. On the cliffs and hills above us I could see flashes of gunpowder. It was Todd Finlay and the Arabs of al-Arabah! It had to be! They'd taken up positions all around us! The camels, donkeys, and horses of Sheik al-Farabi's men were scrambling around in a panic, bucking off their riders. Several men were hit by bullets. They screamed and fell. Others were arming themselves with rifles and shooting wildly up at the cliffs.

I heard Mary yell out. Her camel was twisting in a circle. My own camel started lurching desperately, trying to run from the danger. I was holding on for dear life, but then one of its bucks was just too violent. I flipped out of the basket, did a perfect somersault in the air and bounced off my camel's head as it swung its neck. Then I did another somersault and landed flat on my face in the red dirt. Little bolts of lightning flashed inside my skull, like a lightbulb that blows out just when you turn on the switch.

I wasn't sure if I was unconscious or awake. As I opened my eyes all I saw were colors and stars. The pain in my head was enough all by itself to send me to the land of Make-Believe, but I didn't lose my awareness of what was happening. I felt someone wrap their arms around my waist and hoist me into the air. The next thing I knew I was hanging over someone's shoulder. My focus cleared enough to see the man's striped cloak. From that alone I knew it was Shika. I also saw that he was carrying the long bundle of cloth that had been on his camel. I turned my head and saw his other hand. There was a dagger in it. A monster-sized one with a silver handle. The knife was setting right against my arm, the blade turned outward. Was the knife threatening me? Or was that just how he was forced to carry it since his other hand was full? I didn't know, but even the thought of Shika with his hands on me made my skin crawl.

My vision cleared a little more and I could see the Arabs of al-Farabi still running every which way, although some had taken shelter behind rocks and crumbling walls. They were firing up at the cliffs. I heard shrieks above us. Some of the bodies of Hazim's men tumbled to the valley floor. It was hard to make out much detail with my head bouncing up and down. Shika was running toward the face of the cliff. Suddenly Hazim al-Arabah sprang out of the entrance of another tomb a little ways down the cliff. He was rushing at Shika. In his hands was that long spear that I'd seen on his horse—the one that had been sharpened on both ends. He was charging right at us, getting ready to run us through!

I screamed. Shika turned. He dropped his rope bundle, reached up and snatched the knife out of his other hand. My eyes now faced the cliff wall. Just in front of us was the tomb that I knew would lead to the time tunnel. I could tell by the way Shika leaned back and hurled forward that he'd thrown the dagger with all his strength. When Shika turned back toward the cliff, I could see Hazim again. He'd dropped to his knees, the silver-handled dagger sticking out of his belly. His chin dropped and he fell forward.

Out of the corner of my eye I saw something else. It was my brother, Joshua. His camel had carried him about fifty yards down the valley, but he hadn't fallen off. He was looking straight at me. Over the echoes of shouting and gunshots I heard him cry out my name, "Becky!"

My mind was in a storm of confusion. Shika had killed Hazim, but was it to defend me? Was Shika a good guy after all? By all appearances it seemed that he was rushing me into the shelter of the tombs. But he could've chosen any tomb for that. He'd chosen this *one. How could he know which tomb was the right one unless he'd been here before?*

He was still carrying the bundle with the sword inside. I saw that there was something else tied to the bundle as well—a stick. That is to say, a torch with a thick glob of tar at one end. As Shika ducked his head inside the tomb, I felt that I had recovered from my dizziness enough to pound on his back.

"Let me go! Put me down!"

To my surprise he did exactly that. The big-eared buck-toothed monk plopped me right onto the dusty tomb floor. But then he put his boot down hard on my shoulder and pinned me there.

"Ow! What are you doing?!"

"Just hold on, little girl," he said, those vampire eyes shining in the darkness.

He reached down and yanked the torch away from the rest of the bundle. I'm not quite sure what happened next. I blinked, and sometimes that's all it takes to miss something important.

"*Make light!*" *Shika commanded in a gravelly whisper.*

The next thing I knew, there was *light. Or at least there was fire. The torch somehow ignited. Maybe Shika had a match or a flint, but I didn't see it. The torch seemed to burst into flames out of nothing.*

Shika turned his cold gaze onto me. He stepped harder onto my shoulder. "Stop struggling! Do you hear? In a few minutes I'll bind you, but for now there isn't time. So I'll just tell you that if you give me any more trouble I'll start snapping limbs one by one. I don't need your bones intact. I just need you to be breathing."

"W-what are you doing?" My voice was less than a whisper. I couldn't get any breath.

"You, little girl, have been selected for a great honor. Now get up! From here you walk under your own power. Let's move!"

He thrust the torch toward my face, ready to burn my flesh if I didn't obey.

"Okay!" I shrieked, throwing my hands over my eyes. I struggled awkwardly to my feet, my eyes now blinded with tears.

"You will go this way," he commanded.

He hadn't needed to tell me. I knew which way to go. I knew it as plainly as if I'd visited here every day of my life. I went to the opposite end of the tomb. The back wall had been carved into a row of gaps and pillars that stretched from floor to ceiling. The pattern had been designed in such a way that the glow of the torch created hundreds of strange and twisted shadows. Just looking at it, it wasn't real obvious that there was a passage that led back behind. Still, I knew which gap to walk toward, and when I reached it, I squeezed in behind the pillar. Beyond it was a raw-looking cave with no carvings at all.

This might've been my chance to run. I don't know. I wasn't sure where I would have gone anyway without Josh and Mary. I just stood there frozen as Shika slipped into the gap and appeared behind me with the torch and bundle still in his hands.

I looked into the cold, glistening eyes of the vampire and somehow found the courage to ask, "Who are you?"

"Who am I?" he repeated, amused. "I've never lied to you about who I am. Well . . . maybe there were some lies. But I am all that I've said I am—a master swordsmith, and a sage of all the esoteric arts handed down from darkest beginnings of human antiquity."

I didn't remember him telling me that last part.

Next I asked, "Are you a monk?"

"No," he scoffed, "but it is a convenient way to travel, and the safest way that I could think to transport such a valuable item as this sword across the lawless landscape of Judea."

"Are you a Syrian?" I asked next.

"No," he confessed. "I guess I lied about that too. But I do admire them. My, but they do know how to make swords! No people in the history of the world ever made a stronger, more flexible blade."

I swallowed hard. "Are you going to k-kill me?"

His whole countenance seemed to get darker. His protruding ears seemed to flare out and I swear I could see a red fleck in his glowing vampire eyes. "On the contrary, you're going to become immortal, Rebecca. Your blood will become part of an instrument of power that will conquer nations, topple kingdoms, and reign supreme to the end of time.

My heart was hammering so hard and I was breathing so fast that I felt sure I'd pass out. Somehow I kept my wits enough to ask one last question, "W-why me?"

"Why you? Now that is an interesting question. You certainly wouldn't have been my first choice. You're a great deal more trouble than I'd have felt you were worth. Still, I've labored as hard as I could to spare your life up to now. I prevented Hazim and his men from pursuing you that night at the monastery. There was murder in their eyes and I don't think it would have boded well for you."

I had a vague memory of a man dressed in a monk cloak coming out of the monastery as we were running away. I'd thought it was brother Nicholas.

Shika continued, "I also gave you water and saw to your every comfort in the desert. But that was only to bring you safely to this moment. If it had been me, I'd have found a subject far less vexing. One of these little Arab girls would have done nicely. But it wasn't my choice, my dear. It was the sword's."

A shiver ran through me, colder than anything I'd ever felt.

"You see," he continued, "during the very last phase of the sword's heating and tempering—just after the final silver plating is applied to the blade—it's not the blood of just anyone that's required. It's the blood of an innocent maiden—the sacrifice of an innocent life. The sword is very choosy about such things, and for this it has selected you. But don't fret too much. We've still a long ways to go before we reach the place where the ritual will be completed. Come! We're wasting time!"

He used the sword itself, still bound in its mummy wrappings, to push me along down the tunnel. My fears had taken over so completely that I felt like I was only half-aware of what was happening. I started walking only because the weight of the sword was forcing me to. I didn't have the power to resist. But I'd only made it a few steps when a voice cried out behind us.

"Monk! Stop where you are!"

Shika and I both turned. Standing back at the narrow entrance leading into the tomb were three people, having just squeezed through the narrow gap. The tallest one was forcing the others to walk ahead of him.

"Becky!" *one of them called.*

It was Josh. The other was Mary. And the last one was Todd Finlay. Mary and Josh moved aside to reveal two ivory-handled pistols in Todd Finlay's hands. They were aimed at Shika's heart.

"Let her go, Monk," *Finlay demanded.*

"What is this?" *Shika asked, utterly annoyed that someone would be so rude as to interfere.*

"The girl is mine," *said Finlay.*

He cocked both pistols with his thumbs.

Shika stood up straight. "May I ask what you want her for? Maybe we can make a deal. You remember me, don't you, Mr. 'Stephens?' We met at the monastery."

"Yeah, I remember you. You're the monk who knew my real name. But you never told me how you knew it."

"It wasn't necessary for me to tell you then. But I might be willing to tell you now. If you'll remember, I also told you that I am a man who is known for making arrangements."

"I don't care *how* you found out my name!" *barked Finlay.* "And I'm tired *of arrangements! I want the girl! She has the stone! The girl and the stone are the only way for me to get what I want!"*

"What do you want?" *he asked calmly.*

"Never mind," *said Finlay.* "You wouldn't understand."

"Try me," *said Shika.* "Trust me. I have no doubt that I need the girl more than you. Tell me what you want."

"The same thing I've wanted for twenty-five years!" *said Finlay.* "The Sword of Coriantumur! I want her to reveal the doorway that will take me to a place where I can find it. I want the Sword of Akish!"

A strange slimy-looking smile climbed the vampire's cheeks. He started laughing. It started out as a low kind of laugh, then got more and more hysterical. Finlay was so shocked by this that he lowered his pistols a little.

"What's so funny?" *he demanded.*

"Oh, how the ways of the Dark One do weave and turn!" *Shika said.* "Don't you realize it, Todd Finlay? Aren't you the least curious how it is that I know who you are? You've been granted your wish! After all these years of yearning and searching, you've arrived at the end of your path."

"What are you talking about?" *cried Finlay, growing more flustered.*

"The *sword! Do you want to see it? Do you want to set your eyes upon the object of all your passions and dreams?"*

Finlay shook his head. "You don't have it. The Sword of Akish was destroyed. To find it I have to go back thousands of years!"

"You *fool!" Shika snapped. "Are you really so dense? So stupid that you can't untangle a simple rearrangement of syllables? I did it not so much to disguise myself as for my own amusement."*

Now even I was confused. What was he talking about? Todd Finlay was no less befuddled than the rest of us.

"My *name!" Shika yelled. "I can't believe you haven't figured it out!"*

Then I gasped, though it sounded like a choke. I figured it out, and the terror burned hotter and hotter.

"Turn it around!" *he said.* "Say it the other way!"

At last Finlay's eyes widened. Mary and Joshua got it too. But hearing it made the mystery no easier to understand, even as his voice echoed back and forth through the chamber.

"I am Akish!"

CHAPTER 23

"Meagan, would you like to participate in the final cleansing?" asked Julu-Tlé, one of the chief women of the village.

She was talking about Pawcali, the son of Kanalha. His body had been lying in a "mortuary" hut at the west end of the village for almost five days now. Every afternoon the women had tended to it, washing it in clover water and herbs and perfuming it with a tree resin called copáli. This afternoon, at long last, was the funeral.

I nodded a little nervously. It didn't exactly sound like my idea of a fun afternoon, but I'd been of such little help to these people over the last few days that I didn't have the nerve to say no.

She gave me a small smile and motioned for me to follow her. I was actually surprised that they were asking me at all. Many of the women of the village didn't seem comfortable around me. I knew nothing about weaving on their complicated looms, making poultices or dyes, or gathering herbs, or grinding corn, or even making a gosh darn homemade tortilla! I felt some were thinking, "Is she of any practical use at all?"

Most of my days were spent with the children, who never seemed to tire of hearing my personalized versions of *Cinderella*, *The Wizard of Oz*, and *The Jungle Book*. And if you don't think they were impressed with my Lamanite version of *Star Wars*, let me just say that I had those kids on the edge of their seats!

I followed Julu-Tlé to the "mortuary" hut. Several other women were already waiting with pouches and pitchers of herbs. As we went inside I could see the body of Pacawli covered by a soft fur blanket. More furs had been placed underneath it. The odor was stronger than yesterday. Mostly it was the sweet odor of copáli, but I could tell that the smell of death was fast taking over. After five days the battle was about to be lost. It was a good thing that today his remains were finally being interred in their last resting place.

"Why did we wait five days before having the funeral?" I asked Julu-Tlé.

She seemed surprised that I had asked. "His soul has been preparing for his journey through the obstacles of the Afterworld."

"Oh," I said.

I was reminded again that we were still a long ways from converting these people to Christianity. From time to time I'd continued to hear the women praying to this deity or that deity, and lighting incense to please malevolent spirits. Yesterday a child who'd been a particularly avid listener of my stories was kept in her hut all day because, according to her birthday calendar, the day had been designated as unlucky for her. The Lamanites had a god for every-thing—sun, moon, sky, clouds, wind, trees, flowers, eyesight, hearing, menstruation, laughing, marriage—you name it! Nothing in life was a coincidence to a Lamanite. There was no such thing as "bad things happening to good people." If you got sick, it was because you sinned. If your husband left you, it was because you'd been cursed by an enemy. If your child died, it was because the gods were punishing you. These beliefs had been ingrained over many generations, maybe for thousands of years. Two centuries ago, when they were living the gospel, such beliefs were likely relegated to "folk tradition" status (much like our traditions about rabbits' feet, or black cats, or the number thirteen), but after the Lamanites fell away from the gospel, these beliefs took center stage again and were taken *very* seriously.

I was determined to just keep my mouth shut and do whatever Julu-Tlé asked me to do. It occurred to me that what these people needed most was the gift of the Holy Ghost. I'd come to learn how critical this gift really was when it came to changing habits and hearts.

Pacawli's wounds had been stitched and repaired as well as could be expected. As I gazed upon his silent features I might even say he looked peaceful. I was given a sponge and instructed to wash his upper body while two other women washed his lower body and feet. Outside the hut waited several old men with a litter that was to be used to carry Pacawli's body to its final resting place. If all of the younger men hadn't gone off with Lamanai to participate in the rescue of the Prophet Moroni, this likely would have been *their* job. But women, children, and old men were all that was left in Seibalche. Even the *youngest* of the old men, like the mayor, Jolom, were still out recruiting warriors to fight in Eagle-Sky-Jaguar's revolution.

After we had finished with the clover water and herbs, Julu-Tlé proceeded to anoint Pacawli's body again in a final glaze of copáli. Afterwards, Kanalha came into the hut and asked us all to leave. Kanalha had a double assignment today. He was not only the boy's father, but also the village shaman. He would be conducting the funeral.

"Thank you," I said to Julu-Tlé as we emerged from the hut. "It was an honor to help."

She gave me a queer look. Maybe it just wasn't logical to her that I should feel honored or thankful about such a thing. Or maybe she just plain didn't like me.

Feeling lonelier than ever, I began to make my way back to the shaman's house on the hill. Of course my thoughts turned again to Apollus. I'd been telling myself for three days that worrying about him was not permitted. My heart just wasn't obeying.

Perhaps I should have worried more about Ryan. After all, he was the one with no battle experience. But in reality, I worried more about Apollus. And not because I realized that I was still hopelessly, madly in love with the oaf. Not *exactly* anyway. Apollus frightened me. He would have thought nothing of being the first to sacrifice his life for a cause. If I'd known for certain that Apollus loved me, I might have felt significantly more secure. If a woman that you love isn't incentive enough to return home in one piece, what is?

Oh, I *hated* this. I *hated* being in love. Hated it! Hated it! But I did my best to swallow such sentiments and climbed the hill.

Kanalha's wives and several of the older children were busily removing all the stones and floorboards of Kanalha's house. My conclusions from a few days ago had been accurate. Pacawli's remains would be interred right underneath the floor of the house. I felt it might be appropriate if tonight I asked the manager for different sleeping arrangements.

As I looked inside the doorway, I suddenly realized a whole *crypt* of bodies had been interred there. For four nights I'd been sleeping right on top of a cemetery! At least thirteen perfect skeletons had been exposed, almost entirely decomposed. I say "almost," because at least two of them still had skin as dried and shriveled as ancient shoe leather clinging to the skull and ribs. There were even the tiny skeletons of two small children. Each of the bodies had been laid side by side. There were other things in the crypt as well: jewelry, dolls, articles of clothing, all of which I assumed had been the favorite possessions of the person while they were alive. Other small skeletons were also in the crypt—*animal* skeletons—but I didn't interrupt anyone to ask about them.

The entire population of the village started to make their way up to the Shaman's house. Many lined the pathway of the hill as Pacawli's remains were solemnly carried past them. Kanalha led the way holding a rounded clay vessel that emitted a heavy blue smoke. Just behind the procession walked a young girl. She was the same teenage girl who'd wept so violently when we first arrived in the village. Her cheeks were still moist. I'd learned that she was Pacawli's fiancée. They were to have been married at the end of the rainy season. In her arms was a small beige dog on a red leash.

The litter reached the top of the hill and entered the house. I noticed that a mask had been laid over Pacawli's face. It was a colorful mosaic of turquoise, obsidians, and bloodstones artistically arranged in the likeness of a fox. This was said to be Pacawli's guardian spirit. The body was carefully laid beside another skeleton in the crypt that may have been Pacawli's mother. The mask was removed. Kanalha set down his incense burner and held up a small piece of blue-green jade for all of us to see.

"For the Lord and Lady of Heaven," he said.

The crowd said in unison, "May he be welcomed into the jade-stone light of bliss."

"May he be welcomed," Kanalha repeated.

He then pressed the tiny stone between the lips of the corpse. Kanalha motioned for Pacawli's fiancé to step forward into the crypt. Curiously, she handed him the little squirming dog.

Kanalha held it up much like the stone. "For his final journey across the Black River."

"May he swim safely to the opposite shore," replied the crowd.

"May he arrive safely," Kanalha repeated.

He gripped the dog by the scruff of its neck. As it hung there kicking and yipping, he raised a white stone knife. My heart stopped. He was going to *kill* it!

"Wait!" I screeched.

The sound came out of me involuntarily. I had no idea how rude or sacrilegious I was being. I just couldn't sit there and watch.

"Why?" I asked. "Why are you going to kill a little dog?"

Even though my "godhood" status had been significantly reduced, Kanalha and the crowd at least had enough respect for me to pause the proceedings. The dog was given back to the teenage girl, who glared at me in contempt.

"Because Meagan," said Kanalha patiently, "the first obstacle in the afterworld is a black river through a black countryside. My son's soul will arrive there at the darkest hour of night. He can only cross this river by holding onto this dog, which can smell the far shore and swim directly to it."

"And this is how he gets to heaven?"

"It is only the *first* obstacle," said Kanalha. "Then he must pass through the grinding mountains, then he must climb another mountain composed entirely of flesh-cutting obsidian chips, then cross a region of ceaseless rainfall where every raindrop is an arrowhead, then pass through a forest of lurking snakes, alligators, and jaguars who—"

I shook my head. "It isn't true. Getting to heaven isn't like that. Remember what Ryan and Apollus taught a few days ago? Jesus overcame every obstacle already. Every obstacle that there could ever be. All we have to do is believe in Him, and repent and . . . Trust me, when we arrive at the gates of Paradise the toll has already been paid. It's important that you understand that. That *everyone* understands."

Kanalha looked up at me through his milky white cataracts. "But . . . this is how it's always been done."

"I know," I said sympathetically. "But if you believe that our arrival in your world brought about any goodness whatsoever, please believe what I'm saying to you now. It's not just about the life of a little dog. It's the whole idea that life itself is precious, and should never be taken away from *any* living thing for no reason. Not unless it's a matter of survival or defense or . . ."

I assessed the blank looks on everyone's faces. Did they understand a word of what I was saying? I sensed an air of restlessness and wondered how much longer they'd tolerate my pleadings. The spirit that had been present on the day of the healings just wasn't here. Oh, how I missed the Priesthood!

But then something occurred that obliterated any disturbance that I might have created. From the back of the crowd I heard several shrieks that made my hair stand on end. Women and children were turning abruptly to look down the hill toward the village.

"Soldiers!" someone screamed. "The forest is filled with soldiers!"

More screams erupted. Children burst into tears. A wildfire of panic and consternation swept through the villagers. I fought my way through to the edge of the hill to see what everyone was pointing at. When I saw it, I felt as if my flesh had been doused in ice water. The forest floor was crawling with warriors—*swarming* with warriors. Where had they all come from? It was as if they'd always been there and something had brought them out of hibernation.

One of the old men spotted a soldier just emerging from the trees at the opposite end of the village and cried, "He has the insignia of Teotihuacan! It's the army of Fire-Born!"

Nothing anyone could have said would have aroused more terror than those words. Within seconds mothers were grabbing up infants and toddlers. Old men were scrambling into the jungle on the western slope. I remained there at the lip of the hill, frozen with indecision, my mind still trying to grasp the fullness of what was happening. Many of the soldiers had flaming torches. They were setting ablaze every standing structure in the village! There had been a few stragglers who did not attend the funeral—old women, old men, and children. I saw them emerging from huts—fleeing, screaming. Oh Father in Heaven! *They were killing them!* Cutting them down like stalks of grain!

Some of the men marching forward in the long wall of soldiers were pointing at us. They'd seen the gathering at the top of the hill. They began charging toward us with full fury. At last I broke my fear-frozen limbs and turned to run with the others. The jungle on the western slope was a maelstrom of confusion. Children separated from their mothers were crying. Some were wandering back the opposite way! I grabbed up one little girl, her face streaked with tears. When she realized I was not her mother she only screamed louder, but I ran with her to the bottom of the hill anyway. A panic-stricken woman with one child already in her arms reached out to me. The little girl reached out toward her.

As I delivered her daughter, I asked, "Where is everyone going?"

"The river!" she replied. "The caves!"

I hadn't even been aware that there *was* a river nearby. It certainly hadn't been visible from the top of the hill. The jungle foliage had hidden it from view. But even if I could have found the river, could I have found the caves? The further I ran, the more amazed I became at how efficiently these people were melting into the foliage. I realized that if I didn't pick someone to follow right away I was going to find myself alone in the forest. I caught sight of the old shaman, Kanalha, with his walking stick. For his age and infirmity he was moving down a jungle path at an incredible pace.

"Kanalha!" I cried. But he didn't wait. I could hardly blame him.

Great jungle leaves slapped me in the face. I was panting and sweating profusely. Kanalha continued scuttling ahead of me. I couldn't see anyone else in the trees to the right or left. With the foliage as thick as it was, I feared I might easily lose sight of the shaman. I batted ferns and vines out of my face, feeling almost as if I was drowning in them.

I called ahead to Kanalha, panting heavily, "How far . . . to the river?"

He didn't answer me, but his pace began to slow. I finally caught up to him, but I was too winded to ask the question again. I just pressed my side with the palm of my hand, fought to catch my breath, and stayed directly behind him.

All at once he stopped. He turned around, but he didn't look directly at me. His dim eyes were focused on the jungle behind us. I realized he looked perplexed.

"What's wrong?" I asked.

"I don't think this is the way," he said.

"WHAT?"

"Forgive an old man. I've taken the wrong path. Come, we must go back."

"We *can't* go back, Kanalha! The soldiers!"

"But I don't know how to reach the caves from here," he said.

"You *have* to know!" I said. "You've lived in these woods all of your life! How can you *not know!*"

"If I were younger and my eyes were not so dim . . ."

I took his hand. "All right then. We'll just keep going down this path. Where does it lead?"

He thought hard, "It goes to . . ."

I began to hear voices behind us. The soldiers were coming. There had been thousands—more than enough to divide up and send hundreds down every jungle path leading away from the village.

"It goes to the poison cenote," Kanalha finally decided.

"The what?"

"It is a cenote. The walls of the pit are very steep, but the water stinks and is not fit to drink. I have used the clay at its edges to make a cream for skin wrinkles that will—"

"Okay, okay," I said, rushing him along. "Is there a place to hide there?"

"Perhaps."

"Then let's keep moving."

Kanalha's energy was finally fading. He was wheezing for breath. The noises behind us were coming closer. As I glanced back I could also see a thick pall of smoke in the east—all that remained of the village of Seibalche.

The pathway widened a bit, but a heavy curl of growth continued to give it the appearance of a winding tunnel. Suddenly we stopped and listened. I caught my breath. There were noises in the jungle *ahead* as well as behind. Still, it had escaped me how close the noises ahead actually were. From around the next bend in the trail—not twenty feet away—appeared several warriors with black faces. The black paint circled their eyes and mouth like a death mask. In their hands were long spears with oversized obsidian points. I turned, colliding with Kanalha. The warriors sprang forward. There was no escape! They were surrounding us! I'd seen how they'd cut down women and children. I was convinced the last seconds of life were passing before our eyes!

But just as the spear points thrust toward my face, someone cried, "Wait! It's her! The Demon Goddess!"

That was a strange title, I thought. Kanalha and I stood back to back. Spears remained directed at our vital organs from fifteen different angles. The man who had cried out stepped forward. His battle helmet was adorned with mirror-polished jade. He leaned in until we stood face to face. I realized the black pigment on his face was actually a permanent tattoo. He peered into my eyes, right down into their depths, I think trying to determine if there was any supernatural power or magic in them. I sneered back with a look of utter contempt. The fact that I could see myself in his helmet only caused me to scowl even deeper, hoping he might feel a curse entering his soul.

"Take them both to Siyah K'ak'!" he commanded.

I needed no translation. The name meant Fire-Born.

Several men went to seize us, but as I turned my lethal gaze onto them, they hesitated.

"Touch me," I hissed, "and I'll give you a disease that will make your flesh shrivel and melt off your bones."

They looked at the man with the jade helmet, unsure what to do.

Kanalha's eyes were as wide as everyone else's. I think he really believed I would do it.

"We will walk!" Kanalha declared at the soldiers with as much venom as his old, graveled voice could generate.

The man with the jade helmet, who I assumed was in command, tried to rant with as much passion as I had displayed, but the fear was thick in his voice. "You have no powers! You are not Ix-Chel! We have been told!"

I stared back, hoping the message of *"Are you willing to take that chance?"* was coming through loud and clear.

He pointed a trembling finger at me, then at Kanalha. "You will come."

We did as requested and walked up the trail, a dozen spearpoints guiding our every step.

Suddenly something rustled in the jungle off to the left. Half of the spearpoints were aimed in that direction until the squad commander barked, "Keep them moving!"

A few minutes later the air began to smell strongly of sulfur. We emerged from the jungle into a small clearing dominated by a sink-hole with sheer edges and a thirty-foot drop into a soupy well of yellowish water—the poison cenote. Anyone who fell in there would drown for sure. Judging by the smell, it seemed a more than appropriate place to meet a man who would orchestrate the slaughter of so many defenseless women and children.

The commander of the Lamanites had made this his temporary headquarters as he awaited word that the destruction of the village had been completed, and probably the destruction of all the other villages in the vicinity too. At present there were only thirty or forty black-faced warriors present, as well as a few other men who might have been stewards or orderlies or slaves. There were also litter-bearers—as well as the portable litter of the great warrior himself. The carrier actually looked rather plain considering who usually sat inside it—just a simple palanquin of light wood with a thin awning and a brightly painted owl emblem with a fist holding a spearthrower. The litter was empty at the moment, but standing beside it was a man I fully recognized.

"Kux-Wach!" said Kanalha as we were brought into the clearing. The old man's dim eyes still recognized his son, but I couldn't tell if Kanalha's voice was filled with excitement, surprise, or alarm.

Kux-Wach saw his father, then he saw me. He glanced off toward the jungle at his left. Then faced us again and pointed at me, his eyes full of wrath.

"That's *her!*" He approached swiftly. "That's the girl. The old man is . . . the village shaman."

What a lowlife, I thought. He wasn't even laying claim to his own father.

As he approached, the squad leader asked him, "Where is Lord Fire-Born?"

Again Kux-Wach glanced toward the trees. "He will be back in a moment."

I realized that the great war general was going to the bathroom. I don't know why I found it so funny. It just made him so human, so mortal. Just an insignificant man who would one day know the puniness of his own soul.

I looked at Kanalha. The old man appeared so devastated, so heartbroken that it made tears prick at my eyes. I wasn't sure if he had anymore strength in him to speak. But then he erupted like a volcano and declared to his son, "It was *you. You* brought down this great evil—"

Kux-Wach threw it right back. "It was *her!* She and the others, and your reprobate stepson, Lamanai. I am a worshipper of the living deities, Fire-Born and Spearthrower Owl, who rule all the lands north and south, from the First Inheritance of our ancestors to the edge of the northern deserts—the kings of the One World!"

"You are traitor to your blood," Kanalha seethed. "I disclaim you. I spit on you. You are an abortion of my flesh."

"I am a *patriot!*" Kux-Wach shrieked. "And you are a senile old fool."

Kanalha's head drooped. The cataracts on his eyes seemed to gloss over forever.

Kux-Wach turned on me. "This is all your doing—you and the other two demons from the darkness of the Maw. Not so powerful now, are you, now that your fraud is revealed? The blood of this people is on your hands, demoness."

It was hardly worth a comeback. This man had betrayed the people he'd known all of his life. His own brother's body still lay exposed in the burial crypt of his father's house, along with all his other ancestors. If those things didn't affect his conscience, what could I say that would?

Nevertheless, I replied, "Look at your own hands, Kux-Wach."

His hand curled into a fist. I thought he might strike me. But at that moment Fire-Born emerged from the foliage with a retinue of ten or twelve bodyguards. He tidily adjusted the flaps that hung down to the knees on his red-leather loincloth, then raised his gaze to look at us.

The conqueror of the Lamanites was far more striking in appearance than I would have imagined. I'd so often been disappointed by the plainness of the features of so many so-called legendary people that I'd gotten into a habit of expecting nothing out of the ordinary. But Siyah K'ak', or Fire-Born, was not an ordinary-looking man. Maybe it was just the contrast that his features had with the Lamanites. This man was not a Lamanite. I wasn't sure if I was looking at a Nephite either. He was a Teotihuacano. The altitude or diet up there had somehow bred an entirely different race of men. For one thing, he stood well over six feet. My best guess was six-foot-four—unthinkable for ancient men. There were no tattoos on his skin, at least none that I could see, except perhaps around his eyes. He almost looked like he was wearing makeup like the Egyptians. His eyes were shaped like nothing I'd ever seen. The corners near the bridge of the nose curled downward, while the opposite corners curled up. It made me think of a falcon's eye. No—a *dragon's* eye. It reminded me of a creature's eyes that I'd once seen illustrated on the cover of an Anne McCaffrey book. Everything about them expressed violence, and more particularly *efficiency* in violence.

He wore a thick leather breastplate, but also on his chest hung a gold chain with a bulky gold and silver medallion that would have given him additional protection. The medallion was another emblem of Spearthrower Owl, but it was heavily encrusted with jewels that were either crystals or enormous white diamonds. As he moved toward us, those diamonds emitted sharp flashes of light that caused me to flinch and squint.

In his lip was a labret composed of more crystal and delicate yellow feathers. His earrings had orange feathers and more crystals, and his nose plug could only have been a ruby. On his head was a battle helmet much like those of his black-faced bodyguards, except it was tufted with long, overarching plumes from some bird with brilliant red feathers. Yellow, red and violet feathers also adorned his arms and legs. His cape was the most striking thing of all, composed entirely of intricately woven feathers and fabrics, iridescent, scintillating, and again keeping to the theme of reds, oranges, and golds. Everything about him reflected his name, as if he'd just emerged from a molten volcano.

His voice was harsh as he gestured toward me and said to Kux-Wach, "Is that her?"

I realized Kux-Wach was kneeling down, his face touching the earth—practically groveling. None of the others were groveling. Maybe Kux-Wach was required to do this as the only civilian in the commander's entourage.

"Yes, Revered One," said Kux-Wach. "She is called Meagan, and my stepbrother—the same who deludes the people into believing that he is the son of Jaguar-Paw—claims that she emerged from the Underworld in the waters of a bubbling cenote."

"Who is the old man?"

"He . . . is my father," Kux-Wach confessed.

"He is the one who claims to have harbored Jaguar-Paw's son for six years?"

"Yes, Revered One, but—"

"Where are the other two?" Fire-Born demanded. He looked at me.

"Where are the other two demons who rose with you out of Xibalba?"

I kept silent, glaring.

Kux-Wach answered for me. "As I said, Revered One, they have gone with my stepbrother and the warriors of Seibalche to—"

"Quiet!" thundered Fire-Born. "I wish to hear it from the demoness. Speak up, devil! Where are the other two?"

I waited, then inclined my ear as if I hadn't heard. "What was that again?"

His face turned red like the ruby in his nose, "You heard me."

I gave a little shrug. "I don't know where they are."

His question made me feel relieved. If he was asking it, he hadn't caught them.

"Is it true what this man has said? Are they marching for Tikal?"

"Tikal?" I repeated. "Which direction is that?"

All at once his muscles relaxed. He gave a sly smile. "You have courage, demoness. Yet to me you appear as nothing more than a creature of flesh and blood. Is it true? If I cut you with my dagger, would you bleed?"

"Very much so," I said quietly.

"Good," he said. "We'll save that for later. For now answer my questions. Why have you been sent here by the Great Maw?"

"Remind me who he is again?"

"The Maw of Xibalba! The Jester of Death! Why have you come forth to challenge the reign of the god of this earth, Spearthrower Owl?"

He thought I was a demoness? Okay, I decided. I'd play along.

"We were bored," I said. "We demons like to stir things up sometimes. And we thought this would be a great opportunity since you so pitifully failed to eliminate the true heir to the throne of Tikal."

"She's lying!" cried Kux-Wach. "Lamanai is a fraud. He and the demons conspired this fraud together."

"I said be silent!" Fire-Born raged.

Kux-Wach continued groveling in the dirt. Fire-Born walked around me. As if choreographed, each of the warriors raised their spearpoints as he moved by, then aimed them at me again after he passed.

"The Maw has given you an alluring form, Meagan Demoness. Tall of body. Lithe of muscle. Hair of white flames. Eyes like glowing amber."

"Please," I scoffed. "Is this a pick up? 'Cause I've gotten better lines from boys in my high school lunch room."

"I am no boy," he flared. "And don't think I am fooled by your disguise. I know that beneath these illusions you are a hideous corpse. A rotting husk."

If he was going for charm, that lost a few points.

"Tell me, Meagan Demoness, if I strike you down and send your spirit back to Xibalba, what will you tell the Great Maw?"

"Tell him?" I said coyly. "I'll tell him that you're scared. The great Fire-Born is as frightened as a little girl."

"I fear *nothing!*" he said angrily. "Not men, not demons, not gods!"

"But you sure fear the son of Jaguar-Paw," I said. "Or you wouldn't be killing innocent women and children."

"I kill whoever I *wish* to kill. And that includes anyone who defies the power of Spearthrower Owl."

"Yeah, yeah, yada, yada. You're afraid. Otherwise you'd spare these villagers and save your strength for the warriors of Eagle-Sky-Jaguar."

"Eagle-Sky-Jaguar may already be dead."

"Let's hope not," I replied. "Or you really *would* be a coward, wasting your time slaughtering the weak and defenseless."

"Where is the son of Jaguar Paw? I will show you how much I fear him. I will rip out his beating heart and hold it in my hands!"

"Then prove it! Leave these villagers alone!"

"The death of these peasants seems to offend you a great deal, demoness. Tell me why a servant of the Underworld would be offended by the death of *any* creature?"

I hesitated a moment, then said, "Because the Great Maw hates cowards more than he loves death. If you continue to oppress the weak, he will rain down a curse on you that will drive your kingdom to extinction."

Fire-Born laughed mirthlessly. "The Maw has no power here. And I will send you back to him to tell him that he may rain down as many curses as he likes. I am Siyah K'ak'! *All* life is in my hands!"

To my horror, Fire-Born reached for his sheath and armed himself with a bright metal dagger. It was different than any knife I'd ever seen among the Lamanites—bright and golden, the hilt bejeweled with rubies. As clever as I thought I was, I was no match for this man's capriciousness and arrogance. In a flash—no warning whatsoever—he drove his blade into the chest of Kanalha! He killed the harmless old man right before my eyes! Kanalha raised his eyes to look one last time, not at his murderer, but at his son. Kux-Wach continued to kneel, too afraid even to look up to see his father's face before he crumpled.

My heart plunged into darkness. What had I done? What had I said? I stared at Fire-Born with revulsion and horror and yes—with *hatred*.

Fire-Born snapped at Kux-Wach, "Throw the body of your traitorous father into the stinking cenote."

Kux-Wach crawled over to the fallen body. Fire-Born saw the terror in my eyes—heard the soundless scream in my throat. He saw how his murder had wiped away every semblance of courage and smugness and self-assuredness from my countenance—and he relished it.

"Is my message to the Maw clear?" he yelled at me. "Take it back to him! *I am Fire-Born!*" He shouted to his men, "Kill the demoness!"

But just as he pronounced my execution, the jungle at our right *exploded*. Something sprang from the foliage—something with a fire-orange streamer on its tail. It was Huracan, the black jaguar!

With a fury that could only have been vengeance for the death of the old shaman it ripped into the black-faced warriors. They were so taken by surprise that two men had their viscera torn completely open before anyone could redirect their weapons. Spears were swinging every which way, more dangerous to each other than to the beast. There were several shrieks as spearpoints accidentally sliced into shoulders and legs. But the jaguar had its target picked out. It leaped at Fire-Born—his master's murderer!

For an instant the conqueror's face blanched white, the true color of his cowardice, but a swipe of the jaguar's paw left four deep red gashes from forehead to chin. Fire-Born fell back in pain. Huracan left him writhing on the ground and lunged toward his next target—the man who now threatened his master's body. Kux-Wach was at the edge of the poison cenote, just about to fling Kanalha's body over the side.

"Huracan!" Kux-Wach cried out, hoping the jaguar would falter at the sound of a familiar voice, but it was too possessed with anger to care about that.

The jaguar reared up and swiped at Kux-Wach with both paws. If not for the ferociousness in Huracan's eyes it might have looked like a kitten batting at a dangling string. It swiped Kux-Wach once, then caught him with its other paw and sent him careening over the edge. The black-faced warriors had recovered enough to fling their spears at Huracan, but I didn't stay to see its fate. I saw my opening for escape and took it.

At first I just tore into the foliage—no thought for direction. I hurdled massive tree roots, ripping plants out of the earth as I ran. Already I could hear men pursuing. I crashed through a hanging vine and got brave enough to look back. Behind me about fifteen yards were the raging eyes of the squad leader with the jade helmet, as well as a dozen of his men, all bent on fulfilling Fire-Born's murderous command. I had no delusions that I could outrun the elite warriors of Fire-Born's bodyguard. Still, I flew as swiftly as my adrenaline could carry me, a prayer pulsing in my thoughts—a plea for one more miracle to finally whisk me away from the sickle of death.

I made it fifty more yards through the undergrowth when up ahead it began to appear that there was some kind of clearing. But then I lurched to a halt. The ground sloped suddenly. It was the riverbank! The river looked thirty or forty feet wide. To my left the foliage was impenetrable. I turned the only direction I could—north—almost back in the same direction I'd come from. I thought I'd collide with my executioners, but Providence had placed a thick patch of brambles between us. To reach me they had to follow around the same path by the riverbank. The blur of a javelin crossed before my eyes, barely missing my chin. I continued on, ignoring several other arrows and spears that also missed. Ahead was another clearing, but to reach it I had to crash through another leafy barrier. I threw up my hands, closed my eyes, and leaped.

As I opened them again I had to immediately throw on the brakes. The clearing was a roadway. My sudden appearance had surprised—*was it possible?*—a *horse!* The red-colored stallion reared up and let out a high-pitched neigh. And the rider—the mighty rider! It was Apollus!

"Meagan!" he cried.

There were *other* horses. I recognized Lamanai. I thought I also recognized Ryan on a golden mare with a woman seated behind him, but the others I didn't know. All of them had their eyes raised to the jungle. They saw the approaching line of warriors. Several leaped off their mounts—including Apollus.

Just as Apollus positioned himself in front of me, the squad leader burst through the brush. Apollus was armed with two weapons—an axe and a dagger. The Lamanite bared his teeth and drew back his spear to impale Apollus through the heart. Apollus leaped toward him and deflected the spearpoint with his axe. The squad leader brought up his other hand—armed with a dagger of green obsidian. He stabbed toward Apollus's throat. But before it struck, Apollus's own blade cut into the squad leader's forearm. And then with his axe Apollus struck down onto his jade helmet. The helmet split. The warrior collapsed.

Other fights were raging within ten paces on either side of Apollus. A warrior from Seibalche—I think his name was Jacobah—heaved his weapon at an attacker while a third man with shining black hair cut down another of Fire-Born's warriors as he emerged from the brush. Could it be—I was almost breathless to think of it!—that the black-haired man was Moroni? I don't know how I knew it. I just knew!

As Jacobah finished off his foe, Lamanai cried from atop his horse, "Enough! We must leave! Back on your mounts!"

It was the only choice. The jungle was writhing with activity as more warriors crashed toward us through the brush. Apollus took my hand. At just that instant a dart from a spearthrower whizzed over my head. I ducked down, frightened. Apollus's voice resonated, "I have you! You'll be all right. Stay close to me!"

I did precisely as he asked. How could I have done anything else? He leaped on the back of his red stallion, then hoisted me up to sit behind him.

"*Chanim!*" cried Moroni. His horse seemed to be the leader of all the other horses.

Fire-Born's troops were emerging from the trees by the dozens. One entered the roadway in front of us, but Moroni swung his sword while still on horseback and cut the warrior down. Spearthrower darts were being hurled at us from all directions. The horse Jacobah was riding reared up in agony as a dart pierced its side. Even before the animal staggered and fell, Jacobah leaped and landed behind another rider. Apollus was kicking his horse furiously and yanking its mane, trying to entice it to run. Not even the death of a fellow horse could make that animal move any swifter than a trot.

"*Chanim!* Run, you mule!" Apollus cried.

But that only seemed to insult it. I was afraid it might even stop. And then from the jungle at our left came a bloodcurdling roar. Huracan emerged from the foliage at the heels of Apollus' horse. He'd survived the spears of Fire-Born's bodyguard! Apollus's horse found its incentive. In fact, all *five* remaining horses began to gallop like the wind. Each rider leaned forward and gripped the horses' manes.

As for me, I gripped onto my Roman warrior, and soon we were out of range of the spearthrowers' missiles, and the din of war faded behind us.

CHAPTER 24

Akish. He'd called himself Akish. I didn't even know what that meant. The only time I'd ever heard the name was when Finlay had said it, and that was only when talking about the sword. But Joshua seemed to know who he was. He'd read the Book of Mormon more times than I had. Besides, he remembered names a lot better.

Joshua had a look of awe. I don't know why, but at this point he didn't look afraid, as if this was all one big adventure and he was enjoying the twists and turns.

"You're Akish the Jaredite?*" he asked.*

Akish got a queer look. "How do you know that name—Jaredite?"

"I know a lot *about you," said Josh. He then started listing off things about him, like he was listing off character attributes on a Pokémon Card. "I know you're a murderer, and a conspirator, and you married the daughter of Jared the king, and then you* killed *Jared the king—"*

Akish's eyes flew wide. "You cannot know these things. Jared, the son of Omer, is not *king. His father reigns, and I have not been given the daughter of Jared to wife."*

"Ohhh," said Josh, like he'd figured it all out. "So that's *why you created the sword—to help you in all your schemes?"*

Akish looked dumbfounded. But then he got a look like he'd *figured it all out too. He stepped toward Josh. "So it's* true. *You children are* also *wanderers out of time. The sword told me this, but I didn't fully understand what it meant until now. Tell me, young man, what era are you from?"*

"You mean where I was born, or where my family lives?"

"Don't tell him anything, Joshua!" I interrupted. "He says he's going to kill me to finish making his sword!"

Todd Finlay stepped toward the bundle on the ground. He'd never taken his eyes off it ever since Akish had told us his real name. He put one of the Turkish pistols back into his sash, then bent down to pick it up, his hand trembling with excitement.

Akish saw him and reacted swiftly. "No touching! Only I may touch it."

Finlay hesitated, then he thinned his eyes and pointed his pistol at Akish. "I should kill you. Then the sword would be all mine."

"The sword isn't finished, you idiot!" snapped Akish. "Its powers now don't even compare with the powers that it will possess after we baptize it in blood. And you will be a part of it, Todd Finlay. You were destined to be a part of it. For now you will help me to bind the two children and the girl, after which we will take the sword to Ephraim Hill in my homeland of Moron. There I will give the sword its final plating of silver."

"But I have silver," said Finlay. He shrugged the gym bag off his shoulder. Using his free hand he undid the zipper five or six inches. Then he reached in and pulled out the silver head with the two black stone eyes.

Akish shook his head as if Finlay were a total dork. "You don't understand. It cannot be just any silver. It must be from the ore of Ephraim Hill where Jared, the son of Omer, slayed the prophets."

"This is from the ore of Ephraim Hill," said Finlay.

Akish looked perplexed, then suddenly very interested. He accepted the statue from Finlay's hand and examined it more closely. I looked over at Mary and tried to signal her with my eyes that she ought to move closer to me. Both Josh and Mary got my signal. They didn't understand why, but they began to move closer to me just the same. Finlay quickly turned his pistol onto them.

"What are you doing? Don't move!"

Mary and Joshua stopped. Finlay kept aiming his pistol at them, but his attention was on Akish as he rolled the silver head over in his hands. I knew that Finlay's pistol was an old kind of pistol. There was only one shot in it. But there was another pistol in his sash. What could we do? We knew if we didn't do something immediately, we'd all be dead. We just kept our eyes on the pistol in Finlay's hand.

"What is this object?" asked Akish.

"It's an oracle," said Finlay. "It may be used to track an enemy, or find something lost."

"You mean it has already been endowed with arcane powers?"

Finlay nodded.

Akish looked delighted. "Do you realize what this means? It's better than I could've ever hoped for. You have saved me an incalculable amount of time. I don't need to go to Ephraim Hill! I can finish the sword right here!"

Finlay reached out quickly and snatched the statue back, pointing the pistol back at Akish again. "I don't need you at all. I can give the sword its final plating of silver myself."

"Is that so?" said Akish calmly. "You're a swordsmith, are you? You know the incantations?"

Finlay frowned. He clearly didn't know any of it.

"Don't be greedy and foolish," Akish warned. "Don't you see, Todd Finlay? This was all meant to be. Your twenty-five-year search. The statue. Your arrival here today. I still don't think you fully understand your own obsession, and why you have felt the sword calling to you for so long through the centuries."

"Show it to me," Finlay demanded.

Akish started to smile. "Of course. It's time for you to see it. If you hadn't asked, I would have offered."

He balanced his torch against the wall, then knelt down and began to untie the ropes that bound the bundle. Those same ropes would likely be used to bind us. Finlay's eyes were glued to Akish and the sword. I almost felt that if we made a break for it now, he'd never react quickly enough to stop us. Mary and Joshua moved a little closer. I began to move further toward the passageway that led deeper into the mountain.

Akish untied the last knot, then began to unwrap the prize inside. Finlay licked his lips. His pistol hand was trembling so badly that I thought he might shoot Akish on accident, which would've been just fine with me. At last the swordmaker got down to the very last fold. He paused there and raised his eyes to look right at Finlay. A wicked grin was still on his face.

"Do it!" Finlay commanded. "Reveal it!"

Instead of tossing aside that last fold of cloth, Akish reached under it and found the sword's hilt. Slowly, he pulled it out. As the shiny copper surface was revealed, Finlay's eyes were as big as moons. The sword reflected in the torchlight like a brand-new penny. It looked heavy, with shiny red and silver jewels and both edges appeared to have been sharpened. The triangle tip looked so sharp that I'd have been afraid to touch it even lightly with my finger. It might've cut right through my flesh like a hot knife cutting butter. Part of me said, "It's just a sword, like any other sword—no different than the terrible curved sword of Hazim." But another part of me, much like Finlay, felt a strange desire to hold it. I know it's totally weird, but that's what kept going through my mind.

Finlay's pistol became shakier than ever. He clenched his teeth and seethed, "Give it to me. Hand it over now!"

Akish was still wearing that evil grin. He rose to his feet, still watching Finlay's eyes. The hilt of the sword was firmly in his grip. He balanced the other end in his palm.

Akish shook his head. "No, Todd Finlay. I already told you. Only I may touch it."

"I'll kill you. I swear I'll kill you!"

"No, you won't. You can't. Not while I'm holding it. Go ahead and try. Pull the trigger. I promise you, you don't even have a fraction of the strength."

Sweat was pouring off Finlay's forehead. He clenched his teeth even harder. I think he was really trying. He really wanted to pull that trigger. But he couldn't. The gun continued to tremble. Finlay's whole arm began to tremble. Then his body. He dropped the statue and brought up his other hand to steady the gun, perhaps thinking if he used both hands he might finally have the strength to shoot. But it didn't work. Finlay couldn't do it. He couldn't make his finger pull that trigger. Tears were streaming down his face. At last, all the resistance inside him failed. The sword controlled him completely. His face almost had a look of surprise as his grip on the gun started to loosen. Finally, against his will, it dropped out of his fingers and fell to the floor.

"Very good," said Akish smoothly. "It's just as I thought. The sword owns you. Not the other way around. Do you know why, Todd Finlay?"

Finlay continued to shiver and tremble. He shook his head, his face a mask of terror.

Akish stepped toward him. "It's because you're a part of it! You always have been. Your blood flows through its veins!"

Akish said something more, but for the first time since we'd traveled back through time, I didn't understand the words. They were dark words. Evil words.

My eyes widened. The sword! Something was happening to it! It was starting to glow! The whole copper blade—everything but the hilt in Akish's hands—was becoming molten hot. We could feel its heat all the *way across the room! Akish raised the sword over his head. Finlay closed his eyes and turned his face up toward the ceiling. Oh my gosh! I couldn't watch! He was going to kill Finlay right before our faces! I wanted to run. We all wanted to run. But our feet were frozen. Something was holding us!*

I turned my face away as Akish brought down his sword in a terrible stroke. I heard the awful sound as the sword hit. I heard the sizzling of blood, and I smelled a most horrible smell.

But then my eyes started turning involuntarily. What was happening? *I was being forced to look!*

"Don't turn away, little one," said Akish. "I want all of you to watch."

It was a hideous scene. Akish was standing over Finlay's fallen body. The sword was still glowing hot, only now it was giving off steam. For just an instant I glanced at Mary and Joshua. They were watching too, their eyes wide with horror.

Akish took his steaming sword and pointed it toward the silver head on the floor. He continued to say strange, eerie words that I couldn't understand. Then the strangest thing of all happened. As Akish touched the tip of the copper sword against the silver head, the silver began to melt. The face of the statue began to bubble and ooze. The stone's eyes dropped off onto the floor. The silver began to climb the sword!

Akish spoke again, and this time I understood his words.

"There," he said with satisfaction. "Climb the blade, O precious metal. We're almost finished now. Only one more step to go. And see? You have been given more than you even asked. Your blanket of silver will be sealed to your flesh by the blood of three *innocent victims. What more could you have hoped?"*

I was petrified. My thoughts were all messed up. I couldn't think straight about anything. *Why was this happening to me? Then in the hurricane of darkness, I heard a faint whisper. It was from the lips of Mary. She was whispering the words of a song. But even though it was just a whisper, she was saying the words in perfect rhythm with the way the song would have been sung.*

"I am a child of God . . ."

Suddenly I realized why my feet wouldn't move. It was fear itself that held them. That was the source of Akish's power. It was the only *source, and without it, he had no power over us at all. I continued to watch the melted silver climb the glowing, steaming blade. It was almost to the top. The statue had been reduced almost to a puddle. But before the last of the silver reached the hilt, I followed Mary's example, and in my mind I began singing the same hymn. I looked at Joshua. His lips were moving. I could tell that he was doing it too. We sang to our Savior—the one who takes away all fear. Who teaches that there is nothing to fear.*

And with that thought my legs immediately broke free of the power that was holding them—and I could run!

"Now!" cried Mary.

She leaped for the passageway that led deeper into the mountain. Josh and I bolted after her. I caught a brief glimpse of Akish's face. He looked shocked.

"Stop!" he shouted.

I think he even pointed that sword at us, now fully plated with silver. But we weren't like Todd Finlay. The sword didn't own us. We were free! We slipped into the passageway and continued to run.

"Stop!" cried Akish again. He'd snatched up the torch. He was coming after us.

"Where is it, Becky?" Mary asked me frantically. "Where is the time tunnel?"

I still had the image in my mind. Every step was familiar to me. We reached a fork where the cave went two different directions, but I didn't even hesitate. I took the fork to the right. I still worried that it was too late—that the pivotal moment that would have taken us back to our own century had passed.

"You can't escape me!" Akish yelled. "The sword has chosen you!"

He was gaining on us. My legs were starting to feel heavier.

"Don't slow down, Becky!" cried Joshua.

My hand went to my neck. I clutched at the seerstone and again thought about the words of the hymn. We rounded a corner and leaped down onto a shelf. Then all at once we reached the lip of a cliff. Josh nearly ran right over the edge. He threw back his arms to stop himself. Mary caught him. We peered into the nothingness below.

"It's a dead end!" yelled Joshua.

There were no other tunnels—no other ways to go. We were trapped. The walls of the cliff were totally sheer. The pit was fifteen-feet wide, but even if we could've jumped, the walls on the other side were sheer too. Mary looked at me in desperation.

Akish appeared at the end of the shelf. He stopped there and caught his breath, but that same wicked grin climbed his face. The sword in his hands was no longer glowing, but it was shining brightly with its fresh silver coat.

"Well, well," he said. "What were you thinking, young lady? The passageway to another time is down that other fork. I ought to know; that's how I got here. Silly girl. You missed *it!"*

He laughed. Josh and Mary looked at me with ultimate confusion, wondering how I could've made such a mistake. Again I looked over the edge of the cliff. As Akish's torch drew closer it revealed nothing different. The pit had no bottom—just an empty blackness.

"I didn't miss *it," I declared to Mary and Josh. "This is it! We jump here!"*

Their eyebrows shot up in disbelief.

Josh shook his head. "There's nothing there!"

"Trust me, Joshua," I said. "Trust me."

Josh and Mary said nothing, but they took each other's hands. Mary also reached out to me. I threaded my fingers through hers and held on. My other hand continued to clutch the seerstone around my neck.

Akish suddenly got a look of panic. He realized we really were going to jump.

"On two!" said Mary quickly. "One-TWO!"

Akish dropped the torch. He lunged toward me. We all leaped at the same time, but just as I was expecting to plunge into the blackness, Akish caught my arm. He pulled me back, causing me to smash against the cliff wall. My grip on Mary's hand immediately broke apart. Joshua cried my name, but his voice faded fast as they fell into the gloom. Akish was lying flat against the edge, holding onto me with all his strength. As the torch that Akish dropped dimmed and snuffed out, I saw the hilt of his silver sword hanging partly over the cliff's edge.

Akish was holding onto the same arm that I was using to clutch the seerstone. I let go of the stone and began to struggle. I struck out at him. I couldn't even see his face. Yet I felt my fingernail jab into the softness of his eye. He lost his grip on my wrist. As I swung my other arm, it bumped something—the hilt of Akish's sword. As I felt myself starting to fall again, Akish's other hand made one last furious effort to seize me. I felt the chain dig into the back of my neck. He'd caught the stone! Instantly the chain snapped. I was falling again! I'd lost the seerstone, but saved my own life.

"NOOO!" *Akish's voice echoed in the darkness.* "MY PRECIOUS SWORD!"

I saw it to my left. The silver blade still had a dim shine, tumbling and turning. The sword was falling with *me! As my body began to pick up speed, a warm, pleasant wind began to flow all around me. I began to see lights. They were brilliant blue and flashing like little forks of lightning.*

I was falling into time.

CHAPTER 25

I sat beside Apollus, my rescuer, my hero, in the fading light of day.

We were both watching the face of Eagle-Sky-Jaguar. He looked almost frozen in time as he stood gazing back toward the jungles that had been his home for the past six years. Many of the people he had known and loved through all those years—the ones who had saved his life when he was a boy—were dead. The final fate of many others was unknown. We never did try to find the caves where the survivors of Seibalche had taken refuge.

Instead Apollus and Moroni had decided that we should ride as far as we could until dark. We now found ourselves in the ruins of a small village on the edge of the river. Lamanai told us that it was once a Nephite village, but it had been abandoned according to a treaty that Mormon had made with the Lamanites thirty-five years before.

Lamanai let simmer the hatred that had been brewing in his heart for so long. "He killed my father," he said darkly. "He killed my *step*-father, and I have yet to obtain my revenge."

"Don't let vengeance be the motive," said Moroni. "Let it be the well-being of your people. And the well-being of *mine*. If indeed you can regain the kingdom of your father, perhaps the Nephites and the Lamanites can finally live together in peace."

As I listened to Moroni the most peculiar feelings welled up inside me. Moroni really believed it—he really believed that it was possible to avoid the terrible fate that I'd read about so many times in the Book of Mormon. Lamanai seemed to believe it too. They really felt that peace was possible. Could the righteous convictions of two great men change the fate of a nation?

They had *me* wanting to believe it. But how could I? And then I remembered the words of my cousin, Joshua. I whispered them to Apollus, out of hearing of the others.

"Joshua asked me once, 'Why *can't* you change the fate of a nation? Why *can't* we save the Nephites from being destroyed?'"

"Did you think he was right?" Apollus wondered.

"No, I didn't," I confessed. "I didn't think it was right to even *hope* for something like that. How could it be right to change history?"

"But haven't we already done that?"

He was referring to Moroni. I sighed wearily. "I don't know. I just don't know."

Ryan overheard and added, "Maybe we can't change the Nephites' final destiny. But there may still be a lot more that we *can* change. Look at what we've already done. We saved the Prophet Moroni! I still can't believe it. I look at him and I still can't conceive that he's the same man who will one day appear at the bedside of Joseph Smith."

The prophet continued to talk to the son of Jaguar-Paw. "You must come with us to Cumorah, Lamanai. My people have been gathering there for four years. My father has been building fortifications and defense works non-stop through all that time. But despite his tireless labors he still believes that this is the final struggle of our people. I believed it too. But you have given me new hope, Lamanai. We will forge an alliance the likes of which has never been known in all the history of our peoples. We are brothers after all—children of the same parents who came across the great deep nearly a thousand years ago. I know that our fathers were great enemies, but you and I can become greater friends. There will be no peace so long as Fire-Born and Lord Crocodile sit upon the throne of the Lamanites. I know that now. When I was captured I was coming to Tikal to make one last plea for peace. You saw how they received my entreaties."

Lamanai pondered this. "Yes, our fathers were great enemies. But I also know that my father had great respect for Mormon. I heard him say once that if Mormon had been *his* general, he might have extended the boundaries of his kingdom to the farthest limits of the One World. Perhaps if our nations can be united, we can make my father's dream a reality."

"But only if it's a nation where we can remain free to worship as we please," said Moroni. "And where Christians cannot be persecuted as they have been in the past."

"Yes," said Lamanai, but on this point he seemed to have some uncertainty. There was still much that the heir of Jaguar-Paw didn't understand about this new religion that had suddenly sprung up into his life from the depths of the bubbling cenote. He still credited Apollus, Ryan, and myself for setting in motion the chain of events that had convinced him to take back his father's throne, but there was still very little to show for his efforts. He had saved a Nephite prophet, but his village had been burnt to the ground. There was still no word from Jolom or the others who had gone to spread the word that Eagle-Sky-Jaguar still lived. Had Jolom failed in his mission? Had he been killed or captured by the loyal subjects of Fire-Born before the message could take hold?

Lamanai accepted Moroni's invitation. "I will journey with you to the land of Cumorah. I will do all that I can as the son of Jaguar-Paw to forge this alliance. But I must leave someone here. Someone who will tell the people where I have gone and when I will return."

They looked to Jacobah, but he shook his head. "Please, Lord Sky. I feel it is my duty to defend the life of Kukalcan."

"I will stay," said Antionum. "I will find Jolom, and I will help him to spread the word. I'll spread it by whispers and by night messengers if necessary. When you return, Lord Sky, there will be a whole nation of the Lamaya here to embrace you."

Lamanai smiled. "By Itzamna, Lord of Creation, let it be true." Then he saw Moroni's reaction and changed his oath. "I mean to say, by the name of Jesus Christ."

"We will go to Cumorah as well," Apollus declared. "If it's a battle for freedom, I will be there."

I gave Apollus a strange look. If I was going to Cumorah it wasn't to become some kind of freedom fighter. It would be to find a way home.

I asked Moroni, "Have you heard of a land called Melek? A place where there is a volcano?"

"There are many lands with volcanoes," said Moroni. "Why do you wish to find this land?"

"Because if we can find that land, we will be able to find the pathway that leads to our home." I didn't feel I needed to go into any more details than that.

Moroni thought hard. "I have read the histories of our people, as well as the stories that are contained in the plates of Ammoron. I believe Melek was the name of the land where the Lamanite converts of Ammon once lived."

"Yes!" I said excitedly. "Do you know where it is?"

Moroni shook his head. "The names of many of those lands have changed. My father still knows all of the old names and places. He will be able to tell you how to find the land of Melek."

"Then I guess," I said wearily, "we're going to Cumorah too."

Ryan nodded, then gave a grunt. "Guess it might be more worthwhile than a first semester at the 'Y.' I can't think of *anything* that would better prepare me for a mission. Besides, there may be other reasons why we're here. Some that might turn out to be completely unexpected."

I noticed him steal a glance at the girl who'd ridden with him on the back of the horse. This was an interesting development. I'd been told that this girl's name was Tz'ikin, but as yet she hadn't spoken a single word to me. Earlier I'd heard her declare that she would be traveling with Moroni toward Cumorah, but supposedly that was only because her homeland was on the way. She struck me as kind of a hard case, but if Ryan was truly interested in her, it relieved some of the guilt I felt over my feelings toward Apollus.

"We should prepare ourselves," said Gilgal, the other surviving Nephite. "If Fire-Born finds out that Lamanai and Moroni are alive, he's also bound to figure out where we're going. Likely he'll send assassins, soldiers, and everything else at his disposal to try and stop us before we reach Nephite lands."

Moroni nodded. "You're probably right. But it *is* the planting season. Soldiers must become farmers, or even the subjects of Fire-Born will starve. God has helped us to come this far. If His hand continues to shield us, we'll be home before the end of the rains."

On those words we decided to retire for the night. Gathering up our meager supplies, we made a place to sleep in the ruins of a building that Moroni said was an old house of worship. But before I went to sleep I decided that I had to talk with Ryan alone. I found him outside as he was returning from checking on the horses.

We sat down together on an old stone fence that was nearly overgrown with vines. I decided that I had to be honest with him. He deserved that.

"I love him," I confessed.

"I know," he replied, and to my relief there was no tone of animosity or resentment.

"How did you know?" I asked.

"You don't hide your feelings very well, Meagan. Oh, you try hard, but you don't usually succeed."

I smiled at him warmly. "Then you understand?"

"Understand? Who can ever understand matters of the heart? But I'll always have kind feelings for you, Meagan. And I'd like to remain your friend."

I threw my arms around him. "Thank you, Ryan. That means more to me than you can know. You really are a wonderful man."

I kissed him on the cheek. But of course my timing was impeccable. When I turned my head, there was Apollus standing in the doorway of the church. At first he looked angry, but then he looked around in befuddlement. You know, a woman doesn't get that many chances to see into a man's heart. In that instant I saw all that I needed to know, and I rejoiced inside.

Ryan grinned, trying hard to keep from laughing out loud. "I think I better, uh . . ."

He got up and walked toward the building, but just as he passed Apollus, Ryan reached up and tenderly massaged the place on his cheek where I had kissed him, then whistled casually as he entered the church. Apollus paid me another perfunctory glance, then pretended I wasn't even there as he walked by.

"Apollus," I called.

"I have to check the horses," he said.

"Ryan already did that."

He ignored me and continued on toward the place where we had tethered them. Of course I followed.

"Apollus!" I said again.

But that young man was moving fast. When I saw him next he was leaning over a broken stone wall watching the horses in the moonlight, not even bothering to acknowledge my approach. I leaned next to him, also pretending to take great interest in the horses.

Finally I said, "That wasn't what you thought."

"Oh? What did I think?"

"Come on. If you must know, Apollus, I was telling Ryan my feelings toward you."

"Such feelings must be quite ambivalent if you were kissing him."

"It was on the cheek. He told me that he wanted to remain my friend."

Apollus nodded. "That's good. A person can never have too many friends."

"Oh, Apollus. I give up." I started to walk away.

"I realized something today," he said suddenly.

I came back. He continued to look at the horses, and past them, at the rising moon.

"What was that?" I asked.

"I realized that horses are the slowest creatures in the world."

I pulled in my chin. "That's what you realized?"

"Yes. No matter how swiftly my horse could have run, it would never have been fast enough. It couldn't have relieved the anxiety I felt, wondering if I would reach you in time."

"Well, as usual, you weren't a second too late. Or a second too early, I might add."

He looked at me. "I realized, Meagan Sorenson, that if I had been too late—if I hadn't been there soon enough to find you—nothing else would have mattered."

I could feel my heart beating. "Nothing?"

He shook his head. "Two years ago I made a terrible mistake. Do you remember what you said to me that night?"

"I told you that I wasn't just a slab of bacon that you could put on ice."

"Before that."

"I told you that the thing you were searching for might be right in front of your nose."

He nodded. "That's right. That's what you told me. I'm only sorry that it has taken me two years to see it."

"Well, I've noticed that men are usually a little slow about such things."

Apollus smiled. It was that same Apollus grin that had always weakened me in the knees and quickened my heart rate. For the life of me I would never let him know how defenseless I was in the face of that grin.

And then he wasn't grinning anymore. His features softened and he just stared into my eyes. This was a look that I'd never seen on the face of Apollus Brutus Severillus. I realized I liked it even more than the grin.

"I love you, Meagan."

My eyes filled with tears and I whispered, "I love you too."

He leaned in and he kissed me. I'd tasted this kiss so many times in my thoughts that I was sure the real thing could never bring me to the same place. Certainly it couldn't go beyond it. But leave it to Apollus. The feeling in that kiss was something that no misery in the course of my existence could ever diminish. It was a gift—one that I don't think a girl gets very often in her life, a glimpse of perfection.

When our kiss ended I was so lost in the feeling that I don't think I could have remembered my own name.

He made that same mischievous grin and said, "You're right."

"Huh?"

He licked his lips. "You're not a slab of bacon."

Men! They could never just play a moment to the end! They always had to throw in some stupid thing. I decided the only way to shut him up was to kiss him again. So I weaved my fingers through his hair and started to do so. But our next kiss, unfortunately, was cut short. Something had upset the horses. Apollus's scarlet stallion was kicking at the earth and pulling desperately at the rope that tethered it to the tree.

"What do you think is wrong?" I asked Apollus.

He listened. Far to the east there was a flash of red lightning as a storm moved in from the Caribbean Sea.

"Could be the weather," said Apollus, but I didn't think he believed it.

He took my hand and we crept toward another stone wall a short distance away. This wall was very near the jungle's edge. As we arrived, we crouched down and watched. Something was out there. I sensed it strongly.

Apollus started to rise, "We should get the others."

I grabbed his arm. "Wait."

A second later my eyes lit up. I leaped over the wall and approached the woods.

"Meagan!" Apollus whispered harshly.

But I didn't stop. I focused into the depths of the foliage. Then I crouched down and held out my hand.

"Huracan," I called softly. "Huracan, is that you?"

Finally I saw it again—the jaguar's yellow eyes. Shyly, Huracan emerged from the undergrowth. It was already licking my hand by the time Apollus leaped over the wall to join me. I gave that wonderful cat an enormous hug.

"That could have been *any* jaguar," Apollus scolded.

"No," I said. "I knew it was Huracan. She's got you beat, you know."

"Oh?"

"She saved my life twice today. You only saved it once."

"I see. Well, I suppose I'll have to do a little better."

"Yes, you will."

Apollus started patting the animal's shiny black coat. But it was obvious that I was the one who had captured this animal's heart. As I scratched its neck, it snuggled against me and began making that thunderous purr.

Apollus tried to paraphrase a line from *King Kong*. I remembered that we'd watched it together the very night before he'd ridden away on Harry's motorcycle.

"It appears that Beauty has tamed the Beast," he said.

I continued to pet the jaguar's head. "Have I?"

But I wasn't looking at the jaguar anymore. I was looking straight at Apollus.

Once more tonight I got a glimpse of that wonderful grin, then he leaned down and whispered in my ear. "Some beasts are never tamed."

I gave him the narrowest, most alluring gaze I could manage. "We'll see about that," I said. "We'll just see."

* * *

The blue lightning became brighter and brighter as I fell through time. The warm wind that at first had comforted me became more violent. Toward the end I felt like I was spinning like a top. The roar in my ears was like a tornado. In fact it was a tornado! Dorothy Gale, eat your heart out! I was inside a tornado!

I made a little grunt as I landed. My blonde hair swirled up around my face, and for an instant the wind lifted me one last time and set me down even harder. It wasn't all that painful, but it startled me terribly. When I came to my senses I found myself on the ground in a very desolate place. The wind was still whipping up around me. The ground had more cracks in it than a jigsaw puzzle. To my relief I saw Joshua and Mary lying nearby. They looked equally shaken up, and their hair and clothes were all in disarray.

As I looked off to the right I could still see the tornado. It was ripping up the desert floor just a short distance away. And yet it seemed to be dying. The blast of wind and dust on my face was going away. A few seconds later the tornado looked more like a dust devil. There was one last burst of blue lightning, and then the curl of wind vanished completely. All the dust and debris that had been caught up inside it floated peacefully to the ground.

We looked at one another, shaken and confused.

"This . . . isn't Frost Cave," said Joshua, stating the obvious.

In fact it was the flattest, thirstiest, ugliest place I'd ever seen—even worse than the desert around the Dead Sea. At least around the Dead Sea there were hills. This place was as flat as a tortilla. I almost wondered if that tornado had taken us to H E-double toothpicks. The sky was gray and thickly streaked in purple clouds.

"What is this?" asked Joshua, his voice sounding more and more panicked.

"Were we too late, Becky?" Mary asked. "Did we fail to jump off that cliff in time?"

I didn't want to answer that. I didn't want to answer it at all. Mary's eyes filled with devastation. I knew what she was thinking. Somewhere a missionary named Harry Hawkins was just arriving home, and Mary wasn't there to greet him.

"Look over there!" cried Joshua.

Mary and I both looked. Something was on the horizon. A tower? It was a thin pyramid as tall as a skyscraper. Maybe taller! For all I knew it was still a hundred miles away. The base of it was blurred out by dust, like a building floating in a dust cloud.

"What is that?" asked Joshua, his voice filled with wonder.

"I have no idea," I replied.

But Mary did. "When I was little girl," she said, "a trader from Persia drew a tower like that in the dirt outside my home. He called it a ziggurat."

"What does that mean?" asked Josh.

"Persia was once called Babylonia."

Josh thought a moment, then it hit him. "The tower of Babel? Are you trying to say that that's the Tower of Babel?"

"I'm just saying it looks like a ziggurat," said Mary.

Josh and I gawked at her. Then we gawked at the tower.

"The Tower of Babel," Josh repeated dreamily.

But something I saw lying on the cracked earth about twenty feet away concerned me even more. It was the silver sword of Akish, lying there as innocent as a newborn baby.

So it wasn't over yet—the adventure of our lives. But what I dreaded more than anything else, was that it really had only begun . . .

EPILOGUE

My father called to me from the cliffs overlooking the underground river.

"Harry, don't touch the pillar! We don't know what it is or what it does!"

Actually, I had no intention of touching it. It made me dizzy just to look up and see it rising all the way to the ceiling. What had caught my attention was something at the pillar's base. Something on the ground just inches from the flowing, silver light. It was a pale white stone—so different in character from any other stone or crystal in the cave that I couldn't resist picking it up.

Marcos came over. In his hands was a shiny steel sword—Apollus's sword. He had found it stuck in a crevasse on the cliffs, just above the swirling rapids. He saw the stone in my hand.

"What is it?" he asked.

"I'm not sure," I replied.

The stone was about the size of a fifty-cent piece. I cupped it tightly in my palm and became aware of a strange feeling pulsing through me.

Uncle Garth and my father were still climbing down the rocky ridge to where the two underground rivers converged. The four us had left Salt Lake City only last night. Three days ago I'd been in Athens, Greece. Just *two* days ago I'd been released from my mission, and already I was embarking on another mission to find our missing loved ones.

A few hours ago we'd discovered the most important clue—a note at the place where we usually camped. On one side of it was written a chilling message from Todd Finlay outlining his motives for kidnapping Joshua and Becky. But on the other side it read,

We have Becky. But Finlay still has Joshua. We
will pursue as far as Galaxy Room. May get help
and supplies from Nephites.
Love Meagan, Mary, Becky, Apollus, Ryan.

So here we stood in the center of the Rainbow Room. I hardly recognized the place anymore. It was as if the Rainbow Room and the Galaxy Room had merged into one. Somehow this union had created a phenomenon more extraordinary than anything that had existed before. And this pillar! What *was* it? What did it mean?

Garth and Dad finally arrived. Dad in particular seemed very interested in the stone.

"May I see it?" he asked.

He stared into the pearly white surface.

"They were here," he said confidently. "They were standing right here. Meagan and Apollus mentioned this stone when they spoke to me on the phone. They said that there were actually *two* stones set in a silver frame. Two *seer stones.*"

"May I look?" asked Garth.

Garth studied it very closely, even holding it up to his eye.

"What are you doing?" Marcos asked him.

"I'm not sure," said Garth. "I just wondered if . . . Well, if it truly is a seerstone, it might be a key to finding my children."

Garth cupped it in his hands and blocked out the light. He concentrated hard, as if *willing* the stone to reveal something to him. At last he lowered it in frustration. "I don't have the gift."

I remembered the strange feeling that I'd experienced. "Let me see it again."

Garth handed it back. I clutched the stone like before, and again I felt a pulsing strength. I put it up to my eye, cupping it in both hands like Uncle Garth had done, and blocking out the light. At first there was nothing. Then something began to appear. I couldn't believe it! Images began to appear beyond my wildest imaginings. In the stone's surface I could see decades, centuries—millenniums! I could see events never recorded and faces unremembered. I felt like I was staring into the fabric and texture of time itself.

"What do you see?" asked Marcos.

"*Everything!*" I replied excitedly. "And yet—"

"And yet what?" asked Garth.

"It's almost as if . . . I can't explain it. I see a lot, but . . . there are some things that I *don't* see—like looking through a pool of water after someone disturbs the surface."

"Can you see enough to know how to find Meagan, Mary, and the rest?" asked Dad.

I hesitated a moment, trying to clear my thoughts. I put the stone up to my eye again. The stone veritably *glittered* with energy, like a tiny version of this very room at the exact moment when the burst of energy struck every seven and a half minutes.

"I see them!" I exclaimed.

"Where are they?" asked Garth urgently.

"I . . . can't quite tell. But I know how to reach them."

I lowered the stone. As I lowered it, I focused directly on the pillar less than five paces away.

"It's a matter of timing," I said.

"Timing?" Marcos repeated.

"Yes. That pillar . . . It's like . . . like a conduit. A *highway!* We can use it to reach them. The possibilities . . . are limitless."

"What do we do?" asked Garth.

"We wait. We wait until the timing is right. The stone will tell me."

"How long?" my father asked.

"It depends on which group we wish to find."

"Which *group?*" asked Garth.

"They're in two different places . . . I think."

"Then we'll have to split up," said Marcos.

"One of us has to go home to tell Jenny and Sabrina and Melody what's happening," said Garth.

I looked at my father.

He raised his eyebrows. "Me?"

"It's the logical choice," I said. "You have an infant son and a wife who needs you."

My father sighed with regret. He looked at me with great

emotion. Then he shook his head. "Here I haven't seen you in two years . . . and now . . ."

"I'll be all right, Dad. We'll *all* be all right."

"I know you will," he said. "I know the Lord will go with you. I just feel a little like Mosiah or Alma saying good-bye to their sons when they went over to the Lamanites."

"I love you, Dad," I said.

Tears filled his eyes. He embraced me deeply. He embraced the others. And then he left us, climbing back through the honeycomb of tunnels.

"How do we split up?" asked Marcos, still clutching Apollus's sword.

"I'll have to go alone," I said. "You'll go with Uncle Garth. The two of you will leave first. I'll tell you exactly when to enter the pillar."

"Which group has my daughter and son?" asked Garth.

I shook my head. "All I know is that they're in two separate places—two separate times."

Marcos looked overwhelmed. "You mean we'll arrive at our destinations and we won't even be able to describe who we're looking for? How can we search? And even beyond that, how will we get back home again?"

I shook my head. I didn't have all the answers. But there was no more time to ponder. I told them to poise themselves before the pillar. They did so, giving me one last intense look, as if to remind me that their lives were in my hands. I waited another moment. I felt the power of the stone.

"Now!" I cried.

As the two of them stepped into the silver light, their molecules seemed to liquefy, melting and mixing into the singular stream of energy. I felt a stab of regret. They neither knew where they were going, or who they were looking for. If that wasn't a leap of faith, what was?

I moved back into the tunnels and awaited my own moment of departure. Those jolts of energy every seven and a half minutes, despite their haunting beauty, seriously rattled my nerves.

Only moments before I was set to leave, a flashlight beam came toward me through the tunnel. Who could it be, I wondered? Had my father returned? To my surprise, it was my sister, Steffanie.

"Harry!" she called jubilantly. "Thank goodness you're still here. I'm not too late!"

"What are you doing here, Steff?"

"I'm going with you," she proclaimed. "How *dare* you try to leave me in the first place!"

"But you're getting married soon! What about your fiancé? What about Michael?"

"If it comes to that, he'll have to wait. You think I can get married with half of my family missing?"

"You're incredible."

"I'm glad that you think so."

In truth I was ecstatic to see her. I sometimes wondered if my blonde-haired, blue-eyed sister could have run us all into the ground. She was the star of every sports team she'd ever played on. I sometimes teasingly called her Miss Amazon. Who wouldn't want to go into battle with a genuine Amazon at their side?

The tunnel shook with another jolt of energy.

"I've been feeling that tremor for hours," said Steff. "What *is* that?"

"You're about to find out," I replied.

Moments later we were in position at the base of the pillar. I took my sister's hand.

"This is it," I said.

"This is *what?*" asked Steff.

"Exactly," I answered.

The two of us stepped forward into the everlasting river of time.

ENDNOTES

CHAPTER I

Like other books in the *Tennis Shoes* series, a basic assumption is drawn in this novel that the lands of the Book of Mormon are found in Mesoamerica: Southern Mexico, Belize, Guatemala, Honduras, and El Salvador. This is based on the consensus of most LDS scholars who have written on the subject. It appears to be the only region of the New World that fits all of the parameters of the Book of Mormon itself, including physical descriptions from the text, correlations with local tradition and secular history, population, and levels of civilization. Also, as non-LDS Maya scholar, Eric Thompson, writes, "Middle America is the only part of the New World in which a system of embryonic writing developed" (Eric Thompson, *The Rise and Fall of Maya Civilization*, 1966, 189).

The Church has never taken an official stand on this subject. Opinions have been expressed in every generation since the gospel was restored, but the stamp of "Thus saith the Lord" has never been applied. One of the most intriguing statements is perhaps one that appeared in the *Times and Seasons* in 1842 while Joseph Smith was editor. In an editorial about the book, *Incidents of Travel in Central America, Chiapas, and Yucatan* by the American explorer John Lloyd Stevens, it was stated that, "It would not be a bad plan to compare Mr. Stephen's ruined cities with those in the Book of Mormon" (*Times and Seasons* 3:927). However, even in this instance, the statement appears to be an opinion, not a conclusive fact.

Therefore, until the Lord speaks on the matter, it will remain the pursuit of scholarship and study. There likely has never been a reader of the Book of Mormon who hasn't pondered where these fascinating events took place. Readers of the Bible have been similarly interested, which has led to centuries of scholarly research in many fields of study to help broaden our understanding of that sacred work. Latter-day Saints will undoubtedly continue to engage in scholarly research to help enhance our understanding of the Book of Mormon. The most important attribute is an open mind. As more information comes to light—and it surely will—we should continually be willing to adapt and learn, always bearing in mind the credentials and background of the individuals who offer proposals.

In 1986 President Ezra Taft Benson issued this resplendent blessing:

> . . . I bless you with increased understanding of the Book of Mormon.
> I promise you that from this moment forward, if we will daily sup from its pages and abide by its precepts, God will pour out upon each child of Zion and the Church a blessing hitherto unknown . . . (Benson, *Ensign*, May 1986, 78).

This blessing is being fulfilled before our very eyes. The increase in scholarly awareness about the Book of Mormon is only a part of it. However, the object is never to use archaeology or geography to "prove" the book's truthfulness. It is merely part of the celebration! We are encouraged to gain a spiritual testimony of the Book of Mormon as outlined in Moroni 10:3-5, and then embark upon the lifelong adventure of celebrating the book in all of its ever-widening facets.

As was written in the 1842 *Times and Seasons* editorial previously mentioned, "Light cleaves to light and facts are supported by facts. The truth injures no one." In the end we can rest assured that empirical knowledge and spiritual testimony will come together in a perfect union.

CHAPTER 2

The giant granite heads mentioned here are found in many locations throughout the "Isthmus" region of Mexico (the states of Veracruz, Chiapas, Tobasco, and Oaxaca). One of the largest heads, found at the archaeological site at San Lorenzo, is presently on display at the museum in Jalapa, Veracruz. Another can be seen in the town plaza at Santiago Tuxtla, which is the village that sits directly below the Hill Vigia.

These heads are generally associated with the oldest known civilization in Mexico, commonly called the Olmec or Olmeca. The name was given to them by archaeologists and means "People of the Rubber Tree." Rubber is a major commodity produced in the region. The approximate dates given to the Olmecs are from 2500 B.C. to 300 B.C.

Certain LDS scholars have suggested that the rise and fall of the Olmec civilization corresponds so closely with the rise and fall of Jaredites that, for all practical purposes, the Olmecs may well have been the Jaredites (David Palmer, *In Search of Cumorah*, 1981; John Sorenson, *An Ancient American Approach to the Book of Mormon*, 1985; Joseph Allen, *Exploring the Lands of the Book of Mormon*, 1989).

A sixteenth-century scholar named Ixtlilxochitl (Isht-lil-sho-chee-tul), who was born of Aztec royalty, wrote in his history of a group of people called the "first settlers" who came to Mexico from a place where the inhabitants had erected a "very high tower to protect themselves against a second destruction of the world." He writes that at this time the languages became confounded and the people were scattered to all parts of the world.

However, he says, ". . . seven men and their wives were able to understand one another, and they came to this land, having first crossed many lands and waters, living in caves and passing through great tribulations" (Ixtlilxochitl, *Historical Works*, 2nd Edition, 1892). According to Ixtlilxochitl, after 104 years of wandering, these people eventually settled in Huehue Tlapallan, which today is the Tuxtla Mountains of Veracruz, Mexico, where the Hill Vigia is located.

Michael D. Coe, a non-LDS scholar, suggests that the Olmecs finally destroyed themselves in a great internal conflict around 400 B.C. Regarding the destruction at a large Olmec site called San Lorenzo, he writes, ". . . there is no evidence of outside invasion. The amount of pent up hatred and fury represented by this enormous act of destruction must have been awesome indeed" (*America's First Civilization*, 1968, 86).

Local traditions about large battles taking place on the Hill Vigia in ancient times are still quite prevalent. Also, references in this novel to Santiago Tuxtla, Lake Catemaco, and the entire region around the Hill Vigia as being an area where there is a significant amount of witchcraft, sorcery, and paranormal activity are based on perceptions widely held today. In Mexico this vicinity has the same notoriety as Salem, Massachusetts, in the United States.

If this land truly is Cumorah, and two wicked nations completely wiped themselves out on its slopes, the coincidence that such local traditions still prevail is interesting to say the least.

CHAPTER 8

Frost Cave, or Spirit Mountain Caverns, is an actual grotto located on Cedar Mountain above Cody, Wyoming. It was discovered in 1909 by a man named Ned Frost when his hunting dogs disappeared into a large opening in the side of the cliff while chasing a bobcat. William F. "Buffalo Bill" Cody touted it as a "Western Carlsbad" and urged President William

Taft to proclaim the cave as a national monument in Sept. 1909. Cody fully expected that it would soon become a major tourist attraction.

However, because of the difficulty of the terrain, and because of limited funds and interest from the National Park Service, congress abolished the site as a national monument in 1954 and turned the cave back over to the city of Cody, Wyoming. In 1955, a group of cavers from Billings, Montana, spent four days and three nights exploring the cave. They produced a map showing eight levels and eight and a half miles of passageways with many open-ended tunnels that they never had a chance to explore. Today however, explorers are familiar with only three levels.

During its development as a tourist attraction, and for the safety of visitors, the lower levels were reportedly sealed off, including the passage leading to a legendary chamber known as "Frost Room" or the "Rainbow Room." The descriptions of this room, exaggerated or not, are similar to descriptions given in the original *Tennis Shoes Among the Nephites*. As far as the author is aware, no one alive today has seen this room or knows how to reach it. In 1966 the cave was closed off to tourists, giving jurisdiction to the U.S. Bureau of Land Management, which now issues permits only to experienced spelunkers (cave explorers).

In his childhood, the author spent countless hours and numerous weekends exploring the cavern in hopes of finding another route to this mysterious room, but without success. In 1986 a group of Colorado cavers located a tight crawlway with air gusting through the opening that appeared to lead to lower levels, but because they could not squeeze through, they left without exploring the subterranean world beyond (Michael Milstein, "Cave's Glory Faded Quickly," *The Billings Gazette*, July 5, 1995).

CHAPTER 13

The year of 8 Baktun, 17 Katun, 8 Tun, 10 Winal, and 10 Kin is the Maya long count equivalent of May 4, 385 A.D., a date selected by the author. The Mayans of the classic period reckoned all of their long count dates from the starting point of Aug. 11, 3114 B.C. We are led to wonder why this date was so significant. Some have suggested that it marked some kind of stellar alignment, but this would not explain why the date itself became important. Some LDS scholars, including Joseph Allen and Bruce Warren, have suggested that this date may correspond to the date of the flood in the days of Noah, or the date of the confounding of tongues at the Tower of Babel, or even to the arrival of the Jaredites in the Promised Land. Whatever the case, this great Mayan calendrical cycle marking this period of world history, and set to last a full 13 "baktuns," or 5128 years, is due to end on Dec. 23, 2012. (It should be emphasized that this point of Mayan folklore does not correlate with the revealed word of God regarding the Second Coming.)

It should be noted that when Lamanai (Eagle-Sky-Jaguar) tells of the Nephites' departure before he was born, he is referring to a treaty that the Nephites made with "the Lamanites and the robbers of Gadianton" in 350 A.D., wherein they lost all of the land southward (Mormon 2:28-29). This undoubtedly led to a mass migration of Nephites from cities and strongholds that they held for generations, including the city of Zarahemla, which they had occupied for over five hundred years. The archaeological record suggests that at this time many ancient cities in the Yucatan and Chiapas regions of southern Mexico were either abandoned or they dramatically declined in population, including El Mirador, Chiapa de Corzo, Izapa, and Santa Rosa (Allen, *Exploring the Lands of the Book of Mormon*).

The names of Great Jaguar-Paw, Spearthrower Owl, Lord Blue-Crocodile, and Fire-Born are all real characters from this period in Mesoamerican history. Their names and other information have been recorded on Mayan glyphs in several locations. The political circumstances of each have been represented in this novel as accurately as possible, according to available data (Linda Schele and David Freidel, *A Forest of Kings*, 1990; David Stuart, "The Arrival of Strangers: Teotihuacan and Tollan in Classic Maya History," 1998). The secular history of this region offers many intriguing insights that may help us to better understand the political climate that led to the final episodes of the Book of Mormon.

CHAPTER 14

The subject of seer stones is one where it sometimes becomes necessary to separate fact from lore. We know that besides the Urim and Thummim, Joseph Smith used several other seer stones, some of which are still in the Church's possession (*Doctrines of Salvation*, vol. 3, 225). Besides interpreting ancient texts, Joseph Smith used seer stones to receive revelations, including many early sections of the Doctrine and Covenants (see headings for Sections 3, 6, 11, and others).

The Adversary has also used seer stones to deceive the foolish and the vain (see Doctrine and Covenants Section 28). The author has made seer stones a part of this story principally for dramatic effect, undoubtedly adding more to the lore of such objects than to the facts.

CHAPTER 15

Many of the foreign words and names that are used in this novel are derived from the ancient Quiché, Chorti, and Yucatecan dialects of the ancient Mayans. The glossary found at the front of this book may help with pronunciations. Some LDS scholars have proposed that certain native languages of Mesoamerica might have similarities with ancient Egyptian and Hebrew, since these were the languages brought by Lehi and Mulek. A preliminary study of the Zapotec language of Oaxaca, Mexico, was conducted by Pierre Agrinier of the New World Archaeological Foundation, in which he found that sixteen to seventeen percent of the words may have Hebrew roots (*SEHA Newsletter* 112, Feb., 1969).

Initially, it may appear that these names seem different in character from names in the Book of Mormon. Actually, it's quite remarkable how at home Book of Mormon names are in the context of Mesoamerican languages. The difference at first glance may be partly attributed to spelling. Mayan today retains many of the original spelling conventions of the Spanish translators of the sixteenth century. In other words, the letters have Spanish pronunciations. For example the letter "X," as in Kux-Wach is pronounced "Sh." The letter "U," especially at the beginning of a word, as in Uaxactun (a Mayan city near Tikal), is pronounced "Wa," or "Wa-shok-tûn." "J" as in the name Jolom (which means "Skull" in Quiché Mayan) is pronounced "H" or "Holom," (which isn't that far from Helam).

In some cases the author kept the Spanish spelling to retain the flavor of written Mayan and also to help readers see and compare. At other times, he stayed with more traditional English phonetic spellings, (which Joseph Smith certainly would have done in his translation). In other cases, an English translation of a character's name was used for dramatic effect. Often these names reveal things about a person's character, as in Fire-Born, which in Mayan is actually "Siyah K'ak'" (literally "Fire is Born"), or Spearthrower Owl, which in Mayan is "Atlatl Cauac" (literally, "Spearthrower Owl" or "Spearthrower Shield"). The atlatl is a war weapon that may have been introduced into Mayan territory from Central Mexico (Stuart, 1998).

With all of this in mind, it may be interesting to see how some Book of Mormon names might be spelled in Mayan. Shiblom, for example, might be "Xib-Balam." (Balam is Mayan for "Jaguar.") Helaman might be "Ji-laman." (Ever notice how the name "Laman" is in Helaman?) And Moroni might be "Mah-rohní." (Translated into English from Mayan, Moroni actually means, "Ancient Hill.") The name Lamanai is taken from an actual archeological site in Belize that LDS researcher Joseph Allen believes to be Jershon, where the converts of Ammon first settled (Joseph L. Allen, "Proposed Map of the Book of Mormon," 1998).

Another language comparison is the common Mayan practice of ending a proper name with the syllable "ha," as in Balamha, Altunha, and Lacanha. This syllable relates to an individual's maternal kinship (the ancestral line of the mother), and may have been used for the same purpose among the Nephites, as with names like Nephihah, Ammonihah, and Moronihah. It's also noteworthy that almost all of the unique names listed in the Book of Mormon that begin with the letter "P"—Pahoran, Paanchi, Pachus, Pekah, Pacumeni—are found in the Chorti-Mayan with pronunciations very similar to the Pronunciation Guide at the back of our current edition of the Book of Mormon.

The words of the short hymn sung by the Lamanites in this chapter are taken directly from phrases found in the *Popal Vuh*, lines 140-155. The *Popal Vuh* is widely regarded as the finest example of ancient American literature ever discovered. It records many of the myths and traditions of the Mayan people that were passed down for generations. Although the only version that we have was written more than a thousand years after Moroni sealed up the Book of Mormon, there are still interesting parallels with reavealed scripture. These include an account of the earth's creation from disorganized matter, a reference to man's first home being a paradisiacal land with abundant fruits and flowers located somewhere "eastward," an account of man's rebellion from the gods and subsequent destruction by means of a great flood, and other examples. (See *Popal Vuh*, new translation by Allen J. Christianson, 2000.)

The hymn found in this chapter is not an exact replication of the translated text, but captures its essential tone. It also reveals a common style of poetry used in Mayan literature known as Chiasmus, or reverse parallelism. This means that lines are arranged in such a way that each idea is repeated in reverse order, emphasizing the elements in the center. The Book of Mormon frequently uses Chiasmus, which was also a common poetic style in ancient Hebrew, but is completely alien to Western, or European, thought and literature. A wonderful example of Book of Mormon Chiasmus is Alma chapter 36, which begins, "My son, give ear to my words . . ." then progresses to its central theme that Christ will atone for the sins of the world, then repeats each concept in reverse order until it ends with the phrase, "Now this according to his word." The *Popal Vuh* is replete with examples of Chiasmus, suggesting that Mayan styles of literature may have Hebrew roots.

CHAPTER 17

Those who wish to study the culture and history of the Nephites and Lamanites are sometimes disappointed that Mormon, in his abridgement of the Nephite records, often chose to simplify, skim, and even disregard cultural and historical details. Mormon stated repeatedly that he did this for the sake of expediency, and perhaps because of the actual space available to him on the plates. He writes in Helaman 3:14, "Behold, a hundredth part of the proceedings of this people, yea, the account of the Lamanites and of the Nephites, and their wars, and contentions, and dissensions, and their preaching, and their prophecies, and their shipping and their building of ships, and their building of temples, and of synagogues and their sanctuaries, and their righteousness, and their wickedness, and their murders, and their robbings, and their plundering, and all manner of abominations and whoredoms, cannot be contained in this work." (See also Words of Mormon 1:5; 3 Nephi 5:8.)

In this novel, many aspects of Book of Mormon culture are expanded upon to reflect the rich diversity of the scriptural landscape and help us to understand how it may all fit together. As more information becomes available, it may date some of the proposed, and sometimes speculative, scenarios, but this is all part of the process of energizing our desire to learn more about this miraculous text.

The suggestion that the culture at Teotihuacan has direct correlation with the robbers of Gadianton has been offered by some LDS scholars (Allen 1989: 107; Palmer 1981: 204; Wirth 2001: 15). During the years leading up to the final battle, Mormon called them simply the "robbers of Gadianton." By this time they were apparently a substantial political force—powerful enough to enter into treaties with the Nephites (Mormon 2:29). The Gadianton society had a long-established tradition of settling in the land northward, where Teotihuacan was located (3 Nephi 7:12). During the fourth century, the Teotihuacan culture had far-reaching influence throughout the Yucatan and as far south as Honduras, "using spies, trade, deceit, and war to accomplish [its] goals" (Diane Wirth, *Book of Mormon Archaeological Digest,* Sept. 2001, 15). Dr. Joseph Allen and others have proposed that the Nephites may have been "in the way" as Teotihuacan tried to expand trade and commerce in the south, which may have been a factor leading to the Nephite destruction at Cumorah.

CHAPTER 18

Jerusalem at this time was controlled by the Ottoman Empire of Turkey, and would remain so until the British claimed Palestine after World War I. In turn, Great Britain (along with the United States), was quite instrumental in bringing about the political circumstances that led to the reestablishment of the Jewish state in 1947.

Orson Hyde offered his dedicatory prayer on October 24, 1841. Suffice it to say that until this date only a small scattering of Jews had made it their custom to settle in the Holy Land, usually at the end of their lives, so that they might be buried in the land of their forefathers. After this prayer of dedication for the final gathering of the children of Israel in the last days, the numbers of Jews who came to settle here increased exponentially.

Perhaps most curious was Elder Hyde's declaration that this barren land would again blossom and produce in its strength. Many visitors to the Holy Land prior to this century found it odd that in spite of the frequent mention of forests in the Bible (2 Kings 19:23; 1 Samuel 22:5; 2 Chronicles 24:7; Nehemiah 2:8), there was hardly a tree to be seen. This was due not only to innumerable wars and destructions, but also to the custom of the proprietors of the land during the Middle Ages taxing landowners according to how many trees grew on their estates. Naturally, most of these trees were put to the axe, which led to much erosion and neglect of the land. When Orson Hyde arrived in Jerusalem in 1841, it truly was a desolate and unfertile place.

Today, however, the scene is entirely different. Newly planted forests abound across the landscape. Innovations in drip irrigation and cloud seeding have made this the most fertile land in the region, a fact emphasized by one of Israel's primary exports—flowers.

The anonymous stranger in Philadelphia to whom Orson Hyde referred in his prayer on the Mount of Olives remained unknown to him throughout his life. This stranger's generous donation of $200 worth of gold coins (a fortune in 1840), made possible Orson's trip to Palestine. In 1924, long after Elder Hyde's death, the truth finally became known. John F. Beck reported that the stranger was actually his father, Joseph Ellison Beck. At the time of his contribution, Joseph E. Beck was a thirty-year-old farmer of modest means who had been impressed by Orson's preaching. His only request when the money was anonymously delivered was that Elder Hyde mention him in his prayer that morning. Later, Joseph E. Beck's family testified of the great blessings that came to him and his descendants, attributing it to that prayer (Howard H. Burton, *Orson Hyde: Missionary, Apostle, Colonizer*, 116, note on 307; Myrtle Stevens Hyde, *Orson Hyde: Olive Branch of Israel*, 120).

All of the incidents of Orson's Hyde's activities on the morning of Oct. 24, 1841, are accurately reported up to and including his wading out into the Pool of Siloam. Only the Arab attack is fictional. It is unclear whether he gave his dedicatory prayer orally or in silence. For the sake of the story, the author chose to have him present it orally.

CHAPTER 19

Tikal (translated "Place of Spirit Voices" or "Place of the Twenty Year Count," depending on the translator), is one of the better-known Mayan ruins in Central America, perhaps best recognized from a single shot in the movie *Star Wars* as the rebel base on the fourth moon of Yavin. Another rendering of its ancient name is "Mutul."

It became a major civilization center at about 200 A.D., around the same time that the Church began to break down and "ites" began to dominate the social classes again (4 Nephi 24-47). Some archaeological remains have been dated as early as 800 B.C., suggesting that Tikal may have been founded by the Olmec civilization or some other people brought to this continent by the hand of the Lord (see 2 Nephi 1:5; Ether 2:12). There was also a considerable amount of construction in the first century B.C. However, many of the towering temples that we see in ruins today were not built until after the Nephites were destroyed.

In light of the conclusion of many non-LDS scholars that Tikal played such a prominent role in the political spectrum of the fourth century A.D., a number of LDS scholars have proposed that it may have been involved in the battle at Cumorah. As the Lamanite kingdom expanded during this time period with its defeats over the Nephites and possibly other rivals, Tikal could have been a more suitable capital for their empire, as it would have been far more centralized than their former capital at the city of Nephi (Allen, "Mormon's Epistle to Yax Ayin," *Archaeological Digest,* June 2001). Many LDS scholars have proposed the city of Nephi to be in the Valley of Guatemala Central, which includes the archaeological sites of Kaminaljuyu, Mixco Viejo, and others (see Joseph Allen, *Exploring the Lands of the Book of Mormon;* John L. Sorenson, *An Ancient American Approach to the Book of Mormon;* F. Richard Hauch, *Deciphering the Geography of the Book of Mormon;* David Palmer, *New Evidences of the Book or Mormon from Ancient Mexico;* Bruce W. Warren and Thomas Ferguson, *The Messiah in Ancient America,* and others).

Some LDS researchers have tried to find a Book of Mormon correlation to the city of Tikal, but without any satisfactory conclusions. The best guesses may be that it was the city of Nephihah, or Aaron, or Antionum, but there are simply not enough details in the scriptures to be certain. Whatever the case, it could easily have been one of the "many cities" in the east wilderness that Captain Moroni built up to protect Nephite lands after he'd driven out all of the Lamanite squatters in 71 B.C. (Alma 50: 13-15).

Tikal is one of many cities in Mesoamerica that shows evidence of defensive earthworks and fortifications that seem to match remarkably well with the descriptions given of Moroni's innovations in the Book of Mormon. In Alma we read, "... *the Nephites had dug up a ridge of earth round about them, which was so high that the Lamanites could not cast their stones and their arrows at them that they might take effect, neither could they*

*come upon them save it were by their place of entrance . . . And upon the top of
these ridges of earth [Moroni] caused that there should be timbers . . . and he
caused that upon those works of timbers there should be a frame of pickets . . .
and Teancum . . . caused that [the Lamanite prisoners] should commence
laboring in digging a ditch round about the land, or the city, Bountiful. And he
caused that they should build a breastwork of timbers upon the inner bank of
the ditch; and they were to cast up dirt out of the ditch against the breastwork of
timbers"* (Alma 49:4; 50:2-3; 53:3-4).

In 1967, non-LDS archaeologists Dennis Puleston and Donald
Callender discovered just such defensive earthworks around Tikal. They
write, "The trench is the most prominent feature of the earthworks, but
when it was first discovered it appeared to be nothing more than a natural
arroyo or ravine. As we followed it, however, it soon became evident that it
was not a natural formation. First, it had a continuous raised embankment
along the south side, and second, it passed up and down over hills, following
a fairly straight line . . . This embankment must have been considerably
steeper and higher a thousand years ago than it is today. That the trench was
impassible is suggested by the fact that at four or five widely separated points
along its length were found what appeared to be causeways across it . . . If the
gates were not a barrier to human passage, these "gates" would have little
reason to exist" (Dennis E. Puleston and Donald W. Callender Jr.,
"Defensive Earthworks at Tikal," *Expedition 9*, (Spring 1967); 40-48).

Such fortifications are not original to Tikal. In speaking of similar earthworks at the site of Becan, which is north of Tikal, non-LDS archaeologist
David L. Webster writes, "I suspect that the ditch-embankment type of defensive system is of great antiquity in the lowlands because of its advantages of
simplicity, adaptability, and efficient use in conjunction with timber palisades."
He even goes on to say that these fortifications were likely "the brainchild of
some local innovator . . . as its widespread occurrence suggests" (David L.
Webster, *Defensive Earthworks at Becan, Campeche, Mexico: Implications for
Maya Warfare*, 1976). Some have wondered if this "innovator" may in fact have
been Captain Moroni (Ted D. Stoddard, "Moroni's Fortifications,"
Explorations in the Book of Mormon, Volume 1, 2000; Joseph L. Allen,
Exploring the Lands of the Book of Mormon, 1989, 199-203, 335-336).

CHAPTER 20
The desert fox in this chapter is known as a fennec, found all over the
Sinai, North Africa, and the Arabian Peninsulas. It generally spends the heat
of the day underground in a burrow, then hunts in the morning and
evening for insects, small animals, and fruit.

Islam, the religion preached by the Prophet Mohammed, began officially in Saudi Arabia in 622 A.D. From the eighth century to the twentieth
century, nations dominated by Islam have been the governing forces in
Jerusalem and the Holy Land (except for a brief period in the eleventh and
twelfth centuries when crusaders from Europe held the territory).

Although this novel contains several villains who worship Allah (an
Arabic word meaning simply "The God," which may have its roots in the
early Semitic forms of "El" or "Al"), it should be noted that Islam is funda-
mentally a religion of high moral principles, with a special emphasis on
prayers, fasting, and almsgiving. Moslems (the name given to followers of
Islam) are highly conservative in matters of morality, abortion, and family.
The villains in this novel who follow Islam are similar to the villains from
any other religion or background. They have rejected the moral teachings of
their community to follow their own greedy motives.

CHAPTER 21

In all, there are ten animals mentioned by name in the Book of
Mormon: horse, cow, ass, dog, goat, wild goat, sheep, ox, swine, and
elephant. There are eleven if you count "serpents," and thirteen if you
include the unusual and unidentified animals known as "cureloms" and
"cumoms" (Ether 9:19). The term "fowl" and "flocks" are also used, but
with no specific type of domesticated bird or animal. There are also those
dangerous "wild beasts" that are listed in several chapters, but again with no
mention of any species.

Many of the animals in the first list of ten were not known to have
existed in the New World prior to the Spanish Conquest in the sixteenth
century. Of the animals mentioned, only two are known to have existed on
this continent prior to the Spanish Conquest—dogs (two types) and, of
course, serpents.

As LDS anthropologist John L. Sorenson writes, "The terminology the
Nephite volume used to discuss animals follows a different logic than the
scheme familiar to most of us whose ancestors come out of western Europe.
Anthropologists tell us that the world's peoples have many different models
for classifying animals or plants . . . When the Spaniards reached the
Americas, they had trouble labeling the native creatures systematically. Yet
the Indians had an even harder time classifying the animals the Europeans
brought along" (John L. Sorenson, *An Ancient American Setting for the Book
of Mormon*, 289).

The Mayans are said to have raised a variety of domesticated animals,
including coatimundis, ducks, turkeys, peccaries, Brocket deer, rabbits, agoutis,

and many others. Sorenson has offered a fascinating list of possible candidates for the domesticated animals that Joseph Smith named. As stated, the Spanish made the exact same comparisons when they first arrived in the New World. The coatimundi was described as "a small dog with a snout like a pig." The peccary was referred to as a "wild pig," while the tapir was given every label from cow, to pig, to ass, to horse. Bison were called cows. Llamas and Alpacas (native to South America, although there is some evidence that they existed anciently in Mesoamerica), have been called cows, sheep, asses, and horses, while the Brocket deer was called a "little wild goat" (Sorenson, 288-299).

In a previous *Tennis Shoes* book, the idea was presented that a curelom may have been a wooly mammoth. This may be true. However, it has also been proposed that mammoths or mastodons may have simply been the animals that Joseph Smith meant when he wrote "elephants" (Hugh Nibley, *Collected Works,* 215; George F. Reynolds, Janne M. Sjodahl, *Commentary on the Book Of Mormon,* Vol. 6, 144-145). The classifications for many prehistoric creatures didn't exist when Joseph Smith translated the Book of Mormon. For someone living in 1829, "elephant" would have been an obvious translation for mammoth. Many experts are convinced that mammoths and mastodons may have existed much later than the times normally assigned to their extinction in certain locations—possibly even as late as 100 B.C. (Jim J. Hester, "Agency of Man in Animal Extinction," in Martin and Wright, *Pleistocene Extinctions,* 185).

Horses mentioned in the Book of Mormon have been a favorite target of its critics for decades. The argument is based on the assumption that because there were no horses in America at the time of Spanish Conquest, and because Native Americans didn't seem to know what they were, they couldn't possibly have existed among the ancient peoples. However, non-LDS archaeologists have begun to question this assumption, completely independent of the Mormon question.

Presently on display in the Maya room of the National Museum of Anthropology in Mexico City are four horse bones discovered in the caves of Loltun near the Maya ruins of Uxmal in the Yucatan Peninsula. Because these bones were found at the same depth as Mayan pottery fragments which appear to date from the Classic period (200 A.D. to 900 A.D.), the conclusion has been drawn that horses existed in Mesoamerica prior to the Conquest (Joseph Allen, "Horses," *Book of Mormon Archaeological Digest,* Volume II, Issue VI). Similar finds have been made in Cenote Ch'en Mul at Mayapan, Yucatan and in other caves in southwest Yucatan (Sorenson, 395).

A better question than whether horses existed in Mesoamerica may be, "Why are horses mentioned in the Book of Mormon so rarely?" There are only three actual references that apply to Nephites or Lamanites—Enos 1:21 (Nephites raise many horses); Alma 18:9-12 (Ammon takes care of King Lamoni's horses); and 3 Nephi 3:22 (Nephites gather their horses and other possessions into one place while they defend against the Gadiantons). There is also one reference among the Jaredites—Ether 9:19. They are never mentioned after the coming of the Savior; never mentioned as being used in warfare; and never mentioned as beasts of burden. It has been suggested that after 18 or 19 A.D., these animals, for whatever reason, disappeared.

Allen has proposed that all it would have taken was a few seasons without rain sometime between 29 A.D. and 1500 A.D., and horses would have become entirely extinct until they were reintroduced by the Spaniards.

CHAPTER 22

To learn the actual facts about the notorious Book of Mormon figure named Akish, the reader is invited to go to Ether, chapters 8 and 9, which make it clear that he is undoubtedly on a very short list of the most wicked characters in history. Of course Satan and his servants would never need time travel to spread their wickedness or hatch their diabolical schemes; however, it is hoped that the concept as portrayed in this book is nonetheless intriguing, as all questions in entertaining fiction ought to be.

The ruins of the ancient city known as Petra are today found in the district of Ma'an, Jordan, about fifty miles south of the Dead Sea. Anciently it was known as Sela, or Selah, the capital of Edom, although it was rendered "Petra" (Greek for "the rock"), in Judges 1:36.

The first historical reference to Petra is on a "List of Enemies," compiled by the Assyrians in 647 B.C. The Nabatean Kingdom conquered the territory sometime in the second century B.C., and is responsible for many of the ruins that can be seen there today. It was known as a major stopover point for all of the great spice caravans from the east, whose tributes were the community's major source of income. At one point there may have been as many as fifty thousand inhabitants. As Joshua alluded in this chapter, most readers have seen a portion of these ruins in the movie *Indiana Jones and the Last Crusade*. One scene prominently features the Corinthian columns of the monument of Al-Khaznah, which dates back to Roman times.

After an Islamic invasion of the seventh century, Petra completely disappeared from the annals of history—except of course to the Bedouin tribes who continuously used its tombs as places of dwelling. It was rediscovered in 1812 (just a few years before the incidents of this story) by a Swiss explorer named Johann Burckhardt (John Lloyd Stevens, *Incidents of Travel in Egypt, Arabia, Petraea, and the Holy Land,* 249).

Isaiah issued a profound curse against the Edomites and Bozrah (which means strong or fortified city) when he wrote, "They shall call the nobles thereof to the kingdom, but none shall be there, and all her princes shall be nothing. And thorns shall come up in her palaces, nettles and brambles in the fortresses thereof, and it shall be an habitation for dragons, and a court for owls" (Isaiah 34: 12-13).

Anyone who visits Petra today can testify of its current state of desolation and the literal fulfillment of this prophecy.

CHAPTER 23

As mentioned in chapter twelve, the characters of Fire-Born, Lord Blue-Crocodile, and Spearthrower Owl are all actual characters in Mayan history. It may be important to give some background on the most recent interpretations of scholars and researchers with regard to this time period, and more particularly on the shadowy figure of the man we know today as Siyah K'ak', or Fire-Born.

According to stone glyphs at both Tikal and Uaxactun, its neighbor ten miles to the north, the military conqueror named Fire-Born arrived in the region from Teotihuacan in 378 A.D., which would have been seven years prior to the Nephite destruction. The glyphs also tell us of the death of another Mayan king named Jaguar-Paw, whose rule in Tikal may have lasted sixty-one years, from 317 to 378 A.D. This would suggest that Jaguar-Paw *may* have been a key figure in many of the events that are mentioned toward the end of the Book of Mormon. If this is true, he *may* have been the chief rival of the Nephite commander, Mormon, when war broke out with the Lamanites in 326 A.D., and a participant in the treaty that was instituted between the Nephites, the Lamanites, and the Gadiantons in 350 A.D.

During these conflicts, Mormon tells us of a Lamanite king named Aaron. This king is mentioned twice by name in the Book of Mormon—Mormon 2:9 and Moroni 9:17. On both occasions this king is an actual field commander, as many kings in Mesoamerica were. It could be that Aaron was a regional or local leader who was situated much closer to the Narrow Neck (Tehuantepec), perhaps a son or relative of Jaguar-Paw. In this case, his authority would have been similar to that of King Lamoni who ruled in the land of Nephi under his father (see Alma 17-24). In Ancient Maya, these leadership roles are distinguished by the terms kalomte, which means "emperor," and ahau which means "lord." Ahau in this case would signify a local leader whose domain is a city or land within a larger kingdom (Peter D. Harrison, *The Lords of Tikal*, 179). Or perhaps the name of Jaguar-Paw is a title and may not represent this figure's personal name.

The coincidence of Jaguar-Paw's death in 378 A.D., along with the arrival of Fire-Born in the same year, suggests that Fire-Born killed the long-time ruler, Jaguar-Paw, and then installed Nun Yax Ayin, or Lord Blue-Crocodile as Ahau at Tikal. (Lord Blue-Crocodile, or First Crocodile, is often referred to as Curl Snout in much of the literature because of the appearance of his name glyph.) Nun Yax Ayin is the son of Atlatl Cauac, or Spearthrower Owl, a foreign ruler who is most likely the king of Teotihuacan (Stuart 1998). Fire-Born may have retained the title of Kalomte or Emperor of the entire region, possibly under the umbrella of the even higher emperor at Teotihuacan. To have pulled off this coup in 378 A.D., and then united a kingdom that may have stretched as far south as Kaminaljuyu, and as far east as Cop·n in Honduras, Fire-Born would have to have been a remarkable military and political leader. Was he also the man who orchestrated the genocide of the Nephite nation in 385 A.D.?

At this point the author would like to present a *personal speculation* that this coup in 378 A.D. may have actually been supported by the Nephites. Rulers among the Nephites could have easily played a major role in the conspiracy. If, as some LDS scholars have suggested, the Nephites at this time were situated in and around Cumorah (El Cerro Vigia) and the Narrow Neck (Tehuantepec), then the initial invasion force of Fire-Born would have marched right through Nephite lands. The wicked Nephites may have been only too pleased to allow the Gadianton forces of Teotihuacan to pass through unmolested in the hopes that their old rival, King Aaron, would finally be dethroned and destroyed. They might have even provided Fire-Born with protection and provisions.

So why didn't Fire-Born attack the Nephites first? Probably by this time the Nephites were not a major power in the area, certainly not as big a prize as the Lamanites at Tikal. The strategy was simple: first strike at the heart of power, then consolidate. The Nephites may have gone along with it at first in the hopes that a change in leadership at Tikal would allow them to finally go home to the land of Zarahemla (Chiapas Valley—see Sorenson, Allen). However, as the Book of Mormon reports, this was not to be. For whatever reason, Fire-Born and his new Lamanite subjects turned against the Nephites, perhaps seeing them as a geographical obstacle to future commerce and a barrier to political ties with the homeland of Teotihuacan.

Again, the author *strongly emphasizes* that this scenario is *only speculation*; nevertheless it is remarkable how Nephite history, as reported by Mormon and Moroni, would have fit so neatly into the political spectrum of fourth-century Mesoamerica.

ABOUT THE AUTHOR

Chris Heimerdinger currently resides in Riverton, Utah, with his wife, Beth, and their three children, Steven Teancum, Christopher Ammon, and Alyssa Sariah.

As visitors to his website are aware, Chris recently returned from another expedition to Mexico and Guatemala to complete his research for *Warriors of Cumorah*, the eighth novel in his award-winning *Tennis Shoes Adventure Series*. He feels strongly that only by immersing himself in these ancient lands and cultures could he capture the essence of what it might have been like to live in ancient America in 385 A.D. As Chris writes, "*Warriors of Cumorah* is my most ambitious novel yet, taking LDS fiction where it has never gone before. I did my best to write a heart-pounding adventure and still include some of the latest cutting-edge research on current perspectives of this period in Book of Mormon history."

It is Chris's hope that fiction such as this will do much to inspire the next generation of researchers and scholars of the Book of Mormon, and also inspire a greater appreciation of the sacred volume itself, which has been called "the cornerstone of our religion."

Chris affirms that another novel in the *Tennis Shoes Adventure Series* can be expected in the future as long as his readers "never grow too old for adventure."

For further information about *Warriors of Cumorah* and other books by Chris Heimerdinger, please become a registered guest at www.cheimerdinger.com.